For Laure

PATRIOT ... OR TRAITOR?

Lind's voice, vibrant and determined, once again filled his silent office. "This is a story I swore I would never tell," the voice began. Grady shivered listening to him. Lind had been sitting here, in this chair, dictating those words perhaps an hour ago. And now he was just a lifeless slab draining his blood onto a blue carpet.

The voice continued:

"For thirty-three years, I served as an officer of the Central Intelligence Agency. I lived in the culture of secrecy, inside that little world whose frontiers are defined by the words 'need to know.' Nothing gave me greater pride or satisfaction than the knowledge that I was a keeper of the secrets, that I was ready to defend the secrets which had been entrusted to me with my life if I had to. And now I turn my back on that lifetime trust. . . .

LARRY COLLINS

BLACK EAGLES

A SIGNET BOOK

SIGNET
Published by the Penguin Group
Penguin Books USA Inc., 375 Hudson Street,
New York, New York 10014, U.S.A.
Penguin Books Ltd, 27 Wrights Lane,
London W8 5TZ, England
Penguin Books Australia Ltd, Ringwood,
Victoria, Australia
Penguin Books Canada Ltd, 10 Alcorn Avenue,
Toronto, Ontario, Canada M4V 3B2
Penguin Books (N.Z.) Ltd, 182–190 Wairau Road,
Auckland 10, New Zealand

Penguin Books Ltd, Registered Offices:
Harmondsworth, Middlesex, England

Published by Signet, an imprint of Dutton Signet,
a division of Penguin Books USA Inc.
Previously published in a Dutton edition.

First Signet Printing, June, 1996
10 9 8 7 6 5 4 3 2 1

PUBLISHER'S NOTE
This is a work of fiction. Names, characters, places, and incidents either are the product of the author's imagination or are used fictitiously.

"He may be a son of a bitch,
but at least he's our son of a bitch."

CONTENTS

Prologue

Nothing moved. The summer air was heavy with humidity, a stifling blanket into which even the mosquitoes seemed reluctant to venture. It reminded him of those Central American jungles which he'd once visited with Juanita, cesspools of silent, sodden heat. Fifty feet below him, the base of the bluff sloped off into the gray, brackish waters of the Patuxent River. No sailing craft, no power boat out on an afternoon prowl, not even a hint of the currents moving below its waters marred the perfect stillness of its surface.

Once this river had been one of the great arteries of the New World. All the broad-beamed merchantmen of the British Empire had made their way along its deep-water passage to the landfall off to his right at Saint Mary's City. For a few brief decades men had marched along this bluff dreaming of the great seaport that was going to rise here. But that had not happened. History had conferred her favors on Baltimore instead, leaving this once promising estuary just a forgotten backwater, an unnoticed footnote to a nation's history.

Not so long ago, he, too, had stood at a crossroads of the nation's history, a witness and an actor in great events and great times. And now?

He moved back across his lawn to the door leading into his office, his private citadel, attached by a short passageway to the main house. A series of bookcases ringed the room, their odd spaces filled with the memorabilia of his career: a portrait of Allen Dulles personally dedicated to him, boarding *Air Force One* with Bill Casey for a trip to Central America, sipping Old Parr scotch with Manuel Antonio Noriega in the dictator's hideaway, L'Escondido in Panama's Chiriqui Province.

To the left of his desk, perched on an easel was an oil of his mother painted in 1935 on the eve of her engagement to a young American millionaire. The artist was Eugenio Suarez, the portrait painter of choice of Madrid's pre–Civil War society. How well he had captured the proud thrust of her chin and those dark, defiant eyes, which even now could admonish him from beyond the grave. So many of his life's turnings had been the result of her insistence that he study Spanish tradition and history.

Of his father there was only one small memento in the room, a photograph taken of him in Hobe Sound astride his favorite polo pony. That was what his father had done best—play polo. Play polo and spend money, that is. His great-grandfather, the John Featherly Lind who had started the chain of Roman numerals after his name, had been the first Lind to leave the Maryland shores to seek his fortune elsewhere. He had found it by speculating successfully, if not altogether legally, on land values as the railroad moved west after the Civil War.

The old man had returned to Maryland at the end of his life to purchase this estate in which Jack Lind IV, the latest of his line, now lived in stately if somewhat strained comfort. Strained because both his father and grandfather had set about dissipating the very considerable fortune the founder of their line had left, a task which they had accomplished with a remarkable degree of success.

The youngest Lind, however, had had other sources of comfort and satisfaction. Prime among them had been the knowledge that by birth, by breeding, by education and training, he was an American mandarin. Most certainly, it was that conviction that had underlain his decision to spend his life in service to the nation.

Lind walked across his navy blue carpet to the green leather-topped expanse of his partner's desk. His was a genuine antique, not a clever imitation produced by some Williamsburg cabinetmaker. Indeed, it was on his desk that Salmon P. Chase, Lincoln's Secretary of the Treasury, had signed the first bond issues to finance the Civil War.

As always, that desk was cleared of extraneous papers and paraphernalia. It contained one photograph, of his wife and three sons taken shortly after his third son's birth; one memento, a representation of the three "hear no evil, speak no evil, see no evil" monkeys given to him as a symbol of the career he'd chosen by the fourteen members of his class's delegation to his Yale secret society, Scroll and Key; and one piece of paper, his daily call list. It was blank.

In front of his desk chair was his tape recorder, the microphone resting beside it, waiting for him to start work again. Thank God this sordid, painful task is almost over, he thought.

As he picked up the microphone, the ringing of the bell at the front gate pierced his silent office. It was not a perfunctory ring; it was a long, imperious demand for his attention. He activated the closed-circuit television installation that allowed him to identify his visitor, demanding with patrician disdain, "Who is there?"

That, as it happened, was not a question he needed to ask. He recognized instantly the face that appeared on the TV monitor on the wall opposite his desk.

"This is Special Agent Kevin Grady of the Drug Enforcement Administration, Mr. Lind," the face replied, flashing a DEA special agent's shield to the TV camera as he did. "I am here with a warrant for your arrest. Open the door immediately."

"Okay, Grady," Lind announced to the closed-circuit TV system, "come on in." His commanding voice had plunged to a tremor freighted with despair.

At the main entrance outside, Special Agent Grady heard a "click" indicating that the metal gate in front of him had been electronically opened from inside the compound. He unsheathed his plastic Glock .38 from his shoulder holster. This was not the DEA's favorite way of serving an arrest warrant. The agency's rule for arrests was "go fast with a maximum of force and a minimum of fuss." He would have preferred to take Lind while he was out shopping for groceries or on his way to dinner at the country club. The trouble was, he rarely left his property lately, leaving Grady little choice but to come onto the property after him.

"I don't expect any trouble," he warned the three backup agents with him, "but stay awake."

Slowly, he pushed the metal gate. It opened to a large gravel courtyard that served as a parking area. Ahead loomed the main house, a three-story Georgian building fronted by a wide marble staircase leading up to its imposing main entrance.

"Holy shit!" whispered the backup agent behind Grady. This estate was far removed from the urban ghettos in which he was used to serving DEA arrest warrants.

Grady turned to the three agents. "You guys," he ordered, designating two of them, "cover each side of the house.

"You run backup on me," he told the agent who'd just spoken. Then he strode swiftly across the twenty-five yards to the marble staircase leading to the house's main doorway. The door, he could see, was ajar.

His foot was on the lower step of the staircase when he heard the sound, sharp, dry and utterly unmistakable: the crack of a gunshot. Grady spun to his left to get out of the line of fire of a round coming from inside the front door.

"Check out the sides and the back of the house," he shouted to the two agents he'd sent out on his flanks. "Stay in cover."

As they started to move, he grabbed the walkie-talkie linking him to their backup vehicles outside. "Shots fired," he said. "Advise the operations desk. Block the front gate with one of the cars. We'll proceed with the arrest unless I advise you otherwise."

For three or four minutes Grady and the third backup braced themselves against the building's brickwork, well out of the line of fire.

"Boss," his walkie-talkie finally burped. "We're out back. It's clear."

"What's out there?" Grady asked.

"Just a big lawn and some bushes. Looks like a ledge going down to the riverbank at the end of the lawn."

"Okay," Grady ordered, "stay under cover in case anyone tries to run out. We're going in. If there's more shooting, call for backup."

Motioning with his head to the remaining agent, he dashed up the steps, his Glock pointing forward. He smashed open the door with one vicious kick, then edged into the house sideways, his body pressed tightly against the door frame so he wouldn't be silhouetted in the open doorway.

Grady moved his extended weapon around the entry hall. It was still and empty. His nostrils caught the acrid aroma of gunsmoke lingering in the air. Ahead of him, an open door gave on to a passageway. At its end was a burst of sunlight. That, Grady calculated from what he knew of the house's layout, should be Lind's office.

"Back me!" he ordered the agent beside him and started down the passageway, again hugging one of its walls. When he reached the office door, he saw the body of the man he had come to arrest sprawled facedown on the dark blue carpet. A bloodstain stretched from the side of his head, seeping across the carpet's fibers as inexorably as a slowly advancing tide. A .38 pistol lay on the rug, a foot or so from Lind's outstretched right hand.

"Mother of God!" Grady gasped. His eyes took a rapid inventory of the octagonally shaped room. Opposite him, a door to the back lawn was open.

"Quick," he ordered the two agents stationed outside "get down to the river and see if there's anybody down there!"

"You," he shouted at the agent who was behind him, "search this place, the attic, the cellar, every closet in the building."

As the agent left the room, Grady pulled his walkie-talkie from his pocket. "Patch me through to the operations desk.

"This is Grady of the New York DO," he informed the duty officer on the Washington headquarters desk that ran oversight on all ongoing DEA operations. "The subject of my arrest warrant is DOA, either a suicide or a homicide, I can't be sure which. We're in the process of searching and securing the property. Tell the Maryland State Police or whoever the hell has jurisdiction to get a crime scene unit out here as fast as they can."

With that done, Grady felt, for the first time since he'd rung the bell at the front gate, the tension level in his nervous system beginning to wind down. Once again, he eyed the man lying dead at his feet. The advance of the blood flowing from Lind's brain was beginning to slow, its color darkening, the edges of the stain just starting to congeal. How many years, Grady wondered, had it been since they'd shared that plane ride to Laos? Fifteen?

Then he noticed the tape recorder on Lind's desk, a red light glowing from its control panel. The machine was on. Grady peered down into its Plexiglas cover. The tape reel inside was moving. Next to the recorder was a carefully aligned stack of tapes. So that was what Lind had been doing in the seconds before they'd rung the bell, before he had decided to kill himself—or perhaps before someone had decided to kill him. Those tapes, Grady realized, could be relevant to his investigation. Freelancing with a potential piece of evidence before the local police arrived might require some explanations down the line. But, what the hell, he thought, there was going to be a lot of explaining to do about this bungled arrest anyway.

He took out his handkerchief and, covering his index finger with it, pressed the rewind button. Once the tape had rewound, he settled into Lind's armchair and pressed *play*.

Lind's voice, vibrant and determined, once again filled his silent office. "This is a story I swore I would never tell," the voice began. Grady shivered listening to him. Lind had been sitting here, in this chair, dictating those words perhaps an hour ago. And now he was just a lifeless slab draining his blood onto a blue carpet.

The voice continued:

"For thirty-three years, I served as an officer of the Central Intelligence Agency. I lived in the culture of secrecy, inside that little world whose frontiers are defined by the words 'need to know.' Nothing gave me greater pride or satisfaction than the knowledge that I was a keeper of the secrets, that I was ready to defend the secrets which had been entrusted to me with my life if I had to. And now I turn my back on that lifetime trust.

"An officer involved in covert operations in the CIA spends his career wandering through a dark forest of moral ambiguities. They do not draw a fine line between right and wrong on the black loam of that forest's floor. Each officer must determine the whereabouts of that line for himself, taking into account the bearings of his own moral compass and the imperatives of his mission. Even when he thinks he has found it, he can, if he chooses, step across it with impunity, secure in the knowledge he will not be caught. Or, in the unlikely event that he is, that he will almost certainly not be punished.

"I stepped across that line."

Grady snapped off the recorder. The tapes were going to become a part of his case file whether his colleagues in the Maryland State Police liked it or not. Once again he reached for his walkie-talkie. "Bring me in a nondrug evidence bag and report form," he instructed his outside backup.

By that time the two agents he'd ordered to survey the backyard and the river bluff had come into the office.

"It's all clear out there, boss," the elder of the two reported.

"What's below the cliff?"

"A wooden staircase going down to a little beach. We went down and had a look at the sand. No footprints we could see."

"Any boats moving?"

"Off in the distance, yeah. But who's to say where they came from, you know what I mean?"

The backups were all newly recruited agents the Baltimore office had furnished Grady to help him make his arrest. The younger of the pair moved around the desk and looked down on Lind's body with a gulp.

"Blowed himself away, did he?" he asked.

"Maybe," Grady answered. "Probably."

His mate, playing the older, more battle-hardened agent, followed him over for a gawk of his own.

"Hey, boss," he queried, "did you know this guy? Personally, I mean."

Grady leaned against one of the office walls, thinking his way through the ramifications of Lind's death, trying to get a handle on how this would play when the press got ahold of it. His subordinate's query was not one he wanted to answer in any detail right now.

"Yeah," he growled, "I guess you could say I knew him." My brother, my enemy, he thought, then corrected himself. *Brother* was a term Lind would never have agreed to. *Enemies,* yes, each in the service of the same ultimate employer, the United States government, cast onto a collision course because the government they both served couldn't make up its mind where its real values lay.

Outside, he heard the wail of an approaching siren. The Maryland State Police were arriving. "You better go out and escort them in," he ordered the agent who'd just questioned him.

He turned for a final glance at the body of the man whose destiny had been inadvertently linked to his for fifteen years. Blood had stained Lind's right cheek and matted his curling gray hair. His mouth was half open, as though he had been trying to suck a last breath of life from the carpet's fibers. He had been a handsome man, and even his violent end had not been able to destroy the angular symmetry and strength of his features.

"What a waste," Grady muttered to the lifeless face of his fallen foe, to himself, to everybody and to nobody, "what a fucking waste."

BOOK ONE

Lind's Tape

The place to open this narrative, I suppose, is in an airplane because, in a very real sense, the story may be said to have begun in a DC-6 flying from Bangkok to Vientiane, the capital of Laos, in the spring of 1968.

The CIA had ordered me to Vientiane to make an attempt at recruiting a major in the GRU, Red Army Intelligence. That assignment had grown out of my work a decade earlier in the agency's Berlin base. I'd belonged to a unit there responsible for an operation that to this day remains a highly classified agency secret. It was what we call in intelligence jargon a "honey trap," a ploy at least as old as the Punic Wars. In its crudest form it involves getting a target into bed with a woman—or a boy if he is so inclined—and then using his lapse to blackmail him into doing your bidding.

The high classification came from the fact that, first, the operation produced a veritable gold mine of high-quality intelligence. And second, because some of the armchair moralists in Congress overseeing our funding would have gone white had they known that the CIA had a dozen German girls on the payroll prostituting themselves for the U.S. government.

The girls were all stunningly beautiful and self-possessed to an unusual degree. They were as far removed from your ordinary hooker as Mother Teresa is from Madonna. I was the case officer for two of those girls. One, an attractive blonde from Dresden named Ingrid, recruited for us a colonel in the Polish UB, *Urzad Bezpieczyenstwa,* the Polish equivalent of the KGB. For three years he served as a CIA agent in the security office of the Warsaw Pact headquarters.

When he finally came out to live in connubial bliss with Ingrid, as he had been promised he would one day, she had run off to Zurs with a ski instructor. The Pole, I must say, took that bit of bad news rather well. He used the nest egg we'd put aside for him for his work with us to get himself a Ph.D. in psychology, married a dental technician, and is now the chairman of the psychology department of a university near San Diego.

The first question we asked him when he came out, of

course, was who among his colleagues might be a suitable target for CIA recruitment. He suggested to us the GRU major that I'd been sent to Vientiane to recruit. The Russian had been one of his closest friends in Berlin. He had also been having an affair with his boss's wife and had had the misfortune to get caught in the lady's bed by her outraged husband.

Now, adultery with the boss's wife is not a career-enhancing move in any field of endeavor. Consequently, the major had disappeared back into the maw of the GRU's Moscow bureaucracy. Now he had resurfaced as Soviet military attaché in Vientiane—still, we'd noted, as a major.

On the strength of that, our recruitment branch had decided I would fly out to Vientiane armed with a letter of introduction to the Russian major prepared by our Pole, extolling the limitless pleasures of life in the free world. I was to use the letter as an inducement to convince the major to join the *A* team.

In those days you could fly into Laos, a landlocked nation fixed like a long rib into the western flank of Vietnam, from either Bangkok or Saigon. I elected Bangkok, thinking a twenty-four hour layover in the Thai capital offered as pleasurable a way as any to recover from my Washington to Southeast Asia jet lag. It was, but I then needed about seventy-two hours to recover from my twenty-four hours in Bangkok.

Anyway, I crawled aboard a DC-6 of Royal Laotian Airlines that spring morning with my head throbbing from my previous night's vodka. It was a steaming hot day, and there was not even a pretense of air conditioning on the DC-6. Getting into the plane sitting there on the tarmac was like walking into an overheated sauna. By the time I got to my seat, my Brooks Brothers shirt was plastered to my body with sweat, and my seersucker suit had dark splotches below each of my armpits.

There were, I noted, two other passengers in the travelers' compartment—a pair of elderly Laotian ladies, chins stained rust red by the betel nut they were both chewing. They were talking a kind of non-stop cackle that sounded a bit like the squawking of an old shortwave radio.

The rest of the passenger compartment was taken up principally by livestock. There were several crates of chickens, two goats, a sheep, a couple of small pigs and a duck. Our four-legged fellow travelers were all somehow tethered to the fuselage. The duck was not. His wings were encircled by a band which prevented him from flying, but which didn't stop him from hopping around the cabin floor expressing his concern in a frenzy of honking.

The door to the pilot's cabin was open, and there was absolutely no sign of anyone inside. This, I told myself, promised to be a very interesting flight. Finally, I heard a shuffling in the aisle behind me. A fellow American, close to my own age, was coming toward me. He was wearing a short-sleeve sports shirt and khaki suntans. Clearly, he was more used to the local environment than I was.

He dropped into the seat beside mine, buckled up his seat belt, and glanced at me with amusement.

"You look like shit," he declared.

"Thanks. As it happens, that is precisely how I feel."

"Enjoyed Bangkok, did you?"

"Yes," I acknowledged, "rather more last night than this morning."

Our conversation was interrupted by the sound of someone else moving up the aisle. I looked around and saw what appeared to be a twelve-year-old boy coming toward us. He was all of five feet two inches tall with sunglasses masking almost half his face. His undernourished frame was wrapped in a dirty white uniform which looked at least two sizes too big for him.

The kid shuffled past us and into the pilot's cabin. Before sitting down, he placed two large cushions in the pilot's chair so that, once seated, he could, by straining upward, just peer out of the cockpit window toward the nose of the plane and whatever lay beyond. When he'd settled into the chair, he took a large black loose-leaf folder out of a side compartment, opened it, and, drawing on the wisdom it revealed, began to play with the knobs and instruments of the control panel.

"You don't think this kid is going to fly us to Vientiane, do you?" I asked my new neighbor.

He gave the practiced shrug of an old Asia hand. "Well, they do place a high value on on-the-job training out here in Southeast Asia." He betrayed the studied indifference of his reply with a nervous little smile.

It took our child genius about ten minutes to get his engines on and his plane moving. Twice he literally had to stand so he could see what was ahead of him out on the runway. Finally, he swung us into takeoff position and gunned his engines. The Laotian ladies were still cackling away, quite unfazed by all this. The bleating and squawking of our menagerie continued unabated.

My fellow traveler nudged me. "You wouldn't happen to remember the words of a perfect act of contrition by any chance?"

"Sorry," I said, "I don't think I ever knew them. I'm an Episcopalian."

He leered at my Brooks Brothers button-down. "Yeah, figures," he sighed. "Too bad. They might come in handy on a trip like this."

The plane lumbered down the runway, and, in one of the enduring miracles of aviation science, actually got airborne. When we reached our cruising altitude, my fellow American extended his hand, as much in relief, I think, as by way of an introduction. "Grady," he said, "Kevin Grady."

I offered him mine. "Pete Tuttle." That was the cover name on the documents the agency had assigned me for the trip. "Are you in the military in Laos?"

"Nope. Law enforcement."

"In Laos? Ours or theirs?"

"Ours. Drugs. I'm a narc."

"They've got you assigned up there, do they?"

"No, I'm based in Chiang Mai back in Thailand."

"So why come all the way up here? I thought after last night all the *R and R* action was in Bangkok."

"It is. I'm just going up to get a look at the place. Visit some temples." From the studied casualness of his reply I was sure that the one thing Grady was not going to be spending a lot of time on in Laos was temple rubbings.

"What do you do?" he asked me.

"Department of Defense," I replied. "Weapons evaluation."

"Well," Grady assured me, "you'll find plenty of weapons to study up there. Killing each other with them is what they do best these days."

"How about you guys?" I asked him. "Is there much there for you?"

"You're Department of Defense." Grady shrugged. "You ought to know about that."

"I don't mix guns and dope," I laughed.

"Then you're about the only guy in Southeast Asia who doesn't. Heroin is all over the place in Vietnam. We figure most of it's coming from the opium poppies they grow in Laos up north of the Plaine des Jarres."

"Oh yeah," I acknowledged wisely. "I remember seeing some cable traffic on that. Somebody in the Pentagon bitching to State about all that heroin getting to the troops. Telling them to light a fire under the embassy."

Grady snorted. "That's like trying to light a fire in a mud puddle. The embassy just gives Washington a soothing stroke and files that stuff in the wastebasket. Besides, the only thing the State Department runs in Laos these days is the commissary."

"That's the end of the goddamned world up there," I said. My knowledge of the geography of Southeast Asia was shaky, but I seemed to recall northern Laos was pretty much a jungle wilderness. "How the hell do they get that stuff out of there?"

Grady offered me a mean little smile. "That, my friend, is what I'd like to know."

This, I suppose, is as good a place as any to describe the relationship between the CIA and that other branch of our national government, the Drug Enforcement Administration.

The *official* CIA line is: "We have nothing to do with international drug trafficking. We do not hire people who are involved in that traffic, nor do we knowingly work with them. When we are alerted to drug-trafficking activity, we report it to the proper law enforcement agencies." That position is regularly reiterated for the benefit of the media, with varying degrees of sincerity and indignation, by our official spokespeople.

Like most of our official positions, however, that is, if you will pardon the expression, *bullshit*. The fact is, the agency has lived on the fringes of the drug-trafficking world for almost four decades. We have, on occasions beyond number, knowingly employed people who traffic in drugs if we considered them able to perform tasks for us that we held vital to our national security interests.

In practical terms, that meant we demanded the right of automatic access to the list of the DEA's overseas CIs—their confidential informants. They also had to clear with us the names of the individuals overseas who were about to become the object of their investigations. We didn't want them operating at cross-purposes with our ongoing operations, or investigating individuals who might be our assets, or trying to recruit as their informants people who were already working for us.

Furthermore, we were not above tiptoeing up to certain DEA prisoners before they came to trial with an offer it was hard for them to refuse: Come to work for us and we'd take care of their legal problems. You'd be amazed how cooperative someone can become when they're confronted with an offer like that. We'd then whisper to the federal prosecutor preparing the DEA's case: "Prosecuting this gentleman in an open courtroom will expose CIA sources and methods." Down would come the gavel—*case dismissed*—and we had a valuable new asset.

I suppose that what irked the DEA rank-and-file most of all, however, was the widely circulated knowledge that we had infiltrated over a dozen of our officers into the DEA. For over twenty years, any time the CIA wanted access to a DEA document or file, no matter how confidential it was supposed to be, we got it.

Those restrictions did not, as you can imagine, make for warm and friendly relations. Nor did we tend to socialize much overseas. By and large, DEA country attachés enjoyed a place on the social pecking order in most embassies just below that of the agricultural attaché. Most of them were ex-cops who liked to talk and break down doors, not activities we in the agency usually got into. Their educational and social backgrounds tended to be distinctly different from ours. Sure, the DEA had one guy from Harvard assigned to Paris. Their higher-ups kept pointing to him with the pride of an unwed mother whose son has just been elected to the town's most exclusive country club.

We felt—unfairly—that DEA agents all tended to wear white socks, smoke Dutch Masters cigars and pick their noses at "morning prayers," the ambassador's daily staff meetings at our overseas posts. So, for all of those reasons, I was less than overjoyed to find Mr. Kevin Grady sitting there beside me in our Vientiane-bound Royal Laotian Airlines DC-6.

Suddenly, the plane sank with the sickening swiftness of a high-speed elevator plunging through a drop of twenty floors. It was an air pocket. We hit bottom with a jolt that had the effect of a blender on my ill-digested breakfast. As I dived for the vomit bag in the pocket of the seat in front of mine, I caught a glimpse of Grady's feet. At least, I noted, he wasn't wearing white socks.

The crisis passed and I leaned back to recover. At the head of the aisle, the door to our pilot's cabin remained open. The force of that sudden down-draft seemed to have driven the little fellow even farther into his seat, so there was no way I could imagine that he would now be able to see out of his cockpit.

Nor was there a second crewman anywhere to be seen. What were we supposed to do if our lone pilot had a heart attack? Ask one of the Laotian ladies if she'd like to step up and fly the plane for us?

"Tell me," I said to Grady, "what do you suppose happened to the copilot on this flight? Doesn't IATA have some rule about always having two pilots on international passenger flights?"

"IATA?" Grady laughed. "Those guys don't even know where Laos is. This airline has its own policy as far as second officers are concerned. It goes back to World War Two. You remember that book *God Is My Copilot*?"

"Sure."

"That's who they use."

"Well," I sighed, "I hope God's checked out on a DC-6. I'm beginning to have a suspicion that if we ever get to Vientiane it will be a miracle."

"My friend, completing a trip on this airline usually requires a miracle at least comparable to the miracle of the loaves and the fishes."

"You're rather given to religious metaphors," I observed.

"I am. It was the nuns. They leave their mark."

Grady smiled, perhaps at the memories his childhood mentors stirred. There was something of Bobby Kennedy in Grady. You could sense the same wiry, coiled intensity to him, the same inner drive struggling for release from the unlikely prison of such a slender, boyish frame. His smile had the spontaneous warmth Kennedy's had, a warmth that drew your attention away from those pain-saddened eyes of his. Grady's eyes, too, had a faraway, forlorn look to them. Had some tragedy marred his life? I wondered.

"How did you get into the drug business?" I asked.

"Probably the same way you got into the weapons business."

"Ah, I'm disappointed. I thought there must have been something in those Irish genes of yours that drew you into law enforcement."

Grady's look darkened a shade. Clearly, my attempt at ethnic humor had struck an inappropriate note.

"Genetics didn't have a damn thing to do with it although, as it happens, my father was a cop in New York. I wanted to be a lawyer."

"What happened?"

"My father was killed in the line of duty one night."

There it was, the explanation for those haunted eyes of his. "Christ," I whispered. "I'm sorry. How did it happen?"

"He got called to an armed robbery in a mom-and-pop store over in Queens. His patrol car was the first vehicle to respond. There was a pair of junkies in the store when my father opened the door. One was rifling the till. The other had the old lady who owned the place. He was holding her in front of him with a gun to her head. He told my father to drop his gun and back out the door or he'd shoot the old woman right there in front of him."

Grady paused. His expression slipped into neutral, and for a second or two he stared unblinking at the back of the seat ahead of him. "My father did what the guy asked. He dropped his gun on the floor and started to back out the door. That was when the junkie whacked him. Shot him three times in cold blood."

I said nothing. You would not want to intrude on a memory so painfully recollected with something as meaningless as a stranger's words of sympathy.

"I was in my junior year at Fordham when it happened," Grady resumed. "I quit the next day and enrolled at the police academy."

"What got you out here?" I asked after an appropriate moment had passed. "Vientiane's a long way from driving a prowl car around Times Square."

"Ain't it just," Grady acknowledged. "I always wanted to get into federal law enforcement. It's the big leagues in our business. Got a law degree nights at NYU but then, somehow, I got turned off by the FBI. J. Edgar Hoover with his white shirts and his short haircuts and all that crap. It just wasn't my kind of law enforcement. Not after being out on the streets of New York. I mean it was a little bit like the Yankees and the old Brooklyn Dodgers when I was a kid growing up. I was a Dodger fan ... couldn't stand the Yankees. For me, the Bureau was the Yankees."

Grady stretched out and popped his ears. The pilot had just adjusted the pitch on his engines for our descent into Vientiane.

"Anyway," he continued, "I was running a Police Athletic League program up in the Bronx on weekends. The court sent me this eighteen-year-old black girl who'd been into heroin. Give her some recreational activity to keep her out of trouble, they told me. She was a wonderful kid. Fun, hardworking, devoted to the younger kids. Ran like the wind on our track team. I really liked her."

Grady looked at me with that suggestion of hostility you will sometimes see in police officers confronted with the incomprehension of the civilians they are supposed to protect.

"Is all this boring you?" he asked.

"Hell, no. Go on."

"She was with me for about a year. Then one weekend she disappeared. Just like that, from one day to the next, gone. Six months later, she calls me. 'I've got to go away someplace,' she said, 'but before I go, there's something I want to show you.'

"She came to get me at the precinct. 'No uniform,' she'd warned.

"She took me to a place I'd never been before, a heroin shooting gallery. You wouldn't believe what it was like. There were two people lying dead on the floor from an overdose. Nobody was paying any attention to them. The place stunk of urine, sweat, crap, every filthy odor you ever smelled and some you haven't, believe me. They were zombies in there. Half humans. You know what it reminded me of more than anything else? Those pictures you used to see of the death camps, Auschwitz and those places. Those people staring up at the camera with their already dead faces. That's how these people looked.

" 'This is what junk is,' the girl said to me."

I whistled softly. "What happened to her? Was she being sent to jail? Is that where she was going?"

"No. She killed herself a couple of days later. She'd just turned nineteen. Poor kid. I guess she'd figured death was the only way she was going to break her habit."

Grady ran his fingers through his thick black hair. "When I heard that, I knew what kind of federal law enforcement I wanted to get into. Sometimes out there on the street, you feel a little bit sorry for a guy you have to put away. It isn't always all their fault they're messed up. But the kind of scum who'll do this to people? They haven't got a corner in hell hot enough for them as far as I am concerned."

You could sense the Bobby Kennedy thing there again, the tenacious terrier sinking his teeth into a larger animal and refusing to let go. Intensity of that sort, you learn in intelligence work, can be a liability; it can close your eyes to things you should be seeing and lure you toward conclusions the facts don't substantiate. Still, it occurred to me that Mr. Grady was certainly not someone you would want on your case if you were a bad guy.

At about that thought, our DC-6 hit the runway with a jolt, bounced a couple of times, lurched off to starboard then finally straightened out.

Grady turned to me as we taxied to a stop. "Want some good advice?"

"As long as it's free."

"It is. Just the thing for a guy like you who appreciates the nightlife in Bangkok. Don't miss the White Rose, the *Rose Blanche*, they call it. You'll see a few things in there you can't see back in Washington, D.C."

Vientiane's Wattay Airport was, well, primitive. Our DC-6 taxied to a halt in front of a couple of two-story wooden buildings. The pilot climbed out, unlocked the baggage compartment and handed us our baggage himself as though he were a Greyhound bus driver.

A couple of Laotians in uniform leaned against the door to the building nearest to us. Their half-closed eyes failed to flicker as we walked past into the street beyond.

"Not much for Customs and Immigration here, are they?" I remarked to Grady.

"They don't give a shit anymore. We've borrowed their country from them to fight the war in Vietnam."

A young man rushed up to Grady and grabbed his suitcase. "See you around," he said, then waved as he headed toward a waiting car.

I found a cab. For discretion's sake—if such a thing was possible in Vientiane at the time—I'd been booked into a

modest hotel called the Metropole. It was on the bank of the
Mekong, the river which runs along the edge of the city, and
modest was certainly the operative word as far as the Metropole was concerned. The lobby was the size of a bedroom,
illuminated by three forty-watt bulbs that gave off a light so
weak you could barely see the tops of your shoes when you
crossed to the stairs.

At each landing a porter was ensconced Soviet-style at a
desk to hand you your keys. Unlike the corridor guardians in
the USSR, however, he proffered me my key with a leer and
the offer of a teenager of whichever sex I desired.

In view, I suppose, of my alleged eminence as a visiting
dignitary of the Department of Defense, I'd been assigned a
room with a river view. The Mekong up there was about
three hundred yards wide, a gulch of muddy sludge which
from the window seemed thick enough to walk on. The far
shore was Thailand. It was terraced and cultivated. The Laotian side had a high bank topped by a dike to stem the annual floods.

A couple of geckos were racing each other up one of the
bedroom's walls. They were, as far as I was able to tell, the
only amenities the hotel offered its guests.

Since I had a pickup appointment for a trip to our headquarters, one of those elementary "stand on a street corner
with a copy of *Time* rolled up under your arm" things, I hur-
ried out without unpacking.

Technically, CIA headquarters was on the third floor of
our windowless embassy in a section designated CAS—
Civil Affairs Section. The acronym was appropriate since
the agency was pretty much running the country. Our real
work, however, was done in a white-walled compound
called KM6—Kilometer 6—on the outskirts of the city. As
it happened, the commanding general of our little CIA Laotian army was Ted Hinckley, the man who'd been my boss
during my tour of duty in Berlin.

Of all the men and women with whom I served in thirty-
three years at the Central Intelligence Agency, Ted Hinckley
was the only officer I knew who was possessed of genuinely
criminal instincts. He was ruthless, as utterly ruthless with
his friends as with his enemies. A notion of morality was as
alien to his being as the notion of orchid culture would be
to an Eskimo. It was Hinckley who taught me the hard lessons of this craft: that expediency takes precedence over mo-

rality; that if an operation is more important than a human asset, sacrifice the asset to save the operation.

He was a star of the CIA. He wound up as Deputy Director for Operations, the chief of our covert activities, in reality the second most important post at the agency after the Director's. What's so fascinating is that he wasn't the agency type at all: Ivy League, ex-OSS, a little family money to stretch out those meager government paychecks. He despised those people, and they in turn disdained him. But he trampled over them all with that cold brilliance of his.

That was because he was so damnably effective. No one ever, anywhere, questioned his effectiveness. He didn't trust anyone else's judgment. He never left anything to chance. He read every goddamn file and cable that came within fifty feet of his desk. No fact, however inconsequential it might appear, ever escaped him.

Hinckley's usual welcome to a newcomer to his station was a scornful dose of silence. Not "Hello, how are you?" or any such nonsense. However, he was actually cordial to me that day when I was ushered into his office. He asked me if I had had a nice trip.

"Particularly the part from Bangkok up here," I said. "That was exciting. We had a cub scout for a pilot. Most of my fellow passengers had four legs except for the guy sitting next to me. He was a narc."

"A narc? What the hell is he doing up here?" Hinckley asked.

"Told me he was interested in temple rubbings."

"Of course. Just like I'm interested in memorizing the Sanskrit alphabet. Those narcotics people aren't even supposed to be up here without my authorization. All they do is cause us trouble, running around, poking their noses where they don't belong. We're running a war here and I can't have people like that constantly getting in our way. Where is he staying, do you know?"

"He didn't say."

"Never mind. We'll find him. Let me give you a quick background briefing on just what it is we're doing here."

Hinckley got up and walked to a large map of the area he'd hung on his wall, a pointer in his hand. Physically, Hinckley was a strangely unprepossessing man. His hair was blond, so light it was flaxen in color. His complexion was pale, almost translucent. From that had come his nickname

"The Pale Rider" after, I suppose, Milton's *Paradise Lost*. You know the line: "Death on his pale horse."

"What we've done in Laos from the very beginning," Hinckley informed me, "is organize, train and equip our own army to do our fighting for us. They're based in this area up here in Military Region Two, north of the Plaine des Jarres adjacent to the North Vietnamese border. Basically they belong to one tribe, the Meo. They hate the Vietnamese. And they are, believe me, terrific fighters. Real killers."

Hinckley gloated a moment or two at that thought. "Fundamentally, they are commanded by their own chieftain, a man called Vang Pao."

He caressed the map with his pointer. "We infiltrate them across the Annamite Mountains down to the Ho Chi Minh Trail. They've done a terrific job for us, gathering intelligence on the Viets' troop movements. Lately, we've been using them to plant a heat-sensing device the Pentagon developed on the trail. It picks up the presence of a lot of humans, beams out a radio signal and, bingo, in come the B-52's.

"Here in Laos we've organized them into what we call Mobile Strike Teams. We wanted to call them Hunter Killer teams, but old Mr. Public Relations, Bill Colby, didn't like the phrase. He was afraid our precious media would interpret it the wrong way. What we do with these teams is turn them loose in the areas where the local communists, the Pathet Lao, have taken over. Our teams slip into a village at night, rout out the Pathet cadres and execute them right there on the spot, in front of the rest of the villagers. It's a very salutary way of getting their hearts and minds focused on the fundamentals, believe me."

"How many of these people do we have under arms?"

"Roughly thirty thousand. You can never be precise in these things." Hinckley returned to his chair and took a Camel from his pocket. "Anyway," he concluded, "that's basically the operation we're running here. We're in charge. The Pentagon people work for us. State . . ." He guffawed at the notion of just how inconsequential State's contribution to his operation was.

Hinckley then opened up a desk drawer and drew out a file. "One of my people prepared this for you," he announced, handing it to me. "It's the best rundown we could put together on your GRU target. Take it outside, read it and bring it back to me."

The officer who'd prepared the report Hinckley handed me had done an excellent job. Nonetheless, it was clear that getting to my major without his fellow Soviets picking up my move was not going to be easy. His employers didn't seem to trust him off the reservation anymore.

"Is this guy around?" I asked Hinckley when I gave him back his file. "I'd like to talk to him."

"He's with the Meo up at our forward headquarters in Long Tien."

"Can I get up there?"

Hinckley thought a moment. "I could always send you up on one of our arms flights. You'll like that trip a lot more than you liked the one you came in on."

You entered the White Rose from a side street just off the Mekong riverfront. It occupied the ground floor of a nineteenth-century *hotel particulier,* undoubtedly the home of one of the city's French colonialist rulers in the years between the two world wars. The riverfront at that point was lined with similar buildings, replicas probably of the homes their owners had aspired to buy in Grenoble or Bordeaux once they'd amassed their fortunes in Indochina. My hangover had eased and a few drinks in the White Rose seemed as good a way as any to begin my stay in Laos.

The public affairs officer of the embassy was sitting just beside the door as I walked in. I'd met him at a couple of cocktail parties back in Georgetown. Fortunately, he didn't recognize me because the Laotian bar girl on his lap was gleefully employing her bare breasts to slap his face. That sort of set the tone for the evening.

There was a bar in the first room you entered. It gave on to a second room, this one long and narrow, its wall faced with bamboo rattan. At the far end was a small stage screened by a curtain decorated in a pattern of white roses. There was a bunch of tiny tables and folding chairs clustered around the stage, and along one wall were booths designed to handle half a dozen people or so. One, I noted, was occupied by a boisterous group of my fellow Americans who were, judging from the decibel rating coming from their gathering, having a very good time.

I picked a seat at the end of the bar facing the stage, ordered a drink and took out a Romeo y Julieta cigar I'd picked up in duty-free on my flight out. For a few satisfying moments I sat there watching the Laotian bar girls gliding gracefully through the shadows in search of someone to buy them whatever colored water passed for champagne in the Rose. To my left, one of the Americans in the booth got up and sauntered over to the bar carrying half a dozen glasses ready for refills.

When he'd finished passing his order to the bartender, he glanced over at me. "Howdy," he said. "I reckon this must be your first time here in the good ole Rose."

"Shows, does it?" I asked.

"Well," he intoned, "you are dressed mighty fine for Vientiane." It sounded to me as though he'd used up at least a dozen syllables working the city's name out of his mouth. I glanced at my clothes. I was still wearing my rumpled seersucker suit with a clean shirt and a striped tie. Obviously, they didn't see many ties in the Rose.

My newfound friend offered me the satisfying smile of a country preacher contemplating a particularly generous collection. "You know," he declared, "down where I come from in West Texas, we'd say you was dressed up like a boomtown clap doctor on Saturday night."

He laughed harder at his joke than I did. Then he clapped a hand the size of a frying pan on my shoulder. "Finelooking cigar you got there. One of Mr. Castro's?"

I nodded. "Like one?"

"Thanks, but I don't indulge. Mind if I give you a little bit of well-intended advice, my friend?"

"Anything that'll help out a new boy in town."

"Well, if I was you, I'd put that cigar away before too long." I could see from the mirth in his eyes just how much he was enjoying all this. "Because in a few moments they's gonna be a little ole girl get up there on that stage, and if she sees that cigar of yours, she's sure gonna take a hankering to it."

He reached for one of the beer bottles the bartender had set on the bar, took a long swig and turned back to me chuckling. "Now, that little girl, she can do some tricks with a cigar that'd put a curl in old Mr. Castro's beard. But you sure as hell ain't gonna want to finish smoking your cigar once she be done with it, I can promise you that."

"Well, thanks," I said. "I'll bear that in mind."

"What brings you out here to Vientiane?" he asked.

"I'm with the Department of Defense. Out here on a TDY."

"Is that right? Well, in that case, we be working for the same people."

"How's that?" I asked.

"I'm an airplane jockey. Air America. Or *Scare America* as we call it hereabouts."

Now, Air America was an organization with which I was more than familiar. It was the solution the agency's brass had come up with to solve our air-transport problems. We owned the company lock, stock and barrel through a Florida proprietary we'd set up for the purpose. A handful of the company's senior officers were actually agency career officers seconded to Air America to run it for us. We vociferously denied that we had anything to do with the airline, although by the time of my visit to Laos, that lie was beginning to wear a bit thin.

"I hadn't heard the 'scare' part," I observed. "How did that come up?"

He hooted in purest glee. "Some of them boys over there"—he waved his beer bottle at the booth he'd just left—"they tend to fly a little bit lower and faster than the rules in the good book say they's supposed to." This time he pointed the bottle and a finger toward one of his companions. "Old Billy Bob over there forgot to take his wheels up one day last week. Strong drink'll do that to a man. He figured he'd go say goodbye to his girl 'fore heading north. Damn fool come in so low over her house he like to take the roof off of it with his wheels. Got a stove pipe as it was."

He laughed gleefully at Billy Bob's escapade.

"Shit," I said, "I gotta take a ride with you guys. I hope I don't get him as the driver."

"Is that right, now? Where you going?"

"Long Tien."

"Oh, you'll love it up there," he said. "It's the asshole of Southeast Asia." He offered me that enormous hand of his. "Hey if you're gonna fly with us, you better come drink with us. Man'll only get himself in trouble drinking alone in the Rose. Albright's the name. Ray Albright."

He shepherded me over to his table with an arm around my shoulders.

"This here's Petey Tuttle," he announced to his friends.

"Defense Department. He helps pay the bills, so you all be nice to him." Then he introduced me to his fellow fliers. Interspersed among them were three or four bar girls, the best-looking ladies, I suspected, that the Rose had to offer.

We laughed and drank for a while until a kind of cymbal clash announced the show was beginning. The lights dimmed, the curtain went up and there on the stage was a lanky girl with her hair fixed in a black pageboy bob, wearing a G-string, high heels, makeup and not much else. For a second she stood there casting a haughty glare at the crowd. Then, with a movement as swift as it was agile, she leaped off the stage, extracted a pipe from the hands of a customer in the second row of tables and sprang back onto her stage brandishing the pipe in the air like a knife.

The crowd cheered while she puffed on the pipe a couple of times to make sure it was well lit.

When it was, she settled back onto a canape on the stage behind her. She opened her legs, pushed aside her G-string and, with a defiant smile, inserted the stem of the pipe into her vagina. Within a few seconds, through some magic manipulation of those precious muscles of hers, she had the pipe sending up regular puffs of smoke.

My pilots whooped in delight.

"How to go, Aw," roared Billy Bob beside me. "That's her name, *Aw*," he confided to me. "She's a Thai from across the river. Man, she's putting up more smoke than a Sioux brave telling the tribe Custer's comin'. You oughta see that little ole girl when she gets goin' on the cigarettes. Thirteen Salems. That's her record."

He announced her achievement with such pride you might have thought it had been his.

When Aw had finished demonstrating her artistry the lights went up, and we resumed talking and drinking. I was to get to know those pilots well during my stay in Vientiane, and I've got to tell you, you will never come across a wilder, more raucous, more take-life-to-the-edge bunch of guys in the world. They were pure excitement junkies. If they hadn't been flying airplanes for us, they would have been racing stock cars or trying to ride motorcycles through the Gobi Desert. As Billy Bob said to me that night, "Man, I don't give a fuck what I've got in the back of that airplane of mine. Pay me enough money and I'll fly you a load of camel shit to the North Pole and land it up a polar bear's ass."

They all wore gold bracelets on their left wrists, two or three of them. Each consisted of four long chain-links of gold held together by smaller links. Four Seasons bracelets, Ray said they called them. "They's only two kinds of money that counts out here, gold and dope," he declared.

I got to know Billy Bob a bit more as the night wore on. He was in his mid-thirties, an ex-marine pilot who had Semper Fi tattooed on his left biceps, the rounded, heavy shoulders of a former linebacker and a nose that was considerably the worse for the wear on it. His was the sly, mischievous grin of the kid who's spent the better part of life getting caught with his fist stuck in somebody else's cookie jar.

By his own admission he had been flying what he referred to as the "Bang Bang Shuttle," running arms from Saigon to Vientiane and on to the Meo tribes for two years. It was, he said, "one helluva a lot more fun than dusting boll weevils." Besides, he confided, "a guy who's got his eyes open can always find a way to pick up an extra buck or two out here humping the odd cargo."

It must have been about half past eleven when Billy Bob yawned and stood up. He smiled down at the bar girl who'd been fondling him with silent diligence while we'd talked.

"Me and Lotus Flower here got some business to attend to," he announced. After a surprisingly formal round of farewells, they left.

I don't think it could have been more than five minutes before one of the waiters came rushing up to Albright. "Mister Ray, come quick quick," he shouted. "Your friend, he dead."

"What the fuck are you talking about?" Albright roared at him.

"Your friend, some man he go boom-boom," the waiter cried, cocking his forefinger and thumb into a pistol to make his point.

We all leaped up, knocking over the table in a cascade of beer bottles and half-empty whiskey glasses, and ran for the door.

Billy Bob was lying on his back up at the corner where the side street joined the riverfront, his head jackknifed at the neck over the open sewer ditch running down the street. His mouth was agape and his already lifeless eyes open, looking on the last vision of his young life, the facade of the three-story building rising above him. Lotus Flower was sitting cross-legged beside his body shrieking hysterically.

I bent over the body. He had a gaping wound the size of a fist exploding out of his left lung. Clearly, it was the exit wound of the round from a heavy-caliber weapon, probably a .45.

"What the hell happened?" Ray shouted at the circle of Laotians drawn up in silence around Billy Bob. Their faces were expressionless: no fear, no concern, no wonder to be seen upon any of them. Sudden and violent death, unfortunately, had become commonplace in their once lovely country.

"Man, he go boom-boom," someone informed Ray.

"American man or Lao man?" he demanded.

"Lao, Lao," they all agreed.

"Where'd he go?"

The blank stares that greeted Ray's question said worlds about how embarrassing such knowledge would be. Finally, one shrugged. "He run away fast."

A couple of cops arrived as we stood there and studied the scene with what can only be described as majestic indifference. Finally, one of them reached down and rolled Billy Bob's body up onto his shoulder so he could get a look at the entry wound with his flashlight.

Through the blood and mud around the wound, I could see, on the torn pieces of Billy Bob's white shirt, splotches of gray-black powder burns. Whoever had killed him must have fired from no more than a foot away. The Laotian cop muttered something to his companion and released his hold on Billy Bob's shoulder, letting his body fall back to the ground with a thump.

I looked at Albright. I don't know if he had noticed the powder burns or understood their significance if he had, but a thought suddenly occurred to me. Billy Bob had not been murdered. He'd been executed.

Once Billy Bob's body had been loaded into an ambulance, I joined the departing spectators. Up ahead, I noticed for the first time another Anglo who had just turned away from our little gathering, his hands thrust in his pockets, his head bowed in what I assumed was grief. I knew it wasn't one of the Air America pilots, yet there was something vaguely familiar about his slender build. Suddenly I realized it was Kevin Grady, my fellow passenger on the trip in from Bangkok.

I caught up with Grady and fell into step beside him. It took him a second or two to sense my presence, so concentrated was his mind on whatever it was he was pondering. When he did glance at me, I could see, even in that poor Laotian street lighting, the dark scowl contorting his features. It was clear my presence beside him was less than welcome.

"You look a little shell-shocked. Was he a friend of yours?" I asked.

Grady turned away and continued to stalk the street, hands in his pockets, his head thrust forward.

"Not really." He glanced at his watch. "But I knew him. In fact, I was supposed to be meeting with him right about now."

"Jesus!" I said, unable to cloak my surprise. "So that's why they killed him."

Grady said nothing for a while. Then he shrugged. "Who knows? You asked me this morning how they got the dope out of here. Now you've got your answer."

So that was what those odd cargoes Billy Bob had been flying around in the back of our aircraft were. And if happy-go-lucky Billy Bob had been going to a meeting with Grady, the odds were he had been a snitch. Murder was, after all, the occupational hazard of the snitch's trade.

"So long," Grady said, "my hotel's down here." He gestured along a dimly lit alleyway running away from the riverfront.

"I'll walk you back to your hotel," I offered.

"I wouldn't if I were you," Grady said. "You never know who might be curious about me around here." He waved his hand and turned down the alley.

As I watched Grady disappear into the darkness, Hinckley's words came back to me: "Never mind. We'll find him."

My flight up to Long Tien was scheduled to depart Vientiane airport just over twenty-four hours after Billy Bob's murder. As it happened, it coincided with Billy Bob's own departure on his way down to Saigon. His body had been packed for the journey into one of those rubberized green body bags that now constitute a part of our technological heritage from the Vietnam War.

Most of Billy Bob's fellow Air America pilots and not a few of his girlfriends had turned up to see him off. They were a sober and somber lot that morning in their post-White Rose incarnation. Somebody had unearthed a rent-a-pastor cleric to say a few meaningless words before they carried the body into the cargo bay of an Air America jet.

As it happened, Ray Albright was scheduled to fly the Air America DC-3 taking me up to Long Tien. He'd flown the plane and its cargo down from Long Tien the previous afternoon. Cordially, he invited me to come up and share the pilot's cockpit with him. Apparently, Air America was no more given to copilots than Royal Laotian Airlines had been.

"Anything new on Billy Bob's murder?" I asked him once we were airborne.

"Nope," Ray replied, "and they ain't gonna be. The book's closed on that one."

"Why do you say that?"

"If you like living life on the edge, my friend, the secret ain't knowin' how to get out there. It's knowing how to keep from falling over the edge once you get to it."

I glanced back into the aircraft's passenger compartment, which had been converted into a freight bay. One side was lined with long wooden cases strapped to the fuselage, leaving an aisle between them just wide enough to walk through. Stamped on the side panels of each was the name of the original shipper, Sea Supply, Inc. of Miami, Florida. On the opposite side were a dozen cases of Tide soap.

Like Air America, Sea Supply was one of ours. In fact, it was one of the first proprietary front companies the agency had established.

"What have you got back there?" I asked Ray, jerking a thumb toward the crates. "M-16's?"

"Naw," he answered, "Kalashnikovs. Them Meo like Kallies."

"Yeah," I said, adopting for form's sake my guise as a Pentagon arms expert, "the sixteen can be too sophisticated for some people." On reflection, however, I considered that a wholly wasted gesture. Ray was not a dope. He would have figured out my real affiliation by now. No one got on these Long Tien flights without clearance from the CIA.

"What's all that Tide for? Got a lot of dirty laundry up there in Long Tien?"

"Laundry my ass. Our fellas got a way they teach them Meo to mix that stuff with gasoline and make up a kind of homemade napalm to fry ole Charlie with." He laughed. "Field Expedient Methodology. That's what they call it."

About an hour out of Vientiane, I got up and made my way to the back of the plane to use the toilet. There was a cleared area about ten feet long between the last stack of crates and the end of the aircraft. When I'd finished with the toilet I got down on my hands and knees and, with a small flashlight, began to explore that open space.

I found what I was looking for in the tiny gutter that ran along the floor where it met the fuselage. Caught in it were a series of chunks of black goo, a bit like the hardened gravy drippings your Thanksgiving turkey might leave in your oven. It could only be one thing—raw opium paste.

Back in my copilot's seat, I thought through the ramifications of my discovery. I had, in a sense, put myself in the position of the husband who sets out to see if his wife is being unfaithful. He finds out she is. So now what the hell does he do about it?

Of one thing I was certain. There was no way these Air America pilots could be flying that stuff out of here on our airplanes without Ted Hinckley knowing what was going on. Absolutely no way. Hinckley ran as tight a station as any in the agency. He prided himself on knowing everything that went on in his command.

That had to mean the station was knowingly and deliberately closing its eyes to the traffic. It was another Golden Triangle situation.

The Golden Triangle, with its massive production of the opium poppy, dates to 1949 when the Chinese Communist Army defeated Chiang Kai-shek's Kuomintang. Two of Chiang's supporters, warlord generals named Li Wen-huan and Tuan Shi-wen, marched their armies, soldiers, families, dogs, cats and cattle, across the mountains southwest of Kunming into an area of northern Burma. There, those peasant soldiers began to grow the crop they knew best, opium poppies.

Shortly thereafter, the Korean War broke out. Our newly formed agency had a desperate need for information from inside Communist China, and an equally desperate lack of the resources we needed to obtain it. So, we turned to generals Li Wen-huan and Tuan Shi-wen.

They were only too glad to help. They began to infiltrate their men into China on a regular basis to study targets and obtain for us information we could never have gotten otherwise. For the better part of the next decade, they were our most important source of intelligence on Red China. The decade also coincided with the rise of the Golden Triangle as the world's principal source of opium for transformation into heroin.

We knew what the generals and their supporters were doing, of course. But there was an unwritten deal between the CIA and the generals. We got the information we needed. And we shut our eyes to their dope traffic. Maybe that swap didn't suit some of our armchair moralists back in Washington, but it happened to be the way things got done out in the real world.

So what was I going to do with this knowledge I'd just acquired? Speak to Hinckley about it? At the best he would consider it a joke. At the worst, he would construe it as an act of such unutterable naiveté that it could only be interpreted as being malign in intent.

Drop it on the desk of the Inspector General back at Langley? Not if I wanted to keep my job and my head, I didn't. Whistle-blowers cause embarrassment all around. The Bible uses the term to *know* a woman in the sense of having had carnal knowledge of her. For Langley, it was important not to *know* about our unwelcome tidings, our shortcomings. It was all right to gossip about them in the dark of a quiet bar or in an office between witting officers. But it was not all right to force that sort of knowledge into the institutional process in the form of an official report or a complaint set out on a piece of paper. Then it became real; it existed, it had to be dealt with.

No, the rule in a case like this was simple: Be a good team player. Keep your mouth shut and your eyes straight ahead. Stopping the drug trade was Kevin Grady's job, not mine.

Rusty Wirth, the officer I'd flown up to see, was waiting for me at the dirt strip runway in Long Tien. The installation consisted of a half a dozen prefabricated warehouses, most of which, I assumed, were meant to store arms like the load we'd just flown up in the back of our DC-3. We got into Rusty's jeep and drove off to his "office," a two-room hut about three miles from the strip.

We talked first about my concerns with my GRU major. After we'd reviewed my memories of his memo, Wirth said to me, "Look, as far as I can see, there's only one time when you've got any chance to pitch him without his minders spotting your move. Every once in a while he goes out for an early morning jog along the Mekong. As far as we can figure, that's about the only time they let him off the leash."

When we'd finished, Wirth warmed up a couple of C-ration cans for lunch. C-rations were Long Tien's *nouvelle cuisine*. Wirth was about five years my junior, a pharmacist's son from Ypsilanti, Michigan. He'd spent most of his agency career in Southeast Asia, caught in the unfolding drama of the Vietnam War. Already, he had that sad, burntout look so many of our longtime officers there acquired.

We took our cans out to the stoop of his bungalow to eat. Running off to our left down to the jungle's edge over a series of nubby hillocks was what appeared to be a field of poppy plants. From our distance their white-flowered bulbs looked like tightly sewn tufts of cotton on an old-fashioned bedspread.

"Opium poppies?" I asked Wirth.

"Yeah."

"So it's true a lot of that stuff is grown up here?"

"Of course it is. They were doing it long before we got here. And they'll be doing it long after we leave."

Then Rusty tossed his empty C-ration can toward an open garbage pit and stood up. "Better get you back to your plane."

Ray was waiting by the DC-3 chewing a toothpick, a bemused grin on his face when we arrived. "Why now, Petey," he said, "I figured you'd want to stay on in this lovely place they got up here." He laughed uproariously. Nobody appreciated Ray's jokes more than he did.

When Rusty had left, he informed me we had to wait for another passenger he'd been ordered to fly back to Vientiane. He had no idea when the gentleman was likely to show up.

"Ain't but one thing for it," he announced. He spread a poncho on the ground in the shade of the DC-3's wing, lay down and in thirty seconds was asleep.

About forty-five minutes later, we heard the sound of a vehicle gunning its way down the dirt landing strip toward our plane. Ray rolled up on one elbow and blinked.

"Well, now," he yawned, "looks like we got us a heavy hitter for our trip back home."

"How's that?"

"That there's General Vang Pao's personal command car. They ain't got no room in there for little guys."

The car braked to a stop fifty yards from the plane, and an American and three Laos got out. They bade one another what appeared from our distance to be effusive farewells. Then the American walked over to us. He was in his late forties with a heavy body that had just begun to go to fat, curly black hair and God-knows-what for eyes because they were screened by dark Ray-Ban aviator glasses. He was wearing a white silk shirt, well-pressed slacks and carried a midnight blue lightweight blazer over one arm. He had to be the most elegant gentleman Long Tien had seen in some time.

"Howdy," Ray said, "Ray Albright's the name. I'm drivin' this afternoon. This here's Petey Tuttle."

Our fellow passenger smiled and shook hands. He didn't bother to give us his name. Or if he did, he mumbled it so softly I didn't hear it.

We all climbed onboard. I offered the newcomer the copilot's chair. "Your turn to look at the scenery," I suggested.

He smiled graciously, slipped into the seat and folded his jacket neatly onto his lap. As he did, I noticed that the index finger on his left hand had been amputated just above the bottom knuckle.

The trip back was uneventful. In fact, I slept most of the way. When we'd taxied to a halt, our fellow traveler shook hands and was the first to climb out of the aircraft. He sauntered across the tarmac to the Air America administration building, where a car and driver were waiting for him. They were, I noticed, the same car and driver that had picked me up on a Vientiane street corner the day I arrived, the chauffeur and vehicle Hinckley usually sent after important visitors or new arrivals.

I decided to follow Wirth's advice and make my pitch to our GRU major while he was out for a morning jog. Since he didn't follow any set schedule for his early morning runs,

I had to take up running myself. I'd been out there sweating off the weight for good old Langley for almost a week before I finally saw the major's chunky figure plodding up the riverbank in my direction.

I gave him just the barest jogger's fraternal nod as we passed each other, and continued downriver for another twenty yards or so until I could feel reasonably certain he wasn't being followed. Once I was convinced he wasn't, I turned around and sprinted back toward him.

When I caught up, I fell into step beside him. For a second he gave me the frightened, bewildered look of a cornered rabbit. Did he think I was going to pull a gun? I smiled as warmly as I could to reassure him.

"Good morning," I said. "I bring you greetings from a dear mutual friend, Lech Gutowski."

It was clear from the scowl the mention of our defector's name produced that I had not announced to the major any glad tidings. Before he could blow this whole approach out of the water with some angry retort, I launched into my pitch.

"He is very well and happy now and hopes you are also well. He has given me a letter he wrote especially for you, which he asks you to read as a testimonial to the friendship and affection he has for you, to the memories of the good times you shared in Berlin."

The major stopped jogging. His chest was heaving and I realized it was not from the exertion of his run.

"*Nyet.* Never will I read something from that traitor. For me he is dead." He wiped his sweaty brow. "You are CIA. Of course you are. I go now to my embassy to report your contact."

With that, he galloped off down the riverbank, back toward the Soviet compound. I made no effort to stop him or talk to him. I didn't need to. He had just slammed the door in my face as firmly as he could. By reporting a foreign agency's approach to his superiors, he was making an unqualified declaration of loyalty and, in effect, putting an end to any effort to recruit him.

I did not have the heart left to jog back to my hotel. I walked. After all, I had just come halfway around the world, spent almost two weeks in Laos, all on the taxpayers' money. For what? A thirty-second turndown.

* * *

It seemed appropriate enough on my last night in Laos to drop by for a farewell drink at the White Rose, where I'd spent such an eventful first evening in Vientiane. None of my Air America pilot friends were there on my second visit. Since Billy Bob's murder, the charms of the Rose had, understandably enough, wilted as far as they were concerned.

I settled down on the same bar stool I had occupied that first night and ordered a drink. I was deep into a weighty philosophical debate with my conscience on the wisdom of picking up one of the Rose's bar girls for company later in the evening. And, if so, deciding which of the establishment's lissome ladies it should be, when a familiar figure took the bar stool next to mine. It was Kevin Grady.

"Hey," I said in welcome, "I thought you'd left."

"Gone and come." Kevin smiled. "And you?"

"I'm out of here tomorrow. Tell me, did you ever find out anything more about that guy's murder?"

"Rumors. That's about all you get out here. We hear he was done by General Vang Pao's people."

"Because he was talking to you?"

Grady grimaced. "Who knows? It's possible."

"Working with you drug guys," I observed, "seems to be a high-risk industry."

"They don't make them any more high-risk, my friend. Speaking of which, how would you like to do the smallest of favors for me?"

"Not very much if it means someone is going to want to take a shot at me."

"Naw," Kevin drawled, flashing his most convincing Good Cop smile. "For a guy who's flown Royal Laotian Airlines, it's a breeze. See where the toilets are back there at the end of the room behind the bar?"

"Right."

"Well, just before you get to them, on the left beside the bar, there's a booth. A guy in a blue jacket is sitting there with a couple of girls. Why don't you just wander down to the can and take a look at the guy on your way in? I'd like to know if you've seen him anywhere, anytime, anyplace since you've been in Vientiane. It'd be a big help."

"Who is he?"

"I'll tell you when you get back."

Well, what the hell, I thought, why not? After a few more swallows of my drink, I started back toward the toilet. The task, however, was going to pose rather more of a challenge to my trade-craft than I had anticipated. The gentleman in the booth was submerged in a felicitous sea of Laotian bar girls. His right arm encircled the shoulders of the girl to his right. His head was examining, at very close range, the bosom and stomach of the lady on his left, and a third girl was industriously pouring fresh drinks for their party. Short of grabbing the back of his head and lifting it out of the second lady's lap, there was no way I was going to get a glance at his face.

The situation, fortunately, had improved somewhat on my return trip from the toilet. He had come up for air and a swallow of the fresh drink number three girl had prepared for him. Since his right arm was still coiled around his number one lady, he grabbed at the glass with his left. The index finger on that left hand of his had been amputated just above the knuckle. A sidelong look confirmed the rest. It was the man who had flown down from Long Tien with me.

"So," Kevin said when I'd settled back onto my bar stool, "you ever see the guy before?"

Why should I tell Grady what I knew? I asked myself. After all, he wasn't one of us. What was or wasn't going on up at Long Tien was the agency's business, not his.

"No," I replied, "never. But then maybe I haven't been spending enough time in the clubs. He seems addicted to bar girls."

"Sure?"

"Sure. So who is he, Kevin? I did my bit. Now do yours."

"His name is Tomaso Riccardi. Tommy Four Fingers to his near and dear."

"And what has Mr. Riccardi done to merit your interest in his health and well-being?"

"He's the *consigliere* on drug matters for the Santo Trafficante Mafia family in Miami."

Shit, I thought, and this guy is flying into restricted areas in CIA aircraft, and riding around Vientiane with Ted Hinckley's personal car and driver. "What the hell is he doing out here in Vientiane?" I asked Grady.

"Pete, my boy, let me put it to you this way. Do you figure he'd come all the way out here from Miami just to watch some Laotian lady put a cigarette in her pussy?"

"Well," I noted, "he's certainly demonstrating a healthy interest in Laotian culture back there in that booth, but you have a point. It seems a long trip for a small reward. So why is he here? Buying dope, I suppose."

"You suppose wrong. Guys like Tommy Four Fingers never dirty their hands with deals like that. They leave that stuff to their flunkies."

"Okay, then what is he up to?"

"If I had to make an educated guess"—Kevin rubbed his hands through the watery circle his glass had left on the bar as though he were hesitating to say something—"it would be this. I think he came out here to oversee setting up a French Connection–style lab for converting opium paste into heroin up in a place called Long Tien."

"Oh, come on, Kevin," I protested. "Long Tien's in the fucking boonies. Why would anybody in his right mind want to put a drug laboratory in a godforsaken place like that?"

"Simple mathematics. You take a hundred pounds of that black goo the peasants scrape off the bulbs of an opium poppy, okay?"

I nodded.

"Usually the first thing you do with it is boil it down to something called morphine base. Simple to do. The stuff that comes out looks like brown sugar. Your hundred pounds comes down to about thirty-five. Now, it's in the next step that things get tricky. That's where you need your French Connection–style lab. But if you get it right, what comes out of your thirty-five pounds of morphine base is, maybe, three pounds of pure heroin. But it will be worth a thousand times what your black goo was worth."

Grady grimaced. "Can you imagine how much easier it is to smuggle those three pounds of white powder out of there than to try to run out a hundred pounds of filthy black goo?"

He had a point. Hinckley, my CIA boss, had to know that this was happening. In fact, given the way he controlled access to Long Tien and ran his station, that Mafia hood could only have gotten up there with Hinckley's knowledge and approval. Were we closing our eyes to the fact that the Mafia was setting up a heroin lab on what was essentially CIA turf?

"Well," I said, "I have a little trouble with that. You know who runs things up in Long Tien, don't you?"

Grady offered me the pained look of a politician to whom a journalist has just asked a particularly stupid question.

"Are you kidding?"

"And if by any chance you're right, how do you figure those good agency folk are going to react to your playing bull in their china shop?"

Grady leaned in close to me, that tenacious terrier look of his almost distorting his features. "Pete, let me tell you two things. First, I'm right. Second, I don't give a flying fuck what those agency guys think."

At the rear of the bar, I noticed that Tommy Four Fingers was standing by his booth preparing to leave. Grady had already noticed him and was now doing a wonderful job of pretending to ignore what was happening. With the three ladies convoying him toward the door as though they were destroyers escorting an aircraft carrier, Tommy made his exit. His amatory plans for the evening were ambitious indeed.

Grady, as I had expected, gave him about a two-minute lead. "I'm outta here," he murmured and set off in pursuit.

His departure left me alone to wrestle with the consequences of what I had just learned concerning my fellow passenger on the flight back from Long Tien.

My discovery of traces of raw morphine on the plane going up to Long Tien and now this discovery at the bar of the Rose were disconcerting. After all, I had nothing but contempt for drugs, both for those who took them and those who dealt in them. Clearly, however, there had to be a bigger picture involved here, one that possessed dimensions of which I was ignorant.

And there was, of course, a second problem. Should I whisper into Hinckley's ear some warning that our friends the narcs were on to what was going on in his station?

That was when I thought of Billy Bob murdered, I assumed, by some of Vang Pao's goons. Being a good team player had its limitations. I asked the bartender for another drink.

Shortly before noon the next morning, as agency protocol required, I went out to the compound to terminate formally my mission. Since the idea of pitching our GRU major had originated in Washington and not Vientiane, my failure to recruit him in no way reflected on Hinckley's conduct of his station. As a consequence, he was, by his standards, positively genial when I came into his office.

"Langley!" he exclaimed with that aggrieved air that station chiefs like to adopt when turning their thoughts to our intelligence Mecca. "If only those guys would learn to trust their guys in the field. Think of the time and money we could have saved on this one if they'd come to us for an advisory first."

At that moment one of the phones on his desk rang. From the manner with which he grabbed it, I understood it was his secure, private line.

"Echelon," he said into the receiver. Nothing in that bland expression on our Pale Rider's face changed as he listened to what his caller had to report. I noticed, however, that he was starting to press the pencil he held in his hand between his thumb and first two fingers. He kept pressing until the pencil snapped.

"All right," he ordered his party, "this is what I want done. Isolate the aircraft. No one is to be allowed within a hundred yards of it. If there's any effort to use its radio, jam it. I don't want anyone to make any contact with the guy or undertake any negotiations with him until I get there."

"Sorry, Lind," he said hanging up, "I've got to go." He was in his office doorway when he stopped and turned back to me.

"Hey," he asked, "didn't you tell me you flew up here with some narc from Thailand when you came in a couple of weeks ago?"

"Yeah," I answered. "A guy named Kevin Grady."

"Then you better come with me," he ordered. "I may need you."

"The Air America terminal at the airport," he instructed his driver. "Fast."

"What's going on?" I asked as we shot out the compound gate.

"Your idiot narc friend Grady just forced his way at gunpoint onto an Air America plane. He's claiming there's heroin in its cargo and wants to seize the plane and arrest some Lao that was on board along with the cargo."

Hinckley resembled a bit those sea creatures who tend to fold their tentacles back into themselves when they are menaced. In a crisis or when he was angry, he tended to draw back into himself. It gave his anger a cold, remote quality that made it more threatening than the heated anger of the more passionate among us.

"And what if it is heroin they're carrying?" I asked.

"What precisely that aircraft is or is not carrying is of no consequence. Only one thing matters: making certain some idiot, however well-intentioned he may be, doesn't do violence to our close working relationship with General Vang Pao and endanger the aid he's giving us."

He stared straight ahead for the rest of the trip to the airport, clearly formulating the tactics he intended to use when we got there. The driver took us onto the runway, to the plane's location in an aircraft bay cut into the side of the tarmac. A pair of uniformed Laotians carrying AK-47's and a CIA officer in jungle fatigues stood guard a hundred yards or so from the plane, a DC-3. Hinckley got out and walked up to him.

"Brief me," he ordered.

"The flight came in from Long Tien about forty-five minutes ago. The pilot went into the admin shack to handle some paperwork, and while he was in there this guy goes into the plane."

"How did he get onto the base in the first place?"

"Showed his U.S. government ID at the gate. Apparently when he got onto the plane he pulled his gun on this Lao in there."

"Do we know who the Lao is?"

"One of Vang Pao's people he sent along to ride shotgun on the load."

Hinckley grunted. "Go on."

"Apparently the guy tells the Lao he's a narc and he's putting him under arrest. Cuffs him to a pipe on the fuselage. When the pilot comes back, he tells him he's seizing the plane because it's transporting heroin. He says he's arresting the Lao and orders the pilot to fly him down to Tan Son Nhut in Saigon. The pilot told him that was fine with him, but he'd have to go back to admin to file a flight plan before they'd let him off the ground. That's how we found out what was happening."

"Exactly what authority is he claiming for all this?"

"Says he's a federal law enforcement officer. Bureau of Narcotics and Dangerous Drugs."

"Since when does he think the BNDD has the power to make arrests on Laotian soil?"

"Maybe that's why he wants to get the plane down to a U.S. military reservation in Saigon."

"Probably. How many people know about this?"

"Him. The pilot. The Lao. Us." The officer gestured toward his armed guards. "Them if they can understand what's going on, which I doubt."

Hinckley had apparently learned all he wanted to know. "Bring me my autovin-autovon speaker phone," he ordered his driver. That was the secure portable telephone that patched him into the military's worldwide secure voice communications system. When the driver gave it to him, Hinckley looked at me. "Come on," he said, "we're going to play Baptist preacher. See if we can reason together with this gentleman."

"Be careful," the officer warned, "he's threatening to use that arm of his on anyone who tries to interfere with him."

"If he's what he says he is, he can't possibly be that crazy," Hinckley snapped, leading the way to the steps up into the DC-3's entrance at the back of the aircraft.

Grady was waiting at the head of the stairs, his .38 leveled at us.

"Stop," he ordered, flashing his badge. "I'm a federal officer and I've seized this aircraft."

"The hell you have," Hinckley retorted without altering his forward progress by so much as a hesitant half step. "I am the CIA station chief for Laos, and you are on this aircraft in gross violation of your orders and your authority. You will immediately release this Laotian gentleman you're holding prisoner, leave this aircraft and return to your station in Bangkok, or I shall have you placed under arrest and sent to Saigon in what passes for irons in this modern age of ours."

Hinckley got the entire mouthful out advancing up the stairs with that cold leer of his on his face. Clearly, he intimidated Grady, who retreated four or five paces back into the aircraft's cabin.

From our new post just inside the DC-3, I could see the Laotian on the passageway near the cockpit, his hands handcuffed to a railing running above his head. A dozen cardboard packing boxes lined the plane's walls. Two of them had been ripped open and their contents, orange and blue boxes of Tide soap powder, tossed out on the floor. They lay at Grady's feet with their tops torn off and a white powder spilling out all over the flooring.

"Stop," Grady ordered us. "One more step and Langley

will have another martyr's name they can carve on your office wall."

This time Hinckley did stop. At about the same instant I sensed that Grady had recognized me. He started to say something, but then didn't. In any event, he did not need words to express his feelings. His eyes did that for him.

"What arrant act of madness has led you to do this?" Hinckley demanded. "Do you know who that man you have handcuffed to the wall like a common criminal is? He's Colonel Li Ten Hua, the executive officer of General Vang Pao, the commanding officer of Military Region Two in Laos."

"I don't care if he's the fucking queen of England," Grady growled. The comparison was clearly inappropriate, but then our Irish cousins are given to comparisons of that sort. "As far as I'm concerned, he's a dope smuggler and he's under arrest. See this powder?" Grady kicked one of the Tide boxes with a fury that sent a stream of white powder pouring onto the airplane's greasy floor. "That's heroin. Pure heroin."

I peered down at it. I had never seen heroin, so I could not be certain what the stuff was, but it certainly did not look like Procter and Gamble's finest synthetic detergent.

"It's of no interest to me if it's heroin or Duncan Hines Shake-and-Bake," Hinckley told Grady. "It is the personal property of a vital ally of the U.S. government in the prosecution of the war out here. You have exceeded your authority by boarding this aircraft and attempting to arrest a foreign national on his native soil."

"The hell I have," Grady replied. "This is a U.S.-registered aircraft owned and operated by a U.S. firm on behalf of an agency of the U.S. government operating in foreign commerce and carrying a controlled substance, namely narcotics, with the intent to distribute same in violation of Title 21 of the U.S. Code of Criminal Justice sections 1952 and 2." Grady paused just long enough to fix a sneer onto his face. "You could look it up."

Whether the legal verbiage gave Hinckley pause or he was just trying to take the edge off the confrontation, I don't know, but he momentarily shifted gears.

"Let me tell you something that may have escaped your attention in your zeal to enforce those laws of yours," Hinckley told Grady. "We have half a million men fighting and dying in Vietnam. The intelligence information General

Vang Pao and his people are furnishing us is vital in keeping those young men alive. It is far more important than any effort of yours, however praiseworthy, to stop the drug traffic. National security concerns are at stake here, and they take precedence over your efforts. That is the beginning and the end of the story."

"National security concerns?" Grady shouted. "Do you know where this dope is headed? Saigon. So it can be peddled to U.S. GI's. Turn them into zombies. That way when Charlie comes to call he'll have an easier job making monkey meat out of them, because the poor zapped-out bastards won't know which end of their M-16's the rounds come out of. This dope and this plane are mine. That's the end of the story."

Hinckley drew his secure portable phone to his mouth and tapped his personal code into it. "I tried to reason with you and clearly failed," he informed Grady. "I am now calling the National Military Command Center for a patch to your ultimate employer, the assistant attorney general for law enforcement. At least he will have been your ultimate employer, because I would not guarantee your prospects for long-term employment in the federal government after this fiasco. I will see to it that he orders you to release your prisoner and this plane immediately and leave Laos without further delay."

And that is exactly what happened. Hinckley got the assistant attorney general on the phone, explained the situation to him and then passed the phone over to Grady. Kevin went chalk white listening to Washington confirm word for word every threat and order Hinckley had uttered. Poor Kevin. He was a man betrayed. He had marched onto that plane to avenge the eighteen-year-old black girl who'd killed herself in New York, in honor of his father shot dead by a pair of junkies. And the federal bureaucracy had betrayed the righteous goodness of his intentions in the name of our higher national security concerns.

"Give Lind your .38," Hinckley ordered. "He will escort you back to Bangkok and return it to you there."

Grady didn't say a word to me from the moment we walked out of the DC-3 he'd tried to seize, until we'd cleared Customs in Bangkok and I returned his service revolver to him. All the way down in the Air America plane

Hinckley had ordered up for us, he sat there beside me on his bucket seat brooding. That slender figure of his seemed to throw off waves of anger and frustration as the stones in a clambake emanate waves of heat.

Finally, slipping his .38 into an airline carry-on bag, he spoke.

"Listen, Lind or Tuttle, or whatever the fuck your name is, don't ever get in my way again. Because the next time I'll have your ass no matter what it costs me. Even if you're Director of the CIA." He spat angrily at the floor. "That patriotic speech of your pal, Hinckley. Half a million GI's. If you swallowed that crap you're a choirboy or a cynic. And you lied through your fucking teeth when you told me last night at the Rose you never saw Tommy Four Fingers in Vientiane. You and Hinckley probably had him over for lunch."

He kind of rocked back on his heels and glared at me a moment. "Your Mr. Hinckley is rotten to the core. And so, my friend, are you. Except he at least knows how rotten he is. You haven't figured it out yet."

In his office at the DEA, New York D.O., Kevin Grady snapped off his tape player and walked to the window. The memories of that flight from Vientiane to Bangkok were as painful, as bitter as they had been on that morning sixteen years before. He stared moodily out across the rooftops of Manhattan toward the gray and sullen waters of the Hudson River, three blocks from the DEA's New York District Office.

He faced this task of listening to Jack Lind's tapes with a mixture of foreboding and curiosity, excitement and sadness. On the one hand there was his professional investigator's zeal to peel away the last of the artichoke leaves, to get to the heart of the matter. On the other, he felt a bit like the distant relative who's been asked to rummage through a dead man's closet for the clothes to dress him in his coffin.

The angry emotions the passages of Lind's tapes had stirred in him were not, he was certain, the last of the bitter memories they would evoke. Lind, it now seemed clear, had meant for this material to fall into his hands. Why? Grady noted that the tapes leaped from 1968 Laos, to 1981 Washington, D.C. Was there something that had happened in those intervening years that even from his grave Lind was still trying to hide?

Curiosity aroused, Grady switched his tape player back on and returned to his job.

BOOK TWO

Casey at the Bat

Lind's Tape

Bill Casey's appointment as Director of Intelligence was welcomed with unabated enthusiasm by those of us at the CIA who believed in an activist agency. After our savaging at the hands of the Church Committee, our betrayal at the hands of Bill Colby, and our mutilation at the hands of Jimmy Carter's DCI, Stan Turner, Casey's arrival was a breath of fresh air. One of his first actions was to make Ted Hinckley his DDO, Deputy Director of Operations, the boss of all our covert activities. In the shake-up that followed, I was given the Latin American Division.

Among the perks to which my new post entitled me was the privilege of lunching in the seventh-floor executive dining room. The tenor of the place is elegant London men's club: muted lighting, oil paintings on the wall, well-made antique furniture. With a little imagination you might think you were in a Pall Mall club, which is hardly surprising since it was in just such an environment that most of the agency's founding fathers first nurtured their craft.

I was there one summer day in 1981, mopping up the dressing of my chef's salad with a twist of bread—something I'd been taught from an early age never to do—when Elsie, the waitress, came tiptoeing up to me.

"Mr. Lind," she whispered, employing a tone of voice so pregnant with concern she might have been announcing Armageddon or at the very least a sure winner in the seventh race at Laurel, "Mr. Hinckley wants to see you in his office right away."

When I arrived, Hinckley commanded, "Read this." He thrust at me a piece of paper.

The paper contained a bulletin which had just ~~come~~ over the Associated Press news wire.

PANAMA CITY (AP) July 31: The twin engine Ott~~er~~ of Panamanian military boss General Oma~~r~~ crashed into a mountainside during a rainstorm this morn~~ing~~ outside the village of Coclesito 100 miles north of here. General Torrijos, his pilot and the five other passengers on board the plane are all believed dead.

I whistled in surprise.

"Yeah," Hinckley said, "tough luck, but this is not the moment to waste a lot of time weeping and gnashing our teeth. What we've got to do is look at the potential consequences of this. Just what are the chances of your friend Tony Noriega taking over down there?"

"I'd have to rate them very high."

"That's what I hoped you'd say." Hinckley got up and walked to his window, which looked down on a long green lawn running off to a line of dogwood trees partially screening the electrified barrier that protected the building. "There are some things starting to take shape around here you haven't been brought in on yet. This could have a major bearing on them. Casey's on his way back from the White House. He wants to see us as soon as he gets here."

The reason Hinckley had summoned me from my chef's salad that morning was simple enough. I was Manuel Antonio Noriega's rabbi in the CIA, the officer who had recruited him, nurtured his career both with us in the agency and in Panama, served as his controlling officer and friend for thirteen years.

I had recruited him shortly after my return from Laos in 1968. Lyndon Johnson had just pronounced John F. Kennedy's *Alianza por el Progreso* dead. It wasn't working. The Latin oligarchies that were supposed to support it were, in fact, quietly sabotaging it. We would, LBJ proclaimed, now throw our support in Latin America to the military classes. They were the solid bedrock, the Pentagon had assured him, on which to build a new, democratic church south of the border. We had trained them. We furnished them with their toys. They belonged to us.

If the military was going to be the wave of the future in Latin America, then it was essential that we at the agency wave a good distance from the shore. Study carefully the young, junior officers of each country in the region, our order of the day, then try to recruit two or three of the most promising of them in each nation.

If our initial selection was good, then it stood to reason that ten, fifteen years down the line, our recruits would rise to major command. Consequently the key military figures, and hence the key players in many countries, would be comfortably installed in the CIA's pockets. I had been ordered to

Panama to review the most promising candidates for recruitment there, then attempt to get at least one of them to sign on with us.

The CIA enjoys a very special status in Panama. We have the usual station chief attached to the embassy as a second commercial attaché or whatever. Our real business, however, is done out at Corozal, a military base bordering the Canal. The Corozal compound includes a tropical diseases lab, various other medical facilities, a veterinary clinic; in short, it provides excellent cover for our activities.

Joe Topanga, the station chief at the time, had prepared dossiers on seven recent graduates of two institutions, the Mexican Federal Military Academy and the Escuela Militaria de Chorrillos in Lima, Peru. Both institutions were held in high regard by the CIA as greenhouses in which the future leaders of Latin America's military were nurtured.

It took me the better part of the day to get through the material. Of the seven, two in my judgment, stood out as possible candidates. The first was the captain in charge of the National Guard garrison in Colon at the Atlantic entrance to the Canal. Personally, he was rock-solid, married, two kids, not a blemish on his character that anyone had been able to detect.

The Panamanians have a quaint local custom they refer to as "The Friday Night Cultural Outing." It is the unwritten understanding in marriages down there that Friday night is Daddy's night off from conjugal constraints. He's free to go where he wants with whomever he wants: he can go out with his mistress, his secretary, chase the bar-girls, play poker, get drunk with the boys and fall into bed at any hour and in any condition he chooses. No questions asked.

Our potential recruit, Carlos Rodriguez-Lara was his name, never missed nine p.m. bed-check with his wife on Friday night. That's an indication of just how rock-solid he was.

On the surface, our second candidate didn't seem very promising. He had just made second lieutenant and was already over age in grade. He was serving as an intelligence officer in Chiriqui Province in northern Panama, up against the Costa Rican border. United Fruit had thousands of acres of banana plantations up there, and our man's principal task was rooting out leftist labor union activists who were trying to organize the company's peasants and tenant farmers. It was an assignment he was carrying out with a considerable degree of skill and an appalling degree of brutality.

The brutality—it included trying to cure some of the labor leaders' hemorrhoids with broken Coca-Cola bottles and billy clubs—would take some explaining in Washington, but perhaps it could be put down to the natural exuberance of the Latin fiber.

Unlike Captain Rodriguez-Lara, there was nothing in this man's file that spoke particularly well of his moral character. There was, however, an incident which suggested to me that Manuel Antonio Noriega might just be the recruit the CIA was looking for.

The Bishop of Panama was a handsome man who wore his cassock with considerable style. His name was Tim McGreavy. Despite that name he was pure Panamanian, the second-generation descendant of an American who had worked on the construction of the canal, married a local girl and stayed on in Panama. Tim's cardinal weakness was of the flesh. He very much enjoyed the company of young ladies, normally a perfectly commendable attitude, but one not widely encouraged among those who wear the purple. Like many Panamanians, he also had a well-developed taste for whiskey.

Late one evening, in the company of a young lady from an excellent Panamanian family, and in what a police report subsequently indicated was a questionable state of sobriety, he struck and killed an elderly woman as he was driving through the streets of the capital. In view of the seriousness of the incident, the first traffic cop on the scene sent out an SOS for the officer in charge of the Panama City Traffic Patrol, Manuel Noriega.

When Noriega arrived, the bishop was sitting in a patrol car, white-faced and almost catatonic. The young lady, weeping, was beside him. One of the traffic patrolmen was busily snapping photographs of the accident scene.

It didn't take Noriega more than a second or two to appreciate all of the possible ramifications of the bishop's dilemma. He ordered the police photographer to stop taking pictures and to bring his roll of negatives to his office in the morning. Walking over to the bishop, he is alleged by our files to have told him: "Your Eminence, this is a terrible tragedy. You go back to your residence before any spectators arrive. We'll see the girl home. Leave the rest to me. I'll handle everything."

The old woman's death was put down to a hit-and-run driver. The next morning, Noriega discreetly delivered the crash-scene negatives to the severely shaken cleric. It was a normal and well-executed quashing of a potentially awkward incident, except for one thing. Some days later, Noriega confessed to his Panamanian contact that he had held out five of the most compromising negatives. The next time Noriega needed a friend in the Roman Catholic hierarchy in Panama, he would know where to find him.

"What about this guy Noriega?" I said to Topanga when I called him to review our list of candidates.

"You saw the business in there about how he beat some poor whore silly in Lima?" he asked. "Because she wouldn't screw him? Didn't like his looks?"

"Yeah," I said, "it shows a very disturbing lack of control. And I sure as hell wouldn't want him out on a blind date with my sister."

"How is Langley going to look at that if we recommend taking him on as a regular agent?" Joe asked.

"My guess is it's not going to upset people. They'll be inclined to put it down to an exhibition of the macho characteristics all Latins have. Besides," I chuckled, "let's look at the positive side. At least now we know he's not light in his loafers. That's one character flaw we don't have to worry about. We're making progress here."

"The guy is smart, or rather shrewd, which for our purposes may be even better," Joe said. "And he's consumed with ambition. Still, there is that dark underside to his character that worries me."

It did not, I must confess, worry me. The people we recruit as CIA assets overseas are not priests. They have character flaws, character flaws which we look for, then set out to exploit systematically. If they didn't have those faults, very few of them would come onto our payroll.

I picked up Noriega's file, weighing it in my hands as though somehow it was the man's psyche my palms were caressing. To a certain degree, recruiting a CIA asset is a guessing game in which timing is critical. In tennis, you want to get the ball when it's on the rise. You don't want to wait until it's peaked. It's the same here. You want to recruit your asset while he's still on the rise, while he's still vulnerable, while he can still use whatever it is you're offering. If you wait too long, he may not need you and the Great White Father up north quite so much.

Manuel Antonio Noriega was clearly on the make that March day. His ambition to succeed came burning through his dossier. Everything we were looking for was there: all the frustrations, the psychological weaknesses, the needs and vulnerabilities that set a man up for recruitment as a CIA asset. You could be sure that in his struggle to succeed, he would grab at any hand offering to help him on his way up.

"Joe," I said, "I think we should try to recruit him."

"It's a gamble," he warned. "He's smart and tough and he's hungry for the dough. He's also devious and totally amoral."

"Gosh," I laughed, "I think you've just described your ideal CIA asset."

Shortly before noon a couple of days later, Langley sent us our OA, the Operational Approval to recruit. That authorized me to take the first step in the process that would eventually make Manuel Antonio Noriega the CIA's most important asset in the western hemisphere.

A separate cable assigned as the code digraph by which Noriega would henceforth become known in the CIA's files if my recruitment was successful—PK\BARRIER\7-7. *PK* was the code symbol we employed for Panama. *BARRIER* was the codeword for our agents in the Panamanian National Guard or police, and 7-7 indicated that Noriega, if recruited, would be the seventh agent the station was running inside those organizations.

The place we had chosen to make the pitch to Noriega was furnished in what might best be described as your standard safe-house drab: a table, half a dozen chairs, a worn sofa and, because we were in the tropics, a wheezing air conditioner. It was a one-story bungalow on a side street running off the Panamanian highway just before it entered David, the capital of Chiriqui Province. In my attaché case was the only furnishing that really mattered, a fifth of Old Parr scotch.

Noriega was precise to the minute, which was in itself a good sign. I introduced myself as Jack Brown, and we settled in for a drink. Noriega was short, squat almost, but there was a suggestion of a coiled, concealed strength to his body. His face, as that prostitute in Lima had noted, had been ravaged by acne. His jet-black hair was plastered to his skull with some kind of glistening pomade, the "greasy kid stuff" of those old Brylcreem ads. There was something reptilian to his eyes. They were half closed and seemed to flicker at you. What struck me most about the man, however, was his air of self-composure. There was an aura of assured serenity to him that seemed wholly out of character with the violence-prone individual I'd been reading about.

We settled back into our seats with our whiskies. Noriega regarded me with just a glimmer of humor in his eyes.

"Brown," he said. "That's a fairly common name up north."

At this stage of our relations I was not authorized by the agency to reveal to Noriega my real name or the identity of the Boy Scout troop for which I was working.

"It is," I agreed with a laugh. "Particularly in my line of work. You know, Lieutenant Noriega—"

"Tony. They call me Tony."

"Tony. We think that you have a real future in intelligence work. We'd like to see you realize that future. To the extent that we can help you achieve your ambitions—and you know there are ways we can help—we're prepared to work with and for you. We're the kind of people who can be there when you need us."

I rattled the ice cubes in my glass, trying to size up his reactions. Our business, after all, is betrayal. When we recruit a man like Tony Noriega, what we are asking him to do, fundamentally, is *betray*—his nation, his government, his leader, the institution to which he belongs. We try to dress up that reality in fetching rationalizations, but when the clothes come off, what you are looking at is a traitor. Young Americans sometimes join the CIA under the illusion that they are going to become James Bonds, performing violent acts of derring-do for the U.S. government. That is not how it works. We get others, the Noriegas of this world, to do our dirty work for us.

"For example," I said, baiting the hook, "there are specialized U.S. military schools that offer courses in intelligence work. They have a quota set aside for officers from friendly armed services. If you're interested, we can see to it that you get one of those places."

That went to the target. Noriega had a well-developed nose for those things that were going to move his career forward, and getting that kind of specialized U.S. training into his personnel file was prime among them.

"You've been very helpful to us in the past"—he had done the odd report for us via his brother, one of our informants, when he'd been a student—"and we would like to think we can continue to work together just as effectively in the future. Perhaps on a somewhat more regular basis."

Noriega nodded slightly. He was coming along.

"We know how tough life is here for young, hardworking officers like you with families to support," I continued. "We'll do what we can to help ease that problem for you. But, above all, to the degree it's feasible, we'll be prepared to try to set things up so you can progress along your career path and we can continue our close association in the pursuit of our mutual interests. You're the kind of young officer who deserves to go places here in Panama. We want to see that you do."

That was the pitch. You don't lay a quid pro quo on the table. Never anything as crass as that. It's unspoken but it's there. For a young officer in Central America in those days, that offer had very real appeal. Here was Big Brother from up north saying, in effect, "I'm ready to number you among my elect."

Noriega got up and poured himself another whisky. He swirled the liquor around in his glass for a few seconds, lost in thought. Then he half raised the glass to mine and said, "Okay."

It was as simple as that. No questions, no doubts, no haggling, no attempt to lay down his own conditions or restrictions on our relationship. He'd made up his mind and that was it. I liked that. No doubt he could be devious, but he could be decisive as well.

Over the next few minutes we ironed out the modalities of our new arrangement. Then we finished our drinks, shook hands, and Noriega left, offering me one of his cryptic half smiles as a parting gift. He had now officially become a paid asset of the CIA.

As soon as I got back to headquarters at Langley, I got Noriega admitted to a U.S. Army–run course in intelligence at Fort Gulick near the Atlantic entrance of the Canal. That initial gesture was meant to show him we were holding up our end of the bargain. In addition, his local handler was instructed to slip him a hundred dollar bill each time they met.

Then we watched and waited. He was, after all, a sleeper, a hidden asset on which we would only begin to realize a return when, and if, he rose to the position of authority we were wagering would one day be his.

That day came much sooner than either he or we could have hoped. It can be dated to October 11, 1968, when a colonel named Martinez led the Panamanian National Guard in a coup d'etat that overthrew the country's democratically elected president. Shortly thereafter, another Panamanian officer staged another coup and ousted Martinez. It was Omar Torrijos.

Torrijos was Noriega's patron inside the Panamanian National Guard. Nine months later, while he was vacationing in Mexico, a couple of his colleagues tried to pull off yet another coup to overthrow him—those things are as contagious as a cold virus down there. Noriega saved Torrijos by opening up the one airfield in the country which the rebels hadn't closed. Torrijos's reward to Noriega for saving his regime was swift and salutary. It could not have suited our designs for PK\BARRIER\7-7 better had we designed that reward ourselves. He promoted him to major and put him in charge of his intelligence service.

The days of slipping a few clean hundred dollar bills in an envelope to Noriega were over. From that moment on, the money began to come twenty, fifty, a hundred grand at a crack. It came in legitimate bank transfers to an account he established in his role as head of the G2. Of course, twenty-five, thirty percent of the money that moved through his G2 bank account was going to get stuck in his palms. We expected that. It was just part of the cost of doing business.

Both Noriega and his G2 now became increasingly important sources of information for us. We instructed him to cultivate his peers in the police, military and intelligence services in Central America. We backed him into the left-wing guerrilla groups springing up in Colombia and Venezuela. They all idolized his boss, Omar Torrijos. He was able to develop a relationship of trust and confidence with some of those people to whom we could not get access.

Soon he had built a network of informants among his peers in Central America, and we were getting a solid stream of inside information from him: who was on the rise in Honduras and whose star was setting in Costa Rica; which politicians were on the take in Central America (a fairly long list, that one); where Castro was making inroads in Guatemala; who was thought to be an agent of his intelligence service, the DGI, in Colombia.

Then, as always seems to be the case when things are running smoothly, they went suddenly sour. The source of our trouble was a man named Jack Ingersoll, who ran the Bureau of Narcotics and Dangerous Drugs, the forerunner of the DEA, the Drug Enforcement Administration.

Ingersoll had divided the world's known drug traffickers into three categories. Category One, at the top of his hit parade, was made up of his primary targets. That list contained 175 names.

It was passed on to us at the CIA for our routine scrutiny. Four CIA assets had been accorded a place of honor on it. Among the four was our old friend General Vang Pao of Laos. That came as no surprise to anyone. It was another name on the list that set the alarm bells ringing in the Latin American division.

Ted Hinckley had taken over the division on the completion of his tour in Southeast Asia. He summoned me up to his office.

"Take a look at this," he ordered, shoving Ingersoll's list under my nose.

There, high upon it, was the name of the man who was fast becoming the CIA's best asset in Latin America, Manuel Antonio Noriega.

"So what about it?" Hinckley demanded. "Is this stuff true?"

I was forced to admit that this was the first time I had heard PK\BARRIER\7-7 accused of being involved in drug trafficking, an admission of ignorance that did not endear me to my boss.

"Get hold of our people over there at the drug agency and find out just what it is they've got on Noriega," Hinckley ordered.

I went back to my office and called Nick Reilly, one of the CIA officers we'd planted inside the BNDD.

"I'll get back to you," he promised.

Two days later he did.

"Since we started shutting down the French Connection in Marseilles," he explained, "some of the major heroin traffickers have begun to move their stuff through Spain to Panama and then up to the States. It seems this guy Noriega controls Customs down there. He's not into the traffic himself, but he's taking a skim for closing his eyes as the stuff goes by."

That had an unhappily truthful ring. Customs was under the overall control of Noriega's G2. Some of the CIA money we'd been providing the G2 had, I knew, been destined for the Guard officers assigned to Customs. So, in a sense, the CIA was helping to finance an organization that was facilitating the importation of heroin into the United States.

I asked Reilly what they planned to do about the guys on their list. Some years later, the *New York Times* would claim that Ingersoll had come up with a plan to assassinate some of the gentlemen on his Category One list. They were wrong. Ingersoll's battle plan was more subtle than that. He proposed to get rid of some of those people by what is euphemistically referred to as *non-judicial processes*.

Here's an example of the non-judicial process in action: in the mid-seventies, the DEA made an important heroin seizure at Port Elizabeth, New Jersey. During the press conference announcing their triumph, some DEA blabbermouth inadvertently revealed the nickname of the French informant who'd given the load to them. Six weeks later, the gentleman in question was found in the waters off Marseilles attempting to swim the Mediterranean with cement blocks for shoes. He was, indeed, a very important drug dealer but, as it turned out, he had never seen or talked to an officer of the DEA in his life. He had been infected, poor chap, with a virus called *non-judicial processes*.

That was not a destiny Hinckley had in mind for an asset as potentially valuable to his division as Manuel Antonio Noriega.

"Those cowboys aren't going to touch one of our people," he declared when I'd outlined the situation to him.

"Ted, the fact is he's apparently taking money to let that heroin flow on to the United States."

"So what?" Hinckley looked at me with that aggrieved air he always wore in the face of heedless innocence. "I do not doubt that he is. Any more than I doubt that some of our citizens, particularly, it seems, those in our black communities, have a problem with heroin. That, however, is their problem. It damn-sure isn't mine. Nor is it the concern of

this agency. Our problem is what is Noriega doing for us
now, and what can he do for us in the future. That and that
alone is our concern."

"Maybe, Ted, but that doesn't mean his activities aren't
the legitimate concern of our drug people."

He pulled a Camel from his shirt pocket and lit it without
offering me one. I don't recall ever seeing Hinckley offer a
subordinate a cigarette. When he'd taken a deep puff and exhaled the smoke through his nostrils, he put one of his feet
on his desk and smiled.

"You remember that day in Laos when we stopped that idiot narc from seizing Vang Pao's dope? We did it in the interest of higher national security concerns. That," he
continued, "is what is at stake here. Never forget, Jack, the
narcs are just glorified cops. They interpret the law the way
Billy Graham interprets the Bible—*literally*. They don't understand the other considerations that are sometimes involved. That's why the interests of this agency are, and must
always remain, paramount."

He stood up, walked around his desk and looked down at
me. "Let's analyze this thing together, rationally, pragmati-
cally, which is the only way to analyze a problem in our
business. First, how much have we invested in Noriega over
the past five years?"

"You mean including all those G2 programs we've been
funding?"

"Of course."

I made a quick calculation. "Getting on close to half a
million dollars."

"Right. And can you name me a better asset this division
has in South America right now?"

I was at a slight disadvantage there. After all, I didn't
know all of our Latin American assets. We had, among those
I was aware of, a major-general in the Chilean Air Force and
a cabinet minister in Brazil. Noriega's take, I acknowledge,
was at least as good as what we were getting from them.

"And you would also agree, would you not, that we are
just beginning to realize the potential of this guy?"

That proposition clearly needed no defending.

"Okay." Hinckley circled back around his desk and sat
down again. "You know, Jack, I've been watching you
closely since I took this division over. You're good. Even, I

would say, very good. For my money, you're one of the smartest operators I've got."

Coming from a man as stingy with his praise as Hinckley, that was quite a compliment.

"The job you did fingering Noriega in the first place, re-cruiting him, bringing him along so well is terrific. He's your baby and you've got every damn right to be proud of him. However, there's just one lesson I don't think you've fully absorbed yet. This is a cruel world we run in, Jack. Get too guileless in this business and you become ineffective." He waved his cigarette toward the ceiling, a gesture I understood was meant to encompass the seventh-floor offices of the agency's senior executives.

"The problem with this place is some of those people up there still think it's amateur night. They just can't bring themselves to turn pro, and because they can't, they go on wasting lives on the altar of their holy innocence. I don't want guys like that in my division, Jack. I want pros. The name of our game is pragmatism. Whatever it takes to get the job done, do it. Noriega is too valuable to this agency to be lost just because some half-witted blacks up in Harlem can't stop putting needles into their veins."

I was troubled by what Hinckley had said—troubled first, because a lot of it was true, but troubled as well by his con-viction that expediency should enjoy pride of place over any other concern in our activities. Surely, there had to be room for something else in there.

"You don't leave much room in that construct of yours for idealism, Ted," I observed.

"Forget about idealism, Jack. Ideals are for the innocent. The graveyards are full of prematurely dead idealists." He leaned forward, the cigarette dangling from the corner of his mouth as if he were imitating Humphrey Bogart, his hands clasped on the desk in front of him. "The question is what do we do?"

"You can always pass the word to Ingersoll to knock it off," I suggested.

"We could do that," Hinckley agreed. "However, I would prefer not to. That would be telling Ingersoll that Noriega is one of ours. You know how cops are. They can't keep their mouths shut. In three months the whole world will know we have Noriega in our pocket."

"Well, what else can we do? Tell Noriega?"

Hinckley took a long drag on his cigarette. "You know," he said as the smoke burst from his lungs, "that's a damn good idea, Jack. That's the way to go. First of all, he's going to be grateful to us for our timely warning. He'll owe us one. Second, the fact that the narcs have targeted him means there's got to be a leak somewhere in his operation. If he's half the operator he's supposed to be, he'll know how to find it and cover his ass."

"He'll put a bullet through somebody's head."

"Probably. That's what people do to snitches in that business when they catch them. That's hardly our concern, however. You go down there, whisper this stuff in his ear and tell him to cool it, for Christ's sake."

I did and that is why, on the day when Omar Torrijos's airplane flew into a Panamanian mountainside, our leading Latin American asset was ready for advancement, his path forward unclouded by even the slightest suggestion that he might be involved with the drug traffic.

Bill Casey didn't enter a room. He erupted into it. His security guard hadn't even had time that day to take his key out of the door to the Director's elevator before Casey was pushing his way into the anteroom of his office. With one hand he thrust the morning's *Washington Post* at his secretary, Betty Murphy, telling her to get him a new book on Vietnam he'd seen advertised on page sixteen; with the other he'd grasped the elbow of his ADC and started to mumble an order about a four o'clock tee-off time at the Chevy Chase Country Club. By then he'd spotted Ted Hinckley and me waiting for him.

He blinked at us in recognition. "Okay, you guys," he ordered, "come on in."

Casey stomped around his desk, then dropped his heavy frame into his office chair with a resounding thump, the sort of gesture that surely must have put many a Washington hostess's teeth on edge when he set himself on their priceless Chippendale dining chairs. His hand shot out to his ADC for his attaché case.

"Thank you," he said, dismissing the young officer with a wave. He carefully placed the case on the desk in front of him, then looked at the two of us.

"So," he said, "that bastard Torrijos is dead." Like his boss, Ronald Reagan, Casey had been a staunch opponent of the new Panama Canal treaties, and had little use for either of their sponsors, Jimmy Carter or Omar Torrijos. "Who the hell's going to take over down there?"

"Bill"—Hinckley and the Director were already on a first-name basis—"it just so happens that one of our best Latin American assets is a high-ranking Panamanian military officer. There's every likelihood he could be the guy."

You cannot imagine the warmth of the smile with which Casey greeted that news. Here was a manifestation of the kind of can-do agency he intended to run already at work.

"Tell me about this guy," he ordered.

"Jack here is his case officer," Hinckley said, turning to me. "Maybe he'd better take over."

I straightened up a bit in my chair as the situation demanded.

"His name's Manuel Antonio Noriega, Mr. Director. He's a colonel in the Panamanian National Guard who's in charge of their G2, intelligence branch." I then proceeded to give him Noriega's pedigree. "He was Torrijos's bagman," I explained, "his enforcer, the guy who did his dirty work for him, broke the bones when the situation called for it."

It was, I'm sure, the first time Casey had heard Noriega's name. It was assuredly not going to be the last. Many in the agency had to stifle a sense of loathing when they worked with Noriega. Not Casey. He came to regard him with something close to real admiration for what he did for the CIA.

"Why's he working for us?"

"Money and access to power."

"You mean the guy doesn't have any political commitments, any ideology?" Casey, of course, had a strong ideological bias, and despite his experiences in World War Two, was always uncomfortable with our professional conviction at the CIA that the best spy is a paid spy.

"Sir," I replied, "Tony Noriega's ideology is right where his heart is—in his wallet."

"Then how can we trust the bastard?"

"Because we pay him well. We make sure some of the things we get him into provide him with an opportunity for some self-enhancement on the side."

I could see a look of skepticism clouding Casey's face. The Director was not above a little larceny here and there himself, but like most people who are so inclined, he was naturally suspicious of those who shared that attribute with him.

"In that case, I want to know exactly what this guy has done for this agency that convinces you he's such a great asset."

"What we've done is back him into the leftist guerrilla movements down there: the M19 in Colombia, the FARC, the Shining Path in Peru, the Farabundo Marti people in Salvador. He's become the best conduit we've got for information on what's going on in all of those groups."

"I mean, what has he *done* for us?" Casey pressed. "The hard stuff on the ground."

"He's built with our money a key network in Central America. That network is one of our best sources of information on what's going on in the region. He also played a vital role in a sting we organized against the guerrillas in Salvador."

"Okay, tell me about that."

Some of Casey's critics liked to refer to his *cold* blue-gray eyes. They never seemed cold to me. Wary perhaps, or skeptical, but not cold. He was too Irish for that. He'd sit there, his eyes half closed behind those outsized, rimless glasses he wore in defiance of the dictates of fashion, looking a bit like a walrus sunning himself on a rock. You'd think he was half dozing until, *wham*, like the seal slashing out at a passing fish, he'd light on some remark you'd just made. He did that now.

"Noriega's been supplying arms to the Farabundo Marti National Liberation Front in Salvador for us—" I started to explain.

Casey exploded. "He *what*? Those are the bastards we're fighting down there, for Christ's sakes! Why are we so pissed off at the Sandinistas? Because they're funneling arms from all over the world to those sons of bitches."

Hinckley intervened. "Bill," he cautioned, "hear Jack out. I think you'll like what he has to tell you."

The look on Casey's face told me he wasn't convinced, but I plowed on anyway.

"Mr. Director, when the Farabundo Marti people came to Noriega and asked him to be their go-between buying arms, he informed us immediately. We told him to go ahead. Those guys are multimillionaires from all the kidnapping and bank robberies they've staged. They were going to get their arms whether they got them through Noriega or someone else. Better, we figured, for us to control and monitor their arms flow."

I sat back, trying to suppress a smile. "Besides, there were some collateral benefits available to us. Noriega suggested we let him take the deal to a buddy of his, a guy name Jorge Krupnik. Krupnik will buy and sell anything, snow to an Eskimo, sand to a Bedouin, whatever. Obviously, Noriega was going to get a few bucks off the top, which is his way of doing things.

"Now Krupnik, just as we figured he would, went to Lisbon to get the arms. The guerrillas wanted U.S. stuff, M-16's because that's what the Salvadoran army uses. There's a flourishing black market in American arms there, stuff the Angolan government captured from Jonas Savimbi and his guerrillas."

Casey was sitting there, taking all this in, absentmindedly playing at his fingernails with a bent paper clip, giving no indication he was reacting to my words.

"The stock of the M-16 is made of kevlar, which is a material through which electric signals can pass with no difficulty at all," I went on. "Unlike wood, for example."

At last I detected a look of interest on Casey's face.

"Our science and technology people have developed a tiny radio transmitter powered by a lithium battery. The whole thing is no bigger than the nail on your little finger. It sends out a signal on a preset frequency and at a predetermined interval, say once every twenty-four hours. Now"—I paused for dramatic effect—"Mr. Director, if you had the M-16 in your hand when the signal went out, you'd never know it. But it's so strong one of our *KH 11* satellites can pick it up at fifty thousand feet."

Suddenly, there was a smile on Casey's face.

"We doctored up a load of these M-16's. Once they arrived and were deployed in the field, we were able to pinpoint by triangulation off the satellites where they were to within ten feet. Then all we had to do was call in a Salvadoran army search-and-destroy team to waste poor old Jose Guerrilla and his pals."

"Holy shit!" Casey exclaimed. "Now that's what I'd call an operation."

"It has its problems, of course," Hinckley cautioned. "Some of our allies in the Salvadoran army are also being killed by the arms we furnished to the rebels, which is not a fact we would like to have widely known. But we have certainly put away our share of guerrillas with the tactic."

"Does Noriega know what we did?" Casey asked.

"No," I replied. "That technology is new and very highly classified. Salvador isn't the only place we're using it."

The Director smiled and turned his attention to his attaché case. "I've got to tell you two guys something—this agency is going back to work." Casey started picking open the combination lock on the black leather case he'd had made especially at Mark Cross in New York, squinting through his bifocals at the numbers on its dials.

"The days when communist guerrilla groups could run wild around the world, getting their arms, their money, their orders from Moscow, kill people, blow up things then go sliding back into the safety of their sanctuaries, are over. Under this President we're going after the bastards."

He'd finally gotten the attaché case open and pulled out a stack of papers. "Read these," he ordered, passing them to Hinckley and me. They were drafts of a National Security Council Directive for Central America.

They floated in somewhat vague terms the idea of using against the Sandinistas exactly the same tactic Moscow had been using around the world for years: raising an underground army of guerrillas to infiltrate a territory or nation, terrorize its population and destabilize its government.

"Those goddamned Sandinistas down there in Nicaragua are pouring arms into Salvador. The Cubans are right behind them. And the Soviets are right behind them. They want to spread their goddamn revolution all through Central America. Well, I've got news for them. They're not going to get away with it," Casey promised. "We're going to kick the Sandinistas' ass out of Nicaragua. And the Cubans right along with them. The President wants this done. And if Ronald Reagan wants it done, then by God, this agency is going to do it."

"The most important thing in an operation like that," Hinckley declared, "is getting the right senior people in place. At the moment we haven't got anybody in the field down there in Central America who's capable of taking on something of this magnitude."

"Then get somebody down there for me who is," Casey grumbled.

"You just met the man I think would be right for the job," Hinckley informed Casey. "Duke Talmadge, the guy we've brought back from our station in Madrid. For my money he's the best covert operator this agency has."

Casey blinked a couple of times to indicate he was listening but not yet convinced. He was for all practical purposes bald, with just a ring of white, wispy hair circling his skull like an elderly monk's tonsure. He was—as his doctors never ceased to remind him—overweight, one of the causes of his high blood pressure. His cheeks sagged with that excess flesh and another roll of flesh drooped down from his chin. But again, as with so much with Casey, those looks were deceiving. He could be surprisingly active physically when he chose to be.

"I've got to warn you," Hinckley went on, "Talmadge can be a loose cannon on the deck. He's not easy to control. I mean, he has been known to go off half-cocked. But he's tough. He's resourceful. He's not afraid to take chances or run a risk if he figures the price is right."

"I think I'm going to love him. But the trouble with this place," Casey stormed, "is you guys have become a bunch of bureaucrats. You've got gray suits, gray spirits and button-down minds to go with those button-down shirts you all wear. There's no gumption, no spark around here anymore. I want covert operators with balls, who are ready to get the goddamn job done and not sit around picking their noses wondering if Congress is going to be mad at them for doing it."

He buzzed for his secretary in the outer office. "Betty," he ordered, "get that guy Talmadge we just brought back from Madrid up here right away.

"Now," he said addressing us once again, "let's get back to the matter of this guy Noriega. It's clear that there is no way in hell we can mount a major operation against the Sandinistas without having the full, unrestricted use of our military bases in the Canal Zone. Without them we're nowhere. Besides, Panama is the ideal place to transship black market arms to a guerrilla force up north. Legally or otherwise. Panamanians take to smuggling like kids in Minnesota take to making snowmen."

He tilted back in his chair and blinked at me a couple of times. "That means we've got to have a government down there we can work with. If some whining left-wing bastards take over now that Torrijos is dead and start screaming that we're violating the new Canal treaties with our operation . . . You know, put a hundred thousand people into the streets of Panama City shouting, 'Gringos go home'. . . . Our little guerrilla program is going right down the tubes."

He thrust out his stubby index finger and peered at me over his glasses. "So that brings us down to you, Mr. Lind, and this friend of yours, Colonel Noriega. I've got two questions for you. Number one, can we nudge this son of a bitch into power down there? And number two, if we do, will the bastard play ball with us and let us get on with kicking the Sandinistas in the ass?"

"Mr. Director," I answered, "I'd like to go down and assess the situation before giving you an answer to number one. On two, my gut instinct is his answer will be yes. He'll see our backing as the key to getting power. And he'll see our operation as an opportunity for him to make some money on the side. There aren't many activities Noriega won't support if the price is right."

At that moment Casey's secretary announced Talmadge had arrived. Hinckley did the introductions. Casey then reviewed our discussion for the Duke.

"Now, this is what I want," he ordered. "Talmadge, I want you to look this thing through thoroughly and come up with some hard, specific ideas on how to throw the Sandinistas out of Nicaragua.

"You, Lind," he continued, pointing at me, "get your ass on a plane to Panama and go see Noriega. You tell him we'll give him our backing to become the boss down there provided he gives us his backing when we're ready to start kicking ass in Nicaragua."

We saluted and prepared to leave.

Casey walked Duke and me to the door. A wide grin had spread across his face. "This is the kind of an agency I want to run, an agency that's not afraid to roll up its sleeves and get the tough jobs done. And you're the kind of guys I want working beside me when we do it.

"By the way," he asked Talmadge, "do you speak Spanish?"

"No, sir," Talmadge answered.

"Spent much time in Latin America?"

"Never been there, sir."

To Casey's credit, I must say that if he was taken aback

by those answers, he didn't show it. "Ah, what the fuck," he mumbled, "nobody's perfect."

Kevin Grady snapped off his tape recorder and stood up. For a second he rose up on the balls of his feet, stretching like a tennis player will just before a match. *Bastards*, he thought. They knew Noriega was into the drug traffic almost from the beginning and didn't do a damn thing about it, except to push him up the totem pole where he could run his deals easier with each advance he got.

Funny thing, he mused. He'd read every paragraph of the DEA's file on Noriega and there was not a word in there about Ingersoll's accusation—not one. Where had that stuff gone, he wondered, then snorted. Sure. You could bet the farm the agency had shortened up the institutional memory by getting its hands on those files and shredding them. No wonder all the administrators of the DEA since then—Peter Bensinger, Bud Mullen, Jack Lawn—had sworn they had nothing on the guy's involvement in the drug traffic. The agency had seen to it they had amnesia on the subject.

He lit a cigarette and prepared to flip the next tape into his machine. As he did, he noted the date on it—1981. He stopped. The summer of 1981—that was when he was running the caper that led him to Ramon, wasn't it? That was when it had all begun. It was then that he and Lind had set out on the fatal course that had ended with Lind's body sprawled on the carpet of his study.

BOOK THREE

Kevin Grady's Sting

A lfie Westin clasped his hands under the protective folds of his overall bib. He tilted back a degree or two on his heels and sent a glob of the spittle generated by his chaw of Old Indian chewing tobacco streaking straight to the base of the cottonwood tree to his left.

"Hey, man," the Cuban standing beside him said in admiration, "you be spitting that stuff like you be shooting some kind of gun."

"Sheet," Alfie acknowledged modestly, "Ah done drowned a running ant at ten feet yesterday."

He sniffed at the moist night air with the seasoned nostrils of a North Georgia good old boy. It was heavy with swelling mist. Overhead, the silvery shafts of the full moon were fighting a losing battle to pierce the onrolling banks of ground fog beginning to envelop the northern corner of DeKalb County where Georgia and Alabama join.

"Got ourselves a good night for treeing 'coon," Alfie observed. "Might not be so good for landing airplanes, though."

The elder of the two Colombians standing with the Cuban beside Alfie stamped nervously on the grass. Juan Machado's son Eduardo underlined his father's concern by rubbing his hands in evident distress. Despite Alfie's urging, the two of them, father and son, had come dressed for the occasion as though they were on their way to a dinner party in Buckhead, Atlanta's most fashionable suburb. Both wore dark overcoats, suits and ties. Some local sheriff spots Latinos dolled up like that driving around up here at three in the morning, Alfie thought, and it'll be "Oh-oh, there goes the neighborhood." Pull them over for a little look-see in two seconds flat.

He had been introduced to the Colombians by the Cuban go-between in Miami. As it happened, Alfie had a commodity the Colombians very much wanted, a five thousand foot isolated dirt and grass landing strip in rural Georgia. He'd brought them up here to check out the strip, set in the upper corner of his thirty-acre soybean and alfalfa farm.

Alfie's was equipped with night-landing lights which

greatly impressed the Colombians. What had really turned
them on, however, was the fact that he had a sophisticated
signaling device with which an incoming pilot could activate
the landing lights by a beeped command from the cockpit of
his Cessna. That signaling device was commonly found in
small rural airports; on private strips it was a rarity.

That had convinced the Machado father and son team to
organize the flight for which they were all now waiting. A
Volkswagen minivan waited at the edge of the strip with
Alfie's sidekick Jimbo Burke, who would drive it up to New
York with the younger Machado and six hundred kilos of co-
caine. Alfie's transportation and landing fee was $300 a kilo,
$180 thousand in cash, a third up front and the rest after
Jimbo turned the coke over to the Machados's contacts in
New York. That, as Alfie had gleefully told the Machados,
"beats the shit out of what Uncle Sam is paying for soy-
beans these days."

"You sure them boys of yours got off on time?" Alfie
asked the Machados. Juan looked at his son. Eduardo was
carrying a state-of-the-art cellular phone the size of a
walkie-talkie.

"*Si, si,*" he assured them, "I check."

"You mean you can talk all the way down to Medellín,
Colombia, on that there thing?" Alfie asked.

"No problem," Eduardo assured him with a proud smile.
"You call up Pablo Escobar, you say, 'Hey, Don Pablo, I
need a thousand keys,' you have 'em, man. No problem."

Alfie shook his head in appreciative wonder at the miracles of modern communications systems.

"Well, I sure as shit hope they don't run into no head
winds or some such thing," he declared. "I don't like the
way that ground fog's been comin' in this week."

"Don't worry," the elder Machado assured him. "They're
first-class pilots. Americans." He glanced at his watch. It
was 11:45. The plane was due at midnight. "You'll see.
They'll be right on time."

"Ah sure hope so," Alfie worried. "You'd hate to have a
plane pokin' around up there half the night looking for the
right hole in that fog. One of them Georgia Highway Patrol
guys hears that, and he's gonna come sniffin' around to see
what's going on."

Machado laid a reassuring arm on his shoulder. "Don't

worry about a thing. Everything's going to be all right. We all get a little nervous on our first operation."

They paced around in silence for a few minutes. Then, suddenly, they both heard it, the faint buzz of an oncoming plane's motor. Juan Machado gave Alfie a warm smile. "You see," he said, "I told you not to worry."

The plane made a tentative pass over the strip to pick up the all-clear signal Jimbo Burke blinked out with his red flashlight. Then the landing lights, in response to Alfie's signaling device in the pilot's cabin, flashed on. The pilot swung the plane to the northern end of the field so he could land into the wind. He must have read its direction from the movements of the ground fog, Alfie calculated. With barely a jounce the plane settled onto the strip and rushed toward the beckoning signal of Jimbo's red light.

"Mr. Westin," Machado beamed, "it's a pleasure working with a man like you. I hope we can do another load together."

"Why, sure," Alfie drawled, "Ah'd like that."

The Aerocommander drew up to their little group, then pivoted around to face down the runway in case the pilot was forced into an emergency takeoff. He cut his engines, then he and his copilot leaped out of the plane.

"Man!" exclaimed the copilot. "Have I ever got to take a leak!"

While he relieved himself, Jimbo Burke pulled up with the minivan and they began heaving the six hundred kilos of coke packed in surplus U.S. Army duffel bags from the plane to the car. As Alfie had suspected, the Machados were not much help in that part of the job.

"Okay," he said as soon as the van was loaded, "you guys get your asses in gear. Anybody stops you," he told Eduardo Machado, "you let ol' Jimbo there do all the talking. No sense you letting some highway patrolman hear that Carmen Miranda accent you got."

They drove off, and Alfie and the pilots rolled a fuel barrel out to the aircraft to refuel it.

"Hey!" he said. "You forgot to give me back my light activator."

The pilot grabbed the gadget, which looked like the electronic devices used to open garage doors automatically, and handed it over to Alfie. As the farmer stuffed it into his pocket, he activated it. The runway lights flared back on in a burst of white light. Alfie pulled a .38 from his overalls with his right hand and at the same time flashed a gold badge at the stunned group with his left.

"Police!" he yelled. "Don't move! You're all under arrest."

In time to his words, half a dozen Drug Enforcement Administration agents in dark blue DEA raid jackets, came charging out of the woods surrounding the field with their weapons drawn. At the head of the field, a truck emerged from the woods, red roof lamp flashing to block the strip in case the pilot should try an emergency takeoff.

The first instants in a drug bust are critical. It is vital that the smugglers realize immediately that their captors are the DEA, not rivals bent on killing them to seize their cargo. And the idea is to put on an overwhelming show of force so their targets don't get any crazy ideas of trying to shoot their way out of their problem.

Juan Machado looked at Westin with a slack-jawed expression of disbelief worthy of someone who's just seen a dead man rise up from his coffin. Beside the plane, the pilot sagged to his knees and began vomiting onto the grass.

"All of you," Westin ordered, "put your hands on the trailing edge of the wing, bend over, spread your legs wide. Wider!" he barked at the copilot, who was slow in complying. Three DEA agents moved up to frisk and handcuff the men.

"All right, gentlemen," Alfie announced to his shaken and handcuffed prisoners. "My name is Special Agent Kevin Grady of the United States Drug Enforcement Administration, and you are now in my custody. You are all charged with violating Title 21, United States Code, Section 841, concerning the illegal importation and distribution of narcotics into the United States."

No matter how many times Grady said those words, he got a chill of satisfaction each time he uttered them. His job did not have many material compensations, but it had its moral ones, and pronouncing those few words was prime among them.

"You have the right to remain silent if you choose," he continued, working his way into the Miranda rights text.

"Where are you taking us?" Juan Machado asked when he'd finished.

"You will be driven down to Atlanta under guard, put

onto a DEA plane and flown to New York, where you'll be arraigned and remanded into federal custody pending a bail hearing. Although, as I suspect you may know, there are very few judges in the federal court system who are inclined to grant bail on a six hundred kilo cocaine-trafficking charge."

"And our lawyer?" Machado persisted.

"You will be allowed to contact him when you get to New York."

The pilot, Grady noticed, was shaking violently as though he was on the verge of a nervous collapse. "What's going to happen to us?" he asked Kevin, fear and concern compressing his voice into a timid whine.

"I don't know, pal." Grady made no effort to muffle a scornful laugh. "But if I was you, I wouldn't make too many plans for the next twenty years or so."

A pair of his men armed with M-16 submachine guns herded the prisoners into a DEA van for the ride down to Atlanta. As they did, Grady walked out of their hearing and called up the operations desk at the DEA's Atlanta regional office on his cellular phone.

"Okay," he announced. "Operation Sugar Coating successfully completed. We've got the plane and three perpetrators under arrest. You guys reading the signal off the van?"

Jimbo Burke, like Grady, was a DEA agent working under cover. His minivan was equipped with a concealed transmitter the size of a button, attached to its rear axle by a magnet. It emitted a constant signal which would enable the DEA to monitor its journey northward.

"Yeah, we're reading him," Atlanta replied. "We got a bird riding shotgun on him. We'll keep our choppers running relays till your guys in the New York DO can get vehicles on them."

The van was heading north to what Grady hoped was going to be a perfectly set DEA trap. Juan Machado had indicated that his six hundred keys were destined for a single consignee in New York. That presented the DEA with an opportunity too great to miss.

The DEA's Colombian foes employed an organizational structure which was as complex as it was secure. It was patterned on the World War Two underground resistance movements and structured in pyramids with descending layers down to the dealers—never Colombians—who ultimately

sold the drug to its final consumers. Each level had its cellular structure with cutouts so that no single arrest would
lead to numerous secondary arrests. At the apex of the pyramid would be the Colombians' top man in New York. Probably no more than two or three people in his organization,
one on the money side and perhaps two on the side that dis-
tributed the powder, would be aware of who he was. They
certainly wouldn't know where he lived. Communications
were carried out behind the protective anonymity of a blend
of cellular phones and public phone booths, leaving no footprints in the sand that law enforcement could follow.

There was, however, one critical instant when that number
one man would be exposed, vulnerable to arrest. He would
have to take physical possession of those six hundred keys
now on their way to New York. That was the moment to
grab him.

The risks were tremendous. The young Machado was
armed; Jimbo Burke was not. Machado had insisted on that.

The Colombian would call a contact when he reached the
city for his final delivery instructions. That was the way
these things always worked. But suppose the guy told him,
"Hey, we were supposed to get an all-clear call from Georgia to let us know everything was okay. We never got it. It's
a setup."

Grady grimaced and walked toward their captured plane.
That was the kind of thought that gave DEA agents ulcers.

"Target just cleared the tollbooth, moving out onto the
GWB," the radio in Kevin Grady's car cackled. The car was
parked at the base of the access road leading from the Henry
Hudson Parkway up to the Cross Bronx Expressway, just
past the eastern terminus of the George Washington Bridge.

"So where do you figure they're headed?" Kevin's driver
asked.

Grady shrugged. "I wish to hell I knew. If I had to guess,
I'd say that Little Colombian neighborhood over there in
Jackson Heights. Or maybe, outside chance, they'll take the
Sawmill or the Hutchinson upstate toward Pleasantville or
Larchmont, someplace like that."

"Dopers? Up there in the suburbs? That's hard to figure."

"A new thing they're into," Grady informed the driver.
"The heavy hitters anyway. It's easier to spot surveillance up
there. No traffic. You know, they look out the living room

window and see the same blue Ford circle the block three times and say, 'Oh-oh, somebody around here doesn't like me.' "

Grady had selected their current parking place with those two possible routes in mind. If Eduardo Machado ordered Jimbo Burke over the Cross Bronx Expressway to Queens via the Whitestone Bridge, all he and his driver would have to do is to join the surveillance team was head up the access road to I-95. On the other hand, if Machado decided to go north after he'd crossed the bridge up toward Riverdale, they could slip into the flow of traffic right behind them.

An hour and a half earlier, Burke had pulled the minivan into a Burger King rest area on the New Jersey Turnpike, just below Elizabeth. One of their tail cars had reported Machado had used a pay phone in the parking area, then forty-five minutes later returned to the same booth, this time to take a call. Clearly, he had been getting his final delivery instructions. Since then Grady and his driver had been playing leapfrog with the van, waiting for Machado to commit himself.

"Cross Bronx," the radio announced.

At those words a welcome jolt of adrenaline surged through Grady's exhausted body. For the past fourteen hours, as they'd monitored Machado's progress up the Atlantic seaboard, his only rest had been a catnap on the plane. Now the grueling ordeal was almost over.

"Let's go," he ordered the driver, nodding his head up the access ramp.

There were four DEA vehicles plus Grady's command car in the surveillance operation. Two were vans, one unmarked, the other painted as A.J. Murray's Plumbing Services. The other vehicles were private cars, the first driven by two female agents, the second by a pair of black agents masquerading as husband and wife.

That was an effort to minimize the chances of arousing Machado's suspicions should either car catch his eye. For all their shrewdness, the Colombians still had a tendency to think that narcotics officers came in life as they did on television, in varying shades of blond, Anglo-Saxon white. An understanding of the many and diverse forms law enforcement could take in the States had not yet fully penetrated their consciousness.

The vehicles bracketed the van, two up front, two behind,

occasionally switching places to make the surveillance as imperceptible as possible. Grady had ordered radio communications held to a minimum. He knew Burke's DEA van wasn't equipped with a shortwave radio and Machado hadn't had one with him when they'd left northern Georgia. However, there was always the danger other Colombians were prowling the frequencies with a Bearcat scanner looking for any hint that a DEA operation was under way. Therefore, the only exchanges as the van moved along the Cross Bronx were indications of the route Burke was taking: "Hutchinson south . . . the bridge . . . Whitestone . . . Grand Central Parkway."

The van's final destination came as a surprise to Grady. "La Guardia," the radio announced.

Sure, the DEA agent thought. The Colombians had figured the anonymity of one of those huge airport parking lots made La Guardia the ideal place to leave their van. Who was going to pay attention to another van in those lots—even one with Georgia plates?

Machado and Burke would park the van, hide the keys and parking ticket, then take off. A while later, the big guy Grady wanted would come by to pick it up. Or, more likely, he'd send some dumb mule to do the job for him. The mule would have orders to drive the van to a new and final destination while the Colombian scrutinized the operation, looking for any hint that the vehicle was under surveillance.

There were, however, two things the Colombians had overlooked. Getting the van back out of the parking lot would mean taking it through a single exit, the toll gate where the driver would have to pay his parking fee. That would make surveillance in the second stage of the operation easier. Second, Kevin could now call on the airport's Customs detachment and the Port of Authority police for backup.

"Let's move in closer," he ordered his driver. As he did, the word *shuttle* came over the radio. The driver turned right away from the main terminal buildings toward the Eastern Airlines Shuttle terminal. As the car began its climb up the fly-over above the far end of the parking lot opposite the terminal, Kevin spotted Burke's van lined up at the lot's automatic ticket dispenser. At the far end of the terminal building, past the long sidewalk used by arriving and departing passengers to unload or load their luggage, the first of his forward vehicles had come to a stop. It was the car containing the two female agents.

"Head for them," he ordered the driver. As they did, he watched the van pass into the parking lot and begin its search for a parking place. When they'd drawn abreast of the surveillance car, Grady got out and slipped into the backseat behind his two female agents.

"Our Colombian's probably going to be coming out of there in a minute or two," he told them, indicating the parking lot's exit. "I want you to take him, but give him a slack rope. He may have to make a phone call. We want to be sure he makes it before we grab him, so don't move until he's committed himself to leaving the airport. Remember, he's armed. He's dangerous."

His warning distilled a bit of DEA wisdom: "Arrest a Puerto Rican, and you'll probably get a fight; a black, a shootout; a Colombian, a war." While he talked he also studied the flow of passengers moving from the parking lot to the terminal.

"There," he said, pointing to a pair of men poised at the zebra pedestrian crossing. "That's him. The guy in the dark blue overcoat standing beside the guy in the army fatigue jacket. The second one's our guy—Burke."

The women slid out of the car and, pretending to chat casually, strolled down the sidewalk in the direction of the two men. Grady saw Burke and Machado shake hands. Burke wandered off while Machado entered the terminal.

With a credit card, he purchased a ticket on the Washington shuttle from the automatic vending machine in the lobby, then headed down the long passage to the shuttle's departure lounge. Once there, he picked up a complimentary copy of the *Wall Street Journal*, started to sit down, glanced at his watch, then changed his mind and walked over to a pay phone.

Some fifteen minutes later, the public address system announced boarding for the three o'clock shuttle through gate four. Machado was handing his boarding pass to the Eastern Airlines attendant at the gate when he felt the cold jolt of a pistol barrel slamming into his neck.

"Police!" a female voice shrilled. "Don't move!"

Machado glanced to his right, away from the gun barrel, only to see another woman training a weapon at him. Slowly, he raised his hands over his head.

"My God! What's happening?" a middle-aged lady in the line behind him gasped.

"Don't worry, darling," her traveling companion assured her. "They're probably just shooting a scene from some movie like that *Cagney and Lacey* thing on the TV."

The van with the A.J. Murray Plumbing Services markings was equipped with one-way mirrors on its rear and side panels, so that agents in the back of the vehicle could run surveillance on the world outside. Grady ordered it into a position in the parking lot from which he and his men could keep the van loaded with cocaine under constant scrutiny. He briefed both the airport's chief of Customs and police on his operation and plan, then climbed into the Murray Plumbing Services van himself. All they had to do now was wait. Fortunately, the wait was not likely to be long. The Colombians weren't going to leave a van with six hundred keys of coke unattended any longer than they had to.

As it turned out, the wait was just over two hours. Shortly after 5:15, a swarthy man in his late twenties wearing a blue-and-orange New York Knicks warmup jacket came strolling down the lane of cars in which the van was parked. It was immediately apparent he was looking for something. As he passed the van, he glanced down to its plates for a second, then continued on to the head of the alley of parked cars. There he turned and began to study the lot.

"Looking for surveillance," the agent beside Grady mumbled.

"Yeah," Grady growled. "Maybe we're about to get lucky."

Apparently satisfied with what he'd seen, the man started back down the line of parked cars, turned at the van, got in. He bent down inside for a minute, obviously picking up the keys and parking check from their hiding place, then started up the engine.

"Stand by," Grady radioed to the four surveillance vehicles he'd already located in strategic positions outside the lot, ready to pick the van up as it started on what would surely be the final leg of its journey.

At that instant the rear doors of a panel truck some twenty yards away flew open. Three Customs officers and three Port Authority policemen, weapons drawn, leaped to the ground and dashed for Burke's van. Behind them came an *Alive at Five* cameraman energetically filming the scene.

Two of the Customs officers ripped the man from behind the steering wheel and hurled him to the ground. One policeman pinioned him to the ground with his knees while another grabbed his arms, twisted them behind his back and cuffed him.

Meanwhile, one of the Customs officers had yanked open the van's rear doors, exposing the pile of GI duffel bags stacked inside. He jerked one out, slit its side with a knife and, shaking it in triumph, sent a cascade of one-kilo plastic sacks of cocaine tumbling to the pavement before the appreciative camera of the *Alive at Five* newsman.

"I don't fucking believe it!" Kevin screamed. "Who authorized those Customs assholes to do that?"

Seething with anger, his face drawn taut from his effort to control his fury, he leaped from the van and walked over to the scene. There, the airport's chief of Customs began, before Kevin's unbelieving ears, to explain the significance of his seizure to the Channel Five camera.

At the cost of considerable disruption to his digestive system, Kevin managed to keep his anger from boiling over until the *Alive at Five* cameraman had finished his work. Exploding, after all, wasn't going to change anything now. The weeks of work setting up the Georgia sting, the risk to Jimbo Burke's life, the whole fucking business was down the tubes.

As soon as the journalist was out of earshot, he stalked over to the Customs chief, a man who, in all probability, stood at least two ranks above Kevin in the U.S. government's civil service pecking order. "You fucking asshole!" he snarled. "Do you realize you blew apart a major DEA operation just so you could get that fat fucking face of yours on the evening news?"

"And so what the fuck if we did?" the Customs chief snarled right back in a demonstration of the good fellowship that so often characterizes the relationships between U.S. government agencies. "This airport is Customs turf, wiseass."

He jabbed a stubby finger into Grady's chest. "There is no way in the fucking world I am going to let six hundred kilos of cocaine off my reservation. Not for you and not for the whole goddamned New York DEA. You don't like it, pal, then just go play crybaby at the Department of Justice."

Grady's desire to whack the guy was almost too much to resist. He clenched and unclenched his fists then, finally spun and slammed one of them into the side panel of Burke's van, scraping the skin off four of his knuckles.

"Let's go," he said to his team.

"Where?" someone asked.

"To bed. Where the fuck else is there to go when you've got assholes like this working for the U.S. government?"

Lind's Tape

I got to Panama City in ample time to watch Torrijos's funeral on television out at our headquarters at Corozal. They drove him to the cemetery on top of an orange fire truck. His uniform, that cowboy-style hat he liked to wear and his canteen were all neatly piled on top of his coffin. At one point, the television cameras focused on our man Noriega in the circle of Panamanian National Guard officers gathered around the coffin at graveside. His face was an inscrutable mask.

"What do you suppose he's thinking?" Glenn Archer, our new station chief, asked me.

"If he's half the man I thought he was when I recruited him," I laughed, "he's calculating how he's going to put a knife in the back of any of those brother officers who might try to stop him from grabbing Torrijos's job."

At that moment Colonel Florencio Flores, the forty-seven-year-old commander of the Guard, plucked their fallen leader's canteen from his coffin. He waved it to the crowd as a priest might offer his chalice of eternal salvation to his parishioners at Mass.

"May this drink inspire me," he intoned. Then he took a long swallow.

Withdrawing the canteen from his lips, he did not splutter or cough. The canteen contained water, surely the first and only time poor old Omar Torrijos's canteen had been filled with anything but scotch whiskey.

"Well," I told Glenn, "now that Omar's gone, all we've got to do is sit down with Noriega and figure out how to put this nice little country of his squarely into the hands of a CIA asset."

Noriega agreed to meet me the next night in an unoccupied officers' bungalow on the grounds of Howard Air Force Base. He didn't want to run the risk of any of his fellow Panamanians seeing him with a gringo in those uncertain days following Torrijos's death.

I began by expressing the routine condolences the occasion demanded, which, I noted, seemed to leave Noriega quite unmoved. Then we got down to business.

"Tony," I said, "we've given a great deal of thought in the past few days to the situation caused here in Panama by Torrijos's sudden death." Noriega had no doubt who the *we* in question was. But over the years, with his conspiratorial turn of mind, he had come to believe the CIA *was* the U.S. government. I had never seen the need to disabuse him of that notion.

"What matters to us is the stability of Panama, a sense of continuity in the institutions Torrijos created here," I went on, "and, above all, having the right Panamanian partner to work with so together we can assure the security of the Canal, the nation and the region."

Noriega took my little talk in silence, not even an intimation of what he might be thinking lightening those saturnine features of his. He just sat there, sipping away at his Old Parr, weighing up my words in some concealed mental balance of his.

Fifteen years of American foreign policy under four different presidents had firmly established military dictatorship as Panama's mode of governance. Torrijos had recently appointed a civilian president and vice-president, but they were just window-dressing to conceal the fact that real power in Panama resided in the office of the commander-in-chief of the National Guard. Our task was to get Noriega into that office as quickly as possible.

"I don't know what your personal convictions and feelings are, Tony. Nor do I know how you analyze the situation caused here by Torrijos's death. But I do know, it is widely felt in Washington that no one is better qualified than you are to take command of the Guard. If that were to be your ambition, then I feel reasonably certain you could count on American support in achieving it."

That got a reaction. Even more unusual, it got a smile. Smiles tended to appear on Tony's face about as infrequently as they did on Ted Hinckley's. For my benefit, he began to analyze the coming power struggle. No one expected Flores, the man who'd taken that parting swallow of Torrijos's canteen, to last more than a few weeks. The struggle for the throne would pit Noriega against two rivals, both colonels, of whom one, a cousin of the dead leader named Roberto Diaz Herrera, worried him.

Fortunately, he explained to me, Herrera was a bit of a flake. He was forever chasing after astrologers and psychics, slicing up lizards to read tomorrow's weather and stock market reports in their entrails, babbling out the infinite wisdom of his latest guru. Tony himself was not above dabbling in the black arts of *santería,* a blend of voodoo and Christianity. But Diaz Herrera went overboard on the stuff. That was his weakness.

To assure his own ascension to power, Noriega explained to me, he would need to secure and expand his power base in the Guard. He did not tell me he would require money to do that; he didn't need to.

I, in turn, nodded with a banker's ponderous wisdom. "It's entirely possible," I assured him, "that we can increase funding for the institutional cooperation between our organizations." My words referred to the unaccountable and invisible CIA funds we channeled to him. In this instance, he would be using CIA money to buy his way to power. Well, that was just fine with us.

The next step, after refilling our whiskey glasses, was to let him know what the price of the bride was going to be. I explained the changes under way in our Central American policy, our plans to build up a guerrilla army to go after the Sandinistas in Nicaragua.

"We would certainly hope," I told him, "that in the event you took command of the Guard, we could count on your understanding and support for that program."

Noriega nodded.

"I mean, clearly we would need to have unrestricted use of all our military facilities here. We wouldn't want to have a bunch of quarrelsome lawyers claiming we were using those bases for purposes not sanctioned by the new Canal treaty."

That was the deal, gussied up in the prettiest diplomatic

language I could invent. We help him buy his way to power in Panama; he, in turn, buys into our campaign against the Sandinistas.

I have no idea what, if anything, Noriega thought about our upcoming crusade. He was not a man to argue. He felt he exposed his hand by arguing. Better, he reasoned, to listen and learn.

"Why don't you just invade Nicaragua and be done with it?" he asked.

That, I explained, wasn't how we did things anymore.

"Well," he said, "if you really mean to do it, you will succeed because you are strong." He then clinked his glass to mine and smiled, a gesture I took as setting the seal on our agreement.

We would want to continue to keep our working relationship a tightly held secret, I told him. Publicly, it would be wise for him to distance himself from our anti-Sandinista policy. That would strengthen him politically at home and enable him to maintain his contacts with the leftist organizations in the region with which we wanted him to stay in touch.

"There are other things I can help you with in this program," he said.

"Like what?"

"Pilots to fly your arms to your guerrillas, for example. Moving arms through the Free Trade Zone in a way that nobody sees them moving."

I could not have heard more encouraging words.

We drank a bit more until Noriega announced it was time for him to leave. Watching him disappear into the damp tropical night, his shoulders hunched like those of a wrestler waiting to begin a fight, a beguiling metaphor occurred to me: He had been a poor scholarship boy when I'd recruited him; now he was about to become the head boy of the whole damn school. *Not bad,* I thought, *not bad.*

I went back to my hotel and decided to put in a call to my wife, Sarah Jane. I tried to do that at least every third day when I was overseas on assignment.

We had met on a blind date for the Dartmouth game during my junior year in New Haven. It was, as they said in the soap operas of the day, love at first sight. Romantic love at least; the other kind before a visit to the altar was much frowned on at the time.

When we were married, the society pages of the *New York Times* and her hometown newspaper, the *Louisville Courier-Journal,* identified me as an employee of the Department of Defense. I detailed the significance of that for her while we were on our honeymoon in Bermuda. My real employer's identity neither surprised nor shocked her. I think she'd already figured that out, possibly with a gentle nudge from one of the several members of her graduating class at Vassar who were employees of the agency.

About my work itself, however, she knew very little. She'd surmised that because of my Spanish background I was involved in Latin American affairs, but that was about the end of it. CIA officers and their wives are forced to find other subjects for their dinner table conversation than "How did things go at the office today?"

When I traveled abroad on agency assignment, she, for the most part, did not know where I was going or how long I would be away. At the moment, for example, she had no idea that I was in Panama or what I was doing here. Nor was it likely she would ever find out. The passports on which I traveled, either in my own name or under one of the pseudonyms Langley assigned me, were kept locked in a safe in my office so that no one could go poking through my exit and entry stamps to determine where I'd been.

Of course, like any good husband and father, I brought home souvenirs of my trips for Sarah Jane and our three young boys. Inevitably, however, they tended to be gifts purchased in the anonymity of some airport duty-free shop through which I'd transited rather than souvenirs of the country in which I'd been working.

That double-life which a CIA officer working under cover is forced to lead has, almost inevitably, an insidious effect on his behavior. His second, cover life is not real; what happens there really didn't happen insofar as his other, honest life, is concerned. And if it's not real, then it doesn't count. The rules that govern your existence back there on the reservation do not apply in that unreal, undercover world. Temptations that could not be indulged in the green and wholesome world of suburban Virginia could be yielded to with little concern in that make-believe existence. One of my superiors in Berlin, discussing the mindset of spies, once told me: "Adulterers do not necessarily make good spies, but spies inevitably make good adulterers." There is, I found in my work, much truth to that. Look at that English master spy, Kim Philby. Sexually, he was never more fulfilled than when he was cuckolding somebody, preferably a close friend.

Anyway, I must say that Sarah Jane had always accepted the constraints and menaces my career placed on our marriage with remarkable good grace. She was a Dabney from Virginia whose father had moved to Louisville to take over the Brown Forman distillery. A notion of service, whether to the federal government or to the Confederacy, was very much a part of the Dabney family tradition. In addition, she, too, had a private income, so we both knew from the outset that we would not have to live our lives entirely on a government salary.

Sarah Jane ran through the familiar litany of our domestic proceedings: Jonathan, our eldest, had hit the winning home run in his Little League opening game; Mrs. Emerson, the second-grade teacher of Tony, the youngest boy, was complaining again about his classroom antics; the Junior League would be holding its annual black-tie Civic Awards dinner in three weeks at the Washington Hilton. She hoped I'd be back in time to make it.

My end of the conversation was, of necessity, rather dreary. I was well, the work was progressing, the weather was fine, which in the case of Panama, it was not. We ended, as always, offering each other the ritual expression of our affections. I then hung up and headed into the sweltering Panamanian evening for the solace of a nightcap or two.

High-priced law firms, whether they are on Wall Street, in London's Inns of Court or on Panama City's Calle 50, always seem redolent with a certain odor. It contains a dash of old leather, a hint of furniture polish, the intimation of rich tobacco. But what it is above all, I thought, sitting in the waiting room of *Arias, Calderon & Torres,* is the smell of money.

The firm specialized in the sale and formation of Panamanian corporations. Hinckley had ordered me to use my stay in Panama to set up half a dozen such dummy corporations, which we could subsequently employ as cover for operations in our contra program.

Clearly, setting up Panamanian corporations was a flourishing business. The air conditioning in the firm's new glass-

and-steel office building had the temperature down to about sixty-five degrees. The pile on the royal blue wall-to-wall carpeting must have been an inch thick. My wing chair was highly polished leather with brass tacking for trim. The desk of the receptionist, a lady of distant and regal allure, was, unless my eyes had gone bad, a Queen Anne antique. The walls of the reception area were covered with nineteenth century English engravings of fox-hunting scenes, a sport I somehow doubted the messieurs Arias, Calderon and Torres had ever practiced.

A buzzer sounded ever so discreetly on the secretary's desk. "Mr. Calderon is on the way out, Mr. Reid," she said. That was the name on the passport I was carrying in my suit pocket for the purpose of these visits. The tone with which she heralded Mr. Calderon's approach would have been appropriate for announcing the arrival of the archbishop of Canterbury.

A lanky gentleman, well over six feet with a fast-moving Adam's apple, appeared. He was wearing a well-cut gray suit and a blue Brooks Brothers button-down shirt. Like his secretary, Mr. Calderon appeared to be of pure Spanish stock. "Mr. Reid," he said cordially, "do come in."

He showed me to another well-polished leather wing chair in his office. As he moved behind his huge partner's desk, I glanced at the gallery of diplomas and awards on his wall. His law degree, I noted, was from Georgetown.

"How may I be of service, Mr. Reid?" he asked.

I explained that I wanted to form a Panamanian corporation.

"Certainly," he said. "Would you like to organize a new corporation of your own or would you prefer to take over one of our existing shelf companies?"

"Perhaps," I suggested, "you could explain to me the difference."

"It's a question of time, really. With a newly formed corporation of your own, we are required to check the index of the Corporate Registry to be sure that there is not a company already in existence with the name you have selected for your corporation. That requires three days. If you decide to purchase one of our existing shelf companies, we don't have to go through that process. With that kind of a company, you and I can do all the paperwork that's required together here this morning."

"That sounds good," I said. "I'll buy a shelf company."

Calderon opened one of the drawers of his partner's desk and drew out a manila folder. "Now, the next question I must ask you is what will be the purpose of the company? Although I should inform you that under Panamanian corporate law, a Panamanian corporation, regardless of what its stated purpose may be, is allowed to undertake any activities it chooses as long, of course, as they are legal."

Did I detect just the slightest indication of a smile on Mr. Calderon's face as he uttered the word legal? Probably it was just my imagination. Three-quarters of these Panamanian corporations were formed for the purposes of evading taxes.

"General commercial activities."

"Do you wish to have your shares registered in your shareholders' name, or would you prefer to have bearer shares?"

That was the key question. Bearer shares are employed to conceal the real identity of the owner or the owners of a company. The Greek buying that oil tanker he's going to register under a Panamanian flag, for example, will employ bearer shares. That way, in case the tanker is involved in a multimillion dollar oil spill, the search for someone liable for damages would end at Mr. Calderon's desk. No one would ever be able to find out the name of the Greek owner of the tanker and sue him or his company for damages.

"I'll take bearer shares," I replied.

"Panamanian law," Mr. Calderon continued, "requires you have three corporate officers and three directors, although they can be the same people. You can name them if you want or we'll provide nominees among our staff here."

"I'll let you provide the nominees," I instructed Mr. Calderon.

He took out his pen and wrote three names on a form he'd picked out of the manila folder. None of them meant a damn thing to me.

Calderon opened up the manila folder and passed me a wad of stock certificates. "These shares represent a hundred percent of the bearer shares in Inland General Trading. Whoever holds these shares is the owner of the company. You may wish to sign them yourself in the place indicated so that no one can take control of the company if you lose them. Or you may decide to leave them blank. Suit yourself."

I looked briefly at the shares. "I'm sure they're in order."

"Now," he said, "I imagine you will wish to request the directors of Inland General Trading to issue you a power of attorney to act for the company in any and all legal matters. With that you can do basically whatever you want in the company's name, buy a villa in Marbella, charter a tanker in Sumatra, buy oil in Saudia Arabia and sell it in the Netherlands. We have a standard power of attorney form we use in these circumstances which is designed to be as broad as we can make it." He took his pen.

"It's Mr. . . ."

"Edward R. Reid," I said, spelling out the last name on my false passport. Calderon wrote it on the form, signed it and got up.

He was back in several minutes with the power-of-attorney signed by his fellow directors of Inland General Trading and notarized by an in-house notary public.

"Now," he smiled, passing it to me "is there anything else I can do for you?"

"I would like to open a bank account in Inland General Trading's name," I told him. "There's a new bank here that's been highly recommended to me—the Bank of Credit and Commerce International, the BCCI."

"Yes, we know them," Calderon said with a gracious smile. "Very aggressive bankers. I can call them and ask them to send over a courier with the necessary forms for you to fill out."

The BCCI was Casey's latest brainstorm. It was fundamentally run by Pakistanis, and we had started using it as a conduit to funnel funds to the Islamic extremist guerrillas in Afghanistan. That way we could conceal from them the fact that their money was coming from infidels in Washington rather than fellow Moslems in Iran or Saudi Arabia. The bank already had a reputation as a haven for money launderers and for dancing close to the edge of legality. The perfect cover, Casey had decreed, for the agency. Who would ever suspect the CIA of using an institution like that?

Fifteen minutes later, I was filling out the forms to open the account. I attached a hundred dollar bill for the initial deposit. The courier who'd delivered the forms then gave me a receipt and a copy of the application with the number of my company's new bank account on it. That was all there was to it.

The whole business had required barely an hour. The CIA now had a corporate vehicle which we could employ anyplace in the world to do virtually anything we wanted to do: buy or sell arms; lease an aircraft, a ship or a safe house; pay an agent or bribe the prime minister of one of our Latin neighbors; hire an assassin to kill someone for us or an explosives expert to plant a bomb in a place of our choosing.

There was no way anyone, any government, any investigative or regulatory agency, any rival service could crack the paper facade concealing the CIA's ownership of the firm. Not once in the hour I had spent in those law offices had I even taken my passport from my pocket to identify myself. Calderon didn't have the faintest idea who I was, or whether my name was Reid, Brown, Lind or Jesus Christ. Once I had left his office, there was absolutely no way anyone would ever be able to determine who was behind Inland General Trading.

Kevin Grady glanced up with a grateful smile as the girl set a styrofoam cup of hot, black coffee on his desk.

"Hey," he said, "I thought in this brave new world of ours, our female colleagues didn't get coffee for us anymore."

"They don't," the girl replied, "except you look like you haven't got the strength to walk down the hall to the Mr. Coffee machine this morning."

"Yeah, I probably don't." Grady took a gulp of the coffee and thought once again about the fiasco at La Guardia. "The last few days have been a bitch."

"Look at the upside, Kev. You got the two Colombians, the plane, the pilot and the six hundred keys. The only thing you didn't get was the credit, thanks to our brothers at Customs."

"And the big guy. It's the ones that get away that hurt the most, Ella Jean."

"Ain't that the truth."

Ella Jean Ransom was in her late twenties. She was black, a graduate of the John Jay School of Criminal Justice who'd served three years in the New York Police Department before signing on with the DEA. She was, as Kevin had frequently had the occasion to notice, a tough, street-smart young lady. They were both assigned to the DEA's New

York District Office Group Six. Grady was its sort of senior agent in residence, Ella Jean was one of the group's newer recruits.

An incident that occurred shortly after Ella Jean had joined the group established a special bond between them. Posing as a hooker, she had gone into an apartment in Brooklyn's Bedford Stuyvesant neighborhood to make a heroin buy. She'd been wired to a *Kel*, a transmitter with a mike and battery pack whose emissions Kevin was monitoring from a car outside the building. That way he would know by listening to the conversation inside the apartment the exact moment when the powder was on the table, so he could break down the doors and make his arrests.

Trouble was, the damn Kel had suddenly gone dead. Storming the apartment without confirmation that a criminal act had taken place inside was risky. At the least, it could lead to disciplinary action on a charge of breaking and entering without probable cause. Kevin, however, had not hesitated for a second. The only rule that mattered to him was: If a fellow agent may be at risk, move.

He'd led the charge on the door. As it happened, he had probably saved Ella Jean's life. One of the three dealers in the flat had become suspicious of her. He'd come on to her like a hungry john, put his hand around her waist and found the Kel.

"Mind if I pay you a compliment, Kev?" Ella Jean asked. Her lithe, almost tomboyish figure was tightly enclosed in purple toreador trousers and a lilac blouse.

"I love to hear them. Particularly from girls like you."

Ella Jean made a face at him. "You're looking like shit these days, Kevin, dear. You're killing yourself with work. This isn't a job for you anymore. It's become an obsession."

Grady sighed. "You're probably right. But what else am I supposed to do?"

"Us girls worry about you, Kev. You're a very unhappy guy and unhappy guys don't make good cops."

"Find me some happiness pills, Ella Jean, and I'll take them, believe me."

"That's not the way it works, Kev." The sad smile of a woman more familiar with compassion than passion made a brief appearance on Ella Jean's features. "Happiness ain't God's amazin' grace falling out of heaven on your shoulders. You have to help it along. And working fourteen-hour days doesn't help it all that much."

"You're right, pal. And I appreciate your concern. I really do."

Ella Jean bent over and kissed Grady lightly on the forehead. "You're a honky, racist, male chauvinist pig, but some of us around here care for you all the same."

With that she turned and left Grady's office, leaving him to face the mound of paperwork that now cluttered his desk.

Fans of *Miami Vice* could never dream how much of a drug agent's life was devoted to paperwork, courtroom appearances and legal depositions, and how little of it was actually spent out on the street hunting down dope dealers.

Grady's immediate task was to fill out a lengthy DEA6 setting out all the details of the North Georgia sting. The *Six* was the basic DEA document, the investigative report which had to follow every DEA undertaking from a banal wiretap, to an aborted surveillance, to a major operation like Sugar Coating. Those Sixes were the building blocks with which a DEA agent gradually built each of his cases. They recorded conversations and meetings while the details were still fresh in the agent's mind, so that six months or a year later, when he had to testify about them in court, the information he would need to refresh his memory would be available to him.

In classic police work, as Grady enjoyed pointing out, time ran backward. A New York homicide detective began his work with a corpse staring up at him. From there, he worked his way backward, identifying the corpse and determining the hour and the place of the killing, until he was able to reconstruct what had happened.

The DEA's tactics were almost diametrically opposed. A successful DEA agent had to fasten onto a criminal act long before it was committed. Indeed, the DEA would frequently set the stage for the crime by dangling bait in front of the criminals, then watching as the bad guys pounced on the lure like kittens stabbing at a running insect.

The Georgia bust had been a classic example. The Cuban go-between, Humberto Martinez, was in fact a DEA informant. Kevin Grady had recruited him when Martinez had been picked up for importing several tons of marijuana into the coves around Myrtle Beach, South Carolina.

Kevin had explained to Martinez how, with a little effort, he could shorten the sentence he was facing. When he agreed to cooperate, Grady sent him out to troll his old Miami haunts in search of someone who wanted to engage his services. He'd found the Colombians who told him they were looking for an airstrip to land a load on. Grady flew down to Miami in his Alfie Westin incarnation and it was off to the races.

Most successful DEA operations came down, as that one had, to one word: penetration. Whether through the use of an informer or a DEA agent working undercover, the DEA had to penetrate the protective circle surrounding a criminal enterprise. Then they work at that enterprise from the inside until the criminals could be seized in the act of committing a crime that would offer them a long vacation in a federal penitentiary.

That was why virtually all DEA agents were expected to go out on the street undercover, hanging out with the bad guys they were trying to put away, rapping with them, adopting their mannerisms and their mindsets. Some, like Kevin Grady, took naturally to it. There was nothing in his New York City background that should have enabled Grady to play the role of a North Georgia good old boy. Yet he'd carried off that role, as he had a dozen others in his career, with consummate skill. It was, he boasted, the frustrated ham actor in him, the kid who'd never gotten past the grade school Christmas pageant.

In fact, Grady owed his progress in the DEA to two skills, of which that was one. The second was his almost uncanny ability to spot a potential informant, then persuade him to the difficult and dangerous challenge of flipping, going to work for the government.

Grady's rule of thumb was to try to move from one penetration to the next. In other words, pick up the CI—confidential informant—who's going to lead you on to your next case from the one you're closing out today. Doing that was his real concern this morning.

The Colombians, the Machado father and son combination, were of basically no use. Colombians almost never became *pajaritos*—little birds. The price was too high. Either they or one of their near and dear died, and they did not die nicely. One favorite stunt down there was peeling off a guy's skin strip by strip until he finally bled to death. It made for a slow death and an exquisitely painful one.

That left Kevin with the pilot. Pilots were good, but this guy had made the papers, thanks to Customs. It would be too dangerous to try to play him back against a new set of Colombians. Nonetheless, remembering how terrified the man had been during his arrest, Kevin went to his file first.

The guy was a second officer for American Airlines, barely three years away from qualifying for a first officer's stripes and a six-figure annual salary. He also had a wife and two kids. Why would a guy like that get messed up in dope, Kevin wondered.

Money, okay, but money for *what*? Was he supporting a major habit? That happened, but it would be very difficult to conceal a habit of that magnitude from the other guys in the cockpit for very long. A girl? Did he have the hots for some stewardess who was milking him?

Kevin lit up one of the Marlboros he was trying not to smoke and thought a bit. The pilot was still in the holding cells. He'd made his authorized call to his attorney, but the gentleman had not yet shown up. This was the best time for a little chat, before the lawyer could start to screw up the plans Kevin had for his client.

The pilot, whose name was Denny Strong, looked even worse under the glaring lights of the holding cell's interrogation room than he had during his arrest. His pallor had gone sickly white, his shoulders sagged, his chin slumped onto his chest as though his neck muscles could no longer support the weight of his head. Clearly, he was a shaken and contrite figure.

Grady gestured to the marshal to remove Strong's handcuffs. He could read the relief on the pilot's face as they came off. Nothing, Kevin had noted years earlier, makes a man think the preacher's at the door faster than slipping the cuffs on him. He pushed his pack of Marlboros at Strong as a kind of peace offering.

The pilot gratefully grabbed one, lighting it from Kevin's proffered match. He blew a spume of smoke at the light bulb with a sigh. "Haven't had one of these in seven years," he mumbled.

Yup, Kevin thought, this is a real worried fellow we've got here. "I know," he said consolingly, "I'm trying to give them up myself. But they do ease the tension, don't they?

"Look," he continued, "I want you to understand you don't have to talk to me for a second if you don't want to. Tell me to take off and I'm out of here. But sometimes it helps a guy to chat with someone like me, you know what I mean? Helps them work their way through all the stuff that's going down here. Particularly someone like you. I mean I know you're not the criminal type. You don't belong in this dump."

His words were spoken in a tone as gentle as that of a mother crooning an Irish lullaby. The last words, in particular, were calculated to offer a ray of hope to Strong. Hope, after all, was a quality he rather desperately needed at the moment.

"No," Strong muttered, "I'd like to talk. Get some idea of what's going to happen to me."

"Well, as you know, ultimately that will be for the courts to decide," Kevin told him. "All I can do is lay things out for you. Basically what you are looking at here is twenty-five years' exposure."

Strong gasped. His body seemed to shrink under the impact of those words. He was thirty-two. Twenty-five years meant he would be fifty-seven when he got out of jail. His children would have grown up without him.

Grady was silent for several seconds. He was in no hurry to proceed until the terrible impact of those numbers had fully registered.

"Of course," he added, "with luck you can probably work that down to twenty years, time off for good behavior and all. Still, twenty is a long stretch."

Poor Strong shook his head in dismayed agreement.

"The case, as you can imagine, is pretty much open and shut," Kevin informed him. "We have a bunch of eight-by-ten glossies suitable for framing of your meeting with the Machados down in Miami. Martinez, the Cuban, was working with us. He was wearing a wire that day, so all the conversations are on tape. And, of course, you guys were all caught with the coke. That powder is going to be on a table there in the courtroom for the jury to eyeball. Six hundred keys. That's an eyeful, all right." Grady shrugged to underscore just how majestically simple it all was.

"Now," he said, "you can be, you know, a standup guy

and not say anything to anybody, go to jail and do the full twenty-five along with everybody else, or you can help us and perhaps then we can help you."

Kevin paused. "That's my job now. To see if together we can find a way that we can work with each other so we can help you. Maybe we can do something for you that's going to look a little better than any of the other rather unpleasant options you're facing."

"What can I do?" Strong asked plaintively.

"Normally what we would want to do is get you out of here and back on the street, see if you can make another connect. See if you could find somebody out there who needs a good pilot to bring another load in.

"Unfortunately, you've been arrested and charged, so we can't do that. With all the publicity in the press, that would be too dangerous. I wouldn't want to expose you to risks like that. Whatever we do, we'll have to do from in here."

Kevin mulled the possibilities in front of him for a moment. "Let me ask you something," he said. "Did you spend much time down there in Colombia?"

"Oh, once I was there for two weeks helping them check out and upgrade their airstrips." Strong spoke with the pathetic eagerness of a pupil trying to impress a new teacher.

"And you remember where those fields were?"

"Sure."

Kevin reflected. That was interesting as intelligence, but it wasn't the hard stuff he was after. Asking Strong about the Colombian drug barons was apt to fall under the same heading. He'd never get his hands on those bastards anyway.

"Tell me," he asked, "did you ever run into any other Americans while you were down there?"

"There was one guy," Strong recalled. "He was married to a Colombian girl. He was from Philadelphia. His name was Ray, Ray Marcello, but everybody called him Ramon."

"And he was involved in the traffic?"

"Oh, sure. He brokered loads."

Kevin spread his hands on the table and leaned forward, his shoulders hunched slightly as though he was about to confide some secret of enormous importance to Strong. "Maybe this is where we can work something out. You cooperate, tell us everything you know about the guy. You'll have to agree to testify against him in open court if we ever get our hands on him. And you'll have to agree to forfeit all your drug-earned assets."

"I can't," Strong gasped.

"Why?"

"I don't have them anymore."

"A girl?"

Strong nodded.

"What did she do with it?"

"I bought her stuff. A condo in Boca Raton. A Porsche. Other things."

"All in her name, I suppose?"

Again, Strong nodded.

"She know how you got the money?"

"Oh, yeah. That was the whole idea. So the money couldn't be traced back to me."

"Right," Kevin said approvingly, "good thinking. We can deal with that." In fact, he was contemplating the prospect with some delight. The DEA's assets seizure people would pick that broad clean so fast she'd be out on the street looking for a bus before she could say "Porsche."

"Can you live with the rest of what I've outlined?"

"What will it get me?" Strong asked.

"Well, first of all, it's going to get us on your side. Instead of trying to nail your ass for the maximum time we can lay on you. Then, if we manage to grab this guy thanks to your help, we go to the judge, tell him how helpful you've been. We stand up for you there in the courtroom, and say, 'Look, your honor, the guy's repented, he burned his bridges. Can we lower that twenty-five-year exposure for him?' "

Strong sighed and twisted out his cigarette. "I guess that's the way it's got to be, doesn't it?"

"Right," Grady smiled. "Now, let's just start slowly by you telling me everything you can remember about this guy Ramon, okay?"

Lind's Tape

The CIA tends to be as conservative in its sartorial standards as its critics maintain it is in its politics. I mean, if you show up in the office without your Brooks Brothers button-down shirt, there's a tendency at Langley to look at you as though you're out of uniform. Duke Talmadge, the guy Bill Casey had selected to head up our Central American operations, loved to go against the grain of that unwritten dress code of ours. He was forever showing up in cream-colored Italian silk gabardine suits with a purple silk shirt, and a red foulard hanging like the tongue of a thirsty puppy from his vest pocket. People walking the corridors got pinched nerves in their necks from swiveling around for a second look at the Duke in his latest raiment.

"Oh, God," they'd whisper to each other. "Talmadge's got his vanilla ice cream suit on again."

The Duke's taste in his wardrobe was just the tip of the iceberg as far as the man's personality was concerned. The mythologists in the media liked to compare him to James Bond, which was most inaccurate. He was five-ten, slender, mild-mannered, in no way physically imposing. He did resemble Bond in one way, though. Women adored him. Months after our first meeting, when his nemesis Senator Pat Moynihan of New York was savaging him in the Senate, a bunch of the girls in the office made up T-shirts with his picture ringed with American flags on them over the words: "I love the Duke."

He was also a very quick study. By the time I'd returned from Panama, Talmadge was ready to give the Director a preliminary report. Hinckley ushered us up to Casey's office where Talmadge passed us each copies of a twenty-five page memorandum titled "Proposals for Destabilizing the Sandinista Regime."

Casey took his, thumbed through it quickly, then hiked his feet up onto his desk. He let his reading glasses slide down to the bridge of his nose, and ordered, "Okay, summarize this thing for me."

"Essentially, Mr. Director," Talmadge began, "as I see it our job here is to take the war to the Nicaraguans and kill Cubans."

Well, those were exactly the words Casey wanted to hear. His feet came thumping back onto the floor, and he sat up, an enormous grin on his face. "Attaboy!" he snapped. "That's exactly the kind of thinking I want from this agency. Go on."

Talmadge waved a book he'd brought with him at Casey. It was called *The Sandino Affair*. "This covers U.S. involvement down there in 1927–31," the Duke said. "Then we were backing the central government fighting the Sandino rebels. What I recommend we do is turn the thing inside out. Create a peasant army like the Sandino rebels did. Infiltrate them into those same mountain sanctuaries the old Sandino rebels were using in the 1930s. Then they strike out, ambush Sandinista army patrols, attack their barracks, overrun their local command posts, break down the government's lines of control and authority over the people in those rural areas, and replace them as their protectors and benefactors."

Well, Casey went for that the way a kitten goes for a bowl of warm milk. It was just what he'd been after, the mirror image of the tactics the communists had been using against us for years—a can-do CIA turning the tables on them and letting them have a taste of their own medicine.

"What we're looking at here, Bill," said Hinckley, who had already studied the Duke's paper, "is essentially a job for covert operations."

"I would agree," Casey replied, "except that one of the problems I have with this agency right now is with your covert operators. They can't fart without getting some goddamned lawyer to tell them it's okay."

"That's because of our congressional restrictions," Hinckley started to explain.

"Fuck Congress!" Casey barked. "They've intimidated you guys in this building."

The Director reached into a drawer and pulled out a bound Top Secret document. He tossed it scornfully onto his desk. "This pile of lukewarm dog shit sums up everything that's wrong with this place."

The object of his wrath was an official 130-page manual, *Principles and Policies Governing CIA Covert Operations,* compiled on the orders of his predecessor at the CIA, Admiral Stan Turner. It was, at that moment, our New Testament, stating in very precise and well-defined terms what we covert operators could and, more important, what we could not do.

"The trouble is right here in this document," Casey barked. "No balls. No imagination. Just play it safe, cover your ass, keep your head down so those assholes over there on the Hill won't shoot it off. Well, that's finished. That's not the kind of agency I'm going to run, and people who believe in that crap aren't the kind of people I'm going to have around here running it with me. I'm throwing this out the window. Right now." To make his point, he picked up the binder and tossed it into his classified waste bin.

Hinckley's face lit with a glow of rare pleasure at Casey's gesture. "That's the kind of language a lot of us around here have been waiting to hear for a long time, Bill."

Casey grunted, his way of expressing pleasure, I suppose, at the notion that he was getting through to us.

"I'd like to lay down a couple of operating principles which I think should guide us as we start thinking about how we're going to put this together," Hinckley went on.

"Okay," Casey told him, "fire away."

Hinckley had been playing with a scheme he called an off-the-shelf commercial, covert operations capability—a kind of have gun, will travel, Rent-a-Green-Beret service.

The idea had grown out of his realization that as a consequence of the Vietnam War, there was a major talent pool out there of National Security alumni, ex-CIA covert operators, pilots used to dealing in clandestine cargoes, Pentagon-trained former SEALs and Green Berets, all of whom were equipped with highly specialized skills and yet had no marketplace in which to sell them.

He wanted to bring them together into an organization he could rent out, for example, to a foreign government threatened by leftist guerrillas or to a commercial enterprise working in an area where its operations might be endangered by a leftist insurgency. Suppose the Uruguayan government was once again assailed by urban guerrillas. Hinckley's firm would take on the job of finding, rooting out and eventually eliminating those guerrillas for their foreign employers on a contract basis.

Now he proposed applying some of those concepts he'd been working on privately to our forthcoming operation. "The first thing I think we want to do is make every effort to bypass the standard government channels."

"What are you suggesting?" Casey asked.

"Embed the operation as far as we can into the private sector. Subcontract our work out to private concerns wherever possible. We're going to need cadres to run this operation— the guys who are going to buy arms undercover, verify we're getting the right stuff, handle the shipping, move the merchandise through Panama to our forward bases, check it out when it arrives, train our guerrillas to use the stuff."

He paused while Casey nodded at that evident bit of wisdom. "We could use regular agency officers to do that. But I think it would be a mistake. I think we should go outside the agency. Hire contractual personnel to do the work for us. Our UCLANs, for example."

"Our what?" Casey growled. "What the hell are you talking about, for Christ's sake? A California football team?"

"Sorry," Hinckley laughed. "I lapsed into agency jargon there. Unilaterally Controlled Latino Assets. They're Cuban Americans we take on a contractual basis to do jobs for us down in Latin America that we don't want tied to the agency. They're ideal for this. They're Hispanics. They'll do anything for a chance to kick Castro in the slats. The good ones have been trained in clandestine operations. We use one of those Panamanian shell companies Lind brought back to hire them. Name some anti-communist Nicaraguan as the company president, pay them offshore in Panama, the Caymans, wherever. That way, if the press or some liberal congressman starts shouting, 'The CIA is running a war in Central America,' we can say, 'Who? Not us! This is just some Nicaraguan patriot trying to get his country back. We haven't got a thing to do with it.' "

Casey never made an effort to conceal his thoughts, and I could see that this suggestion delighted him.

"It's a way of insulating the President and the CIA from what we're doing down there. It ensures our ability to deny legally, openly, any knowledge of the operation or our involvement in it. And since we'll be running this thing outside the official government circuitry, there's no reason that it should be subject to congressional scrutiny or oversight," Hinckley concluded.

The Director gobbled that up. "Yeah," he said. "Congress is just an obstacle to the successful accomplishment of foreign policy anyway." His glance encompassed Talmadge and me. "You guys let those principles of Ted's guide you as we go about setting this up. Talmadge, I want you to run operations in the field. Lind, you're going to be in charge of the logistical side of the operation, hiring people, buying arms, setting up the air service and the channels we'll need to get the arms to the guerrillas. And keeping your friend Noriega warm."

The Director stretched and stood up to indicate our meeting was over. "One last point, gentlemen," he concluded, "Once we get this thing up and running, I want to keep the loop very tight. There are too many goddamned people with cold feet around here. You two report directly to me," he said, indicating the Duke and me, "or to Hinckley in my absence. Forget everybody in between. You need anything, you come to me. Anybody gets in your way, you come to me. And remember, I'm behind you on this one hundred percent, and so is the President of the United States."

Despite the apparent urgency of our contra initiative, the operation actually moved forward with glacial slowness. Such is the way of the government machinery. It wasn't until mid-November that the paperwork for National Security Council Directive #17 authorizing nineteen million dollars to recruit, arm and train a first contingent of five hundred guerrillas was ready for the President's signature.

It was on the same day the final draft of the directive was ready that a top-secret cable from our Panama station landed on my desk. That cable, as it turned out, was to mark a milestone in our relations with Manuel Antonio Noriega.

PK\BARRIER\7–7 INFORMS STATION HE HAS BEEN CONTACTED BY COLOMBIAN LAWYER GUIDO MORO REPRESENTING MEDELLIN DRUG DEALER JORGE LUIS OCHOA. OCHOA WANTS PK\BARRIER\7–7 USE HIS CONTACTS WITH M19 TO SEEK RELEASE OCHOAS NIECE MARTA KIDNAPPED BY M19. PK\BARRIER\7–7 REQUESTS GUIDANCE.

. The M19—the Movimiento de 19 Abril, the Movement of April 19th—was among the revolutionary movements in his area with which we had asked Noriega to establish contact. Its leader was typical of those middle-class Latin males who seem incapable of growing out of their grad school mindset, the kind of person who thinks you become a revolutionary by memorizing a few lines of Karl Marx and growing a beard. Jaime Bateman was his name. Jaime should have been studying to be a dentist, but he wanted to be Che Guevara instead.

He and his middle-class revolutionary pals had just made what would turn out to be a major strategic error in their tactics for the great proletarian struggle. They had kidnapped Marta Ochoa of the Medellín drug family, convinced they could use her as a pawn to extort drug money from the family to finance their revolution. Fifteen million dollars was the sum they had in mind.

A marriage of convenience had sprung up during the 1970s between the world's various terrorist networks and drug traffickers. Each needed what the other had. The drug dealers had money, lots of it. The terrorists had people, techniques, the knowledge of how to move arms and gather intelligence surreptitiously.

Since penetrating those terrorist networks was one of our primary national security concerns at the CIA, the idea had occurred to us that a good way into them would be to exploit their ties to the drug trafficking world. It is, after all, a lot easier to bend or buy a drug trafficker whose ideology is in his wallet than it is to convert a dedicated terrorist to sweetness and reason.

So we had begun to brush up against people we knew were moving drugs when we thought they might get us inside those terrorist networks. If dealing with people like that was the price for a penetration that might one day forestall a car bomb outside one of our embassies, well, that was a price we were prepared to pay.

Go ahead and give Ochoa's lawyer whatever help you can, I instructed Noriega. If Tony's assistance contributed to the girl's safe release, it would certainly enhance his standing in the eyes of the drug dealers in Medellín. And who could say? That might one day turn out to be just the sort of penetration we could use.

Marta Ochoa was finally released unharmed some five months later for a ransom in the neighborhood of 1.2 million dollars. Noriega's role as an intermediary was vital. It was whispered at the time that he had skimmed $300 thousand off the ransom money as it went by as a fee for his services, something I doubt unduly surprised or upset the good folk in Medellín. There was a saying that was beginning to make the rounds those days: A sparrow can't fall out of the sky in Panama unless Noriega gets a cut of its feathers.

Sparrows, as it would soon turn out, weren't going to be

the only thing falling out of the Panamanian skies on which PK\BARRIER\7–7 would be getting his cut, thanks to those relations he'd established with the Medellín cartel at our behest.

BOOK FOUR

A Fine White Powder

Lind's Tape

Like the rest of Miami Beach, the Hotel Fontainebleau—"Fountain Blue" as it tends to get pronounced—is a fading lady, an aging glamour queen in need of a facelift. In its high season it can still attract the older members of the lox-and-bagel set from up north, but their progeny long ago abandoned Miami Beach for the ski slopes of Colorado or the sands of the Caribbean.

Fifty, it struck me, sauntering through its lobby one March morning in 1982, was the very flower of youth in the Fontainebleau. I headed downstairs to the commercial arcade in search of the florist shop. *Florarte* was its name.

The proprietor did not notice my arrival. He was busy describing to a lady with a blue-rinse hairdo the glories of the gardenia and orchid centerpiece he was going to prepare for her dinner party that night.

"Such flowers you have!" she gushed.

"Flown in fresh every day from Bogotá," the proprietor proudly assured her as I turned to contemplate his cold-storage display locker. His assistant, a Latin lady in a very tight tank top, came over and offered to help me.

"Thanks," I told her, "I'll wait until the boss is free."

I followed her twitching buttocks as she slunk back to her desk. On the wall behind the desk was an old sepia portrait of José Martí, the patron saint of Cuban independence. It was bracketed by a pair of framed certificates. The first attested to the proprietor's service in Brigade 2506, the Brigada Cubana, which had landed at the Bay of Pigs; the second, from the Cuban American Society of South Florida, bore witness to Felipe Santiago Nadal's service as "a tireless fighter for the freedom of his beloved homeland."

When Nadal was finally done with Madame Blue Rinse, he came over to me.

"Can I help you, sir?" he asked.

I turned and smiled.

"Juanito!" he cried. *"Hombre!"* Then wrapped me into a back-thumping Latin bear hug.

"How long has it been?" he asked. "Ten years? You no change. Not one bit. What brings you back to Miami?"

"You," I said.

At that, the lights went blinking on in the quick-moving mind of Felipe Nadal. "Work? We go back to work?"

"Come on, Felipe," I suggested, "let's go get a cup of coffee."

Felipe was one of our UCLANs—Unilaterally Controlled Latino Assets, a rather typical example, in fact, of that special breed. He'd been born in Cienfuegos, Cuba, studied physics at the University of Havana, and fled the island in 1961 after getting into a punch-up with a *barbudo*—bearded one—or Castro henchman. When he'd arrived on our shores, he'd signed on with Brigade 2506 but wound up in a battalion which sat out the landing in Guatemala.

Because Felipe was young, smart and burning with the desire to throw the communists out of his homeland, the Miami station had signed him on as a contractual employee when he received his discharge from Brigade 2506. He got the same basic training we gave to all of our Cuban-American mercenaries, the low-intensity conflict stuff, weapons, explosives, infiltrating frontiers, field survival.

Those UCLANs constituted a highly specialized labor pool into which we at the CIA could dip for covert operators whenever we needed them: drivers, pilots, small arms and explosives instructors, skippers to run boats in and out of Cuba with our agents and sabotage teams. We'd sign them up for six months or a year, and when they'd finished their work with us, they'd return to Miami's Little Havana—Sector 60, the cops called it—and go back to pumping gas or bartending or whatever, until the next call to service came. People used to joke that every Cuban in Miami was an employee of the CIA, wanted to be an employee of the CIA, or wanted you to think he was an employee of the CIA.

Felipe's career trajectory had been fairly typical. He'd begun working on our boat service ferrying arms and people to the Cuban coast, first from Alligator Key, then from a rather splendid villa we used on Riviera Drive off the Ponce de Leon Highway in Coral Gables.

It's worth noting here that it didn't take some of our skippers—I don't know if Felipe was among them—long to figure out that the Miami Customs Patrol officers were getting stiff necks from looking the other way every time one of our boats sailed by. From that realization, a minimal effort of thought was required to understand it would be a nice idea to stop off in the islands on the way home for a bale or two of marijuana. That became an accepted part of the job for many UCLANs, a kind of hazardous-duty pay to which our Miami station conveniently closed its eyes.

Felipe did some work for us on Lake Tanganyika in the Congo, served a term in Vietnam, and did a three-year stint we'd arranged for him with the DISIP, the Venezuelan security service. Since 1978, he'd been running his flower shop in the Fontainebleau.

We wandered into one of the hotel's coffee shops, took a back booth and ordered espressos.

"Hey, Juanito," he said, squeezing my hand affectionately. *Juanito* was the hispanicized version of *Jack* our UCLANs used with me when we worked together. "You look good, man, real good."

He pointed at my blond hair, a possession which, when combined with my fluent Spanish, had always amused my dark-haired Cuban friends. "You still pure gold, man. Why no gray? No *chicas* giving you problems?"

"You know me, Felipe," I smiled. "I'm a gringo, remember? Faithful husband."

Felipe grimaced to indicate just how distasteful such a notion was to him. "Hey," he asked, "how's Hinckley? They still use that fucker's blood for freezer fluid?"

Hinckley had run the Miami station before leaving for Southeast Asia. His chilly demeanor had done little to endear him to our more warm-blooded UCLANs. "Sure. He's a big shot now. Still a laugh a minute, though."

Felipe leaned forward and dropped his voice two or three registers, a sure sign he was about to reveal a secret. For Cubans, secrets tend to be bits of information that are meant to be shared provided their sharing will enhance the raconteur's standing in his listener's esteem.

"It was here in this hotel," he whispered, "upstairs in room 814 Hinckley gave Santo Trafficante and one of his guys the pills for Fidel. You remember? The ones that were going to kill the son of a bitch?"

Poor Felipe shook his head in sad recollection of that abortive effort to put his homeland out of its misery.

"How do you know that?"

"The other guy who was there that day told me the story a few years ago. What the fuck was his name?" Felipe banged his head with his fist. "My memory's getting terrible. He only had four fingers on his left hand. Anyhow, what's up? We got work to do?"

"Maybe. I'm going to need some people to help me move arms around. Quietly. Check them out, make sure they're okay, repackage them, forward them to our clients."

"Where, man?"

"Central America."

"For the *causa*?"

The *causa* was the liberation of Cuba from Castro's rule. "Yes," I replied, "indirectly, but yes."

"I'm your man, Juanito. You tell me, I go."

"You remember that company, Biscayne Financial Services over on Biscayne Boulevard?" That was an agency front we had employed to pay our UCLANs, provide them with false identification cards, documents, passports and whatever else their assignments might require.

"Sure."

"I'll be in touch in a month or two. I'll tell you the roses are ready for delivery and you go over to Biscayne. They'll give you your startup money and the walking around paper you'll need. They'll tell you where to go and what to do when you get there."

"How long you figure this will last?"

"It's hard to say, Felipe. A year. Two, three. You'll get expenses and ten G a month, offshore so you won't have to worry about the IRS. Can you be away from the shop that long?"

"For the *causa*? No problem, man, no problem." Suddenly a light flashed in his eyes. "Riccardi," he said. "That was the guy's name. The one with the four fingers up there with Hinckley that day."

My next stop was Victoria, Texas, a little crossroads community an hour's drive west of Houston. Finding what I was looking for, the municipal airport, was easy. Finding anything in Victoria would, I think, be easy. Once there I spotted my sign, Albright's Aerial Services, hanging over the door of a rundown, one-plane hangar.

The door to its office was open. The proprietor was sitting in the office, his booted feet hiked up onto his desk, tilted back in a chair, a ten-gallon hat covering his eyes, an irregular snore rumbling his nasal passages as he dozed in the midday heat. It was Ray Albright, the Air America pilot with whom I'd flown up to Long Tien in 1968, a trifle beef-ier, his face—or at least that part of it which was available for viewing—a bit puffier than it had been back then.

"Hey!" I asked. "Anybody home?"

Ray stirred, tilted back the hat with an indifference that did not bespeak great entrepreneurial energy, and fixed me with a puzzled expression. Clearly, he'd recognized me but hadn't yet been able to figure out just where we'd met.

"Don't I know you from somewheres?" he asked.

"Vientiane, 1968."

"Sheet, yeah, you're that weapons guy I met in the Rose the night they killed poor old Billy Bob. What's your name again?"

"Back then it was Pete, Pete Tuttle."

Ray's cowboy boots came thumping down onto the floor. He reached into a small fridge behind the desk, pulled out a Coors Lite and tossed it to me. "Have a silver bullet, Petey."

He took out a second can for himself, stripped off the top, helped himself to a long swallow, then wiped his mouth with the back of his hand.

"Them were the days, weren't they, now?"

"Ever find out what happened to Billy Bob?" I asked.

"Naw. He was talkin' to some people it don't do no good to talk to is what I reckon."

"How's business?" I waved my Coors toward the seem-ingly deserted municipal airport of Victoria.

"Sucks." Ray pointed to the Cessna in his hangar. "That's the business. I fly an air taxi down to Houston or Dallas Fort Worth. Oklahoma City when we got us a good football team up there. Teach a few housewives how to fly. Trouble is, I have to diddle half of 'em to keep up their interest in fly-ing."

Ray had been a victim of Air America's demise at the end of the Vietnam War. The airline's ties to the CIA had be-come such a well-known secret the operation had begun to be a liability. We closed it down. People like Ray and his merry band of brothers in Laos had been pastured out to more mundane and less profitable activities such as crop dusting or running the kind of charter service Ray was oper-ating.

"So what brings you down to this godforsaken corner of God's own country, Petey?" Ray asked.

"You."

"Me?" Ray exploded in laughter.

"Yeah. I work for the guys who used to own your airline. The real owners, I mean."

"Sooooo," Ray whistled, "that's why they let you ride up to Long Tien with me."

"Yup. We're looking for a few good pilots to do some interesting flying for us."

"You know me, Petey. Like Billy Bob used to say, I'll fly camel shit up a polar bear's ass if the price's right. Where's this flying at, if you don't mind my asking?"

"Central America. The Caribbean."

"Nice country down there from what I hear. Figure they got any places like the Rose to keep a man amused at night?" He guffawed. "You remember that little ole girl Aw? Wasn't she something else?"

"Yeah." I smiled in fond recollection of those distant evenings. "Tell me, do you stay in touch with your old Air America gang?"

"Hell, yeah. Four or five of us, we get together real regular like for a night out up in Vegas or some such place."

"Well, you might pass the word. You ever hear of Southern Air Transport?"

"That name rings a bell somewheres."

"They'll be getting in touch with you in a couple of months. Fill you in on all the details."

"I'll be here. What'll we be flying?"

"Best we cover that when the time comes."

"No sweat, Petey."

"Jack," I said, smiling. "The name's Jack now."

New York City

"You know what I think, Kevin? I think this guy is having you off."

Kevin Grady put on the resigned smile of a man who has spent too much of his life tilting with the resistant windmills of the federal bureaucracy to respond to such a challenge. The speaker was his boss, Richie Cagnia, the group supervisor of the DEA's New York Office Group Six, the investigative unit to which Grady was assigned.

"Rich," Grady assured his boss, "he's doing the best he

can for us. He's just a poor jerk who got his gonads caught in the grinder and can't figure out how to get them back out again."

"He's dumb, all right," Cagnia agreed. The gentleman whose intellect they both held in such low esteem was Denny Strong, the American Airlines copilot whom Grady had convinced to become an informant.

"Anybody who's looking at twenty-five years' exposure because he can't keep his dick in his pants has to be a prize jerk. The point is," Cagnia declared, waving a piece of paper in his hands, "I can't go waltzing over to Judge Parker's chambers and go to bat for your guy with what you've got in here. This is just a handful of smoke."

He laid the paper on Grady's desk. "Come on, read that thing again."

The *thing* was labeled *File G3-82-0003*. It represented a distillation of the information Kevin had been able to extract from Strong about the man who was now the subject of the file, a gentleman identified as Marcello, Raymond aka Ramon.

Information received from SG3-82-0049

—that number was the informant code Grady had assigned his American Airlines pilot—

indicates that Raymond Marcello, an American citizen residing at an address unknown somewhere in Colombia, South America, is actively involved in the transshipment of multi-hundred kilo quantities of cocaine to the United States. SG3-82-0049 met Marcello in October of last year in Medellín, Colombia, South America where Marcello was associated with a group of Colombian drug smugglers who were preparing to import approximately 500 kilos of cocaine into the United States. Marcello asked SG3-82-0049 if he could find him a pilot capable of flying a second load of cocaine to the United States and a secure landing strip to receive it. SG3-82-0049 said Marcello spoke fluent Spanish and told him that was because he had a Colombian wife and had lived in Colombia for several years. SG3-82-0049 stated that Marcello appeared to be completely accepted and trusted by his Colombian associates despite the fact he was American.

> Marcello is a white male, approximately 40 years in age, 5'10", 160 pounds with dark, curly hair graying at the temples. He is NADDIS Negative

—that meant his name was not carried on the DEA's master computer file of known drug smugglers or drug smuggling suspects—

> Subject cannot be identified further at present. An investigation on the basis of the foregoing information has been opened.

"Come on, Kev," Cagnia said, "what is this guy Strong supposed to do if he finds a pilot and a strip for Ramon? How does he make contact? That's not in here, is it? What's he supposed to do? Go back down there to Medellín, stand on a street corner and holler, 'Yoo-hoo, Ramon! I've got a pilot for you!' This Ramon has to have given that American Airlines pilot of yours a contact somewhere. A number to call. Something. Where is it? He's holding out on you."

"He swears to me he didn't get one because he didn't intend to follow up on it."

"Oh, horseshit, Kev. Believe that and you'll believe the Ayatollah is Mother Teresa's confessor. He just won't cough it up is all."

"Richie, I want this guy Ramon indicted. That's the only way I can keep this case open. And if I'm going to get an indictment, I've got to get Strong to go in and testify before a grand jury. That's why I want to keep him sweet."

Cagnia turned to Ella Jean Ransom. "Have you talked to this pilot?"

"A couple of times, yeah."

"How do you read him?"

"I agree with Kevin. I think he's one scared little rabbit and he's coughed up everything he knows."

"Kev," Cagnia sighed, "between pals, why are we going through all of this anyway? Why have you got such a hard-on for this guy Ramon? I mean, we may never come across him again. Or if we do, it may be five years from now. Why are we wasting our time here?"

"Richie, what would be going to the Super Bowl in this business of ours? What's the one thing we can do that's going to give everybody from the Administrator right on up to the Attorney General an instant orgasm?"

"I doubt this Attorney General knows what an orgasm is, Kevin." Cagnia glanced at Ella Jean. "Excuse me for being so uncouth."

"Rudeness in the pursuit of accuracy is not a sin." She smiled.

Kevin ignored them. "Ever since those guys down in Medellín formed that so-called cartel of theirs, we've been drowning in a sea of white powder. We've never had a drug curse like this. The only place it hasn't hit is the ghettos."

"At a hundred bucks a hit, how do you think the brothers are going to go for that shit, man?" Ella Jean asked.

"I don't know. It's the only blessing of poverty as far as I can see, and let's pray to God it stays that way. But what I want to say is the best thing we can do right now, bar none, is get a penetration into those guys in Medellín. Put an informant onto Pablo Escobar's dinner plate."

"And you are crazy enough to sit here and suggest to me," Cagnia asked, "that we might do it with this guy who might be called Ramon, who all we know about him is he brokers loads? Who might be an American or might not be? Whose real name may or may not be Marcello? Who lives somewhere—we don't even have a clue where—in Colombia, which is a very big country?

"Forget the guy, Kev," Cagnia snorted. "I admire your tenacity, but let your pilot pal do his twenty-five. He earned them. Let's you and me get on to something else. I mean we don't even know whether this Ramon really exists or whether the pilot just made him up to get some time off his sentence!"

"Oh, this guy exists, all right, Richie."

Cagnia got out of his chair and walked over to the window to glance down at Fifty-seventh Street. "Are you two holding out something on your Uncle Richie?"

Grady glanced at Ella Jean, then opened his desk drawer and drew out a small black loose-leaf binder.

"Ella and I have been doing a little moonlighting. Our friend Marcello was born in Ardmore, Pennsylvania. Father's a surgeon. Very wealthy, distinguished gentleman. Mother's deceased. One sister, a lawyer with an old Main Line Philadelphia law firm. Went to Milton Academy outside Boston, one of those fancy New England prep schools that cost Daddy twenty K a year. Graduated Lafayette College in Easton, Pennsylvania, in 1969. Mediocre student. Became one of your sixties, long-haired weirdo freaks. Ran a rock group called No Exit. Big in the anti-war stuff. Known to our cousins in the FBI for his activities, arrested in two anti-war demonstrations, one in New Haven and one at the Pentagon. Released on probation both times. Busted for selling grass to an undercover cop in Easton, Pennsylvania. Got off with six months suspended because Daddy apparently knew the judge. Moves to Bogotá, Colombia, in 1970. He's back in this country for about six months in 1976, married to one Lucinda Rodriguez, Colombian national. Worked as a real estate agent for the Green Doors Realtors in Rehoboth Beach on the Delaware shore for six months. Then all of a sudden quits in a big rush and goes back to Colombia. Nothing on him since. Until our pilot friend caught up with him brokering loads for the cartel, that is."

"Okay, you guys have been doing your homework. But tell me first why you're keeping all this good stuff in the drawer. Why not put it into a Six so I can show it to the Assistant U.S. Attorney and take it to Judge Parker?"

"I want this guy for myself, Richie. I don't want anybody else stepping on him. Once all that background information gets into the files, who knows what other government agency might develop an interest in him?"

Grady knew that since Marcello's address was outside the United States, any information on him officially recorded in the DEA's files would automatically find its way into the hands of the CIA. Since his encounter with the agency in Laos, he'd become more than a bit paranoid about the big brothers at Langley. That was not a place in which Kevin wanted this information to come to rest. He snapped his little folder shut and slipped it back into his desk drawer.

"Richie," he told his supervisor, "we will never, ever penetrate the cartel with a Colombian, would you agree with that?"

"It's unlikely, yeah."

"About as likely as penetrating the Mob with the Attorney General. Our only possible chance is with an American. It's obviously got to be an American we've got something very major on. But above all, it's got to be an American those Colombians really trust. You know how they operate. They want a guy's family in easy range to make sure he stands up straight. They don't trust Americans as a rule, but maybe, just maybe, they'd trust an American who's married to a Colombian and got a couple of kiddies down there they can get their warm and friendly hands on if they have to."

Cagnia whistled softly. "That's tough stuff, Kev."

"It's a tough world."

"Besides, if this Ramon of yours is doing regular business with those Medellín cowboys, he's got to know how they reward informers, right? Why would he flip in the face of that?"

Grady shrugged. "Who knows? It's just a hunch."

"You seem to be living on hunches these days."

"Maybe. But I think this guy's soft. Spoiled rich kid. Easy life, all that prep school stuff. Goes off and plays hippie, shouts about the war. Why? Because he's got Daddy's dough to fall back on. Gets caught selling grass but Daddy saves his ass. I'll bet he goes into the coke business down there because he figures, what the hell, lots of easy money and nobody can ever lay a hand on him. He may talk tough, but I'll bet the guy's a marshmallow inside."

"You make him sound positively adorable."

Once again a strained smile appeared on Grady's face. "There are very few things, Richie, that I enjoy more than sitting down with guys like this one and explaining to them just how much fun it is to do twenty-five years in one of our nicer Federal institutions where you see the sun once a day if you're lucky. Then you talk to the guy about the roomie he's likely to have, except how he won't be much like the fellows he lived with back at the old frat house. He'll be black, weigh about 300 pounds, and like to bugger college boys when he hasn't got anything else to do, which, in the can, is about ninety-nine percent of the time. It makes people think, Richie. Particularly people who have brains, which is the one thing I suspect our friend Ramon probably has."

"All that's great, Kevin, but remember even if we do get an indictment, we still won't know where the hell the guy is. It's like having a thousand-to-one shot in the Irish sweepstakes."

"Maybe, Richie, but if we want to penetrate the cartel, what better shot have we got?"

The Piper Cheyenne had dropped down to wave-top levels twenty miles off the Panamanian seacoast. Now, it skimmed the Pacific's long gray swells like some enormous seagull in search of prey. Ahead, the pilot could make out the coastal ridge and, dead ahead, the visual landmark that was his beacon, the twin spires of Coronado Beach's luxurious highrises.

The resort, an hour's drive north of Panama City, was a weekend refuge for the city's wealthy. To his left, two miles from the building, was the pilot's destination, the small landing strip used by the resort's tenants for their private aircraft. He cast a glance back into the cabin at his cargo: a dozen dark green U.S. navy duffel bags he'd stowed on the plane in the predawn darkness at Pablo Escobar's Hacienda Napoles ranch, a thirty-minute flight from Medellín. Nervously, he mumbled a hastily recollected prayer to the Virgin, however inappropriate invoking her name on behalf of a man running 400 kilos of cocaine might appear to be.

Two hundred yards off the sandy swath of beach, he pulled up to clear the coastal ridge. His reckoning was perfect. The strip was directly in front of him, a russet Volkswagen minivan waiting for him in the early morning sunlight.

He cut back the throttle and settled the Piper onto the paved strip, letting the craft slip down the runway to the van. There he pivoted around, braked to a stop, and threw open his cabin door. The trio of his fellow Colombians waiting by the vans began to wrestle out his load of duffel bags. The pilot did not cut his motor. This was an in-and-out operation.

When the last duffel bag had been hauled from the cabin, one of the ground crew slammed the door shut, giving it as he did a thump with his fist as an *All Clear* signal. The pilot gunned his engine and shot the Piper back down the runway and out across the Pacific's gray expanse.

He did not look back. If he had, he might have seen the three olive-drab Toyotas of the Panamanian Defense Forces, roof lights flashing, screeching up to the men who'd unloaded his plane.

The trio were handcuffed and taken to the nearby Chorrera barracks, where the beating began. It was done systematically and dispassionately under the disinterested gaze of an officer called Pedro: first each man's back and kidneys with a bamboo stave, then his testicles, and, to complete the task, a dozen solid fist blows to his face.

Finally, with a grunt, Pedro ordered the beating to stop.

"We'll inform your boss in Medellín he can have you back," Pedro announced, "for half a million U.S."

The three Colombians were silent. None of them knew whether Don Pablo Escobar's sense of loyalty to his employees extended deeply enough into his bank account to accommodate a demand like that.

"Tell your boss when you get back to Medellín this isn't how things are done up here," Pedro continued. "Tell him he has to work things out first."

"How? With who?" one of the three blubbered through his swollen and bleeding lips.

"He knows," Pedro replied.

The town of Leticia lies two thousand miles up the Amazon River from the Atlantic Ocean, on the southernmost tip of Colombia, in the heart of the planet's largest ecological reserve. It is an area that is at once an environmentalist's fondest dream and worst nightmare. Across the brown gulch of the Amazon from Leticia—a strip of water so wide the naked eye can barely see the farther shore—lies Peru. A ten-minute stroll down International Boulevard from the center of the town, across an unmarked frontier, is Brazil. For hundreds of miles around Leticia, the banks of the Amazon and its massive spider web of tributaries are wrapped in the jungle's luxuriant cloak. What little human life there is, is primitive and poor: Ticuna Indians fishing the side streams in pirogues as they have been doing for centuries, gliding through the high grass along the banks, spearing a fish with one swift and lethal swish of their two-pronged spears.

From ten thousand feet, the outline of the Aerocommander skimming over the jungle's green canopy would have resembled a moth flitting over a dark carpet. The plane's pilot, however, had dropped down to 500 feet to better pick up the ground bearings that would point him toward his destination, a narrow dirt strip scratched into that green blanket rolling along below his aircraft.

Willi Fernandez, the pilot, was barely twenty-three years old, a recent graduate of the Colombian National Civil Aviation School. He'd been flying professionally for less than two years, yet he was already earning twice as much per month as a captain with Avianca, the Colombian national airline.

Willi was a drug pilot, a member of the select aerial stable of Pablo Escobar, the Medellín drug baron. The curious dictates of geography had linked that vast, primeval Amazonian watershed to some of the most glamorous and sophisticated locales in the world. It was here, in these impenetrable jungles, that Colombia's drug lords concealed the laboratories in which they converted the raw paste crushed from the coca leaves of Peru, Bolivia and Ecuador into pure white cocaine hydrochloride powder to sear the nasal passages of North America.

The products of the jungle around Leticia serviced the appetites of Jay McInerney's Wall Street yuppies and their model girlfriends; Hollywood hot-hots and starlets; pimps from Chicago's South Side and their high-class hookers; athletes of the NBA, the NFL, the major leagues and their excited female fans; rock stars and their groupies. A generation of affluent, middle- and upper-class, largely white Americans had developed an insatiable appetite for Colombian nose-candy.

As a result, the jungle around Leticia had undergone a boom that dwarfed in importance the rubber boom that had once brought prosperity to the Amazon Basin. From this remote swath of jungle, a veritable tidal wave of fine white powder was pouring north to the United States, creating an industry whose annual financial dimensions were already calculated in billions of dollars.

Willi Fernandez, a minor if grateful beneficiary of that boom, was, like most drug pilots, a flying fool. He had to be. The planes he flew were chronically overloaded and under-fueled. That was for the simplest of economic reasons. Most of the *pasta basica,* the brownish puttylike paste made from the leaves of the coca plant, arriving in Leticia came from Peru's Upper Huallaga Valley. The valley was under the control of the *Sendero Luminoso,* the Shining Path guerrillas. They charged a landing fee of fifteen thousand dollars on all drug flights coming into and out of the valley, a fee payable by wire transfer to a Panamanian bank account. The Sendero were the world's most vicious guerrilla organization; they were also its wealthiest.

In order to maximize his profit on each drug flight, Escobar saw that his planes carried just enough fuel to get them to their destination. The weight gained was used to cram an extra sack or two of pasta into the plane. Fortunately for Fernandez, the weather today was bright and clear.

In the rainy season, these were the moments when a drug pilot earned his money. Then, dense banks of swift-moving rain cloud could smother visibility all along the river, swallowing up landmarks in an horizonless bowl of gray mist.

Willi picked out the contours of his first bearing, Monkey Island. Swinging his Aerocommander out of Peruvian airspace, he crossed the Amazon and began to fly upstream along the Colombian shore, checking out each tributary emptying into the river until he found his next bearing, a modest sized stream, its mouth marked by a narrow stone island set like a lizard's tongue into its junction with the big river. He flew up the tributary, each of its twists and bends seared into his memory.

When he found the one he wanted, he bisected it on a heading of 231 degrees, flew for two minutes, and there below him was the welcoming slash of his strip slicing open the jungle floor.

While Willi watched, the ground crew swarmed into the plane to transfer his load of pasta basica onto a flat-bottomed motor launch hidden under the dense foliage arching over a stream bordering his landing strip.

When the job was finished, Willi flew back to Leticia to berth his Aerocommander on its grass strip alongside the dozens of other private aircraft that made that remote Amazonian town's airport look like Aspen, Colorado, in high season.

Once he'd taken off, the boatman and his crew motored five miles up the Amazon to another tributary. Three minutes into its course, the boatman nosed his launch up against what appeared to be a thick wall of jungle foliage.

He idled his motors and screeched out an imitation of a macaw's shriek. From somewhere behind the wall of foliage came an answering screech. Then two of the branches spread apart just enough to allow the motor launch to slide past.

Behind the foliage wall was an open-water passage up to a dock concealed under the immense branches of a swetiana tree, as old as it was enormous. A 300-yard path passing over a pair of land bridges led back into the jungle. Both bridges were mined. Spread out beyond the second bridge, under the canopy of the jungle, was a cocaine conversion laboratory.

By the standards of the Amazon, it was a modest operation. It consisted of half a dozen open-sided buildings with wood planking for floors and sheets of corrugated metal covered with branches as camouflage for roofing. There was a dormitory slung with hammocks for the thirty local *campesinos* who worked the lab; a food hut; a hut in which the chemicals were stored; a hut for the diesel generators which powered the lab; two working huts for the conversion process itself. The jungle provided the outhouse.

"Every time you go out to take a shit you have to shoot a snake," was a common lament among Leticia's lab workers.

The chemical process carried out in the lab was relatively straightforward but it could be dangerous. Some of the chemicals it required, ether, hydrochloric acid, acetone were highly volatile. Ignore the rules for using them and the result could be a devastating explosion.

What counted most for the lab was security. Its operations were governed by rules as rigid as those ordering life in a Benedictine monastery. First, each day's production was picked up daily by the boatman who'd unloaded Willi's pasta. He took it to a *calletta*, an underground hiding place lined with cement cut into a hillside. That way, if the lab was raided, the *Federales* would be able to seize only one day's production. No one at the lab besides the boatman knew where the calletta was located.

All the chemicals, fuel, equipment and machinery the lab needed had been brought to the lab site before anybody else was allowed into it. The thirty campesino laborers and six armed guards assigned to it arrived on the day the lab was ready to start operations. Once they got there, nobody was allowed in or out except the boatman. The lab's employees worked in two shifts, twenty-four hours a day, seven days a week. It was only when the last kilo of pasta had been processed that the lab was closed down, usually for good, the campesinos paid off and allowed to return to Leticia or their farms.

For the Federales and the DEA, those tight security arrangements made discovering a lab in the immensity of the Amazonian jungles a daunting task. At first they had called on technology for help. Helicopters equipped with heat sensors were sent out to overfly the jungles at low altitude, trying to pick up traces of the heat given off by the lab's drying devices.

Once the helicopters had registered a heat trace, a paramilitary squad was sent charging into the area, weapons drawn, shouting for everyone to freeze. Alas, in almost every case what those SWAT teams found was not a lab in full operation but a group of terrified Ticuna Indians huddled around a baking kiln.

And so the DEA had now resorted to a tactic that long predated any of the technology the narco-traffickers had brought to the jungle—informers. The Federales had assiduously circulated the word that the gringos would pay money, big money to any campesino who fingered a lab for them. Those sums could, depending on the size of the lab discovered, run as high as twenty thousand dollars. To campesinos struggling to earn fifty dollars a month from their lands, two hundred dollars when they were working in a lab, such sums were almost beyond imagining. The tactic was beginning to work. *Informer* had become the dirtiest word in the vocabulary of Don Pablo Escobar.

There were few prospects the drug pilot Willi Fernandez contemplated with more delight than a night on the town in Leticia. It was, its residents liked to boast, Dodge City with tropical palms. Everybody had money. There were the hotshot pilots like Willi; the "cookers" from the labs; lab owners; heavies in town from Medellín and Cali; guards from labs that had wound up operations, tossing away their earnings with frenzied delight; Peruvian Indians who'd spent a fortnight paddling a load of pasta down the Amazon in a pirogue and now had more money in their pockets than they'd seen in a lifetime.

Willi slung a heavy gold chain around his neck, snapped on his new Rolex Seamaster, gave himself a last admiring glance in the mirror of his hotel, and headed out into the warm tropical night.

His first stop was a bordello, the Monterey on International Boulevard, its entrances screened from the street by a wall and garden. Its owner, Johnny Sanchez, known all over Leticia as El Gringo Negro—The Black Gringo—liked to boast that his establishment was "a whorehouse known from Patagonia to Paris."

To Willi's surprise, a small knot of clearly agitated people were gathered at the steps leading into the Monterey. Leticia's senior police sergeant was there along with two of his men. El Gringo Negro was standing in the doorway gesticulating excitedly to someone just inside the door. The door opened and two of his bouncers rolled a bloodstained corpse down the steps to the feet of the three policemen.

"All right, all right!" the sergeant shouted up at El Gringo Negro. "Just what the hell happened?"

"He got all angry when the waiter gave him his bill. He said that the waiter wasn't showing him sufficient respect. Then he pulled a gun on him. Enrico here"—he indicated one of his bouncers—"shot him before he could shoot the waiter."

"Is that right?" the sergeant demanded of Enrico.

"I swear," replied the bouncer. "Exactly."

The sergeant stared at the others gathered on the steps above him. One was clearly a young lady of the house, softly sobbing her eyes out, evidently grief-stricken either for the loss of the dead man or for the potential income he had represented.

"You know him?" asked the sergeant.

"I was with him," gasped the girl.

"And that's what happened?"

"Si, si," she sobbed.

The sergeant turned to his two patrolmen. "Okay" he announced, "we take a vote. Did he deserve it or not?"

"Yes," said the first policeman.

"Yes," agreed his colleague.

"Case dismissed," said the sergeant. "Get him out of here," he ordered El Gringo Negro.

Willi smiled. Letician justice had been served. He entered the Monterey's lobby and went into its main room, a large dance floor ringed by crescent-shaped booths. To the left of the entrance was a long bar.

The place was packed. There was just the faintest whiff of gunsmoke in the air and, beside one of the booths, two waiters were busily mopping up the deceased's blood. Otherwise, nothing suggested a killing had just taken place.

Willi strolled over to the bar and ordered a cognac. There was almost no brand of whiskey or cognac known to man that was not stocked behind the bar. The pilot surveyed the action, looking for a lady who was available. A certain discretion was always advisable in making your selection at the Monterey. In view of the ease with which guns were drawn, it wasn't clever to hit on a woman who had already been fingered by a local heavy.

The fifty-odd girls on duty at the Monterey had been recruited principally in Bogotá, Cali and Medellín. To fill out their ranks and add a touch of the exotic to his establishment, El Gringo Negro had added half a dozen girls from Rio de Janeiro. He recruited the girls himself. It was the part of his job he liked the best.

Willi was sipping his cognac when one of them, a blonde with a beehive hairdo and a white silk dress which encased her body so tightly she had to cruise the bar at half-speed, slithered up to him. She eased her hands into his crotch and cast him a beguiling smile.

"Boom-boom in my room?" she asked

Willi caressed her buttocks in reciprocation for her introductory gesture and pondered her suggestion. As he did, he saw, from the corner of his eye, El Gringo Negro moving toward him.

"Hóla," he said, dropping a friendly hand on Willi's shoulder. "I'm afraid it's going to have to stay in your pants tonight, my friend. Your boss just called from Medellín. He wants you up there right away."

Of all the major drug barons whose names were associated with the city of Medellín, only one was a native son—Pablo Escobar. He had been born on a lovely two hundred acre *estancia*, a horse and cattle farm in the rolling hillsides of El Tabla, the high plateau country ringing the city to which its wealthy retreated for weekends and vacations. Unfortunately for Escobar, he did not owe his birth on El Tabla to membership in that elite caste. He was born there because his mother happened to be a domestic in a rich man's home, his father an overseer of the man's animals.

Escobar earned the first of his billions of dollars in the unlikeliest of locales—the graveyard. He pillaged cemeteries under the cover of darkness, ripping up tombstones which he carted off to a garage workshop. There he shaved off their inscriptions, honed, washed and polished them until their marble or granite gleamed like new. Then, with the aid of the obituary column in the local newspaper and a suitably soulful demeanor, he set out to sell his stones to the newly bereaved.

He expanded his trade to dealing in stolen cars. One day a friend asked him to drive a truckload of pasta basica from

Peru to Colombia. Pablo Escobar had found his calling. He never looked back.

He was, quite literally, awash in money which he spent with gleeful and ostentatious abandon. His favorite residence was the Hacienda Napoles, a short flight from Medellín, its entry gate surmounted by the wreckage of the first of his planes to crash smuggling drugs.

The place was so enormous it contained over fifty miles of roads and two dozen artificial lakes. He had also built himself a zoo that would have been the pride of a medium-sized city. It contained elephants, giraffes, hippopotami, zebras, anteaters. There were hundreds of white doves in the area around his swimming pool. He liked to sit out by the pool at night with his guests while his employees drove the birds into the branches of the trees overhead until they formed a white blanket stretched out against the equatorial night. All that, as one visitor noted, despite the fact that a considerable number of that immense flock inevitably found it necessary to defecate while they were entertaining Pablo and his friends.

Physically, Escobar was an unprepossessing man. His handshake was limp and wet. He rarely looked an interlocutor in the eye. One of his constant affectations was a little hat he wore perched on the top of his head like the yarmulke of a Jewish grocer in a kosher delicatessen in Brooklyn. He was short and overweight, although a little excess weight never dimmed a man's social standing in Latin American society. It was, after all, graphic proof of the fact he had the money to eat well.

He was referred to as El Padrino, the Godfather, a nickname in which he delighted. When it came to savagery, to sheer bloodthirstiness, however, the dons of Sicily had nothing to teach Pablo Escobar.

According to the Mafia's old-fashioned concepts, when a man broke his vow of *omerta,* silence, he paid for his indiscretion himself. Escobar had refined that Sicilian notion, bringing it to a higher plane of retribution. When Escobar killed someone, he was doing him a favor. If a man betrayed Pablo Escobar, it was his near and dear who first paid the price of his treachery. Shoot a man's son, or rape his wife, in front of him before you kill him, was Pablo's recommendation. That made more of an impression, and impressions counted for much in his uncertain trade.

Escobar had summoned Willi Fernandez away from the

pleasures of Leticia's bordellos just to turn him around and point him back to the Amazonian Basin. Twice in the past six months, the Federales, acting on information from paid informants, had raided Escobar's jungle labs. He had decided the time had come to put an end to the Federales's information flow by administering a dose of preventative justice.

Escobar climbed into Willi's plane with a pair of bodyguards armed with Uzi submachine guns and ordered his pilot to take off. The control tower obligingly instructed Avianca's Bogotá shuttle flight to hold its departure until Escobar's plane was airborne.

The drug baron almost never visited his jungle labs. The installations were too primitive for his tastes. Therefore, his unannounced arrival at the lab to which Willi Fernandez's planeload of pasta basica had been delivered the previous afternoon was the cause of considerable consternation. The lab boss ran over the bridges leading to the landing to greet him, aware that whatever it was that had provoked Escobar's visit, it could only mean trouble.

"Assemble every son of a bitch who's working in this lab," Escobar told him. "Right now. Line them all up."

"Some of the campesinos from the night shift are sleeping," blurted out the lab boss.

"Wake them up."

Escobar and his guards were already storming across the bridges toward the lab site.

"Everybody," Escobar repeated. "In two lines, right here." He indicated with a flick of a riding crop he was carrying where he wanted the men assembled.

The illiterate campesinos working the site came tumbling out of its huts, some with hands still dripping chemicals, the workers from the night shift driven bleary-eyed and half-dressed from their hammocks.

When they'd been lined up, Escobar turned to the lab boss. "They all here? Double check."

The lab boss recounted his flock. Escobar and his two bodyguards, their Uzis trained on the workers, looked on. By now the lab's six local guards had arrived and their weapons, too, were trained on the gathering.

The campesinos stared slack-jawed and uncomprehending at the weapons pointing at them, slowly coming to the knowledge that some terrible calamity was about to overtake them.

"All here, Don Pablo," the lab boss announced.

"No one's missing, you're sure?"

"Si, si," the boss assured him.

For at least a minute, Escobar stared at the assembly, slowly caressing his left palm with his riding crop, his dark eyes as cold as black pebbles on a wind-glazed beach. He paced the two lines of men, scrutinizing their anguished and puzzled faces.

Finally, he strode back to the center of the clearing.

"One of you bastards betrayed this lab to the Federales," he announced.

A gasp of collective horror burst from the campesinos, an emotional ejaculation like that a group of spectators will emit when suddenly they see an automobile spin wildly out of control during a race or a downhill skier cartwheeling into a terrible fall.

Escobar took one step forward and jabbed the man before him with his riding crop.

"Your name?" he barked.

For a second the man was so terrified he couldn't remember his own name. When he had, Escobar moved on and repeated the process with the next man in line. He continued that way, working his way slowly along the line, name by name, campesino by campesino.

Then he started in on the second line. He'd passed the third man and was facing the fourth when he spun and sent a vicious slash of his riding crop across the cheek of the campesino he had just addressed.

"You're the son of a bitch!" he roared.

"No, no!" the man—his name was Diego Nader—shrieked. "I swear to Christ! I swear to the Holy Mother of God! I swear to all the saints! I don't even know no Federales."

"Lying bastard!" Escobar's riding crop slashed another cut into the man's face, already pouring blood from his first lash. "You think the Federales don't talk to Don Pablo Escobar?"

"I swear, I swear, I never talked to nobody," Diego cried, tears now streaming down his cheeks along with the blood drawn by Escobar's riding crop. He sank to his knees and began desperately kissing Escobar's feet. The drug baron whacked his skull with his crop.

"Pick him up," he ordered the lab's guards. "Tie up his wrists—tight.

"Not behind his back," Escobar snarled as they started to work. "I want them in front of him." The drug baron had already decided how he would deal with Diego Nader.

"Take him down to the landing," he ordered.

"Jesus, no!" begged Diego. "Not the piranhas!"

"No, not the piranhas," Escobar answered. "Why should I be nice to you?"

He stabbed the lab boss's chest with his riding crop. "Bring a drum of kerosene and a pail down to the landing." He turned to the lab guards. "March them down there, too, all of them."

Like a group of prisoners of war, the twenty-nine remaining campesinos were marched to the edge of the waterway, then formed up again into two lines.

Diego, sobbing helplessly, knelt on the ground in front of them.

"Take a rope," Escobar ordered, "and tie it to that rope around his wrists."

When the guards had finished, Escobar pointed to the large branch of the swetiana tree arching out over the stream.

"Throw the rope over the branch," he commanded.

"They're going to hang me!" Diego cried.

"In a moment you'll wish I were," Escobar laughed. "Hoist him up until his feet are just out of the water."

Once Diego was dangling from the branch, his body convulsed by sobbing, Escobar paused to contemplate his handiwork. Then he pointed at one of the campesinos standing in line. "Fill that pail with kerosene," he ordered, "and douse our little bird with it."

Diego screamed, now fully aware of the agony that was about to be his. A flight of jungle birds burst screeching from the branches overhead at the sound.

"You!" Escobar indicated another man with his riding crop. "Set the bastard on fire."

"Oh, Jesus, no, Don Pablo," the man begged "He's my neighbor!"

"You want to get up there with him? Torch him, I said," Escobar replied.

Weeping hysterically, the man stumbled toward Diego, whose body was now flip-flopping with the wild, spastic motions of a freshly landed fish.

"Jesus, Jesus, forgive me, Diego," he begged his neighbor. Then he plunged a flaming newspaper on his body.

Diego screamed as a pillar of fire engulfed him.

Escobar contemplated the spectacle for a few seconds, then turned to the two guards holding on to the rope by which Diego was suspended over the stream.

"Lower him into the water," he ordered.

With a hiss and cloud of smoke and steam, Diego's tortured body slipped into the stream.

"Now pull him back out again," Escobar commanded.

There was little movement left in Diego's red and blackened body when it came out of the water. He had only the strength left to groan in agony. The quality of Pablo Escobar's mercy, however, was to be decidedly strained.

"Soak him in kerosene again," he said. Then he plucked another campesino from the line with his riding crop. "Now you torch him," he ordered.

Escobar repeated the process until the fun had gone out of his game and his point had been well made. Diego Nader's remains were left dangling from the tree branch like a blackened side of beef on a spit.

"Keep your campesinos lined up here for half an hour so they all realize what happens to informers," Escobar ordered the lab boss. "Then back to work."

With that, he climbed back into his motor launch, well satisfied with his morning's labors. Diego Nader had never, of course, spoken so much as a word to an officer of the Federales in his life. His had been nothing more than an expedient sacrifice to Escobar's concern for maintaining tight security in his labs.

For Escobar, his victim's agony was already forgotten. The drug baron's mind was now concentrated on his next problem. He needed a new staging area to move his cocaine north to Mexico and the United States, and he knew just the country he wanted to use for that purpose—Panama. His problem was the man who was now, for all practical purposes, running the country—Manuel Antonio Noriega.

To say that Noriega was satisfied contemplating the crumpled figure waiting on the living room couch would have been an understatement of considerable magnitude. He was positively delighted, although nothing in his usually dour demeanor indicated it. Guido Moro was the personal emissary of Don Pablo Escobar. The message Noriega had sent to Medellín in the form of three badly beaten drug dealers had clearly gotten through to its intended recipient.

Wordlessly, Noriega went to his bar, filled a pair of tumblers with Old Parr and ice, handed one to Moro, muttered *"Salud"* and sank into a leather armchair. He knew Guido Moro well. The attorney had been one of the two emissaries sent to ask him to intervene with the M19 after the kidnapping of Marta Ochoa. The second emissary had been a priest, the personal confessor of that devout drug runner, Jorge Luis Ochoa. A priestly presence, however, was not necessary for the business to be transacted tonight.

Noriega said nothing. He simply sipped his scotch and stared disinterestedly at his visitor. That was meant to make Moro uncomfortable and, perhaps, just a bit more vulnerable than he normally might be. It was a tactic Noriega had mastered during his days interrogating prisoners.

Outside the bungalow, both men could hear the sporadic splash of the Pacific's water on the rocks below la Playita. It was stifling hot but the bungalow was well air-conditioned. The machine served a dual function. Noriega had equipped the bungalow with the latest audiovisual recording system, and its gentle hum was meant to mask any inadvertent whir or click the recorders might produce.

Noriega liked to invite his officer friends of the United States Army's Southern Command here for Saturday night romps. "Colombian Nights," he called them, because both the girls and the coke came from his southern neighbor. The footage he shot during those evenings he considered an investment in the future, the assurance that a guest's friendship would be as enduring as it would be silent.

He had the equipment on now, just in case some slight misunderstanding should arise about what was said here this evening. Señor Moro, quite unaware that even the clink of the ice cubes in his glass was being recorded, bowed slightly and conveyed his client's warmest personal regards to Noriega. Don Pablo, he said, "wished to assure him of his desire to work closely with him in the future."

Noriega sipped his Old Parr as though he was meditating

on what he'd just heard. He'd been preparing for this little chat for some time.

"Those people in Medellín think they can treat us up here like a bunch of savages," he began. "Indians. They think they can get away with anything they want."

"I think all your friends in Medellín regret what happened at Coronado Beach, Colonel." The lawyer's tone caressed Noriega's rank with just the proper touch of reverence. "They wish to be sure that it doesn't happen again. That's why they sent me here tonight. They hope we can find a way by which we can all work together in the future."

Those, of course, were exactly the words Noriega wanted to hear, but his facial expression did not change. He took another long drink of his scotch. "What do they have in mind?"

"Essentially, a mutually satisfactory way of assuring safe passage of their product through Panama."

"By air?"

"Yes. My principal client owns a controlling interest in a Panamanian air-freight company called Inair which has scheduled flights to the U.S. He would like to be able to use Inair as a vehicle to move his product north."

That was news to Noriega. He knew Inair's Panamanian owner well. He hadn't realized Escobar was the man's silent partner.

"You are aware that the Panamanian Defense Forces control the airports here? The tower. Security. Customs. Immigration."

"Indeed we are. That's why we've come to you."

Noriega got up and went to the bar to pour himself another scotch. It was one of those sweltering Panamanian nights outside, the kind when a man's shirt becomes a second skin. Yet, Moro noted, Noriega's uniform was impeccable. His short-sleeve khaki blouse was pressed to a starchy tautness. The crease on his trousers, the lawyer thought, looked sharp enough to slice an orange. On his left breast he wore a paratrooper's badge and three rows of ribbons.

Just what the hell were they for? Moro wondered. After all, the last time a Panamanian soldier had fired a rifle in anger was a quarter of a century before Noriega's birth.

Noriega returned with his second drink and settled back into his armchair. He was more relaxed now. To the lawyer, it seemed that he might even be smiling.

"You know," he began, "on occasion we have Panamanian National Guard flights coming into our airports which get special handling. They have access to a particular controller on the control tower team. We give them a special radio frequency to use on their way in to be sure everything is ready for them. When they land, a Defense Forces jeep picks them up and takes them to our Military Police hangar so they can discharge their cargo under the proper surveillance."

"Obviously, if something like that could be arranged for our incoming shipments, I know your friends in Medellín would be properly grateful." Unless I've very badly read the man, Moro thought as he uttered that phrase, that is exactly what he's proposing.

"Perhaps it could," Noriega agreed. "But we would have certain conditions."

"Such as?"

"Each trip has to be arranged and coordinated the right way beforehand. No trips get made without our knowledge."

Moro smiled agreeably. "I'm sure that will be no problem." In fact, he wasn't sure of that at all. The cartel's leadership didn't like exposing all its cards to anybody, whatever the advantages doing so might bring.

"There will be a service charge, of course. A transit fee."

"We'd expect that. I'm not mandated to discuss financial details," Moro countered, "but I'll be happy to convey any proposition you'd care to make to my principals."

"It will be one-thousand-U.S. a kilo. That's not negotiable," Noriega declared. "If they can't handle it, tell them to find another way to ship their product, because next time they try to do it through Panama, they won't get their people back alive. If they're ready to do things my way, I'll send one of my officers to see them in Medellín and work out the details."

Noriega had already decided who he'd send. It would be Captain Luis Peel, the officer who served as his liaison with the United States Drug Enforcement Administration. The symmetry of that appealed to him. That way Peel would know exactly who had paid for protection and couldn't be given up to the gringos, and who could be tossed to them as proof of Noriega's determination to fight drug trafficking. And with his friends at the CIA counting on his support for their little war on the Sandinistas, no one was going to be anxious to disturb his operation.

He swallowed off his whiskey to let Moro know their talk was over. As he walked the lawyer to the bungalow door, he stopped. This time he really was smiling.

"By the way," he told Moro, "I still have that four hundred kilos of cocaine in safe keeping. Your people can have it back if they'd like. For eight thousand dollars a kilo."

The son of a bitch, Moro thought. He's just made himself three million dollars.

"I'll inform them of your generous offer," he assured Noriega.

Lind's Tape

Felipe Santiago Nadal was ordered to pick up his delivery of roses in the early fall of 1982. Although Felipe did not know it at the time, his summons was part of a mobilization of a number of veteran agency UCLANs for the upcoming campaign against the Sandinistas. His first assignment when he arrived at the offices of Biscayne Financial Services was to go out and get himself a passport photo. That was fixed by one of our technicians into the Nicaraguan passport, which would be his basic travel document in his work with us. That passport was not some mint-clean and suspect new document, but a year old passport with an impressive collection of visas and entry stamps already affixed to its pages. Documentation like that made it easier for us to point the accusing finger at someone else if something went wrong.

Felipe also got ten thousand dollars in cash and instructions to meet a Mr. Juan Lopez at the Marriott Hotel in Panama City on September 15.

I don't think Nadal was unduly surprised when I opened the door to room 327 that September afternoon. My pseudonym was the result of Casey's order that all agency officers working on the contra program in the field were to employ cover identities. That was part of his effort to conceal our involvement in the project. When I'd gotten us up room service, I explained to Felipe just what his job in our operation was going to entail. Essentially, he was going to be our freight forwarder in Panama, ensuring the safe passage north of the arms for our guerrillas which we elected to funnel through the country.

I waved to the window looking onto the Bay of Panama. "There's a ship over in Colon unloading our first container of arms right now."

"Where are they coming from?" Felipe asked.

"Israel, Haifa. On a ship called the Orient Star. They're AK-47's mostly. With ammo and some Chinese mortars." I'd flown out to Haifa myself to purchase them from the granddaddy of the international arms trade, Shaul Eisenberg. The deal was signed in the name of one of those Panamanian shell companies I'd set up and paid for with untraceable CIA money which had gone via the BCCI to a numbered Liechtenstein bank account.

Obviously, neither Felipe nor I were going to go down to the Colon docks to watch the Orient Star swing our container ashore. The literature contains too many stories about long wooden crates whose contents are prominently identified as "Agricultural Machinery" tumbling onto the dock, then splitting apart before their embarrassed owners' eyes to reveal a cargo bearing only a notional resemblance to plowshares.

What I had done, I explained to Felipe, was sublease a warehouse inside the Colon Free Trade Zone in the name of the Panamanian shell company to which the arms were being shipped. Noriega had arranged that through the man who held the principal lease on the property, a close friend and silent business partner of his, I have no doubt.

Our Colon freight forwarders would hook up the container to a tractor as soon as it was ashore and haul it to the warehouse. Because the container was going into the Free Trade Zone, it would not be subjected to any Customs inspection. When the arms had left Haifa, the Israelis had conveniently closed their eyes to that "Agricultural Machinery" label on the cases.

I explained to Felipe how to get out to the warehouse. He would sign for the container's delivery, using the name in his Nicaraguan passport. I had listed him, using that name, as the president of our shell company.

Later in the afternoon, I explained, a man named Pedro would join him in the warehouse. Pedro, courtesy of Noriega, would bring with him a kit for affixing the official Panamanian Customs seal to freight cargoes and a sheaf of empty bills of lading. The two of them would make out new paperwork identifying the contents of our arms crates as automotive equipment in transit for Salvador. Pedro would show Felipe how to put on the Customs seals which would guarantee they'd get their crates back out of the Free Trade Zone without a Customs inspection.

He and Pedro, I said, would then pack a half dozen of those crates into Pedro's van and proceed to Paitilla airport, where I would meet them that night. We'd then make a test run of the arms north to Honduras to check out the final leg of our system.

I had dinner in a small *parrillada,* a meat and fish grill, on the Via Israel facing the bay opposite the hotel. At precisely 11:15, I got up and left, ostensibly to return to the hotel.

The car I was looking for, a black Hyundai, was waiting as I had been told it would be in the parking lot of the Convention Center opposite the Marriott. A copy of *Hóla,* the Spanish gossip magazine, was sitting on the top of the dashboard in front of the apparently dozing driver.

"Pedro?" I asked.

"Juanito?"

I got in and we drove off.

"Everything go okay this afternoon?"

"No problem."

Pedro, as I would come to learn, was not a man to use five words when one or two would do. He was a major in the Panamanian National Guard. He was some piece of work, Pedro del Rica was. Before joining the Panamanian National Guard, he'd been a bouncer at the Ancon Inn, the bar-bordello opposite Ancon Hill where Roberto Duran had sharpened his boxing skills punching out hapless GI's from Southern Command.

One night as Pedro was hastening a marine's early departure from the premises, the jar-head had smashed a beer bottle on the bar and employed its jagged remains to perform some primitive plastic surgery on Pedro's face. His gesture had left Pedro with a welt of scar tissue twisting upward from the left-hand corner of his mouth, contorting his features into a kind of perpetual sneer.

That was an altogether accurate reflection of the character of the man behind the grimace. Hurting people was what Pedro did the best and liked the most in life. He was Noriega's human Doberman, held snarling on a chain from which he was occasionally released to do his master's bidding. Tony had assigned him to be our liaison for this arms for the contras operation.

We drove in silence along the seacoast to the entrance of Paitilla Airport. The security guard at the gate disinterestedly waved Pedro through. Clearly, both he and his car were well known here.

The National Guard hangar was set a bit apart from the rest of the airport's buildings. As I had been assured, the airport was deserted. Felipe was waiting for us in the hangar beside a Cessna Titan and our pilot, Teofilo Watson, one of the airmen Noriega had recommended to us as experienced in the sort of flying we were going to need. The boxes of AK-47's he and Pedro had brought up from the warehouse in the Free Trade Zone were already stowed on board.

We flew out over the Bay of Panama, then up the Pacific coast, staying fifty miles out to sea, along the shorelines of Panama, Costa Rica and Nicaragua to make landfall again over the Gulf of Fonseca, set into the seacoast of Honduras between Salvador and Nicaragua.

From there it was a short overland flight to Tegucigalpa, the capital of Honduras. Dawn was coming up when we flew in. Talmadge had given us a frequency to use with the control tower, which immediately furnished us landing instructions. As we came back down the taxiway toward the terminal buildings, a jeep containing a pair of uniformed men scuttled out to greet us. They indicated we should follow them, then guided us to a dilapidated hangar well away from the main terminal building.

Talmadge was waiting for us together with Gary Ellis, our young station chief, and a couple of Felipe's fellow UCLANs. At the back of the hangar, a Honduran officer surveyed the scene with the befuddled look of someone who's wandered into the wrong cocktail party.

Talmadge ordered his people to transfer the AK-47's to a van for the journey up to the Nicaraguan border and a contra training camp. Then we got into Ellis's car for the ride across the city to an agency safehouse in one of the capital's nicer neighborhoods.

Tegucigalpa—*Tay Goose,* as we gringos tend to call it— means *hill of silver* in Indian dialect, presumably because silver was mined there in precolonial times. Alas, there is little evidence of whatever riches those hills might have yielded in Tegucigalpa today. Honduras is the poorest nation in Central America. The city is set in a basin ringed by a series of steep hillsides. The rural poor, forced to migrate to the city from their nation's impoverished countryside, were clustered onto those steep inclines, the front door of one shanty looking out onto the rooftop of the shanty below.

Our safehouse was surrounded by high garden walls, something found throughout well-to-do areas in Central America, products of a concern both for security and privacy. Ellis had very thoughtfully stocked the villa with food, whiskey and some excellent California cabernets. Talmadge had a well-developed taste for the good things in life.

The Duke explained that we were going to be doing a little business entertaining that evening, the lieutenant colonel in charge of intelligence and security and the major who ran the airport. The former was a member of that intelligence network Noriega had organized for us, so he was already on the CIA payroll even though he didn't know it. The Duke wanted to secure their friendly cooperation in our contra enterprise.

Talmadge, despite his lack of Spanish, was the genial and considerate host that night. He kept everyone's glass full, exuded charm and confidence, suggesting, without ever dropping any revealing details, just how important his clandestine work in Europe had been. When he turned the talk to our crusade against the Sandinistas, I was a little taken aback by his opening phrase: "I'm addressing you with the full support and authority of the President of the United States."

As you can imagine, those are pretty heady words when they fall on the ears of a colonel or a major in Central America making four or five hundred dollars a month. They conjure up some intriguing perspectives, both in terms of prestige and career advancement as well as of the chances of dipping into Uncle Sam's passing gravy train. The Duke did everything he could to reinforce those impressions. It was hardly surprising, then, that they promised us their full, continuing support.

Once they'd left, I sensed something was troubling Ellis. "You've got something on your mind, son," I suggested.

"I've been hearing some things about those two."

"Like what?"

"Like they're involved with drug traffickers, providing

them basically with the same kind of services they're going to give us."

I must admit that that information did not unduly surprise me. In Latin America, running arms and running drugs are frequently overlapping enterprises. And the officials who have their hands out to protect or ignore one activity will in all likelihood be on the take for the other as well.

"Well, that bothers me, too," I told Ellis. "I don't like drugs any more than you do. The fact is, however, we need these guys, and most of all, we need what they can do for us. As long as they're doing the job we want them to do, that's what counts. What they do on their own time, when they're not on our payroll or punching in on our time clock, isn't our concern. We don't have to know. That's what's called the pragmatic approach."

I turned to Talmadge for his reaction.

"What the fuck," he declared, "whoever said you had to make revolutions with altar boys?"

Later, after Ellis had left and we were having a nightcap, he gave me a quizzical smile. "If those two guys are into moving drugs," he asked, "what does that tell you about your friend Noriega?"

"Duke," I sighed, "I'm not sure I want to know." After all, the Panamanian part of my operation was a success thus far, thanks largely to Noriega. Who was I to spoil it?

BOOK FIVE

Ramon's Run

MEDELLÍN! announced the billboard's bright red scrawl. A PLACE FOR GOOD MEN WHO WANT TO WORK AND LAUGH. That cheerful welcome greeted visitors wheeling out of the traffic circle beyond Medellín's modern airport, nestled in the highlands above a metropolis that evidently preferred to be known for the industry and good humor of its residents, rather than for the other activities more frequently associated with its name.

Raymond Marcello—*Ramon* to his many friends in the city—guffawed his approval of the billboard's message. He loved Medellín, for a good reason. The work he had performed with such success in this city, brokering loads of cocaine, had made him a very wealthy man, and the prospect of adding considerably to that wealth on this trip contributed to his evident good cheer this morning.

It was a clear, warm day—but then all Medellín's days were clear and warm. Medellín's boosters had baptized their metropolis "The City of Eternal Spring." Close to the equator, the city was the orchid capital of Colombia, the nation's most important industrial center, the heart of Colombia's world-famed coffee-producing regions.

It was also, with the possible exception of Beirut, the most dangerous city on the face of the planet. The annual per capita murder rate in the prosperous community of Medellín made places like Detroit and Washington, D.C., citadels of law and order by comparison. That spate of killings was due almost exclusively to the rivalries engendered by the flourishing cocaine traffic.

Despite his affection for Medellín, Marcello kept his residence in Bogotá to preserve the distance he'd established between himself and his Medellín associates. Recently, from his drug profits, he had bought an estate twenty miles northwest of Bogotá, thirty hectares of rich, low-lying hills, ideal for racing horses. Once he'd retired on his drug millions, he and his wife would make that their principal residence, an ideal environment in which to bring up the two young children he so adored.

Anticipating already the delight of those days, Ramon left

the *Tabla* behind and started down Las Palmas Road snaking along the valley wall toward the city below. The view was spectacular. From time to time, through the gaps in the high pines lining the road, Ramon could glimpse the familiar landmarks of the city: the Plaza de Toros de la Marcarena; the glass-and-steel tower of the Torre Coltejar, the sky-scraper headquarters of Latin America's largest textile firm; the spires of the Cathedral of the Virgen de Villanueva, an edifice which was, Medellín's citizenry liked to boast, the largest brick cathedral in the world.

Ramon's immediate destination was a cathedral devoted to more temporal concerns, the Medellín Intercontinental Hotel, a boomerang-shaped hostelry whose owners had, over the course of the past decade, become the innkeepers of choice to the elite of the world's coke trade. Ramon took his usual third-floor suite overlooking the swimming pool and the rooftops of El Poblado, the Beverly Hills of Medellín, where the city's newly rich drug lords dwelled in luxurious walled compounds. He unpacked, then set his black leather Hermès picture folder containing portraits of his wife and children on his bedside table. That gilt-trimmed picture frame was his special icon; he was a drug trafficker who never went anywhere without a picture of his wife and kids.

Then he picked up his phone and called his close friend and *socio,* business partner, Francisco "Paco" Garrone. Paco was a descendant of an old Medellín family, one of the Basques and Galicians who'd followed the footsteps of the *conquistadores* in the seventeenth and eighteenth centuries. Paco was a lawyer by profession, although the number of wills and contracts he had drawn up in the past few years would scarcely have filled a single drawer in a filing cabinet.

"Hóla, socio!" Ramon trumpeted into the phone. "I'm back. And I've got just what we've been looking for, my friend."

Half an hour later Ramon left his Mercedes with the door-man of La Marguerita, an elegant restaurant three-quarters of a mile down the Las Palmas Road from his hotel. A dozen men wearing loose-fitting Panamanian style *guayabera* shirts flopping down over their waistlines milled around the restaurant's entrance. It was not, however, the dictates of fashion nor a concern for their bulging waistlines that had determined their mode of dress. They were the bodyguards of the drug barons lunching inside; the ample folds of their shirts concealed the sidearms they all carried.

Ramon nodded to a couple he knew personally. Most were products of the desperately poor barrios that clung to the steep hillsides rising above the valley floor. Two decades ago, the best schooling those barrios offered the impoverished kids growing up in them was at institutes that turned out some of the world's cleverest and most quick-fingered pickpockets.

Today those schools trained assassins, teaching modern urban killing techniques like *el asesino de la moto,* shooting someone from a motorcycle, the driver steering, the passenger riding pillion making the hit. The honor graduates became bodyguards. The less fortunate stayed behind to serve as *sicarios,* the hired guns the cartel turned to for their contract killings. Still, their trade had its compensations. As once Medellín's pickpockets had traveled the world in search of fat wallets, so now its sicarios traveled the globe to execute those unfortunate or unwise enough to cross Medellín's drug lords.

Ramon took a table on the terrace overlooking the valley floor and ordered a bottle of chilled Chilean chardonnay. A few minutes later his socio arrived. Paco was a stocky man just under five feet eight with a Clark Gable mustache to compensate for his fast-receding hairline. As always, he was impeccably dressed in a dark blue Brioni silk gabardine suit he'd bought on a recent trip to Rome.

The two men gave each other a vigorous, back-thumping Latin *abrazo,* a display that usually conveyed more artifice than affection. Then they sat down, clinked wineglasses, and set out exchanging the prerequisite gossip of their trade: who had been killed, which of their associates had been arrested by the gringo cops, who had scored a major coup running cocaine into the United States.

Eighty percent of the cocaine flowing north to the United States was under the control of Medellín's drug dealers. Yet there was not a single coca plant flowering in the Medellín countryside. The city had become the cocaine capital of the world not for any geographic or natural reason, but because of the human qualities of the people who lived there, qualities well represented in the stocky gentleman seated opposite Ramon. The *paisas,* as the inhabitants of Medellín liked to call themselves, were hustlers, and they were proud of it.

They were, they boasted, the Jews or the Lebanese of Latin America. They could cut a finer deal, spot the opportunity to make a quick buck, better than anybody else south of the Rio Grande.

For men like Paco and Ramon, selling cocaine was a business just like any other. Sure, it was illegal, and there were more contingent risks associated with it than there were with, say, the coffee business, but it was a business all the same.

As soon as they had ordered lunch and the waiter was out of earshot, Paco laid his chubby hand on Ramon's wrist. "So," he hissed, "give me your news."

"I've found a perfect setup for us," Ramon replied, kissing his fingertips. "I've got a first-class pilot who has an Aerocommander 1000 on a six-month charter in West Palm Beach, Florida." The Aerocommander 1000 was the drug traffickers' transport of choice. It had a three thousand mile range, and it could land on short, rough dirt strips. Above all, its engines could fly three-quarters of their useful life on diesel rather than high-octane aviation fuel. Diesel was cheaper but, above all, its presence on a farm was a lot easier for a farmer to explain to a curious policeman than a few barrels of aviation fuel.

"What this guy does," Ramon continued, "is he ferries supplies down to the oil companies over in Lake Maracaibo. He makes the trip once, twice a week. He's been doing it so often nobody pays any attention to him anymore."

"How do you know that?" Paco asked.

"I spent time with him out at his hangar. A retired Customs guy comes by maybe once every two weeks, checks out his paperwork. End of story. It's the simplest thing in the world. One night he flies out just like he always does, files his usual flight plan with Miami Air Traffic Control, but when he gets off the Venezuelan coast he just ducks down here instead of going on to Maracaibo. He loads up, flies right back on his same flight plan like he's coming back from his usual run."

"And he's ready to do it?" Paco asked. "He's not a DEA plant, you're sure of that?"

"Positive. But the best thing is this." Ramon gave his partner's hand a squeeze. "His plane's stripped down to carry that oil field equipment. He's got a bladder in there for extra fuel. He can take a thousand keys, man, a thousand keys!"

Paco whistled softly in awe and admiration. A thousand

kilos of powder was a score brokers such as he only
dreamed of. It was the granddaddy score, all right, the coup
that would make them both very rich and legends inside the
traffic.

"He'll do it for seven hundred thousand dollars," Ramon
whispered.

"How much up front?"

"A hundred thousand. We charge five thousand a key.
That gives us a profit of over two million dollars apiece, my
friend." Ramon let the figures roll slowly on his tongue, savoring them as a Parisian gourmet might savor the first bite
of a fresh black truffle.

"It's gonna be tough to put a thousand keys together,"
Paco warned. "People are gonna be scared. But for that,
socio, we got to try. Real hard."

Lind's Tape

Vic Craig's office was at the U.S. Customs Regional Headquarters at the Miami International Airport, so when I called,
he suggested we meet for breakfast at the Viscount Hotel,
just outside the airport itself. Clearly, Vic was a regular in
the hotel coffee shop. We'd barely slid into our booth when
the waitress came over to take our order, a smile warm
enough to light up Stockholm on a January afternoon spread
over her face.

"Why, Renee," Vic laughed, "you look good enough to
eat this morning."

Renee shifted a wad of chewing gum into her cheek with
her tongue and snickered. "Ah'd try something else if ah
was you, honey," she advised Vic. "My old man done beat
up on me something fierce last night."

Vic looked at me and shrugged. "Story of my life, Jack.
In that case . . ."—he turned back to Renee—"give me that
Mexican ranchero breakfast, the number six. I need some-
thing that's going to stick to my ribs this morning."

In defiance of all the conventional wisdom, I ordered
scrambled eggs and sausages.

"So," Vic asked as soon as Renee had disappeared with
our order, "how're things back at the ranch these days?"

"Better. We've got a director who's ready to get down to

work again now. Morale's improved about five hundred percent."

"About time."

Vic was a perfect example of something the CIA has done very well over the years, infiltrate people into other federal agencies: the DEA, of course, the Treasury, Customs and the military. For the last twelve years he'd been assigned to the Customs Service. They, of course, were totally unaware of where his first loyalties lay. Ninety-five percent of the time, he did his work like any other Customs officer; the other, critical five percent, he responded, as he was doing now, to our concerns.

"So what brings you to South Florida?" he asked. "Not a hankering for Key Lime pie, I don't suppose."

"They've given me Latin America," I told him, then provided him with a quick rundown on what he needed to know about my arms supply program for the contras.

"Where will you want to fly your stuff to?" he inquired.

"For the moment, the place that concerns me most is Costa Rica. What I need from you first of all is a little overview on how to get my flights in and out of the country without attracting undue attention."

Renee placed Vic's mound of Mexican breakfast food in front of him. He looked at it with an air of respect. Bran flakes and skimmed milk it was not. "They got enough calories in here to feed half of Ethiopia," he sighed, then dug in.

"To get back to your problem, Jack," he said after he had digested his first few mouthfuls. "There are two ways to do it, the easy way and the hard way."

"Give me the hard way first."

"Okay, where do you want to fly your stuff out of?"

"Opa Locka." Opa Locka was a private airport of some importance in the Miami area.

"Obviously in this case, your pilot isn't going to want to file a flight plan with Miami Air Traffic Control, right? He's just flying up to Lauderdale to see his sister."

"Something like that."

"So, he pulls his transponder and takes off."

The transponder was the signaling device required by law on all aircraft flying into and out of the U.S. Attached to a plane's altimeter, it gave off a characteristic signal that both identified the plane to air traffic control and automatically registered its altitude for traffic control purposes.

"That means," Vic continued, "our civilian radar here at Miami International isn't going to pick him up. But the military radar at Homestead or the Navy's Boca Chica station down in Key West can get him. So he's got to stay below the horizon, underneath their radar."

Vic paused to digest another huge mouthful of what looked like refried beans. "That means he's got to fly no more than fifteen feet off the deck until he's at least sixty miles out to sea, which ain't easy flying. Same thing when he comes back home. And it helps if he can come up into the blind spots between radars."

Vic paused to catch his breath and let his stomach come to grips with the first part of his breakfast.

"It can be done," he assured me. "It's done all the time. But if the guy runs into weather, if he gets nervous and slips up over the horizon, then alarm bells are going to start going off all over the place."

"Okay," I noted. "Now tell me about the easy way."

"He files a regular flight plan with Miami Air Traffic Control for Port au Prince down in Haiti. Goes out normal as can be, his transponder squawking away like it was a seagull. When he's seventy miles or so offshore, well out of the range of our approach radar, he pulls his transponder, changes course, and goes to wherever the hell it is he wants to go."

Vic now turned his attention to the tortilla lapping over his plate. Once he'd handled a couple of mouthfuls of that, he waved his fork at me.

"When he's ready to come home, he just flies in on the same bearing he went out on like he was really coming back from Port au Prince on the back end of his flight plan. The thing of it is, Jack, Haitian Air Traffic Control is hopelessly, completely, fucked up. They don't even know what day of the week it is down there. There is no way we or the DEA or anybody else are ever going to be able to find out whether your pilot really completed his flight plan and went on in to Port au Prince or not. That's not a bit of knowledge we would want to see circulated too widely around here, although I suspect some of your friendly South Florida dopers are already onto it."

"You make it sound easy."

Vic burped and pushed away the remains of his breakfast. "You don't know how easy. This part of the country's a fucking sieve. The dopers come in over the Gulf Coast, get down between those offshore oil drilling platforms that make even our military radar a blur, and come right on in. We can pick up a Russian missile popping out of a silo, for Christ's sakes, but do you think we can pick up an Aerocommander full of dope sneaking into the country? No way."

"Listen, Vic, the other thing is, as I indicated earlier, we want to keep this as discreet as possible. For a whole range of national security considerations." I offered him my award-winning commander's smile.

"Sure, I understand."

"So really, we'd appreciate not having a lot of your Customs people coming around while we have a few cases of M-16's or AK-47's or whatever lying on the floor."

Our exporting those arms without the proper paperwork was technically illegal. It violated the Neutrality Act and about five other U.S. statutes. Okay, we had a Presidential Finding, and our congressional oversight committees had given the overall idea a green light, as covers for our actions. But, on the face of it, it was still illegal, so it was thought best for all concerned that we did not force the knowledge of what we were doing onto other government agencies.

"No problem. Where are you going to be working out of?"

"Hangar One at Opa Locka. First Aviation Services."

"I'll take care of that myself. Just be sure you keep me current on what's going on so I can cover for you."

We picked up the check and strolled to the cash register. Renee rushed over to say goodbye. Vic kissed her playfully on the cheek.

"How about saving some for me tomorrow, honey?" he grinned.

Black Eagle was the code name we'd assigned the contra arms supply program. It was the most important aspect of the job I'd been given by Casey when we instituted the contra program.

To distance the agency from the operation, I'd installed our command desk in the National Security Council office of

Vice President George Bush. Once I'd finished setting up the basic mechanics of the thing, then our man in Bush's office would be responsible for implementing the plan: contracting the jobs out to different carriers, scheduling flights, making sure the arms were where they were supposed to be when they were supposed to be there. The idea behind that was if one of our planes went down somewhere, they could haul me up in front of Congress, question me all day long and I could swear to them, "Gentlemen, I know nothing about that flight." And I'd be telling the truth.

The Israelis, as a result of their invasion of Lebanon, had come up with a gold mine of captured PLO Soviet bloc arms which were ideal for our purposes. They'd leaped at the opportunity to sell them to the contras, but were insisting the arms flow through the U.S. on their way down to Central America, to conceal where they were coming from.

Black Eagle had been assigned to pick them up in Israel and fly them back to fields in Texas, Florida and Arkansas. That was easy. They came in consigned to an American-registered Israeli firm covered by perfectly legitimate U.S. Government End User Certificates. It was getting them out of the United States and down to our guerrillas in Central America that had been taxing my imagination since I'd been told to handle the problem.

Opa Locka Airport, my destination once I'd squared things away with Vic Craig, was a short drive up Fourth Avenue from Miami International Airport past the Hialeah race track. First Aviation Services was run by an ex-U.S. Army military police major named Derrick Watts. He had a pair of N–November registered Cessna Titan 404's in his hangar on lease from Pacific Air, the company to which we'd passed, via the Vice President's office, our basic arms-forwarding contract. *N* was the letter with which the serial numbers of all U.S.–registered aircraft began.

I was not pleased looking around Watts's hangar. There were cases of AK-47's and C-4 plastic explosives, clearly labeled as such, stacked openly in one of its corners.

"Get that stuff covered up and keep it covered up," I ordered. "We don't want anybody who happens to come wandering in here to see that stuff, for Christ's sake!"

"Don't worry, Jack," Watts promised. "Nobody wanders in here without my clearance. Except maybe Customs which is your department."

"I've taken care of Customs. They won't be coming around. But I still want that stuff concealed all the time."

Watts took me into First Aviation Service's office, a spartan place furnished with his desk, a Formica-topped table, and a sofa and a couple of armchairs which the Salvation Army would have turned down. Our first three pilots were there waiting for me to brief them on the operation. One of them, I was pleased to see, was my old pal Ray Albright.

We sat down around the table and Watts passed out the ritual plastic mugs of Nescafé.

"The first thing," I announced to them, launching into my briefing, "is none of you are to take off with any of your own ID on you. No driver's licenses, no credit cards, nothing with your names on it. When you're ready to leave, the major here will give you traveling ID kits. You hand them back to him on your return. Clear?"

They nodded. All three had flown for Air America, so this sort of security arrangement was routine to them.

I spread a map of the Caribbean out on the table and explained to them essentially what I'd learned at breakfast from Vic Craig.

"We've equipped your planes with Loran," I informed them. Loran was a fairly sophisticated navigational system. The pilot programmed into it the coordinates of his destination, and the instruments gave him his heading, a constant readout of his true speed, and his wind correction factor.

"You file a regular flight for Port au Prince and go out on a heading of about ninety-five degrees. Hold that course until you pass Matthew Town on Great Inagua Island. You can work off their radio beacon as a navigational aid. When you get there, you pull your transponder and fly south, down through the Windward Passage and the Jamaica Channel."

Although I didn't bother to point it out, that routing would take them right past Port au Prince in ostensible fulfillment of their flight plans.

"Now for Christ's sake, don't go flying over Cuban airspace on that leg of your trip. Anything happens to you in there, and, believe me, we'll hang you out to dry. We aren't going to know your name—not even the name we've put on the fake ID you'll be carrying."

At that, I stopped and looked each of them in the eye to make sure my warning had registered. It had.

"When you've passed Kingston, take a heading of 210 degrees. That'll give you landfall here." I indicated the place on my map, at the mouth of the Colorado River in northern Costa Rica. "You'll be able to recognize it from this island set into the bay at the river's mouth. Any questions so far?"

"How about radar?" someone asked.

"There isn't any. It's just a big black hole down there. The only radar they've got in Costa Rica is at the airport in San Jose, the capital. The city's in a bowl of mountains and the signal bounces off them, then dies. The government down there wants to buy some more sophisticated equipment," I laughed, "but I don't think that'll be part of any aid package they'll be getting from the U.S. government in the near future.

"Now, when you cross the coast, you call up 124.6 VHF radio band until you get a reply. When you're answered, identify yourself with your registration number. We've installed an ADF on the landing strip you'll be heading for."

An ADF emitted a nondirectional beam, a radio signal which an incoming plane could pick up and home in on.

"It emits on 89.75 megacycles," I went on. "Once you've identified yourself, they'll turn it on for you. You ride it to your destination which is here"—again I pointed to my map—"a town called Muelle about fifty miles due west of your landfall.

"A river runs through Muelle which will be your landmark. It bends twice, here and here." Again, my fingers traced out their route. "The northern end of the strip abuts this second curve, and you'll make your approach across the river and onto the strip. Don't get your feet wet. They've got crocodiles in the river."

The strip belonged to an ex-Kentucky tobacco farmer named Jim Tulley who'd set up a cattle ranch down there. The Duke had signed him up. Tulley's politics were well to the right of the John Birch Society. The idea of killing communists filled him with a zeal similar, I suppose, to that which must have motivated Torquemada when he had a heretic on the rack. But hell, he was eager to help and needed the money we were paying him for the use of his ranch. Running arms for us was a much more profitable pastime than cattle raising.

I'd assigned Felipe Nadal and a couple of other UCLANs to oversee things on the ground for us. They would, I explained, to the pilots, handle the unloading of the planes,

give them a bed, bath and meal and gas their planes for the
return trip. That would be over the same route they'd used
coming out.

"How about Customs coming back?" someone asked.

"Don't worry about Customs. They won't be a problem.
That base has been covered." I gathered up my maps and papers.

"From now on," I instructed the three men, "the major
here is in charge. Any questions, any problems, you take
them to him."

Despite the legends surrounding it, the so-called Medellín
cartel was anything but the rigorous economic entity college
professors teaching first-year economics refer to. It was, in
fact, a rather loose confederation of senior dealers grouped,
as a consequence of Marta Ochoa's kidnapping, around Pablo Escobar and the three Ochoa brothers—Jorge, Juan David and Fabio.

They practiced, however, a form of vertical integration of
which the professors would certainly have approved, seeking
to control the flow of their product from the mountain hillsides of Peru through their jungle labs around Leticia and on
to their own Colombian-controlled distribution networks in
North America.

In their product's long voyage from the coca bushes of
Peru's Upper Huallaga Valley to the nostrils of Manhattan or
Los Angeles, there were two times when the traffickers were
particularly vulnerable to arrest. The first was on the street
corner, or in the bar or nightclub where the powder was
passed from its retailer to its final consumer. Colombians,
therefore, never retailed coke. As the Brahmins of India left
the job of cleaning out their toilets to the Untouchable caste,
so Colombia's drug barons left retailing their powder to
Americans, white or black, or Jamaicans and Dominicans.

The second dangerous passage was moving the powder
from Medellín, usually by private plane, to a clandestine airstrip in the U.S. and then on by vehicle to the hands of the
Colombian distributor who would take charge of it. The cartel associates had a few private channels for that which they
reserved for their own use, such as Pablo Escobar's Inair cir-
cuit out of Panama. The demand for powder in the U.S. was
becoming so enormous, however, that those private channels
could accommodate only a modest percentage of the cocaine

required by the inflamed nostrils of North America. Filling that gap was the role of private load-brokers like Ray "Ramon" Marcello and his socio, Paco Garrone. They took the risk of finding the pilots and planes to move the coke, the strips to land it on, the means to move it on to its final destination in New York, Miami, L.A., Houston or Chicago.

Kevin Grady, sitting in his office in New York contemplating Ramon Marcello's profile in his loose-leaf folder, might reason that Ramon owed his evident good working relations with the Medellín traffickers to the fact he had a Colombian wife. The truth was more subtle. Ramon, as far as the leadership of the cartel was concerned, was an established success.

He and his socio had successfully brokered a dozen loads. All had arrived where they were supposed to arrive, on time and safely. More important, every kilo package which had been handed over to them had been delivered present and accounted for when the powder was delivered. Success like that meant Ramon was a serious man, and the cartel liked to do its business with serious people.

Putting together a thousand-kilo load, however, was an extraordinarily difficult challenge even for an experienced broker. No single member of the cartel would contemplate putting a thousand kilos on any one brokered flight. The risk of losing that much refined coke was more than they were prepared to take.

That meant Ramon and Paco had to organize a group pool, two hundred kilos from one major dealer, two hundred fifty from another and so on, until they'd found their full complement of a thousand kilos. Negotiating that took six weeks of nonstop work and enough cups of *cafe tinto,* strong black Colombian coffee, to jangle the nerves of a battalion of Olympic athletes. The associates were finally forced to make two potentially fatal compromises to put their load together. First, Paco had to agree to fly to Florida with the load and assume responsibility personally for delivering it to whoever would be assigned to receive the powder in Miami.

Second, Ramon would have to remain at the airstrip from which the coke had left Colombia under armed guard until word reached Medellín that the coke had been delivered safely. He would be a hostage to the trip's success. If the coke failed to arrive, if the operation was a DEA sting, Ramon would be a dead man. It was not a pleasant prospect, but that was the way the Colombians did business.

The pilot Ramon had selected was a wiry skydiving freak named Bill "Sunshine" Ottley. He flew oil-drilling equipment to South America in his chartered airplane so he could earn the money to go around the world jumping out of other people's airplanes. He had never flown dope before, had never been involved with the police. That was good; it meant he probably wasn't under suspicion.

But it also meant he might panic if something started to go wrong. Ramon decided that since he was going to have to put his own life on the line to make this trip work, he had to get Ottley down to Colombia for a final review of every detail of the flight.

For their departure site, Ramon and Paco had chosen a dirt strip on a ranch near the Colombia-Venezuela border. Finding the strip would be easy because just beyond it was a massive oil refinery which would serve as a bearing from which Ottley could fix his final approach.

The ranch itself belonged to two brothers who would have 250 kilos on the load. The brothers, Juan and David Otero, would assemble the coke from the other dealers who'd be using the flight, and serve as the cartel's supervisors for the trip.

Ramon drove Ottley out to the strip. He paced it half a dozen times taking measurements, checking the firmness of the soil, before pronouncing it acceptable. Then he insisted on taking the Oteros' Cessna to reconnoiter with the Colombians the route he was going to follow in and out of the area, making a careful note of every landmark along the route, quizzing them on the zones in which aircraft of the Colombian Air Force might be patrolling, demanding everything they knew about radar coverage. Finally, he made half a dozen touch-and-go landings on the strip before giving the operation its final go-ahead.

That evening, the three men went to Paco's weekend ranch in La Ceja to review one last time all the details of their trip. They decided they would make the flight in ten days' time, leaving the U.S. on a Thursday evening and flying back into West Palm Beach on a Saturday morning, when the vigilance of the Customs Service would be at its lowest. At noon on Thursday, Ramon would call Ottley at his hangar. If he used the number six in his first sentence, it would mean the trip was on. If he used the number seven, it would mean there had been a problem at the Medellín end and it was off.

The flight plan Ottley had worked out would put him over the Oteros' ranch at approximately 8:00 a.m., Friday. Ottley would spend the day sleeping, and leave on his return flight well after nightfall. That would put his Aerocommander on the ground in West Palm Beach about 6:00 a.m. on Saturday.

When they'd nailed down the last details of their plan, Paco bounced up from his desk with a grin of childish delight on his face.

"Gentlemen," he announced, "I think we've earned the right to a little party."

He strode over to the double doors giving onto his ranch's formal dining room and threw them open. A massive feast of Colombian delicacies was spread out on the dining room table. Ringing the table were half a dozen delicacies of another sort, young ladies wearing high heels, dainty white aprons and, unless one counted the ribbons in their hair, very little else.

"November Eight Oner Oner Victor X-Ray," Ray Albright called into his radio, then repeated that registration number of his Cessna Titan 404 a second time for his unseen audience. Below him, the coastline of Costa Rica was already slipping past his wings.

"November Eight Double Oner Victor X-Ray," came the reply, "we read you. Welcome. We're turning on our beacon now."

Albright switched frequencies, picked up the signal from the ADF beacon and adjusted his heading so that he was riding straight up the signal. As he approached his destination, he began to check out the features of the terrain below his aircraft on the detailed map he'd spread out on his lap.

While his plane was now down to less than a quarter of a tank of fuel, he was still carrying a twenty-five hundred pound load, and some of the stuff back there, Ray reasoned, would make a pretty good bonfire if something went wrong. You'd want a little room to land that on, and to Ray's experienced eyes, the dirt strip below looked a hell of a lot shorter than the thirty-five hundred feet he'd been promised.

Trying to put the CIA guy's crack about crocodiles out of his mind, Albright feathered the Cessna down as gently as he dared, aiming to set his wheels onto the strip as close to its northern tip as possible.

When he'd rolled to a stop, an excited Latino rushed over to the plane to open the cabin door for him. "Hey, man, great!" he shouted. "You're our first customer."

Albright yawned. "Yeah, well, if you're figuring to stay in this business any length of time, I'd put me a couple hundred more feet on that runway if I was you."

While he was stretching beside his plane, two more Latinos and an American came over to greet him. The American looked to be in his mid-sixties, about five-ten with a gray crewcut, a sun-burnished face and, given his age, a remarkably lithe figure.

"Tulley's the name, son," he announced, "Jim Tulley. I'm the agency straw boss around here, so if there's anything you need, just let me know. Felipe here"—he pronounced it "Phillipee"—"will take you over to my house and get you a bed and some breakfast while we unload your plane."

Tulley's home was an unpretentious ranch house. One side looked out on the San Juan River, whose course had provided Ray his incoming landmarks. He walked through the living room to glance out the back terrace.

"Hey!" he gasped. "What the hell's that?"

"A volcano," Felipe informed him. "Called Arenal."

"Looks just like they do in the picture books," Albright declared admiringly.

He munched down some breakfast, stretched out on Tulley's couch and fell asleep. It was four o'clock in the afternoon when he woke up. Felipe was reading a book in Spanish in one corner of the room.

"Say, where can a man find a cold beer hereabouts?" Albright asked him.

"Come on," Felipe offered. "I'll take you into Muelle."

They drove down *Ruta Quatro* to the main highway running up from the nearest big town, Ciudad Quesada. As they started north to Muelle, Albright's nostrils picked up a sour stench.

"What the hell's that smell?"

"Sugar mill," Felipe informed him. "They grow a lot of sugarcane around here."

"Sugar!" Ray shook his head in wonder at life's unfathomable mysteries. "And to think it stinks like that!"

Muelle turned out to be little more than a bend in the road

and a bridge across the San Juan River. There was a school, a hairdressing salon, a general store and a bar.

"This is it?" Albright asked.

"Yeah."

"Well, at least you boys don't have to tire yourselves out arguing about where you're going to go at night."

Felipe led the way into the bar, Los Tres Gatos. It was fronted by a wooden panel screening off a dark room in which there were half a dozen tables.

When they were well into their beers, Albright noticed Felipe was beginning to get nervous, a state of mind he betrayed by blinking incessantly.

"What's bothering you, man?" he asked "You're blinking like a bullfrog in a hailstorm."

"Listen," Felipe said, "I gotta ask you a favor, a big favor."

"Shoot."

"My mother, she's dying of cancer up in Miami. She hasn't seen her brother, my uncle Pedro, in thirty years. That son of a bitch Castro wouldn't let him out of Cuba. He finally got himself a visa to come down here to Costa Rica. Trouble is, by the time he's going to get his papers for the States, my mother, she's going to be dead. He's sick, man. He'd give you five thousand dollars cash if you'd take him back with you tonight."

Ray turned that one over in his mind. The chances this guy Felipe's mother was dying of cancer, or even alive for that matter, or that his pal Pedro was really his uncle, were about as good as the Texas Rangers' chances were of getting into the World Series. What did figure to be real here, though, was that offer of fifty hundred dollar bills to help old Pedro beat the Immigration Service. That CIA guy Lind had told them Customs weren't going to be any problem when they came home. The boss down here claims he's an agency man. This whole deal had to be pretty well covered.

"Why not?" he told Felipe. "I can use a little company in the cockpit at night."

He landed back at Opa Locka at seven the next morning. There was no one around except Watts, who didn't even bother to ask who Uncle Pedro was. While Ray was turning in the plastic ID card which identified him as Rick Alden, an employee of Pacific Air, and getting back his own papers, Uncle Pedro disappeared.

Later, leaving the airport, Ray spotted him waiting in line for a bus to downtown Miami.

Shit, he thought, soaking wet Uncle Pedro doesn't figure to weigh more than seventy-five kilos. That made his transportation fee up here 125 dollars a kilo. If things were going to be as easy as this was, there was some other shit a man could bring back from down there which would pay a hell of a lot more per kilo than Uncle Pedro had.

Bill "Sunshine" Ottley's Aerocommander made its first pass over the Oteros' dirt strip seven minutes ahead of the arrival time called for on his flight plan. As soon as he taxied to a halt, Paco and Ramon ran to his plane with the fervor of the *gendarmes* rushing to greet Charles Lindbergh at Le Bourget airport in 1927. Ottley reacted to their excited queries about his flight with monumental indifference. "A piece of cake," he intoned wearily. "Get me a bed to go to sleep in."

While Paco took Ottley to the Oteros' ranch house, Ramon and the Otero brothers began the job of unloading the coke from the four-by-four that had brought it to the strip from its hiding place. The coke was packed in one kilo bags, each tightly wrapped and sealed to keep out moisture. Nothing destroyed the drug's properties quicker than exposing it to water. Each packet was stamped with the symbol of its owner, usually a series of letters such as D-E-C which represented a code only the recipient of the coke in the U.S. would be able to decipher. Occasionally, names were employed. Reagan and Bush were two favorites. The cartel's leadership was not without a sense of humor. The packets were stuffed into green U.S. Army–surplus duffel bags, then each bag was padlocked and a list of the number of packets it contained and their identifying seals was wired to the lock.

Ramon and the Oteros counted each packet and verified its seal as they were loaded. When the job was finished and the bags loaded onto the plane, Ramon locked the cockpit doors. From that moment on, his life could be on the line if some of those bags turned up missing.

The rest of the day dragged by, Ottley asleep in the ranch house, Ramon and Paco on guard by the plane. Their conversation took wild swings between exultation, as they contemplated what they'd do with the two million–plus dollars that would shortly be theirs if the trip went right, and nervous reappraisals of everything that could go wrong to deprive them of that fortune and, in Ramon's case, his life.

The sun was just caressing the horizon when their pilot emerged from the ranch house. He was energetically scratching at the armpits of his Washington Redskins T-shirt.

"You boys have a good day?" he inquired politely of Paco and Ramon.

Ramon marveled. The guy was about to risk spending the rest of his life in prison flying maybe thirty million dollars' worth of cocaine into the United States, and he seemed about as concerned as if he were flying a planeload of Girl Scout cookies to a 4-H county fair.

As Paco and Ottley prepared to board the plane, Juan Otero handed Paco a slip of paper. On it was the name of his contact in Miami, named *Pichu,* and the number of Pichu's beeper. A Volkswagen van, Juan Otero explained, would be left beside Ottley's hangar during the night. The keys would be under the driver's seat. Otero then handed Paco a mobile phone of his own. Once Paco had loaded the drugs and left the airstrip, he was to head to Miami. When he entered the city, he would find an isolated public telephone booth and make a note of its number. Then he would call Pichu's number on his mobile phone. When Pichu's beeper came on, Paco would trip in the number of the public phone booth he'd selected.

Exactly thirty minutes later, the phone in the booth would ring. He would then receive his instructions for delivering the load. There was no way even the most sophisticated of intercept systems could penetrate that arrangement. It was a classic example of modern technology married to the needs of crime.

Ottley yawned again and gave a final scratch to whatever it was that was troubling his armpits. "If it's all the same with you boys," he announced, "I reckon it's about time we got this here show on the road."

Ramon and Paco embraced. This time the emotion engendered by their Latin bearhug was genuine. Ottley went through his preflight maneuvers with the same methodical indifference that had characterized everything he'd done. Finally, he pointed the Aerocommander down the runway, built up the power on his engines and, with a parting wave, unleashed his brakes. The plane accelerated down the runway, lifted off with room to spare, and banked north toward the Atlantic Ocean, thirty million potential dollars and Ramon's physical well-being disappearing into the evening sky.

Ramon watched the plane go with a sense of relief and fear, dread and excitement. In twenty-four hours it would all be over one way or the other. Now, for him, the worst part began. He was a prisoner—a well-cared-for, well-treated prisoner, but a prisoner nonetheless.

To Paco's admiration and relief, Ottley brought the Aerocommander onto his airstrip almost thirty minutes ahead of schedule. The Volkswagen minivan the Oteros had promised him was parked as they had said it would be beside the hangar. There was no sign of life anywhere. The whole thing seemed almost too perfect.

With a frantic energy engendered by nervousness and fear, Paco began to transfer the duffel bags full of coke from the plane to the minivan. There was still no sign of life anywhere near the hangar.

"Man, why you so wrought up?" Ottley asked him. "I told you they ain't going to be anybody coming around here this time of the morning."

Paco didn't reply. Finally, they heaved the last bag into the van. "Okay," he said, "I'm outta here."

"Don't you want to stick around while I brew us up a nice cup of Nescafé?" Ottley asked.

Paco looked at the pilot as though the man were mad.

"Drive carefully," Ottley cautioned as Paco got into the van. "Like they say, the life you save might be your own."

Forcing himself into a state of calm he didn't feel, Paco started out for Miami, making certain he stayed well under the posted speed limits. This wasn't the moment to excite some passing patrolman's curiosity. On the outskirts of the city, he found a shopping mall virtually deserted at such an early hour of the weekend. There was a phone booth at the far end of the parking lot. He went into it, jotted down its number, then, as he had been instructed, dialed Pichu's beeper and left the number of the phone booth on it.

Thirty minutes later, precise almost to the second, the phone in the booth rang.

"What's your name?" a voice asked.

"Paco."

"And what's mine?"

"Pichu."

"Where are you?"

Paco described the shopping mall's location.

"Okay," the voice ordered, "go to the corner of Flagler and LeJeune. You got a map, right?"

"Yeah."

"There's a McDonald's there. Park the van in the parking lot and for Christ's sake don't forget to lock it. Come inside, get a breakfast tray, and sit down at my table. I'll be wearing a San Francisco 49ers warmup jacket. You know what they look like?"

Paco did. NFL and NBA hats, T-shirts, and warmup jackets constituted a kind of worldwide clothing currency, their colors and designs known even in parts of the world where footballs were always round and San Francisco was a saint, not a city.

"Okay," the voice commanded, "take off now."

Forty minutes later, Paco walked into the McDonald's. He filled a tray with coffee, orange juice and a pair of egg McMuffins and, having spotted the man in the 49ers warmup jacket, strolled over to his table. The man, from his looks a Hispanic, nodded to Paco as he sat down.

"The van in the lot?" he whispered. It was not, Paco realized, the voice of the man he'd spoken with in the phone booth.

"Si," he replied.

"Put the keys beside the tray."

Paco did as he was told. A minute or two later, the man deftly palmed the keys. He leaned toward Paco. "The bus runs right past the restaurant. Go downtown somewheres, get yourself a taxicab, and get the fuck out of here. Give me a ten-minute head start before you take off."

Very casually, the man began to stack the litter from his breakfast onto his tray, stood up and, without looking back at Paco, dumped the remains into the refuse bin and left the restaurant.

Paco ate his breakfast slowly, the ten minutes seeming to take an hour to creep by. Finally, he, too, got up and strolled to the bus stop. He glanced at the parking lot. The van was gone. Thirty million dollars' worth of cocaine was off to its final destination on the street corners of the United States. Waiting for a bus to come along, he studied the street and the restaurant. He couldn't spot any sign that he was being followed.

A sense of exultation began to sweep through him. They'd

done it. They had pulled off the big score. For a second he had a crazy idea: he'd take a suite at the Fountainebleau, get some Miami call girls in for company and have a party. Then wisdom prevailed. The celebration could await his return to Medellín. He would head instead for Miami International Airport and the first plane out of the United States.

It was shortly after noon when the two Otero brothers came into Ramon's bedroom. One glance at their smiling faces told the American everything he needed to know about the success of his operation.

That evening he flew out of Medellín for Bogotá, back to his wife and children. It was all over for him now, he swore to himself as his flight took off. When he next came back to Medellín, it would be as a visitor, not as a narco-trafficker. The two million dollars that would make him a multimillionaire would be transferred, he knew, into his Panamanian bank accounts Monday morning. That was the way the Colombians did business. They expected you to honor your debts to them, but they honored theirs to you.

He lowered his head gratefully against his seat rest, the tensions of the last weeks beginning to rush from his psyche like the first bursts of water gushing down a sluiceway. He had done it. He had pulled it off. He was a retired senior citizen at age forty-one.

Ramon glanced out the window as his Avianca flight banked south, leaving behind the lights of Medellín. Then he closed his eyes and let the blissful slumber of success overtake him.

Lind's Tape

It took some time, but before long, we had our contra program up and running full blast. In addition to Panama, we had secured the active cooperation of Honduras, Salvador and Costa Rica. Honduras was run by a military dictatorship lurking under a thin facade of democratic rule. Getting their help was a cinch. We saw to it the Pentagon gave them all the nice new military toys to play with they wanted.

Costa Rica was different. They have no army which probably explains why they have enjoyed a relatively stable democracy for decades. State got them to close their eyes to what was going on with generous batches of U.S. economic aid. If some of that aid stuck to a few sweaty political palms as it passed down the line, well that was just the cost of doing business down there.

My asset, Noriega, could not have been more helpful. In fact, you can say that without Noriega, we couldn't have had our war against the Sandinistas. There was never any discussion of his questioning our use of Southcom—Southern Command—bases in the old Canal Zone to sustain the war. Our electronic eavesdropping equipment and our overflights out of Howard Air Force Base were so good, two Nicaraguan army officers couldn't communicate with each other on walkie-talkies from fifty feet apart in the jungle without our picking up their conversation.

As a consequence of all that, I was starting to spend a great deal of my time in Panama. "You look bored," our station chief, Glenn Archer commented to me on the latest of those interminable visits of mine. "What are you doing tonight?"

"Are you volunteering to give me a tour of the sinful delights of old Panama?"

"Better. The French ambassador's giving a reception for some visiting cultural dignitary who's responsible for bestowing the blessings of French culture on our Latin neighbors. Why don't you come along? His parties are fun."

Well, why the hell not? I thought. "What party disguise shall I wear?"

"Oh," Glenn said, "I'll tell them you're a Defense Department contractor down here checking up on the performance of some of your goodies."

The French ambassador's residence in Panama City is set at the crest of a curling uphill drive, right at the summit of a neighborhood called, appropriately enough, Bella Vista. When we arrived that evening, the residence's terrace was already crowded with guests milling about under half a dozen strings of Japanese paper lanterns. You could sense from the *haute couture* dresses, the understated but significant jewelry of the women, the burnished elegance of the men, that the ambassador's guests were *rabiblancos*, the White Doves, the descendants of those families which had ruled Panama for over a century.

Glenn and I split up so that I would be spared the taint of

being associated with the local CIA station chief. For a
while I chatted with the French military attaché, a Foreign
Legion major who'd served in Algeria with the First Foreign
Legion Parachute Regiment and dangled a vile-smelling
Gauloise cigarette out of the corner of his mouth to indicate
how tough he was. Then I talked to a bubbly, dark-haired
lady journalist from Lyons named Nicole who gave me the
names of what she considered to be the three best restaurants
in the city. It had been worth the drive up here for that information alone, I thought, edging through the crowd at the
bar for a refill of my whiskey.

As I started to move away from the bar with my fresh
drink, I felt my elbow strike a hard object. Turning, I discovered two things. The first was that standing immediately behind me was a woman of such stunning beauty I quite
literally gulped. Her hair was the black of purest ebony,
framing her face in a pageboy cut. She had high, accentuated
cheekbones and taut red lips stretching along a wide mouth
above her squared chin. Her eyes were blue-gray, and at first
glance seemed to offer a promise of angelic softness. Rarely
has a first glance been so ill-informed.

The second discovery was less felicitous. That hard object
my errant elbow had struck had been her champagne glass.
Half its contents were spreading in a dark stain over the pale
blue silk sheath she was wearing.

"Oh, shit!" I groaned. "Didn't I read somewhere that
champagne was good for silk?"

"Not in any of the books I've read." I couldn't figure out
if that was a hint of a smile or a sneer on her face as she said
those words. "Perhaps you saw it in some original Chinese
text on silkworms."

As she was replying, I'd taken her half-empty glass from
her hand and whipped my handkerchief from my breast
pocket. I looked down on my handiwork. She was standing
with just the suggestion of a slouch, her pelvis tilting
slightly forward so that her sheath stretched taut over the flat
surface of her stomach and across her slender, muscular
thighs. It was there, toward her lower stomach, that the
champagne had splashed.

"May I?" I asked.

She gave me that smile of bemused tolerance beautiful
women will sometimes bestow on a man attempting a ploy

so banal as to be barely worthy of attention. "I'll do it," she responded taking the handkerchief from my hand.

As she dabbed the front of her dress, I ordered her another champagne in my most commanding voice and took my card from my pocket. It was, of course, a standard white calling card engraved with my name and nothing else.

"Please," I said, "I'm staying at the Continental. You must allow me to have your dress cleaned for you."

"Don't worry," she assured me, "champagne's not such a terrible problem. But if you see me drinking coffee later in the evening, please stay on the far side of the room."

I laughed and, once again apologizing as profusely as I knew how, offered her a fresh glass of champagne.

"You speak a rather pure Spanish," she observed. Delighted at any excuse to get away from my mishap, I launched into a description of my mother and my Spanish heritage. "My name's Lind," I offered, my biographical sketch completed, "Jack Lind."

"Juanita Boyd."

"That name doesn't seem to have a very Panamanian ring to it."

"Not originally, perhaps. My great-great-grandfather came here from the Firth of Forth while the Colombians were still ruling Panama. We've been here ever since. What brings you to Panama?"

"Airplanes," I lied. "I'm with Northrup Aviation checking out the performance characteristics of some of our aircraft over at Howard Air Force Base."

At that moment the French ambassador glided up and slipped his arm through Juanita's. "Would you mind terribly, dear boy," he asked in perfect Oxford English, "if I stole our charming Juanita away? Our guest of honor is dying to meet her."

Clearly, the guest of honor had no desire to meet a glorified airplane mechanic, because the ambassador left no doubt his invitation did not include me. I was about to offer Juanita yet another abject apology for my awkwardness when I thought better of it.

"See you when the coffee arrives," I said with a wink. Juanita laughed. The ambassador looked gratifyingly perplexed as he swept her away.

I returned to the cocktail party two-step, drifting rather from one knot of people to another. Boyd, I learned talking to a pair of French bankers, was the name of one of Panama's oldest and most powerful ruling families. Juanita, apparently, was the Panamanian princess in all her splendor, the perfect representative of the class that ruled the isthmus.

As I chatted with the bankers, I caught a glimpse of her out of the corner of my eye. The cultural dignitary who was our guest of honor was alight with Gallic gestures, obviously making a desperate effort to impress her. I noted with pleasure that he did not seem to be succeeding. She was all haughty, cool disdain, her face frozen into that same distant smile she'd offered me when I'd volunteered to sponge the champagne from her dress.

It was a half-hour later, I suppose, when, with the charms of the reception beginning to wear thin, I decided to head off into the night. As I was looking for my host, I saw Juanita crossing the terrace to the bar.

"So," I said, moving to the bar behind her, "have you figured out how to save Latin culture from the ghastly onslaught of *Dallas, Dynasty* and the Big Mac?"

For a second or two, she fixed those blue gray eyes of hers on me. Her gaze was neither sensual nor suggestive. Rather, it was cool and appraising, the sort of regard a first-class equestrian—which I later learned Juanita was—might cast on a new jumper she was considering for her stables.

"He was reciting *Le Cid.* I left after the third act."

At that moment a sudden impulse grabbed me. The likelihood that this stunning creature was free for dinner, that if she was, she would choose to share it with a gringo airplane mechanic, was not a proposition on which you'd want to wager the family farm. Still, I thought, what the hell?

"Then why not leave here and have dinner with me? I'll tell you how the play ends."

"A gringo who reads Corneille? How unusual."

"I'm an educated airplane mechanic."

Juanita sighed. "The ambassador just asked me to stay behind with a few others for dinner with our guest of honor."

"Sounds like terrific fun."

"Doesn't it just."

"In case your cultural dignitary doesn't get to it before the cigars and cognac, the pretty young boy gets the girl even though he killed her daddy. There may be a moral in the story for the fathers of all beautiful girls. How's your dad, by the way?" I asked with what was meant to be a wry smile.

Juanita glanced over her shoulder toward the ambassador and the circle of people tightening around his guest of honor. "Where are you planning to have dinner?"

"Las Bovedas," I said, pulling from my memory the name of one of the three restaurants the lady journalist from Lyons had given me.

"Give me half an hour to develop a migraine and I'll meet you there," Juanita said. She drifted back toward the ambassadorial circle, leaving me to depart in a far more exhilarated frame of mind than the one in which I'd arrived.

The restaurant, Las Bovedas, was located in the oldest part of the Panamanian capital on a point of land shouldering out into the bay. The Spanish conquistadores had decided to relocate the city there after that Welsh brigand, Henry Morgan, had burned and sacked Old Panama a few miles farther up the seacoast.

To protect Panama—or Castilla del Oro, Castille the Golden, as it was then referred to—from both British pirates and Pacific storms, the governor general had surrounded his new city with a massive sea wall. Indeed, so huge, so expensive were his walls, that it is said that when Charles II of Spain got the bill for them, he walked to the window of his palace at L'Escorial and shouted, "If they cost so damn much, if they're so enormous, I should be able to see them from here!"

To reach that tip of land you have to thread your way through a maze of crowded alleyways lined with pale green wooden houses which date from the days of Ferdinand de Lesseps's French Canal Company. Their wrought-iron grillwork, their arcades and their sagging balconies, gave the place, I thought, trying to avoid running into the pushcart vendors clogging the alleys, just a touch of the French Quarter in New Orleans.

I finally found the restaurant and parked in front of what was a memorial of sorts to the builders of the Canal. For a dollar, the twelve-year-old kid apparently running the parking concession assured me he would look after Mr. Hertz's car as though it were his own.

Las Bovedas—the word means *vaults*—had been fitted into the old stone vaults which once had served as cells for the conquistadores' prisoners. I took a table, ordered a drink and began to wonder what the chances of Juanita's showing up really were. As I was assessing the probabilities, the Frenchman who ran the place, a bearded hulk from Marseilles, came over to say hello.

"Tell me," I asked, "is it really true the Spaniards used this place as a prison?"

"For sure," he swore. "Downstairs they had the cells they used for prisoners condemned to death. They locked them up, opened the sea gates and let the incoming tide drown them."

"Cost-efficient capital punishment."

He laughed. "I'm going to open a bar down there. I want to give it an English name—the Old Watering Hole."

Juanita arrived, as it turned out, exactly when she'd said she would, half an hour after I'd left the reception. Her punctuality amazed me. Beautiful women, after all, rarely arrive anywhere on time. Tardiness is a discourtesy to which they seem to feel their beauty entitles them.

The owner rushed to welcome her with a ceremony that might have been appropriate for the wife of the president of Panama. Several of our fellow diners rose to greet her as she strode toward our table. Most of the men who didn't eyed her with evident interest.

"How's the migraine?" I asked as she sat down.

"Headaches are such a blessing for people who never have them, aren't they? The evenings I would have wasted without them."

"Ah yes," I replied with the wisdom of the ages, "a good old-fashioned headache, the female's eternal fallback position."

Juanita smiled. "I never use a headache as an excuse for that. I just say no."

And I'll bet you do, too, Juanita, I thought. There didn't seem to be a great deal of feminine readiness to submit to the impositions of the macho Latin male in her character. "This is a fascinating neighborhood," I told her. "All these old wooden buildings. It's a miracle a fire hasn't swept them away."

"Or the termites. They're all infested with them. We say the only reason they're still standing is because the termites inside all link hands to hold them up."

The waiter had appeared.

"Do I dare order you a drink?"

"Why not? I'll stay an arm's length away."

"You're an impressive man," she said as we clinked our glasses. "You attend the best reception in town this evening, then find your way to the chicest restaurant in the city."

"And wind up having dinner with the best-looking woman in Panama."

"Please," she protested, "flattery will get you everywhere." She nodded at my gold wedding band. "I assume you're not wearing that to ward off the advances of hungry females."

"I would never sink so low," I assured her. "To ward off the advances of hungry females, I mean. But yes, I'm married. With three children, to answer the next question."

"Have you been married long?"

"Twelve years."

"Ah, you gringos. You do marry young, don't you? Was she your childhood sweetheart?"

"Sort of. I met her on a blind date for the Yale–Dartmouth game in my junior year in New Haven."

"And she went to Vassar or Smith."

"Vassar."

"With friends who all had nicknames like Muffin or Bootsie and wore cashmere twin sets with a single strand of cultured pearls."

I gulped on my drink, half choking with laughter. "How do you know all this?"

"I went to Manhattanville for two years."

"Ah, ha." Manhattanville was a very exclusive sort of college-finishing school just outside New York, run by the sisters of the Sacred Heart for the daughters of wealthy Catholic families. It would be just the place Latin America's oligarchs would send their daughters to give them a final gringo gloss.

"So you must have run through that collegiate social ramble a few years after I did."

"To an extent." She arched an appraising eyebrow in my direction. "Although I must tell you the magic of those noisy, gin-swilling football weekends in New Haven, Cambridge and Princeton always escaped me somehow."

I'll just bet they did, I thought. Evenings at El Morocco would have been more to Juanita's taste.

"Where are you living now?" she asked.

"In McLean, Virginia, outside Washington."

"Why there? I thought Northrup Aviation was out on Long Island somewhere."

"Most of my work is with the Pentagon," I lied.

"And so," she offered me the hint of a smile "while you gallivant around embassy cocktail parties in Panama spilling champagne on unsuspecting women, your wife stays home to drive the children to school in the car pool and play den mother for the cub scouts on Thursday afternoons."

I winced. "You seem to have a pretty good grasp of American suburban life." I had guessed Juanita was between twenty-eight and thirty. As it turned out, she was twenty-seven. "Have you been married to one of my countrymen?"

"Ah, no. Marriage is a sacrament I have yet to encounter."

"I would have thought that in a society like Panama's there would be a lot of pressure on an attractive, highly eligible woman like you to marry."

"You can't imagine how much."

"How do you resist?"

"I have an understanding father."

"Who I bet you manipulate shamelessly."

Juanita gave her black hair a playful toss. "Well, men are made to be manipulated, aren't they? And as you may have guessed, I have a fairly independent turn of mind. Now back to you," she smiled. "What are we going to get you for dinner?"

Juanita convinced me to try the *corvino,* a tender Pacific sea bass found in the waters off the Panamanian coast.

For a while we worked our way through the usual new-to-each-other conversational mill, what were my impressions of Panama and so forth.

"You know," she told me, "we often call Panama the heart of the universe, which speaks volumes about our capacities for self-delusion. And we are all, without exception, split personalities as far as you gringos are concerned."

"How so?"

"Half of our being hates you for the way you're always interfering in our affairs. The other half of us wants to be just like you. That's why my father sent me to Manhattanville. That's why all our rabiblanco families send their children to finish off their education in the States."

"I didn't think split personalities were the inevitable byproducts of our system of higher education."

"You know, Jack," she replied, "at the risk of appearing ungracious, I must tell you, you gringos are utter hypocrites as far as Latin America is concerned."

"What do you mean by that?"

"You love to go around preaching to the world about democracy, but the fact is the only kind of democratic government you want down here is a government that's ready to do what you want it to do, not what the people who elected it want it to do."

"Juanita," I tried to interject, but she was off and running.

"We've lived under a military dictatorship in this country for the past thirteen years because that's what you Americans wanted us to have. You wanted the military in power here because you were sure you'd get along better with them than you would with the civilian government we'd elected. You could give them lots of nice guns to play with. Like a mother gives a baby his rattle. Keep them nice and docile and ready to do your bidding."

What Juanita had just enunciated in a crude but not altogether inaccurate fashion was the policy we had in fact been following. That wasn't something I was anxious to discuss, however.

"Come on, Juanita," I pleaded, "you people down here want to blame everything on the gringos. If the sun doesn't come up tomorrow, whose fault will it be? The gringos."

"Jack, do you realize this little nation gets more military aid per capita than any other country in the world except Israel? To defend us from what? Castro and the communists coming storming out of the jungle like the Assyrians coming down like the wolf on the fold? Grabbing the Panama Canal? That's what your generals in the Pentagon want you to believe."

She took a long swallow of her Chilean chardonnay. "Well, if you will be so kind as to pardon my French, what the generals at the Pentagon are telling you is bullshit. The real reason the gangsters like Noriega who run our National Guard want those arms is so they can be sure the people who live in this country they stole with your help will never be strong enough to take it back from them. It's us those arms might kill one day, not communists."

"Look, I don't pretend to be any expert on Panamanian history." That, of course, was less than candid, because it was a subject of which, in fact, I had considerable knowledge. "But, as I recall, that guy Arnulfo Arias the soldiers overthrew was a fascist and a son of a bitch."

"So what if he was? At least he was our son of a bitch. We're the ones who elected him president, honestly, democratically. You didn't. The truth is you wanted him out because he was anti-American and you whispered to our soldiers, 'It's okay, go get him.' "

That was at least a half-truth. We knew the coup was about to take place, but on the orders of Lyndon Johnson's White House, those glad tidings never got passed to Mr. Arias. Juanita was right. He was regarded in Washington as an anti-American bastard, and no one was going to lift a finger to save him.

At that point we were interrupted by the waiter setting our fish before us. When he'd left and we'd savored a bite or two, she sighed. "Why am I attacking you like this?" she said. "It's hardly your fault the U.S. government is behind these people, is it?"

Well, that was not a remark calculated to put me at ease. Any objective historian would undoubtedly conclude that the U.S. government agency for which I was working had played a critical role in installing, then keeping, the military in power in Panama.

"No," I assured her, "but I very much admire that independent turn of mind of yours. It must be rather rare down here."

"It is. I have never understood why, just because I was born a wealthy woman in Latin society, I cannot lead the life I choose to lead. I mean, if I want to jump horses, I jump horses. If I want to fly my own plane, I fly my own plane. If I want to have a lover of my own taste and choosing, I have him. Why shouldn't I?"

I ignored the latter remark. It seemed like the wise thing to do. "You fly your own plane?"

She teased me with those angelic blue eyes of hers. "Afraid to trust our life to a lady pilot, are we? Yes, I fly. A Piper Seneca. I'll take you up in it one day if you can stifle your male chauvinist misgivings."

"Tell me, how do your male colleagues here react to your political thoughts?"

"Badly. Politics in Latin America is a men's club. So people are forever raising their eyes to the ceiling and muttering, 'There goes Juanita. She's at it again.' "

"And I suppose your refusal to marry the right young man from the right nice family is a part of this rebellion of yours?"

"Oh," Juanita assured me, "I'll get married one of these days. To an older man, probably. One I'll choose carefully."

One you can control and whose eyesight where your prospective lovers are concerned will be a little less than twenty-twenty, I thought. I decided, however, that that was an observation I'd better keep to myself. We laughed and chatted away, I skirting the shallow waters of Panamanian politics until coffee arrived.

"What traces of the old Spanish settlement are left here?" I asked her, shifting conversational gears. "What's left of the Camino Reale and Portobelo?" Portobelo was the Royal Way's—the Camino Reale's—Atlantic terminus, the funnel through which the treasures of the Incas had flowed on their way back to the court of Castille.

"More than you might expect. Ruins, of course, but interesting ruins."

"I'd love to see them. Do you suppose I could lure you into being my guide?"

Once again Juanita gave me that cool appraising look of hers. "How long do you expect to be in Panama?"

"Hard to say. A week, ten days. I don't know exactly."

"Perhaps," she said, finishing her coffee with a quick swallow. "For now, I really must go."

I settled the bill and walked her outside. The parking lot kids rushed up to her like autograph hounds to a movie star. "Senorita Juanita," they cackled in chorus, making her name sound a bit like a singsong parody of those old Chiquita banana singing commercials.

We walked to her car. She was driving a dark blue Porsche 911E. When she'd unlocked the door, she turned. Quite deliberately, she placed a pair of cool, distant but not entirely unpromising, kisses on each of my cheeks. "It was pleasant. Better than listening to the end of *Le Cid*."

"How about that guided tour?" I prompted her.

"Call me," she said. She opened the door and slid into the Porsche's beige leather seat, exposing as she did a riveting glimpse of her long, elegantly muscled leg up to her midthigh. She started the engine, smiled quickly, and was gone.

* * *

The SAC, the Special Agent in Charge, of the New York District Office of the DEA, walked to his office door and locked it. He then turned to the men he'd assembled there—his assistant, his six group supervisors, and five carefully selected senior agents.

"Okay, you guys," he announced, "absolutely nothing of what you're about to hear is to go out of this room, understand? Not a word."

Listening to him, Kevin Grady suppressed a smile with some difficulty. Bob Walker was sneeringly referred to by his New York subordinates as "Captain Video" for his remarkable faculty in getting his face in front of the nearest TV camera. Discretion was not a quality for which he was well known in the DEA.

"This here's Eddie Gomez from Washington headquarters," he announced, pointing at the heavyset man sitting beside his desk. "He's here to talk to you about something all of you, as hardworking employees on the U.S. government payroll, don't see much of—money. Eddie, take over."

Gomez stood up with the slow gestures of an aging football player whose joints are beginning to be assailed by arthritis. He had jet-black hair and the dark complexion of a Mexican or a Sicilian, identities he had often assumed with great success in his undercover work. He was, in fact, Spanish born, the son of Loyalist parents who had fled Spain in the aftermath of the Spanish Civil War.

"How do we judge a guy's performance in the DEA?" he asked the little assembly. "One question: How much powder did he put on the table in the last year, right? Seize loads, they tell us. Kilos are headlines. Everybody's happy.

"Well," he continued, "maybe we shouldn't be as happy as all that. Suppose we seize a hundred kilos, which by anybody's standards is a lot of cocaine. We let the media know its street resale value is, say, ten million dollars. Everybody gets excited, 'Hey! Wow! That's major stuff.'

"But what is the reality here? How much did those hundred kilos we seized really cost Pablo Escobar or whoever was trafficking the stuff? How much of his money did Escobar actually have tied up in that coke? Two hundred thousand dollars max. Forget about what the papers said. That's the reality. That's the extent of the hurt we did. Two hundred thou."

Gomez looked from face to face. "On the other hand, suppose we could get our hands on the money he was going to make off that coke, the ten million that's going to go flowing back to him? Now you've really hurt the son of a bitch. The reality is we get more bang for the buck with money cases than we do from seizing powder.

"Just to give you an idea of how persuasive this money thing is, the Treasury ran a random check on twenty dollar bills in circulation in the country a while ago. Eighty-five percent of them turned out to be carrying microscopic traces of cocaine."

Gomez's audience emitted a kind of collective gasp. Even for men hardened to the extent of drug trafficking, his figure was a revelation.

"The importation and distribution side of the cocaine traffic basically runs the same way whatever city we're talking about, New York, L.A.," he continued when his audience had digested his statistic. "Now, you all know how tough it is to penetrate those Colombian networks. They're Colombian from top to bottom. No gringos in there, thank you, until you get down to the ant army that's out selling on the street."

Gomez paused for effect. "But now, let's take a look at the other side of the business, the money side. For openers, the Colombians have a basic problem here. You take a mule, give him a suitcase full of coke, and tell him, 'Hey, take this up to Pablo in Queens,' the chances are he's going to do it. I mean, what else is he going to do with all that coke? He doesn't know anybody in New York who can make a thirty kilo buy."

Gomez chuckled. There were aspects to this thing he contemplated with some delight. "But give that same mule a suitcase with a million bucks in it and tell him, 'Hey, take this down to the bank in Panama for me,' and wheels may start turning. A million in cash, he knows what he can do with that. He may decide to go south, all right, but to Rio de Janeiro, not Panama."

There were some approving grunts as several agents started to see where this was headed. "Now, the top guys like to stay close to their money, so on the money side, you don't have five or six protective layers between the top and the bottom guys. Maybe just two. And our Colombian friends have some chinks in their armor there. It's like the pilots. We know the Colombians prefer to have American pilots fly their dope. On the money side, they have got to go to outsiders to service them if they're going to move their money in a sophisticated way. That gives us a chance to run a penetration on them.

"The problem is how do we do it? What's our wedge in the door? We've been looking at that for months in Washington. Now we think we've come up with the answer."

Gomez paused and smiled a smile of purest triumph. "My friends, your DEA is about to become a full-service banker for a few carefully selected drug dealers. We're going to offer them a complete array of financial services just like your friendly Chase Manhattan neighborhood banker. We have now secured from the Department of Justice the formal authorization which will allow us at the DEA to, in effect, launder money for the Medellín cartel."

Somebody behind Grady let out a long, low whistle.

"Right," Gomez said, sensing the agent's unspoken concern. "We're into a very sensitive area here. That's why this has got to be held top secret. First of all, we obviously don't want the bad guys to learn we've been authorized to move into this area. Right now they're convinced we can't do this sort of thing, so they're not too wary. But above all, we don't want this to leak out into the press."

Gomez gave his audience the grimmest regard he could muster. "I mean, they'll shriek, 'Holy shit! The DEA's providing a criminal service for the people they're supposed to be fighting.' They won't see the intelligence we'll be getting on the cartel's infrastructure, the assets we'll be able to identify and seize, the arrests we'll be able to make from wiretaps and surveillance.

"But guys," Gomez's voice took on a warning air, "the real secret here is this. The point of all these exemptions and authorities we've gotten from the Department of Justice is that the DEA is going to be able to make money for laundering the cartel's dough. Suppose we launder ten million dollars. The going commission a money launderer would take on that is six percent, or six hundred thousand dollars. Well, we're going to take it. That six hundred thou will be ours. It will cover the expenses of our investigation. In other words, guys are going to be paying for their trip to the slammer themselves."

"Jesus!" the supervisor of Group Two exclaimed. "You

mean some of our suits down there in Washington actually have got some brains!"

Gomez smiled. "You'll have to follow the same rules and regulations with this money that you do with regular government funds."

"Does this mean we can fly first-class along with the rest of the money launderers when we travel?" Richie Cagnia, Kevin Grady's boss, asked.

"Don't count on it," Gomez laughed.

Grady raised his hand. "Gomez," he asked, "can you explain in terms a dumb New York mick can understand how this thing of yours is supposed to work?"

"Sure." Gomez enjoyed explaining his system even more than a car salesman enjoys extolling the merits of his top-of-the-line model. "A money launderer is valuable to a drug trafficker because by some device or facade he is able to circumvent our currency regulations. As you all know, a bank or a business is required by law to file a CTR, a Currency Transfer Report, on any cash transaction over ten thousand dollars, even for changing small bills into larger ones, right? Anywhere where there's no paper trail in existence, you got to file a CTR.

"Now, what your typical money launderer is going to do is fly out to Hong Kong or down to the Cayman Islands first-class, not coach like us schmucks, and open himself up a dozen companies at fifteen-hundred dollars a crack. With each one he gets the key document he's going to need, a corporate resolution authorizing John Doe or whatever name he wants to use to transact business on behalf of the corporation. With that, he can walk into any financial institution in the U.S., open up a bank account in the corporation's name and start to do business."

He looked up to see if everyone was still with him. "So now our drug trafficker comes to call and says, 'Hey, I got a million dollars cash I want to get down to Panama. Can you help me?'

" 'No problem,' our money launderer tells him. He's already opened up maybe ten bank accounts in the name of the ABC Company, Hong Kong, in different banks in the New York area, where there happen to be thousands of banks. He goes to them and deposits one hundred thousand dollars cash in each one."

Gomez spread his arms wide at the simplicity of the device. "What happens when he does it? The platform officers, very correct guys, all fill out CTRs on the transaction. For Part One, the part that reads 'identity of the person making the deposit,' the money launderer gives the banker his New York State operator's license to establish who he is. With that, the guy records his name, address, date of birth, and uses his driver's license for ID on the form. This, of course, is a joke, because the driver's license is fraudulent, but our friendly banker has no way of knowing that.

"Now the banker goes on to Part Two of the form, the entity on behalf of whom the transaction is being conducted. He puts down the ABC Corporation, of Hong Kong. Then he fills out Parts Three, Four, and Five, the type of account, commercial, the type of transaction, cash, and where the money has been deposited, Citibank, 2 Jane Street, Brooklyn.

"By the end of the day, our money launderer has deposited a million dollars cash into the banking system perfectly legally, and the forms he's filled out are absolutely useless to the government. Two days later, he calls each bank and orders the money wire-transferred to the ABC Corporation's bank account in Panama. Once it gets there, all the money launderer or his drug trafficker has to do is withdraw it in cash, take it across the street, and deposit it in another Panamanian bank account, and that money has disappeared forever without a trace."

Gomez waved his stubby hand at Grady. Kevin noticed he was wearing a diamond pinkie ring on his little finger, the unofficial badge of the Mob. Must be a leftover from some undercover operation, Grady thought.

"To come back to your question, 'How are we going to work this?' We're going to set ourselves up undercover as money launderers. We'll offer the bad guys exactly the same services a money launderer would. And, like I said, we'll charge them the regular money launderer's commission for moving their money down to Panama or wherever.

"But," he cautioned, "a word of warning here. We don't want to get into this thing capriciously. We're not going to go out and launder any old two-bit hood's money for him. We want the right vehicle here. It requires a good high-level CI with the right contacts, someone who can interface our little operation with the people in the cartel who are going to be interested in a service like ours. But it's important you folks all know this is now available. That's why I'm here to-day to tell you if you've got the right vehicle, we're here waiting for you."

Lind's Tape

"Stop here," Juanita commanded.

Here, as far as I could see, was absolutely nowhere. We were driving through the Panamanian jungle along a narrow two-lane blacktop paralleling the Canal three or four miles from its course, on our way to the first stop in the tour she'd agreed to give me. The jungle was a wall of foliage so dense one would, I thought, get hopelessly lost if you wandered more than twenty feet into its luxuriant embrace. To the left, the road dropped off to a slight depression. Piercing the jungle's green fastness on the far side of the depression was what looked like the opening of a tunnel.

I parked in a cleared space and we got out of the car. "Come on," Juanita said, setting off through the underbrush covering the left bank.

For our day's outing, she'd stretched her black hair tight behind her neck in a ponytail. She was wearing no makeup whatsoever; she knew how hot it was going to be tramping through that jungle. If anything, she was even more stunning without makeup than she had been with it. Those blue gray eyes set against the background of her pale skin glowed with a luminosity mascara had somehow dimmed; the promising curve of her lip seemed fuller, even more sensual than it had been when it was glossed with lipstick. She was wearing a sheer white silk blouse which she'd unbuttoned down to her midriff so that it exposed the gauze-like lacework of the brassiere. For slacks, she had on a pair of stonewashed blue jeans which clung so tightly to her buttocks and legs you could almost have mistaken them for a pair of Lycra exercise leggings. On her feet, she was wearing calf-high Castujano leather riding boots hand-tooled in Toledo, Spain.

As we reached the bottom of the depression, she looked around at me as though, for the first time that morning, she was becoming fully aware of what I was wearing. She pointed to my Adidas sneakers. "They *are* wonderful for walking around the jungle," she observed.

"What's wrong with them?" I asked, since there had been no mistaking the sarcasm in her voice.

"For a bushmaster snake, nothing at all. He'll set his fangs into them as easily as if he was biting into a breakfast toad."

Now I realized why she had on those Spanish cowboy boots. "Christ, I'd forgotten about snakes."

"Well, let's hope they forget about you."

"Look at the positive side here. I have you to rush me back to Panama City if I get bitten."

"Jack, dear, the car that can drive faster than a bushmaster's venom works hasn't been invented. You'll just have to expire right here in my arms."

"There could be worse ends."

"Good. As long as you think that way, we're off." She marched toward the tunnel-like opening in the jungle wall I'd noticed from the car. A tunnel was exactly what it turned out to be, a sort of pathway piercing the dense foliage. Twenty, maybe thirty feet overhead, the branches of the trees lining the path crisscrossed and interlaced like the laths of a half-woven basket. A diffused light seeped down into the tunnel through those openings. Occasionally, a golden pillar of sunshine, its course unimpeded by leaves or branches, sank in a bright shaft through the dimness. Up ahead, I saw thousands of fluttering yellow-white objects suspended in the tunnel like outsized snowflakes tossed in a gentle wind. They were butterflies.

Juanita took my hand and we strode off into the passageway. Below my feet I could feel the uneven texture of a sheet of stones. I glanced down. In that half-light you wouldn't even be able to see the snake that bit you. On either side of us, the noise of insect life rose in a noisy tide. Suddenly, an eerie half-human shriek soared above it.

"A howler monkey," Juanita told me.

After we'd been marching for a quarter of an hour, we came on a running cut hacked out of the jungle to allow the passage of a high-tension power line which ran at right angles across the tunnel's path. Juanita bent down, and in the bright light of the clearing, brushed the growth from the stones at our feet.

There was a regular pattern to them, regular enough at least to make it clear they were a cobbled path.

"Look," she said, pointing to the uneven indentations in some of the stones. "Cart tracks."

We were both squatting on our haunches. "This is what's left of your Royal Way. Those marks were made by the Spaniards' wagons."

The heat, the humidity of the jungle, was overpowering. I peered back down the tunnel, half expecting to see the ghosts of Spanish soldiers struggling along those stones, beating their mules to get them to move faster, whipping the captive Indian slaves pushing and tugging at their wagons. What a hoard of treasure, what a wealth of gold and silver, had been forced over these stones on the journey back to Spain.

"Just think of Balboa and his Galicians and Basques hacking their way through here for the first time," Juanita sighed. "And wearing those rusty iron corsets of theirs. How did they survive?"

"Hard men for hard times."

She got up and dusted herself off, pointing as she did to what looked like a clump of gray-green leaves dangling from the branch of one of the trees above us. I stared up at it. The clump began to move.

"A sloth," Juanita noted. "Come on. We're off to the next stop."

"Hey," I laughed, "you're a very energetic guide."

"You said you wanted the full tour." Again, she grabbed my hand. "Now all we have to do is get you back to the car before the snakes find out you're here."

The next stop on Juanita's tour was Portobelo, a two-hour drive away over on the Caribbean seacoast. In the heyday of the Spanish Main, Portobelo had been the Atlantic terminus of the Royal Way. All the galleons of the Spanish conquest had dropped anchor in its wide bay. From their holds they'd disgorged furniture, cloth and rice; out of their cabins had marched those ardent Jesuit soldiers of the Cross burning to bring the faith of Christ to the heathen Indian with their gospel of convert or perish.

In turn, those seamen of the Main had crammed their holds with pearls from the far Pacific islands, the plundered treasures of Cuzco, silver hacked by Indian slaves from the mines of Bolivia; the wealth of a continent riding off to Castille in ships not much bigger than a Greyhound bus.

And now?

There was nothing. Portobelo was a desperately poor, desperately underpopulated fishing village. Juanita walked me down to the water's edge.

"Can you imagine?" she asked. "Once they stacked silver bars on this beach like they were fireplace logs. Right here where we're standing. Thousands of them." She pointed at the bay. "Somewhere out there, if he knew where to look, a scuba diver could find the bones of Sir Francis Drake. Isn't that an irony? The body of the man who saved England from the Spanish Armada dumped overboard in a sack here in the heart of the Spanish Main?"

"Well, if you think of it, maybe they were better off leaving him here. I mean, London traffic probably couldn't handle two Nelson's columns. By the way, did you hear how they got Nelson's body back to England?"

"No, but I can see you're dying to tell me."

"They stuffed him in a coffin and filled it with rum to preserve the body during the trip back. When they got to Portsmouth, the coffin was dry. The crew had drilled holes in it to get to the rum. That's why they call the sailor's grog ration in the Royal Navy 'Nelson's Blood.' "

"How disgusting. Now I know why I've never liked the taste of rum."

Juanita led me up to Portobelo's old walls. A dozen rusted Spanish cannon lay in the weeds, their wooden caissons eaten away centuries ago by rot and termites. Most of the Spanish fortifications, she explained, had been hauled off to serve as fill for the Gatun Locks of the Canal. We stood there side by side on the ruins of the walls looking out into that vast and empty sea, and, I, naturally, had to get poetic.

"Imagine what you would have seen looking out there four hundred years ago? And now you can't even see a single fishing boat." Swept away by the thought, I began to quote Shelley's *Ozymandius* for Juanita.

"Jack, dear," she interrupted, "they fish at night. During the day they sleep. But if you meant to impress me with the fact you know Shelley as well as Corneille, you did."

She was indefatigable. By God, she was going to give me the full-bore tour I'd asked for whether I still wanted it or not. We went to the Portobelo cathedral, where she insisted on introducing me to the Black Christ, a three-hundred-year-old statue of the Savior laboring under his cross carved from the wood of the cocobolo tree. Then it was back to Colon, across the Atlantic mouth of the Canal at Gatun, and out to Fort San Lorenzo on a head of high ground looking down on the mouth of the Chagres River.

By now it had become so humid, simply walking was like doing aerobics in a Turkish bath, but she insisted we clamber over it all, describing how Henry Morgan had stormed the heights with two thousand men in December 1671, massacred three hundred Spaniards, then set sail up the Chagres to lay waste Panama City.

Finally, well after three o'clock, she announced at last that we could go to Colon for a bite of lunch at the Balboa Yacht Club. There is nothing in that institution that would remind you of similar such organizations in, say, Newport, Southampton or Palm Beach. However, given our exertions and my voracious appetite, it looked as welcoming that afternoon as ever any three-star French restaurant did.

"Do you realize," Juanita asked as we were finishing our coffee, "there are countrymen of yours who have spent twenty years living in the old Canal Zone and have never taken the trouble to see what you've seen today?"

"That's because they didn't have a guide like you."

"It's because they're smug, complacent and immensely self-satisfied. You're interested in what's around you. I like that."

We drifted out to the car and started back to Panama City.

"You had your coffee by the Caribbean," Juanita reminded me as we left Colon. "When we get back, you can have a drink looking out at the Pacific. Our charms may be limited, but that's one thing we can offer you won't get anywhere else in the world."

She tilted her seat back and leaned her head against the side of the car, contemplating me again with those soft blue-gray eyes of hers, that bewitching half smile she seemed to favor so much playing at the corners of her mouth. Was that smile meant to be inviting or mocking, I wondered.

It was hard to tell, and in any event I didn't have much time to study it. We were out on the open highway, and in Panama there is a direct correlation between keeping your eyes firmly fixed on the road and your life expectancy. "You seem to be studying me like a horse," I joked.

"Maybe." The smile lengthened just a touch. "We'll check

your teeth when we get you back to Panama City. You know, you're rather handsome, Jack, in a primitive sort of way."

"Primitive? Why primitive? Does that mean I'm supposed to bare my teeth and beat my chest?"

"No. It means they managed somehow to suppress the effects of those aristocratic Spanish genes of yours. Your features are all angles and jutting lines. Was your father a New Englander?"

"Nope. A southerner."

"Puzzling. I dated a descendant of Cotton Mather once in New York. He had a face that looked a bit like yours. It seemed to have been carved out of New Hampshire granite."

"Indicates character."

"And you're a man of great character, are you?"

"Oh, absolutely."

She emitted a kind of *sotto voce* laugh. "We'll see about that."

I had the air conditioning on in the car. Juanita buttoned up her blouse a bit, then crossed her arms under her breasts, emphasizing their seductive challenge. Her legs, wrapped in those skin-tight jeans of hers, stretched out at an angle toward my side of the floorboard. She caught me casting, at the peril of our lives, an admiring glance at them and smiled.

"Usually I prefer my men a little darker and more menacing, but . . ." She shrugged. Then she reached over and, with a playful smile, touched my hair which at the time was blond, thick and curly.

"Know why I did that?" she asked.

"My dandruff is showing."

"For good luck. We have a superstition about men with blond hair. We think it's magic. Touching it brings you good luck. It goes back to the Aztecs, I think. Something about their gods being fair-haired."

I gave my hair a poke with my fingertips. "Will it work for me?"

"Perhaps." Juanita twisted her shoulders as though something was itching her back and she was rubbing against the seat of the car for relief. The gesture may have relieved whatever it was that had troubled her, but it certainly did nothing to relieve the sense of excitement that had been rising in me for some time now.

"Ah, Jack," she sighed, comfortable once again, "I'll bet

you're hopelessly square, aren't you? A girl would have her work cut out with you, I suspect."

"Come on now, Juanita. You're too smart to buy into all those tiresome clichés about Latin and Anglo-Saxon men. Don't forget what that woman said, 'Latins are lousy lovers.' "

"Oh, no, they are not, Jack. Believe me, they are not." Juanita volunteered that affirmation so readily I understood it had sprung from a considerable reservoir of experience. Some women are tempted to hide their awareness under the blush of false innocence. Not Juanita. She might have had her faults, but artifice was not one of them.

The sun was setting as we approached the capital. By the time we'd reached the outskirts of Panama City, it was already night. Darkness is a swift-falling curtain in the tropics. We had, I noted with considerable relief, been able to spend the better part of the day together without once stumbling on the rocks of a political discussion.

Juanita lived in a new glass-and-steel tower called the Monte Carlo in Paitilla, a neighborhood built on the second arm of land embracing the Bay of Panama opposite the arm on which the city had been built in 1671.

"Can I offer you a drink?" she asked as I parked the car.

"I'd like that," I said.

Juanita had the penthouse. From her terrace she had a spectacular view of the bay and the line of freighters, their navigational lights gleaming, waiting their turn to enter the Canal.

"Let me fix you a drink and you can admire the view while I take a shower and change into some clean clothes. I was dripping sweat all day."

A moment or two later, she returned with a scotch and soda. "You know," she said, passing me the drink, "I've been rather selfish. You'd probably like a shower, too."

"Yeah," I answered, "I could really use one after that heat."

She led me to her bathroom, an elegant pink marble chamber with a sunken bathtub and a large shower stall enclosed by walls of frosted glass.

"There," she said, indicating the shower. She opened a linen closet and took out a large bath towel. "I'll let you go first."

With enormous relief I peeled off my clothes and got into

the shower stall. Like most wealthy Panamanians, Juanita kept her air conditioning set to near freezing so, turning my back to the shower door, I could take a real delight in savoring the splash of the warm water showering my skin.

I began to sing—not loudly, but just loud enough so that I didn't hear the soft click of the door to the shower stall opening. Nor did I realize Juanita was in there with me until I felt her bare breasts pushing up against my back muscles and her hands circling my thighs to allow her fingernails to embark on a slow, lascivious journey up my inner legs.

I started to turn toward her.

"No, no," she whispered, "stay just like that."

I stood frozen like some kind of a statue while her fingers continued their exquisitely pleasurable voyage, each advance as unhurried as it was deliberate. By the time her hands had joined at their common destination, any supplemental effort on arrival would have been superfluous. Their work had long since been accomplished.

For a moment or two her hands played there, caressing me, taking measure of the situation. Then she reached for the soapdish and with the same leisurely movements proceeded to lather my chest, stomach and thighs. Once she'd finished, she slipped the hand that was clutching the bar of soap between our two bodies and proceeded to lather herself in that same unhurried manner.

That done, she put the soap back in its dish and half slid around me as I turned toward her, so that suddenly we were slithering against each other, caressing ourselves with our soap-slicked bodies.

"Shower like this often?" she laughed.

She turned up the force of the water pouring from the shower head, so it came sluicing down our squirming bodies, rinsing away the last of the soapy film. Then, without a word, we made our way across the marble floor to her bedroom.

Juanita was a confident young lady. The covers of her bed, I noticed, rolling her eagerly into it, had already been turned down. Given my intense state of arousal, our lovemaking was unfortunately short-lived. When we'd finished, Juanita lay beside me, her face profiled against the pillow, those blue-gray eyes of hers contemplating me once again, still challenging and, I thought, just a trifle mocking. Playfully, she tweaked my lip with the fingernail of her index finger.

"Well," she murmured, "not *quite* as square as I was expecting."

With that, she propped herself up on her elbows. "I'll get you your drink," she announced, and like some proud young lioness in search of prey, she strode out of the room.

She returned with my drink and a vodka on the rocks for herself. Pulling the covers around us as protection against the arctic blasts of her air conditioner, she slipped back into bed beside me. For a while we lay there side by side, savoring the warmth of each other's bodies, neither of us talking and I doing my best not to think. It was not a moment for that.

After a while Juanita began to stir, slowly at first as though she'd dozed off for a moment or two. Once more her fingers set off on an exploratory expedition, this time tweaking the nipples of my breast, then crawling down my rib cage toward my waist. She rolled over on her side and looked at me again. This time there was no doubt. Those eyes of hers were laughing. Whether they were laughing with or at me, I don't know, but laughing they were.

"Certainly didn't think you were going to get out of here as easily as all that, did you?" she asked. Without waiting for an answer, she rolled over on top of me and, using her long legs as levers, jackknifed my legs wide apart. Then one of those hyperactive hands of hers went straight to its target. She found it not only willing but ready. With a deft move she slipped it into her waiting port of call and set it into place with a thrust of her pelvis that was so determined it sent the bones of our groins together with riveting firmness. Then she began to move.

"The mills of the gods grind slowly, but they grind exceeding fine," someone once wrote. I suspect that whoever it was that penned those lines had a woman like Juanita, not the Divine, in mind. She drove me up to a dizzying peak of excitement with those slow gyrations of hers, and then, with maddening suddenness, stopped.

"Change," she said, and sent us gasping into a new position. That delirious carousel kept spinning like that from position to position until, it seemed, Juanita had exhausted the full repertory of the Kama Sutra. In any event, she had certainly exhausted me. The end was not merely a release; it was a sheer, blissful deliverance.

I tumbled back onto the bed from my knees where, as far

as I was concerned, our journey had ended. I kissed Juanita, took a long drink of my now lukewarm scotch and soda and, with appalling discourtesy, fell asleep.

It was after ten when I awoke, caught for just a fraction of a second in that state of panic that overtakes you when you wake up and don't know where you are. The room was dark. I patted the bed beside me. Juanita was gone. I found the light, turned it on and stumbled groggily into the bathroom. This time, the shower I offered myself was ice-cold.

As I left the shower stall, Juanita was waiting in the bathroom doorway with a fresh scotch and soda. She was wearing a sort of mini-kimono, a scarlet silk jacket embroidered with fire-belching dragons which belted at her waist and ended just below the crest of those long, gorgeous legs of hers. Her hair was brushed and glossy, and she'd put on just a touch of makeup. She looked as though she was ready to go out night-clubbing, or set to go on making love for the rest of the night.

"That was a little better," she chuckled, handing me the drink. "I think you deserve this."

As I took a long and grateful swallow of the drink, Juanita opened the door to her linen closet and took out a terry-cloth bathrobe. It came, I noted, from the Ritz Carlton Hotel in New York.

"Put this on and come out to the dining room. You must be hungry."

"Hungry? I'm collapsing."

"Well, we certainly don't want that. Come on."

The dining room was off the terrace looking onto the bay adjacent to her living room. Juanita had set the table, a small vase of delicate white orchids as her floral centerpiece, five candles flickering in a massive old silver candelabrum, the lights dimmed so we could look out at the lights in the bay and the silhouettes of the ships waiting their passage to the Atlantic.

From her refrigerator she brought us a tray of smoked salmon snacks set on squares of toast. When they were gone, she went to the oven for a dish of cannelloni which was warming there. With it she brought a bottle of Antinori Chianti Classico, which she handed to me with a corkscrew.

Like so many Latin women, Juanita was clever about little things like that. She always let the male play out those meaningless charades that flatter his sense of self-importance, convinced that such gestures made it easier to keep the areas that really mattered firmly under her own control.

It was a lyrical, magical end to a magical day. Except that it was not quite over.

When we'd finished, Juanita poured us each a brandy and we went out onto her terrace to look at the bay.

"What a spectacular sight." The banality of my remark was hardly worthy of the vision before us.

"You should be here when a tropical storm hits. It's unbelievable. Will you come and watch one with me some night?"

"Only if I'm asked."

"You will be."

Juanita turned and, opening her mouth, offered me a long kiss, her twisting tongue sharp with the lingering taste of brandy. She was wearing nothing under her mini-kimono, nor was I, of course, wearing anything underneath my robe. And so, somewhat to my surprise, it started all over again.

This time it was a protracted, frantic effort to drive ourselves to the summit we sought. We're mad, I thought, my heart thumping in my rib cage as I responded to Juanita's commanding thrusts. Yet some dark force inside me which I had never known compelled me on, reaching out to grab that final ecstasy as a racing driver forces himself to find that perfect arc of a curve below which is failure, beyond which lies the darkness.

It was well after two o'clock when I left. The streets of Panama were deserted. I was an exhausted, troubled man. Never had I experienced anything quite like whatever it was that had seized me that night in the arms of Juanita Boyd. I hammered the heel of my hand against the steering wheel.

"What the hell am I doing?" I asked myself out loud.

The agents of the United States Drug Enforcement Administration entering Bill "Sunshine" Ottley's little office in West Palm Beach that afternoon were the very picture of courtesy and affability.

"Just a routine investigation, Mr. Ottley," the senior agent, a man called Gallagher declared, showing Ottley his gold agent's shield.

"Questions for a frequent flier," his sidekick laughed.

"Always glad to help, boys," Ottley assured them.

"How'd you like a nice cup of Nescafé?" Treating the law with friendly respect had been a vital part of Ottley's *modus operandi* for years.

The agents demurred. Gallagher withdrew some papers and a black notepad from his pocket. "Now, as I understand it, you fly pretty frequently between here and those oil fields down at Lake Maracaibo, is that right, sir?"

"Yessir," Ottley declared, "a regular little bus ride for me, you might say."

"Right," Gallagher continued. "You went down last Thursday night, I see."

"Yeah. Some guys busted a well cap down there and I had to fly in a replacement." Gallagher made a note in his pad while Ottley warmed with the inner satisfaction generated by his successful lie.

"Did you see anything unusual, observe anything along the route coming or going that struck you as strange?"

"Not that I can recall," Ottley said, feigning intense concentration to show the DEA agents that, as a good citizen, he was eager to help them as much as he could.

"Didn't divert from your flight plan at any time either coming or going?"

"No sir, no need for that at all."

"Right," said Gallagher, closing his notepad. "I wonder if we could just have a look at the aircraft and we'll be on our way, sir."

"Sure thing," Ottley smiled, "she's sitting right out here in the hangar."

"You have her on a six-month charter out of Southland Aviation, I understand, Mr. Ottley," the second agent asked.

"Yeah. I figure it makes more economic sense that way."

Gallagher murmured his approval of Ottley's evident financial wisdom, pulling as he did another piece of paper from his pocket. "This here's a copy of a court order from the U.S. District Court for the Southern District of Florida, Mr. Ottley. It authorized the DEA to attach a recording device to this aircraft before you took delivery of it from Southland Aviation."

"A what!" stammered Ottley.

"Oh, just a routine thing. Like those black boxes you're always hearing about on the television when an airliner crashes. You know, they keep a taped record of each flight you make, the altitudes you're flying at, the compass headings you're flying on, on how long you're flying on each heading. It's just another way of corroborating the fact you're flying in conformity with your flight plan."

"Holy shit!" Ottley had forgotten for the moment that friendly modus operandi he prided himself on employing in his dealings with law enforcement. "You can't do that. That's fucking unconstitutional."

"Afraid not, Mr. Ottley." There was still a smile on Gallagher's face, but his once-friendly eyes were somewhat less engaging now as he stared at the pilot. "Of course, as long as you stayed right on your flight plan and didn't go sliding off anywhere you weren't supposed to, you've got nothing to be concerned about. Nothing at all. It's just routine, Mr. Ottley, pure routine."

"Kevin, dear, you must be doing something right these days, although for the life of me I can't imagine what it might be." Ella Jean Ransom grinned down at her colleague as she uttered those words. She'd crossed her arms in front of her chest so he couldn't quite make out what the piece of paper she had clutched in her right hand was.

"Why do you say that?"

"Because God is being good to you. You remember that guy Marcello down in Colombia we drew a bead on a while ago?"

Grady had to think a moment. "Oh, yeah," he recalled finally. "That guy called Ramon the American Airlines pilot gave us."

"The same lovely fellow," Ella Jean chuckled. "Look what the NADDIS coughed up for us this morning."

The NADDIS, the Narcotics and Dangerous Drugs Intelligence System, was the DEA's master computer bank on which all its vital information was stored and cross-indexed. When he had launched his investigation into Raymond Marcello's drug-related activities, Grady had entered Marcello's name into the computer with the notation that any further information concerning this suspected felon should be communicated to Special Agent K. Grady or Special Agent E. J. Ransom New York DO Group Six.

He smoothed the computer printout Ella Jean handed him onto his desk. It was from the DEA's Miami office. A recently arrested drug pilot named William Ottley, it revealed, had, in the course of a confession to arresting agents, "iden-

tified one Raymond Marcello, aka Ramon, an American citizen resident in Colombia, as the principal agent in the organization and dispatch of a load of one thousand kilos of
cocaine from Medellín, Colombia, to West Palm Beach,
Florida." Marcello, the printout said, had been indicted together with three Colombian co-conspirators in a sealed indictment returned by the federal grand jury for the Southern
District of Florida.

"Holy shit, Ella Jean! A thousand keys!" Grady whistled.

"Yeah," Ella Jean purred with the contentment of a cat
contemplating a particularly succulent mouse. "He be a big
man, your friend Mr. Marcello."

"Let's go see Richie."

Grady and Ella Jean walked down the hall to the office of
their group supervisor, Richie Cagnia.

"Look what the tooth fairy just sent us," Grady announced, passing the printout to Cagnia.

"Hey, you got a heavy hitter, all right," Cagnia agreed
when he'd digested the printout's information.

"A heavy hitter who is now looking at twenty-five years
without parole on two counts which a judge may or may not
decide to let him serve concurrently if he's ever arrested and
convicted."

"Yeah," Cagnia agreed. "Hard time makes for hard
choices. That might make him think a bit. Trouble is, we
still got a problem here. We don't know where he is. I mean,
we can't very well go over to the State Department and say,
'Please ask the Colombians to extradite this guy for us'
when we haven't even got an address on him. You know the
Colombians. They're not big into extradition even when
they got the perp sitting right there in front of them with the
cuffs on."

"Richie, I don't *want* this guy arrested," Grady stressed.
"I don't *want* him extradited. I want to get my hands on him
while he's still a virgin. Look at the potential here. As far as
we know, this guy's never lost a load. He's got nobody
pissed off at him down there. They gotta love him in
Medellín. And he's American. So he's got to know with
what we have here one day, sooner or later, we're going to
nail his ass."

"So what do you want to do?"

"Ask Miami to have the U.S. Attorney's office down there
unseal that indictment and drop it on the table in the middle

of the night when nobody's looking and the press can't find it."

"And then what?"

"We send our friend Ramon a message, a friendly word of warning."

"How do you figure on doing that? Sending off a postcard of the Statue of Liberty addressed to Mr. Ray Marcello, Colombia, South America?"

Grady smiled that ice-cold smile of his. "Richie, I have a better way. I think I know the perfect conduit."

The telephone operator at Philadelphia's Broad Street law firm of Wanamaker, Schuyler and Alton reacted to the words "Drug Enforcement Administration" with a distaste similar to that she might have displayed sipping a spoonful of curdled milk spilled by mistake on her morning bran flakes. Common criminality, and certainly the kind of crime associated with drugs, most emphatically did not fall into the spectrum of law practiced by the partners and associates of her 180-year-old firm. What ever could the representative of such an organization want with one of them, particularly one as distinguished as Mrs. Priscilla Hoagland, whose specialty was the creation of trusts for the firm's wealthy clients?

Indeed, the first reaction of Mrs. Hoagland's secretary when she was informed of the call was to insist that there must be some mistake. No, the caller, who had one of those dreadful lower-class New York accents, had insisted, there was no mistake.

"This is Priscilla Hoagland speaking," the lady lawyer announced coldly when she came onto the line. "How may I be of service?"

"I believe you're the elder sister of a Mr. Raymond Marcello, now resident in Colombia, is that correct?"

"Indeed I am."

"Then, Mrs. Hoagland, I think that you ought to be aware of the fact that your brother is the object of two federal grand jury indictments, one here in New York and one in Miami, for conspiracy to import cocaine into the United States in violation of Title 21 of the U.S. Code, Section 846, conspiracy, and Title 21, Section 841 (a) sub-section 1, possession with the intent to distribute. Are you familiar with those sections of the code?"

"Mr. . . ." she paused. "I'm sorry, I didn't get your name."

"Grady. Kevin Grady, Mrs. Hoagland."

"As I am sure you will understand, Mr. Grady, that is not an area of the law with which I am familiar."

Ella Jean, who was monitoring the conversation, grimaced. "A real tight-ass broad you got there," she whispered to Grady.

"Well, Mrs. Hoagland," Kevin went on, "I'm very sorry to have to tell you that each charge carries a mandatory twenty-five-year jail term. You know how tough we are on drugs these days, and one of those counts relates to a load of a thousand kilos."

Despite her efforts at composure, Priscilla Hoagland made just the faintest of gasps on hearing that figure, a sound that rang like the Angelus in Kevin Grady's ears.

"I've got to tell you, Mrs. Hoagland, that looking through the case file, I had the hardest time imagining that your brother could be involved in something like that. I mean, he seems like such a fine young man, what with his good family background, Lafayette College and all."

Grady let the words hang in the air for a second or two. Mrs. Hoagland had, in the meantime, regained her composure. "Mr. Grady, I am sure that you will understand that I cannot speak to my brother's innocence or guilt of the charges you mentioned."

"Oh, I understand that, Mrs. Hoagland." Kevin was now purring along in his finest father confessor mode. "I just thought that you ought to know. As an elder sister devoted, as I'm sure you are to your brother's welfare I mean, the Italians are a bit like the Irish that way, aren't they, very close?"

That remark did not elicit a reply from Mrs. Hoagland. Her Italian ancestry was not something about which she frequently reminded her associates at Wanamaker, Schuyler.

"But, really, what I wanted to tell you, Mrs. Hoagland, is this. We're here to help if we can. The warrants for your brother's arrest have been drawn up and sent on to the Justice Department for referral to State with the usual request for extradition." No such arrest warrant, of course, was in existence. "As you probably are aware, as a United States citizen resident in Colombia, your brother's subject to immediate extradition in response to a U.S. bench warrant."

"I am not cognizant with the terms of our treaty with Colombia."

"Yeah, that's the situation," Grady continued, freighting his voice with all the false sympathy he could muster. As he did he was thinking to himself, "We might serve him, that is, if we had the faintest damn idea where the bastard was." That, however, was not a flaw in the government's case he was about to reveal to Marcello's attorney sister.

"What I wanted to say to you, in strictest confidence, is this: should he decide, before he's arrested and extradited, to come in and talk to us, I think that in view of his background, the fact he has no priors, no previous arrest record, except, of course, for that insignificant business selling marijuana in Easton . . ."—Grady deliberately dropped that into the conversation to be sure Mrs. Hoagland was well aware of how much they knew about her brother—"that we could try to work something out for him . . ."

"To cut a deal, as they say in your trade," Mrs. Hoagland said icily.

Oh, oh, Grady thought. "Look, Mrs. Hoagland, let me be up front with you here. Your brother has nowhere to run. The Colombians will extradite him in a flash to show us how serious they are about fighting drugs as long as we're not asking them to extradite any of their fine citizens. Even if he runs off and lives like a monk in the Brazilian jungles for ten years, those charges are still going to be out there waiting for him. So will the time. You know that as well as I do. Under the circumstances, Mrs. Hoagland, I honestly believe the best, in fact, the only realistic course open to him is to have a talk with us. With his attorney present if he desires. If he doesn't like what he hears, he can leave a free man. Of course, we'll still go after him with our usual procedures. But at least that way he'll have a chance to see if there's some light out there for him."

Grady paused, hoping there would be some indication from Ramon's sister that his point was getting across. However, she remained silent. *Lawyers,* he thought, cursing silently.

"In any event, Mrs. Hoagland, I thought I owed it to you to give you the name and the phone number of the assistant US attorney handling the case in the event your brother or his lawyer wants to get in touch."

"Well, I'll take the information, Mr. Grady," Mrs. Hoagland's reply was almost begrudging. "Just in case I should be in touch with my brother."

Like in the next three minutes, Grady thought, passing her the information. What a shame no judge would ever authorize a wiretap on her line in a circumstance like this.

"Remember, Mrs. Hoagland," he concluded, "your brother is in a pretty impossible situation. He's going to have to get his help wherever he can find it. It just might be here with us."

"You know something, Kev?" Ella Jean laughed when they hung up. "You missed your vocation. You should have been a priest."

Lind's Tape

In the two or three days that had followed that wild Sunday with Juanita Boyd, some instinct, some pang of guilt perhaps, some fear I was standing on the edge of a precipice, stayed my hand each time I reached out to call her. It was only when the end of my Panamanian sojourn was fast approaching that an intense desire to see her again stifled that hesitation of mine. I called her apartment. Naturally, there was no answer.

There was no answer for forty-eight hours, forty-eight hours during which I alternated between listening to my libido's fury and despair at my earlier timidity and another, more fatalistic voice assuring me that this, perhaps, was the better way.

She finally answered her phone the morning before my departure. As it turned out, she was already going to a cocktail party at the home of one of her wealthy rabiblanco friends that evening. She invited me to come along but, on reflection, I realized that was not the smartest thing I could do. Suppose I ran into someone at the party who really did know something about high-performance aircraft? Just how was I going to handle a chat about, say, the inherent aerodynamic instability of swept-wing fighters?

Better, I decided, to ask her to join me for dinner after her party. We agreed to meet at De Lesseps, a restaurant named after the French canal builder. Its main dining room was a museum of sorts, a picture gallery of old photographs taken during the construction of the Canal: the massed steam shovels assaulting Culebra Cut; the victims of yellow fever dying in their hospital beds; canal workers in straw hats and suspenders playing poker in their barracks; black workers hacking through the jungle; and, of course, that classic of T.R. in his white suit playing at driving a Bucyrus steam shovel.

I was staring, fascinated, at that array of photographs when Juanita arrived. Once again, she was right on time. She was wearing a black shantung silk suit with a ruffled collar at her neck, a little like those you see in oil paintings of Elizabethan ladies. Watching her cross the room, I felt a sensation I had never known before, a longing so intense, so physically real, that it was almost painful. I had been the prince of fools. Why had I been so stupid as to let those precious nights in Panama go by without seeing her?

She offered me her cheeks for a quick kiss. Pulling away after my embrace, she arched an eyebrow and flashed that smile I found so beguiling. "Well rested?" she asked.

"Is that a challenge," I chuckled, "or are you seriously interested in my health and well-being?"

"Both, my dear Jack, are vital to my continuing interest in you."

"In that case, I'll take it as a challenge. Come on, I've ordered us a bottle of champagne."

We slid into the booth which I'd reserved and, with evident good cheer, I signaled the waiter to open the champagne waiting in its ice bucket. I had been expecting some reproach from Juanita, some twisting of a verbal knife into me for my not having called her before I had. Nothing of the sort happened. If my lack of attentiveness had upset her, she certainly gave no signs of it. Rather, I noted unhappily, my failure to call seemed to be a matter of considerable indifference to her.

"Goodness," Juanita noted, "you seem to be in an exuberant mood tonight."

"I'm celebrating."

"What?"

"Being here with you."

"Where did you learn to lie so charmingly?" she asked.

There were a number of answers I could have given her for that, of course, none of which seemed appropriate to the occasion. So instead, I offered her my most engagingly sincere look. "Lie to a woman like you? A man would have to be mad to think he could get away with that."

"Jack, dear, all men—even pillars of gringo rectitude like you—lie to women."

The waiter had filled her champagne glass while she was telling me that. She picked it up, swirled the liquid a second or two, then gave me that mocking smile of hers over the rim. "Fortunately, we women know how to return the favor. *Salud.*"

"Is that a promise you intend to keep?" I laughed, returning her salutation with a gesture of my own champagne glass.

"Not as long as that inquisitive nature of yours stays within reasonable bounds." She gave a playful toss to her black hair. "So you've been forewarned. Indiscreet questions get inaccurate answers."

"I'll remember that," I noted, shifting gears. "You certainly stirred up a few emotions in me Sunday night."

"Did I just?" Juanita teased me with a half-smile and shrugged her shoulders yet again, folding open as she did the black silk of her bodice. "I trust that with that stern character of yours, you'll be able to keep those emotions firmly under control."

"Oh, I will," I promised, "at least until dessert."

"Good. I wouldn't want the pangs of an uneasy conscience troubling that cheerful disposition of yours."

"Why should they?"

"Oh, I don't know. We tend to look on things like marital fidelity a little differently than you gringos do."

"In other words, adultery isn't such a big deal down here, is that it?"

"Oh dear." Juanita caressed my hand with the tender touch she might have used to stroke the back of a pet cat. "Do I detect an undertone of guilt in that voice of yours? Did I leave you awash in a sea of remorse Sunday?"

"Not for a moment," I lied. "It was a sea of bliss."

"Good," she replied, giving my hand a parting squeeze. "Bliss was exactly what it was meant to be. And," she added, some ambiguous warning signal flashing for a second in those soft blue eyes, "all it was meant to be."

I was in the process of swallowing a mouthful of champagne, and the icy liquid caught and burned a second in my throat.

"Now what the hell was that supposed to suggest?"

"Nothing. Everything. What is it the Bible says? There is

a time and a place for everything under the sun. Why think? Why question? Why not just enjoy?"

For the moment, the waiter confronted us with joyful prospects of a different order by laying our menus onto the plates before us. We were seated side by side in our booth. Occasionally our knees brushed, and when Juanita moved I could hear the deliciously promising rustle of her silk dress beneath the heavy linen tablecloth which dropped over our laps and hung almost to the floor. Focusing on what I wanted to eat was not the easiest of exercises.

With the ordering ceremony concluded, we began to chat again. Suddenly, Juanita raised her champagne glass, took a sip, then looked up at me, her blue eyes teasing, that mocking half-smile of hers making its appearance on her lips once again. "Do you have any idea what it is that makes you so attractive to women?"

"I can't for the life of me imagine."

"That's it. That's the explanation. You're sexy and attractive but you don't realize it. That gives you an air of, I don't know, an undiscovered territory."

I almost burst out laughing at that. After Sunday night, nothing might seem more unlikely than the notion that there was any undiscovered territory left in J. F. Lind IV. "I thought you were interested in me for my mind. I mean, a man who can quote Corneille and Shelley and all that."

The waiter, at that moment, was in the process of setting our first course, a gourmet salad of smoked duck breast, slivers of foie gras and avocado, in front of us. Juanita's hand had slipped beneath the tablecloth but I, caught up in watching our food arrive, had not noticed its disappearance. It headed with unerring accuracy toward my groin, there to tighten around what was a sudden and rapidly stiffening erection.

"Of course I'm interested in your mind, darling," she purred. "Talk to me about Kierkegaard."

I spluttered, almost choking from laughter and surprise. The waiter, poor devil, looked at me as though he was afraid he was about to be called on to perform the Heimlich Maneuver, a procedure with which I'm sure he had only a passing acquaintance. Juanita relaxed her grip and smiled at me, her eyes wide with innocent concern. "Poor darling! Are you all right?"

In a sense, that crazy stunt of hers set the tone for the rest of the evening. After dinner, she suggested we go to a disco. Her choice was a club on the top floor of the El Panama Hotel, the first of those classic honeycomb buildings designed by Edward Stone to employ marble screens and waterfalls as a way of producing natural cooling in tropical climates.

Juanita's dancing—whatever music we were dancing to, whether it was salsa, mambo or rock—was sheer, controlled sensuality. Watching her gyrate in front of me, occasionally giving a haughty toss to her black hair, her eyes half closed, a faint and distant smile on her lips, each twist of her pelvis an ode to eroticism, reminded me of that scene in which Melina Mercouri danced in *Never on Sunday*. A man, it suddenly occurred to me, might kill for a woman like Juanita.

In any event, by the time we got to her apartment, I knew, for the first time in my life, what the phrase *overcome by desire* meant. That evening, there were no stopovers on the way to her bedroom. Moonlight was flooding the room, so she didn't bother to turn on a lamp. She marched to the window, glanced out at the Pacific a second, then pivoted around, unzipping her dress as she did with one quick and provocative movement. She arched her shoulders and shimmied so that the dress dropped to the floor in a rustling of silk, leaving her standing there etched in the moonlight in her white silk bra and panties.

I doubt that I have ever, before or since, undressed as quickly as I did that night. We were wrestling gloriously toward our second ascent to the mountaintop when Juanita rolled over on top of me and brought our proceedings to a sudden, agonizing halt. I saw her hand reach out to her bedside table, then heard a faint crackle like the snapping of a small lightbulb.

She began moving again drawing us back toward our climax. As she did, she thrust a handkerchief under my nose.

"Sniff," she commanded. "Take a deep breath."

I squirmed beneath her as an overpowering burst of ammonia assaulted my lungs. "What the hell are you doing?" I gasped.

"Seeing to your continuing education," Juanita laughed. She started to move faster, thrusting us into a climax that seemed as if would never end, a dizzying, slow-motion explosion.

It was only, of course, a physiological illusion provoked by the drug she'd given me, but as illusions go it was pretty damned convincing. It left me with a heart that was pounding away like that of a four-minute miler, five seconds after he's hit the finish tape.

"What in God's name was that?" I said.

"A popper. Amino-nitrate. It dilates your blood vessels. Next time, we'll try applying cocaine to you. They say that has an extraordinary effect."

"The hell you will." I was still panting furiously. Suddenly, half hysterically, I burst out laughing.

"What's so funny?" Juanita asked.

That was not a question I was prepared to answer. I had just started thinking about the lie-detector tests all CIA officers are administered from time to time, and I was asking myself, "How the hell am I going to slip this little episode past the box unnoticed?"

Meanwhile, she had gotten out of bed, wrapped herself in her scarlet kimono jacket and padded barefoot to the window. For a few moments, she stood there, smoking, staring out at the Pacific, saying nothing. I lay in bed staring up at the ceiling. A troubling parade of images formed and reformed there, of Sarah Jane and my boys, of a kind of domestic tranquillity I had come to treasure. And standing by the window smoking was a different, far more troubling reality.

"What are you thinking about?" Juanita asked, turning, finally, away from her contemplation of the sea.

"Us."

"Don't."

"As far as I'm concerned, that's easier said than done."

Juanita walked back across the room, sat on the bed beside me and, almost absentmindedly, began to pick at the hairs on my chest.

"Don't think, Jack," she admonished. "Just be."

I looked into those soft blue eyes of hers. For once, they were not teasing but gentling as she looked down on me, the curves of her breasts swelling against the scarlet silk of her kimono.

"It ain't easy," I told her. "Not when you're getting on a plane to go back to Washington tomorrow."

"Never be obsessed with the future, Jack. *Que será, será.* Some things are meant to be. Some aren't. We'll see."

* * *

It was party time on board Avianca's Flight 090 outward bound from Bogotá to Aruba, the resort island in the Lesser Antilles off Colombia's Caribbean coast. As they always did half an hour after takeoff, the stewardesses had just begun to push their trolleys covered with rum punches down the 727's aisles. Ninety percent of their passengers were off to the island to have fun, to lie on its silvery sands, to scuba dive and snorkel through the turquoise waters of its reefs, to gamble in its casinos or party in its galaxy of discos, nightclubs, restaurants and seaside hideaways.

In that exuberant atmosphere, the man in 22A, his shoulders slumped, his gaze fixed despondently out his cabin window, struck as discordant a note as a pallbearer might in a throng of Mardi Gras revelers.

"How about a nice rum punch?" the stewardess asked him brightly. "You look like you could use one."

The man turned toward her, the gesture seeming to demand an inordinate amount of his strength. His eyes were wet. He had been weeping.

"No thanks," he murmured, "just a cup of black coffee."

Ray "Ramon" Marcello turned back to the window. He could not bear the sight of the two young children, roughly the age of his own kids, playing in the laps of their parents in the seats across the aisle from his.

No party was waiting for Ramon on the island of Aruba. He was flying to the holiday resort to try to buy the second half of his life back from the United States government. In a sense, he was going there to learn if he would have to watch his beloved children growing up through the glass partition of the visitor's room in a federal penitentiary. Never had he experienced a depression comparable to the one overwhelming him now.

Suppose this negotiation didn't work? Suppose he had nothing to offer the government? Would they snap the handcuffs on him, push him into a private plane, fly him back to Miami to spend a quarter of a century, all that mattered of the rest of his life, in jail?

His fingers felt for the reassurances of the two hard, round pellets sewn into the seams of his blue jeans. They were cyanide capsules. If the DEA tried to kidnap him in Aruba, all they would deliver to Miami would be a corpse. Weeping silently, he leaned against the window, reliving yet again the nightmare of the past two weeks.

He had just come back to Bogotá from his lovely new farmhouse out on the savannah when his sister's call had come in. His first instinct had been to run. His emergency flight kit was ready in his safe: three passports, one British, one Costa Rican, one Italian; twenty thousand in cash, U.S. dollars, Colombian pesos and Spanish pesetas. The passports came from his friend "Picasso," who worked in the *Perservancia,* the casbah of Bogotá rising behind the Hilton Hotel. Picasso trafficked the passports stolen by Bogotá's skilled pickpockets; one hundred dollars for a passport plus another fifty for fixing its new owner's photograph to its pages.

But what were his choices if he ran? Settle in Brazil like that English bank robber had? He had the money. But what about his wife and children? Would they follow? Or would his wife say, "Screw you. You're a fugitive and a drug trafficker" get a divorce, grab his country house, and marry the first son of a bitch who made a pass at her so his children could have a brand-new daddy to love and raise them?

He had decided to call a drug lawyer in New York whose name he'd once been given. Ramon made the call, naturally, from a public phone booth. The jerk had refused to tell him what time it was until Ramon had wire-transferred a fifty thousand dollar retainer to his New York bank account. Drug lawyers were like that.

"Just how bad is my situation?" was Ramon's first question when the lawyer was finally ready to talk business.

"Very, very bad," was the answer.

"Suppose I stay out for four, five years, and turn myself in when everyone's forgotten all about this? Won't they give me a much lighter sentence then?"

"I'm sorry," the lawyer had replied, "but that's not the way it works. I'm representing a guy who was out for seven years, then turned himself in. He got thirty-five years last week. I saw him off to the penitentiary this afternoon—in chains.

"You'll do the time, too, when you get caught, and the chances are very high that eventually you will get caught," the lawyer predicted. "Or you come up here and see if you can work something out with these people."

I paid this son of a bitch fifty thousand dollars to hear this shit? Ramon thought. "Something like what?"

"Like a reduction in your sentence in return for your co-operation with the government."

Well, Ramon thought, there was no way he was going to fly up to New York to do that. The DEA would just grab him, toss him in the slammer, and that would be the end of it.

"Tell them it's crazy for me to come up to the States," he had urged his lawyer. "If I stay in place down here, I'll be much more use to them."

They had agreed, and picked Aruba as a neutral meeting ground. Could he cut a deal, Ramon wondered. Years ago a pal in a Bogotá bar, the San Antonio Rose, had told him, "Those guys at the DEA, they deal in ruined lives. They sell hope to guys who've run out of it. And they don't sell it cheap."

By nightfall, Ramon thought, he would know what the price of restoring a little hope to his shattered life was going to be. And more important, if he could afford to pay it.

Ramon took a cab from the airport at Oranjestad—Aruba belonged to the Dutch, which explained names like that—to the Concorde Hotel. A note at the reception desk informed him that his attorney, Mr. Malcolm MacPherson, was waiting for him in room 622.

MacPherson was short, as unkempt as he was overweight, balding, and wearing thick bifocals. He was also an arrogant intellectual who made no effort to conceal his smarts from those beholden to him like Ramon. Imperiously, he waved Ramon to an armchair in the well-furnished sitting room of the suite he was paying for with Ramon's money. Drug lawyers traveled first-class.

The assistant U.S. attorney handling the case and two DEA agents would be arriving shortly, he explained. They were taking a room at the hotel for the purpose of their meeting. The very fact they had decided to come should be interpreted as a positive sign. It meant they wanted to talk. That was not always the case.

"And suppose I just take my chances and go to trial?" Ramon asked.

"Young man," MacPherson replied, "I am without question the best narcotics lawyer in New York City and one of the ten best such lawyers in the nation." Unnecessary modesty had never hindered the flow of MacPherson's thought.

"I must tell you I have lost the last twenty-five cases I have brought to trial."

Ramon groaned.

"That result does not reflect any lack of ability or effort on my part. It demonstrates, rather, the temper of the times and the readiness of juries to convict in narcotics cases however flimsy the evidence may be."

"And what happens if these guys just grab me, stuff me into a plane and fly me back to Miami?"

"They won't. You've been seeing too many movies. They don't work that way. This is the United States government we're dealing with here, not the Gestapo."

Ramon, for whom the distinction had been somewhat blurred since his days as a sixties rebel, started to protest, but his attorney waved him to silence.

"Let me make one thing clear. You are entitled to get up, walk out of the negotiation, and leave this island a free man at any time you choose. The government will make no effort whatsoever to prevent you from doing so."

"You're kidding me!"

"Mr. Marcello, you have paid me fifty thousand dollars to listen to sound legal advice, not fairy tales." His tone took on a few extra decibels for emphasis. "However, if you decide to leave, these DEA people will pursue you with renewed vigor, and when they catch you, as they will, you will find their welcome considerably less cordial than you are going to find it now."

At that moment the phone rang. MacPherson picked it up. "Right," he said, and turned to Ramon. "They're waiting for us down on the fourth floor."

It seemed to Ramon that his knees were refusing to function as he tried to force himself out of his armchair. For a second he swayed uncertainly, then lurched toward the door. As he passed in front of his attorney, he stopped.

"Hey," he asked, almost in despair, "will these guys shake my hand?"

The assistant U.S. attorney waiting for them in room 427 greeted MacPherson, then gave Ramon a firm handshake and turned to the two men behind him.

"This is Special Agent Grady and Special Agent Cagnia of the Drug Enforcement Administration," he announced.

They all shook hands, and the U.S. attorney waved them

to the circle of armchairs drawn up in the middle of the room. Chatting amiably, he poured each man a cup of coffee from the tray he'd ordered earlier from room service.

Kevin Grady watched as Ramon crossed and uncrossed his legs and flicked his tongue along the line of his lips. Mouth's dry, Kevin thought.

Buddy Barber, the U.S. attorney, opened the meeting with the cordiality of a sales manager discussing regional sales prospects with his salesmen.

"As you know," he informed Ramon, "the government is on occasion prepared to make a deal with someone who is in a position to furnish us with something more important than what we already have in hand." He smiled warmly at Ramon. "We think this might well be the case here."

"What are we talking about, sir?" Ramon asked. Barber was younger than he was, but in the circumstances the *sir* seemed appropriate.

"What we do is go to the judge, explain to him in great detail everything you've done for us, the risks you've run, and ask him to give that strong consideration in imposing sentence on you. In other words, we go to bat for you. And our experience is that in almost every case, the judge will listen very carefully to our recommendations."

"How much time could I hope to get off my sentence?" There was just the trace of a quaver in Ramon's voice as he asked the question.

"Depending on how complete and how effective your co-operation is, up to half."

"Only half?" Ramon appeared stunned by Barber's reply. "Wouldn't it be possible to get it down to, say, five?"

He really wants it, Grady thought. He wants it so bad he'll say yes and worry about the consequences later.

"That is possible," Barber said, "but very unlikely."

Grady scoffed. "Hey, pal," he said, fixing that tight, cold smile of his onto his lips, "you know what they say out there on the street, don't you? If you can't do the time, don't do the crime."

Grady and Cagnia had chosen the good cop/bad cop roles. Kevin preferred to play the good cop, but that role often went down better with the older man, so Richie had taken it here.

"Ray," Cagnia intervened, "in this sort of thing, it's all very much up to you. For CIs—confidential informants, that is—who really climb on board with us, who are ready to go the extra mile, run that extra risk, we reciprocate. We really do try to get that time down to an absolute minimum and, above all, see that you can serve it at a good facility."

"Right," Kevin laughed, "instead of in one of those places we've got where buggery is the national pastime."

Cagnia and Barber made the ritual grimaces his remark had been designed to produce.

"The procedure in a case like this, and your attorney will confirm this for you," Barber explained, "is that we draw up a legal document which you sign. Under its terms you will plead guilty to one of the charges pending against you. We will then drop the other charges. Sentencing is delayed until we've completed our work together so that we can intervene on your behalf before the sentence is imposed. When you have signed, Agent Grady will debrief you of everything you can possibly tell us. You will be granted use-immunity covering the information which you have given us."

"May I intervene here?" MacPherson asked.

"Please do."

"What that means in layman's terms is that the information which you have furnished the government cannot be used against you in a courtroom in any future criminal proceeding, even if the deal you've made with the government should have fallen apart. In effect, you will have sanitized the past criminal activities about which you've told the government. Therefore, should you decide to cooperate, it's in your interest to get out and into the record everything there is to know about your past activities. It is the crimes which you neglect to tell the government about for which they can nail you should something go wrong, not those you've already confessed to."

"I concur," Barber nodded. "Now, as part of this agreement you will have to agree to stand up eventually in an open courtroom where everybody can see you and testify against anyone we've been able to arrest thanks to your efforts. And you will have to be prepared to identify for us and forfeit all the assets you've accumulated through drug trafficking."

"My money!" Ramon gasped.

Grady stifled a smile. It was always the forfeiture provision that made them gag.

"How will my wife and kids be able to live?"

"We'll be prepared to return a part of your assets to you for your living expenses while you're working with us," Barber assured him. That was the arrangement the DEA preferred. It avoided the need of paying a CI a regular stipend, which never looked good when it came out in the courtroom in front of the jury.

"How about my wife and kids down there in Colombia if something happens?"

"We're prepared to get them out of there, on a military plane if necessary, and place them in the witness protection program in the United States."

"And how about buying some life insurance for me? If I get killed or something?"

Ramon's lawyer chuckled. "Mr. Marcello, these people aren't going to buy you anything. Except maybe a little time."

Kevin laughed harshly. Time to play the bad cop again. "Sure, we'll get you a nice policy at Lloyd's. Like the movie stars get for their tits." He turned to Barber. "Why are we wasting our time on a guy who's going on like this? We've got the State Department ready to get the Colombians to sling him out on his ass. Let him do his twenty-five. Life insurance, for Christ's sake!"

As he pronounced his last words, Kevin could read the panic flickering in Ramon's eyes. He'd grabbed on to that slender hope of getting his time down, maybe way down, which was just what Kevin had wanted him to do. They were going to send Ramon into the lion's den, tell him to stick his head right there in the lion's mouth. A guy did that for only one reason, to win his life back. For a few minutes Ramon had begun to believe in that possibility. Now he sensed they were going to yank it away from him. He was scared. Our little pal Ramon, Kevin thought, is ready for his tumble.

Cagnia moved in behind Kevin for the last push.

"Look, Ray," he said, "what we're asking you to do is dangerous, sure it is. We know that. But is it any more dangerous than what you've already done? Putting yourself and your family on the line for a thousand keys of powder? For what? Money, right? Here you're taking a risk, sure, but what are you going to be taking it for? To get the best years of your life back."

That did it. Ramon caved in. In DEA parlance, he flipped.

The lawyers drew up the legal papers covering the deal, Ramon and the assistant U.S. attorney signed them, and the lawyers and Cagnia left Aruba. Kevin and Ramon stayed behind to set their new relation into motion.

Kevin's first job was to measure just how hard it would be one day to get a jury to buy Ramon's testimony. To do that he had to flush all the negatives out of Ramon's character and past: Did he have a drug problem? Was he a chronic liar? What was his real criminal record? Had he left a trail of kited checks behind him back in the States?

When Ramon began to protest at the detailed, highly personal questions, Kevin patiently explained to him that in front of a jury and a good defense lawyer, Ramon's virtues were going to be a good deal less evident than his failings would be. It was much better for them to determine together just what those failings were so they could prepare to address them, rather than waiting to see them exposed unexpectedly in a courtroom.

In reality, the negatives in Ramon's case were a lot less troublesome than those Kevin was used to dealing with. Ramon's coke-snorting days were behind him. The guy was very much in love with his wife and kids. His criminal activities seemed confined to his dope smuggling, an activity he'd managed to convince himself wasn't all that much of a crime.

With that opening phase of their work completed, Kevin got Ramon to walk through in detail the thousand-kilo load he'd run into West Palm Beach. That was the critical step in putting together his evaluation of his new CI. A good cop is always suspicious of information come by too easily; felons who volunteer information are often lying. On the other hand, Kevin had to know if Ramon was going to play ball or not.

To do that, Kevin possessed a concealed weapon. It was Ottley's confession. That provided him with a secret yardstick against which he could measure Ramon's answers to see just how honest he was being. Ramon passed the test. Not only was he telling the truth, but he was volunteering additional details that showed his cooperation was real.

Knowing that, Kevin was able to move into the heart of the debriefing, picking out of Ramon's brain every detail he could about the coke traffic, places, names, dates, the little tricks, Ramon's evaluation of all the players. For every name he needed a description: age, race, height, weight, identifying features, address if possible. All of that would get logged into the NADDIS computer once Kevin got back to New York. It was a slow, painstaking process, and it consumed most of their second day on the island.

Finally, Kevin snapped off his tape recorder and gave his watch a glance.

"Five o'clock," he noted. "Do you realize the federal bureaucracy has already been shut down for almost an hour? Let's have a swim and a beer. Did you bring a bathing suit?"

"Shit, no," Ramon laughed. "I thought a striped suit was going to be more appropriate."

"Well, come on. Let's go buy you one on Uncle Sam. He owes you after that day's work."

A raft was moored a couple of hundred yards out to sea off the hotel's beach. The two men swam out to it and flopped down side by side on its planking to catch the last rays of the warm afternoon sun, Kevin humming softly, Ramon doing his best to conceal his sullen anger from his agent controller.

"I envy you going to Lafayette," Grady remarked after they'd been resting for a few minutes. "It must be great, a college like that."

"Yeah," Ramon acknowledged. "It wasn't bad. Seems better now than it did then, though."

"What did you major in?"

"Dope and broads mostly. I did just what I had to do, you know? Just enough to keep the grades above the low-water mark so I could hold on to my draft deferment. Beyond that, my attitude was pretty much, fuck it."

Interpreting silences was not a skill at which Ramon was particularly accomplished, but it was not difficult to sense the unspoken reproach in the man lying beside him. Did DEA agents go to college, he wondered. Probably not.

"Did you go to college?" he asked Grady.

"Fordham. I wanted to go to Brown. Got in, but they wouldn't give me a scholarship and my old man couldn't swing the full tuition, so I had to go to a commuter campus and live at home."

"Tough luck."

"What the hell, Fordham was okay. The Jesuits are pretty

good as teachers go. Not much into the social scene, though.
I mean you wouldn't mistake the place for *Animal House*."

"How old are you?" Ramon asked.

"Forty-two."

Almost subconsciously, Ramon twisted the gold wedding
band on his finger. The agent's fingers, he noticed, were
bare.

"You married?" he asked.

"Not anymore," Grady replied.

"Divorced, huh?"

"No. I'm a widower. My wife died of cervical cancer
about a year ago."

"Ay!" Ramon's response was both spontaneous and
deeply felt. "That must have been terrible."

"The most painful event of my life."

"Did you have any children?"

"No." Grady uttered his answer in a voice heavy with
pain and regret. "I guess it's probably better we didn't. DEA
agents don't make good bachelor fathers." He rolled over on
his side, away from Ramon. The CI felt a curtain coming
down between them. He'd just gotten a glimpse into the private world of Kevin Grady, but that was all he was going to
get, a glimpse.

After a few minutes had passed, Grady sat up and looked
down at Ramon. The informant sensed that their conversation was about to take a new direction.

"You know, Ramon," Grady said, measuring his words
with care, "CIs almost always fuck up at some point."

"Keyin, I've been down there in Medellín, remember?
Fuck up once and I'm dead. I've got no illusions about that."

Grady nodded in acknowledgment of his CIs evident wisdom. "What I was going to say is this. A fuck-up we can
forgive. What we don't forgive is a CI who double-crosses
us."

"Yeah, sure. I mean, why would you?"

"You listen to Barber," Kevin continued, "and he'll feed
you some pablum about what happens to a guy who double-
bangs us. You know, we drop the deal, put the guy away.
Don't buy it. That's not the way it works."

"What do you mean by that?"

"A guy like you, for example, Ramon. Don't ever forget
we can always whisper into some Colombian's ear a few

words about the wonderful job you're doing for us down there in Medellín."

"Jesus!" Ramon gasped, horrified. "You wouldn't do a thing like that!"

"Don't tempt us is all I'm saying."

"It's outrageous. It's fucking unjust."

Criminals screaming about justice always tended to give Kevin Grady a pain in the ass. "Listen," he told Ramon, "you went to the same catechism classes when you were a kid that I did, right?"

"Yeah, probably."

"Well, where in there did they teach you justice is a part of God's plan for the world? You leave the justice part to us. Just don't ever get it into your mind to double-bang us."

His words left Ramon stunned. "And so what am I supposed to do when I get back down there?" he asked, his tone a shaking whisper.

"Eventually, pretty much what you've already done. Organize a load. The bigger the better. Tell them you've got a safe strip to land it on. But this time, try to do it with their plane, their pilot. Maybe get that guy Paco back on there again. . . ."

"Jesus Christ, Kevin," Ramon protested, "the guy's my friend. Our kids went to Disney World together."

Grady's eyes took on that chill, blank look they'd had back in the hotel room before Ramon had cut his deal. "Betraying your old pals and associates is the name of the game when you're a CI, my friend. It's the informant's currency."

"His thirty pieces of silver, you mean."

The smile in which Grady indulged himself was unintentionally close to a smirk. "There are no friends in your new line of work, Ramon. They're criminals, all of them. They'd give you up in a second to save their skins. This is the way you make a believer out of a judge. It's how you show him you've burned your bridges to the past. You're not giving up some half-ass stuff and saving the real stuff for a future deal."

He whacked Ramon on the thigh. "Come on," he said, "let's swim back and get a beer."

The roof fell in on Ramon later that night when he was alone in his hotel room trying to sleep. The terror his coming betrayal of his Medellín associates inspired, the enormity of what he'd done, of the risks he'd accepted for himself and his unwitting family, overwhelmed him. One image kept recurring in his mind: he was walking down a narrow path, each of its sides surmounted by a perfectly smooth twenty-foot wall. The path had no beginning, and as far as he could see, no end. Where was it taking him? Was it taking him anywhere? Or was it just a path to nowhere like those parallel lines that meet only in infinity?

He decided to go for a walk to compose himself, to exhaust his body so sleep might temporarily obliterate his fears. He strolled down the beach road toward the beckoning beacon of a lighthouse. That flashing light, he thought, was a metronome of the dark hours, a promise of the light beyond the night.

The lighthouse was set on a spit of land at the end of a fifty-foot seawall. To its north, a heavy surf from the open oceans smashed along its base, hissing and seething over a mass of boulders twenty feet below him. To the south, on the seawall's leeward side, the water was still and quiet. Ramon squatted down on his haunches and peered into the raging white foam at his feet, letting the boom and crash of the surf sweep him into its rhythm. It would be so easy to tumble down onto those rocks, one small gesture, a slip of the feet really, a few seconds of pain and panic while the waves battered him against the rocks, and then it would be over. They would rule it an accident, never a suicide. He'd lost his footing, maybe had a few too many drinks. The insurance would pay. His wife and children would not have to live with the stigma of a father who'd been a drug trafficker and then an informer for the hated gringo police. He would be a memory for them, a fond memory.

So absorbed was he in his thoughts that he didn't hear the footsteps approaching along the seawall until Kevin Grady was there beside him. The agent, too, squatted down onto his haunches. For a second he stared into the churning sea.

"I thought about it once too, Ramon," he said finally, his voice so low each word had to struggle to survive above the din of the surf. "I thought I couldn't bear to go on living with the pain and loneliness after she died. It was something she said to me one day near the end that saved me: 'The candle's light is never so lovely as when it begins to sputter. Only a madman would blow it out.'"

The agent gently rested his hand on Ramon's bare forearm. For a second, it seemed to possess a warmth of its own, as if Kevin's was a psychic healer's touch.

"Come on," Kevin said, "let's walk back to the hotel together."

Kevin gave Ramon his final briefing at the hotel the next morning. "We'll go for the load, the big load we talked about," he said, "but don't hurry it. We want you down there with your eyes and ears open for a while. Anything you hear, gossip about a load coming up north, any new trick they're using, what the big guys like Escobar and Ochoa are doing, if they're thinking about leaving the country, who hates who this week, we want to know. Don't you try to decide what's important and what's not. Give it all to us. We'll decide."

The DEA agent never dwelt overlong on the risks a CI was running in his briefings. CI's were people who, after all, had already put themselves in harm's way and didn't need a DEA agent to sketch out for them what danger was all about.

"Keep checking your six o'clock like any good pilot to see who's out there behind you," he advised Ramon. "But otherwise, the main thing is be who you are. Just go right on living your life the way you always lived it. That's what those guys down there expect. The CI's who get into trouble are the ones who pretend to be something they're not, the ones who play at being tough guys because they saw it in a movie somewhere. Be straight up. That's the key. And remember, we're behind you one hundred percent."

"Sure," Ramon laughed, "except behind me is three thousand miles away in New York."

"Figuratively speaking. But I mean it. As far as we're concerned, we're on the same side now."

Ramon started to get up, then sat down again. He slowly twisted his wedding ring off his finger. "If anything goes wrong," he told Kevin, "would you see that my wife gets this? For the time being, I'm going to tell her I've lost it. I think I may tell some people that I see in Medellín that we're divorced. It may be smarter that way."

"I will, I promise," Kevin declared, taking the ring. "But don't worry. You're going to do all right." He stopped his flow of thought. Eddie Gomez and the talk he'd given them in New York had just entered his mind. "One last thing. If you run into anybody down there, a big guy, who wants help moving money out of the United States, tell him you've got a friend up there, maybe an accountant kind of guy who moves money for the Mob. Suggest that the guy could, you know, do something for them. Put them in touch with the right people."

Grady walked Ramon to the door and clapped him on the shoulder. *"Suerte"*—good luck,—he said. "I really mean it."

BOOK SIX

Hell in a Little Glass Vial

There was something grotesque about the scene in the formal dining room of Jorge Luis Ochoa-Vasquez's Hacienda Veracruz near Barranquilla on Colombia's Caribbean seacoast. It was almost a vulgar mimicry of the imperial India of viceroys and maharajahs. Behind each chair stood a footman, poised to cater to his assigned guest's merest whim. The flatware was Georgian sterling, the porcelain was Limoges, the three-piece glass settings, baccarat crystal.

Those wineglasses were not filled, however, with some rare Richebourg of Chateau Margaux. Most contained beer. A couple were filled with scotch whiskey and ice. The elegance here was provided by the surroundings, not the guests.

The occasion was a convocation of the drug barons of the Medellín cartel, a kind of board of directors' luncheon of the world's cocaine traffic. The footmen ringing the walls of the dining room in their white ties and tails were the only well-dressed men in the dining room. Otherwise, there was not a tie in sight, and only two of Ochoa's guests had bothered to put on jackets. The rest wore open-necked sports shirts in colors not too distant from the plumage of Amazonian parrots.

The place of honor at the head of the table was occupied, as always, by Don Pablo Escobar. The main course chosen by Ochoa's chef was *pernil de cerdo,* a Colombian delicacy of marinated pork accompanied this midday by fresh buttered peas. Those peas were giving Escobar trouble. Poor Don Pablo was finding it difficult to get them onto his fork and, once they were there, keeping them on it until they'd reached his mouth. The consequence of his ineptness was a steady dribble of peas onto the table or carpet. Each time one of those errant green balls went rolling off his fork, the footman behind him would have to shoot forward and sweep the offending object into a little silver dust tray.

Opposite Escobar sat the host. Jorge Luis Ochoa was in his mid-thirties, a shortish man, with prosperity's paunch just beginning to swell out over his waistband. He was good-looking in a brooding Latin way with a full head of wavy black hair and dark eyes. Jorge Luis was regarded by his fellow dealers as their Crown Prince of Conspicuous Consumption. If it was expensive and flashy, Jorge Luis was sure to want it. Watches, jewelry, gold baubles, expensive sports cars, extravagances like his own private zoo, Jorge Luis gobbled up possessions the way kids gobble up candy on Halloween night.

Curiously, in view of his occupation, Jorge Luis was a devout Catholic. He was forever jumping into his Porsche Carrera and tooling down to Cali for a pilgrimage to the shrine of the *Virgen de la Merced,* the patron of Colombia. Rare was the Sunday he did not attend Mass and receive communion to ask, his enemies suggested, the Divine's pardon for the lives that had been blighted during the previous week by his cocaine.

Next to Ochoa sat Carlos Lehder Rivas. He was the only member of the cartel's leadership who regularly consumed the drug with which they were flooding the affluent world. Indeed, some of the men at the table were convinced that Lehder, an ardent admirer of Adolf Hitler, had fried away what few brain cells God had given him at birth with the excesses of his coke addiction.

Next to him was Gustavo Gaviria, a remarkably ordinary man who owed his presence at the table to nepotism. He was Pablo Escobar's first cousin. Gaviria's lone distinction stemmed from his arrest in 1976 with a load of thirty-nine kilos of cocaine. That had been, at the time, the largest cocaine seizure on record. Like the young ladies in the Virginia Slim ads, the cartel's leaders had come a long way.

Opposite Gaviria was Jose Gonzalo Rodriguez "El Mejicano" Gacha. There was, in fact, nothing Mexican about Gacha except for his taste for Mexican ranchero music. He came from the emerald-producing areas of Colombia, and was looked on as the cartel's expert in setting up and running their clandestine jungle labs.

Bracketing Escobar at the end of the table were the only two men in the room wearing suit coats. Eduardo Hernandez was the cartel's financial adviser, a handsome, well-educated and soft-spoken man in his mid thirties.

Opposite him was the least well known and certainly the most interesting man at the table, Gerardo "Kiko" Moncada, known to many of his associates in Medellín as "Don Chepe" and to his many foes in the United States Drug Enforcement Administration as the Phantom. The files at the

Washington headquarters of the DEA and its Bogotá field office were thick with reports on every man at the table with one exception: the file of "Kiko" Moncada. His dossier was pencil-thin, and it did not contain a single photograph. No DEA agent, no informant, no journalist or wandering paparazzi had ever succeeded in photographing Moncada.

If Escobar was acknowledged to be the criminal brains of the cartel, Moncada was looked on as the brains, full-stop. He was the Chairman of the Board of Coke, Inc., yet very few people in either Colombia or the world his cartel furnished with drugs were even aware of his existence. With Hernandez, the financier, he was the only member of the cartel to possess a university degree. His was in electrical engineering. He understood, as none of his associates did, how the drugs they sold affected the chemistry of man's brain, and the ravages coke was capable of producing in human beings. More than any other man at the table, Moncada was a thinker. The consequences of one of his thoughts this morning were going to have a devastating effect on the fabric of American society.

The men in Jorge Luis Ochoa's dining room that summer day had every reason to be satisfied with the flourishing state of their enterprise. Since 1976, the amount of cocaine moved out of Colombia had tripled. Not all of that, of course, was shipped through the Medellín drug barons. Their rivals in Cali had their share of the marketplace as did a loose assortment of small-time dealers, *independientes,* based in Bogotá.

As always, Pablo Escobar opened their discussion. "Well," he grunted, "we finally got that son of a bitch Noriega in line. I had one of his officers out at my ranch last week, this captain called Luis Peel, who's supposed to be in charge of shutting down the drug traffic in Panama."

Escobar roared with laughter. He admired the symmetry of that. "You know what he did? He gave me the name, the home address and the photograph of every drug agent the gringos have up there in Panama."

"Pablo," Jorge Luis interrupted, "why go after those guys? That'll just start a war." Ochoa frequently intervened to attempt to control the more violent instincts of his bloodthirsty associate.

"Who's talking about going after them? I'll just send them and their wives a Christmas card to let them know I'm thinking about them." Escobar roared again. No one appreciated his humor more than he did.

Moncada, meanwhile, had pushed his chair back from the table and coughed to get his colleagues' attention. He had decided it was time to take over the meeting.

"What I want to talk about today," he announced, "is where this business of ours is going. Two of my men have just come back from a month in the States. I sent them up there to study the conditions of the marketplace." Moncada looked on the cocaine trade as a marketing and merchandising opportunity.

"The one thing they noticed everywhere they went is that the street prices of our powder are falling, in some places dramatically."

That was not the sort of news any of the men at the table were anxious to hear.

"Now, part of the reason for that," Moncada continued, "is over-supply, which we can deal with since, basically, we control the supply. The second reason, however, is more subtle and I think is going to pose a major long-term threat to our business unless we do something about it."

He leaned forward to take a sip of his coffee and let a little curiosity build in his audience. Moncada's eyes were partially obscured by eyelids which drooped like half-pulled window shades. The effect was to give a suggestion of calculated menace to his regard.

"Who sniffs our coke in the States?" he asked. "Basically, our customers, probably eighty percent of them, are white. Middle-aged. Affluent. Plus the younger people from say, thirty-five on down who have got money to spend. We're very big into the trendsetter industries, the movies, television, music, sports, things like that. The poor people up there by and large don't use our product. How can they when powder retails at a hundred dollars a gram?"

Nothing in Moncada's declaration came as a surprise to anyone at the table.

"What troubles me is this," he continued. "My people came across evidence everywhere they went that those well-to-do whites who've been our prime customers for the last decade are beginning to turn off our product. That's the reason why the street price is falling. Now I'll tell you why they're going off it. For the last seven or eight years sniffing coke for most of those gringos was a kind of once or twice a week habit, the Saturday Night High. People thought they could take the powder or leave it. That it wasn't addictive. Well, in the last two years or so, a lot of people have been finding out that that's not the case, that coke can be addictive, even very addictive. All of a sudden there are scare stories flying around everywhere about people whose habits got out of hand, who wound up in clinics, losing their jobs, wives, homes, having cardiac seizures. Suddenly, a lot of those customers of ours up there are getting worried. They're stopping or cutting back."

Moncada sighed, a lament, perhaps, for all those middle-class consumers the cartel was losing. "The other thing that's happening is that the damn gringos, especially the young, wealthy ones, the trendsetters, have decided they want to be healthy. They drink Perrier water instead of champagne. They go white if they see a piece of red meat. They spend more time in their gyms than the Puritans did in church. Now you all know how the gringos are. They're like lemmings. One of them jumps off a cliff with a hula hoop on, and pretty soon they all want to do it."

Moncada wagged a warning finger at his associates like a schoolteacher admonishing a group of kids who haven't done their homework. "Unless we can do something now to enlarge our market up there, this is going to have a serious long-term effect on our business, believe me."

"Ridiculous!" snapped Carlos Lehder. "I know the gringos better than anyone else here. After all, I spent enough time in their goddamn jails. As long as the gringos have noses on their faces, they'll find a way to stuff them with coke." To underscore the wisdom of his observation, he blasted a fog of mucus from his own coke-ravaged nasal passages.

Fabio Ochoa, the youngest of the three Ochoa brothers present, dismissed Lehder's remark with a contemptuous little ripple of his hand. "Our people are telling us the same thing Kiko's been hearing," he said. "What are we going to do about it?"

"We need to develop a new product line, a new marketplace and, above all, a new price structure," Moncada replied.

"How?" Escobar growled. "We're already trying to push the stuff into Europe."

"I'm not talking about Europe."

"Then what the hell are you talking about, man?"

"The black ghettos in America."

"Are you crazy?" Escobar demanded incredulously. "Those damn niggers can't afford to buy a can of beans for dinner. How the hell are they going to afford our powder?"

"Right now, they aren't. That's what I want to change."

Moncada leaned forward and clasped his hands on the table before him. "Look," he said, "we know one thing. Back in the fifties and sixties when heroin was the American drug craze, the blacks were big consumers. That proves they're a potential market for drugs."

"So what are we supposed to do?" Escobar was as bewildered as he was angry. "Slash the price we're getting for our powder just so a bunch of blacks can get high?"

"No," smiled Moncada, "we've got to find a way to offer blacks coke in a form and at a price they can afford. Look, everybody who's studied drugs knows that if a drug can be inhaled or smoked, the high it produces is much stronger."

"Kiko," Jorge Luis interjected, "so what? Everyone also knows you can't ignite cocaine powder with a blow torch."

"How about *basuco*?" the "Mexican" asked. "The Indians found out how to smoke that."

Basuco was a form of brownish paste produced when too much ether was employed in the process of transforming cocaine base into cocaine powder. It was a foul-smelling product which no American consumer was going to buy. The lab owners often gave it away to their illiterate Indian workers as a kind of bonus. The Indians had discovered that when it was mixed with tobacco, it could be lit and smoked.

Jorge Luis Ochoa emitted a low whistle. "That stuff is murder," he said. "It turns people into zombies. Do you know they had a doctor down there in Peru like the one that was in that movie *One Flew over the Cuckoo's Nest*, remember? He'd cut a piece out of people's brains so they couldn't remember what it felt like to smoke basuco. It was the only way they could find to get them to stop smoking the stuff."

Moncada smiled. "Yes, well that gives you some idea of just how potent smoked powder can be. Get powder into a smokable, inexpensive form, and we will have found the way out of the problems caused by our shrinking middle-class marketplace."

He drew a small, clear plastic vial from his pocket and held it up clenched between his thumb and forefinger so the others could see it. It was about two inches long and filled with what looked like large crystals of unrefined cane sugar.

"This, my friends, is it," he announced. "This is going to transform our business. It is going to be our magic grail. It is cocaine in its purest possible form. Yet you can ignite these little crystals in here one by one with a cigarette lighter, burn them and inhale the smoke they give off."

He paused a second for dramatic effect. "Imagine the most intense orgasm you have ever experienced and multiply it by fifty," he commanded. "That, I am told, is the effect of one deep puff of the fumes of these crystals. It will twist your brain into knots in three seconds. One good puff, just one good puff is enough to hook some people. It can drive people crazy, and I mean literally, crazy, with the desire for more."

Escobar whistled in awe. "Where the hell did you find that stuff?"

"In Cali." It was another of Moncada's idiosyncrasies that he served as a kind of informal liaison between the rival cartels. "One of their chemists came on the technique for making it out of cocaine powder purely by accident."

"How the hell does he do it?" Escobar growled.

"That's the beauty of it. Any damn fool who can bring a kettle of water to boil can make this in his kitchen. You dissolve cocaine powder into a mix of ammonia, water and bicarbonate of soda, boil it, plunge the residue into a pan of ice-cold water. These crystals are what forms when you do that."

"Mother of God!" Escobar whispered in awe. "And that stuff is really as strong as you say it is?"

"Stronger. But the beauty of this is that because the hit is so incredibly strong, you can dilute the powder when you're converting it and still wind up with rocks that will blow people's minds away."

Moncada caressed his little vial as a soothsayer might caress a good-luck charm. "What this means is we can transform our whole marketing operation. The street dealers in the States won't have to sell the product in hundred-dollar envelopes anymore. They'll be able to sell these little crystals for twenty dollars a piece and still make three or four times more money out of a kilo of product than they used to do packaging it up in little bags for sniffers. It will change our marketplace up there overnight."

"Si, si, si," Escobar whistled. "Twenty dollars a hit, the blacks can afford that, all right." He guffawed. "If that stuff's as strong as you say it is, those idiots will be buying that before they buy their breakfast cereal. So what do we do? Convert it down in our jungle labs from the powder?"

"Why bother?" Moncada replied. "The people down in Cali have a better idea. One of their distributors has contacts with those two black street gangs they've got up there in L.A., the Crips and the Bloods. He's going to give them a little lesson in home chemistry." Moncada chuckled, beaming with the satisfaction that image had produced in his imagination. "Once those clowns see the money they can make off these rocks, there'll be no stopping them. They'll do the dog-shit work for us. All we'll have to do is sit back, rake in the profits, and watch the fires burn. You talk about the ant army! We'll have an army of idiots out on the streets peddling the stuff for us in no time at all."

"You make that stuff sound really dangerous," Jorge Luis Ochoa mumbled.

Escobar sneered. Concern for the well-being of his customers rarely moved him. "Hey! Who cares if we fry up the brains of those blacks? We'll be doing the gringos a favor, right? Solve their race problem for them. Get rid of one of their races." Escobar guffawed in appreciation of his wit.

Moncada, in the meantime, had wrapped his fist around his little vial and plunged it back into his pocket. "That's the future of our business, my friends, right there in that plastic vial." He laughed, just a hint of hysteria mingling with his glee, too. "Before we're through, we'll be selling these crystals to the gringos for what one of their Big Macs costs. And our jungle labs won't be able to keep up with the demand for powder!"

Lind's Tape

It was one of those stiflingly hot tropical nights, the kind of an evening when it seems you could squeeze the moisture from the air with your fist. I was stretched out on the balcony of the apartment of one of our junior counsels, sweating profusely and in a state of considerable nervous apprehension.

First, I was not an invited guest in the young lady's flat. She had gone out for dinner and a night of disco dancing with one of our young officers attached to the Corozal station. Hers was an embassy apartment. The housing section had a duplicate set of keys with which I had let myself in after she'd left on her date.

The building was set at the end of Calle Thirty-two just a few yards from the Avenida Balboa and the Bay of Panama. Next to it, at the corner of the avenida and the calle was a modest two-story building painted white with brown stone trimmings. That structure housed the Libyan embassy, which explained my presence on our young counsel's balcony.

The embassy was surrounded by a protective wall surmounted by a black iron grille. Crouched at its base, directly in my line of vision, were two young men dressed in black jeans, black long-sleeved T-shirts, gloves and hoods. They were, in fact, U.S. Army noncommissioned officers, members of a top-secret outfit called Yellow Fruit, a division of the Quick Reaction Team of the Army's Intelligence and Security Command. They specialized in surreptitious entry and the installation of electronic surveillance devices.

On the building's second floor was the office of the embassy's third secretary, an engaging fellow who spoke fluent Spanish and English, and who was in constant and very discreet attendance at every radical gathering in the city. In reality, the gentleman, Said Abou Khalidi, was as much a Libyan diplomat as I was.

He was a Palestinian and he was Yassir Arafat's PLO pointman not only for Panama, but for all Central America, Colombia and Venezuela. If things went as I hoped they would during the next forty-five minutes, there would henceforth be very few of Mr. Khalidi's words, plans, contacts and conversations of which we would not be aware.

At precisely ten minutes past midnight, I heard the sound for which I was waiting, the metallic crash of crumpling car fenders, followed, instants later, by an angry barrage of shouts and curses.

The Libyans, quite naturally, had equipped their embassy with an array of hi-tech security devices, including a dozen closed-circuit TV surveillance cameras. At night those cameras were monitored on screens in the porter's lodge just behind the main entrance to the embassy on the Avenida Balboa.

As luck would have it, the traffic accident whose sounds had just rung in my ears had occurred right in front of the porter's lodge. At this very moment the drivers were, I assumed, squaring off for a fistfight over who was responsible for the crash. They were a pair of Hispanic agency employees brought in for the occasion. Off in the distance I heard the wail of a siren, and could just see the reflection of the blinking red rooflight of the approaching patrol car.

That would be the officer Noriega had assigned us. Once the situation was under control, he would summon the embassy night watchman, as the only witness to the accident, to join him in his patrol car to complete a detailed accident report form. Twenty minutes was what the two young men crouched at the wall below had said they'd need; twenty minutes was what they were going to get.

As the clamor died, I heard the words *He's out* in the earpiece in my left ear. I gestured to our two Yellow Fruit operatives. They looped some kind of a rope over the spikes of the grille topping the embassy wall. The first one climbed up. He surveyed the embassy's inner courtyard for a second, beckoned to his partner, and dropped into the compound. The partner followed.

Noriega had furnished us with a blueprint of the embassy and the details of its security system, which he'd gotten from the contractor who'd installed it. We also knew that on the PLO representative's desk was a big table lamp, a rather garish device mounted on a long, tubular, shiny metallic stand. It was one of half a dozen such lamps furnished to the embassy by their local decorator. Working off a similar lamp, we'd set up our scheme.

What the two Yellow Fruit operatives had to do was, first, unscrew the lamp's baseplate. The lamp's power cord passed through a hole in the side of the plate and fed up into the light socket. They would disconnect the wiring, then rewire it so the power would pass through an omnidirectional microphone the size of a little finger. The mike was equipped with its own power pack. They would then run a second wire from the mike to the base of the metal stand, converting it into an antenna, hook the original electric wiring back up to the light socket, and reattach the baseplate. The mike worked twenty-four hours a day off its power pack, and every time our friend from the PLO turned on his lamp, he would be recharging the power pack for us.

I lay on the terrace trying not to look at my watch or think about the consequences of our getting caught. You could imagine the headlines: U.S. Army Personnel Caught Violating Diplomatic Premises on the Soil of a Friendly Nation. That wouldn't do anything to lower Bill Casey's blood pressure.

Lying there, trying to force my mind into other channels, I began to think about Gadhaffi and his Libyan capital, Tripoli. To the best of my knowledge, we had no CIA operatives under cover there. We had to work at one remove, through the Mossad and Egyptian Intelligence.

I had recently recruited a young officer now assigned to our station in Buenos Aires. His father was Panamanian, his mother American. He'd been brought up in the States, went to Penn, but had spent so much time in Panama people here looked on him as a Panamanian.

Suppose I asked Noriega to recruit our Panamanian for Panama's diplomatic service, then assign him to their embassy in Tripoli? That would give us for the first time in years a CIA agent inside Gadhaffi's capital. It would be a coup of considerable magnitude. You could say what you wanted about PK\BARRIER\7-7's character flaws; the fact was, he was one hell of an asset.

Sixteen long minutes after they'd entered the building, I saw the first of our army noncoms climbing back over the grille. The second followed an instant later. The operation had worked. From now on the PLO's Mr. Khalidi wouldn't be able to light a cigarette in his office without our microphone picking up the noise of his match scratching his matchbox.

"Socio!" Ray "Ramon" Marcello swallowed up his friend and associate Paco Garrone in a Latin bear hug, his open palms thumping Paco's shoulder blades with well-feigned enthusiasm. It was almost, he thought, as though he was looking for the right spot in which to stick the knife.

The two men had not met since they'd successfully run their thousand-kilo load into West Palm Beach. Their reunion, therefore, had all the earmarks of a celebration. The locale was Garrone's law office, a well-furnished suite on the tenth floor of a standard steel and glass tower in the center of old Medellín.

Garrone waved Ramon to a leather armchair and ordered

his stunning blond secretary to bring them cafe tintos and thimble-like glasses of Aguardiente Cristal, a clear, licorice-flavored liqueur jokingly referred to in Medellín's late-night discos as "The Breakfast of Champions." The two clinked glasses like a pair of Red Army colonels downing a toast of vodka, then refilled their glasses from a Lalique decanter on Paco's coffee table.

Paco Garrone was a rarity in Medellín, a man as tasteful in spending money as he was skilled in making it. The decoration of his office suite was built around a collection of pre-Columbian antiquities, a collection which he had assembled with care and knowledge. None of his colleagues could rival the beauty and variety of his pieces.

For a few minutes the two friends gossiped about their lives and trade. Suddenly, Paco, an observant man, pointed at Ramon's finger. "Hey, socio," he asked, "where's your wedding ring?"

Ramon rubbed his now carefully tanned finger and offered his friend what was meant to be a wan smile. "She left me."

"Hombre! Why?"

"I got caught with my hand in the cookie jar one time too many, I guess."

Paco slapped his knee. "They're crazy, these women," he lamented with a fine macho appreciation of the situation. "Never mind. There's plenty of others out there." He gestured toward his reception room, where his gorgeous blond secretary awaited his largely nonexistent clientele. "Take Conchita out to dinner. She'll get your mind off your troubles in a hurry."

Remorse, genuine remorse, tugged at Ramon's bowels. Here this guy is really sorry for me, he thought. He's trying to do something to ease this imaginary pain of mine, and why am I sitting here? Because I'm trying to find a way to send him to prison for a quarter of a century—in my place.

"So what's going on out there?" he asked his friend. "What's on offer?" Ramon's conscience might have been uneasy, but it was not so uneasy that it was going to imperil the deal he'd made with the DEA.

"The usual. Nothing's changed. How about your friend Ottley? Will he make another trip for us?"

Ramon laughed. "Ottley? He's so busy spending the money he made on his last trip he hasn't come up for air yet.

But if we can get a plane, we can do a plane gig. I've got a really good guy with a secure strip in northern Georgia."

"He doesn't have a plane of his own?"

"Oh, sure, he's got an old Piper Cub, but what good is that going to do us?"

"Those guys up at the compound don't like to risk their own planes." Paco sipped his *aguardiente*. "You know what they're really interested in up at the compound these days? Money. All from this new thing they got, this 'crack' stuff."

Ramon chuckled. "So what else is new?"

"Not making money, my friend. Moving it. Finding a way to get their money out of the United States. That's their biggest problem right now. They don't know what to do with all the cash they've got up there. Millions of dollars. Millions."

Ramon suddenly recalled Kevin Grady's parting words. He tried to appear wholly indifferent to his Colombian colleague's suggestion. Colombians in the drug trade were as wary of eagerness as a cat is of sudden movements.

"So why," he asked, "don't they just stuff it into a couple of suitcases and fly out with it?"

"My friend, do you have any idea how much space a couple of million dollars in twenty-dollar bills can take up?" Paco leaned forward, his hands clasped together as if in prayerful awe before what was involved here.

"Since you left, I've gotten very close to a guy named Hernandez, Eduardo Hernandez. He's the man in charge of the money for the cartel. He's responsible for finding ways to get their money out of the States.

"Their real problem," Paco explained, "is to find ways to bend the banking system up there. Okay, once in a while they'll put the money in a bunch of sacks and try to fly it out in someone's airplane. But that's dangerous and expensive. They've lost too many flights that way. What they need is people who can back their money into the system legally for them, so they can get it into the international marketplace."

"Where do we fit in? We're not bankers."

"If you know somebody up in the States, if you could find us a connection, then maybe we could get into this."

"Ah." Ramon tried as hard as he could to indicate to his associate that the light was dawning at long last.

"They pay a percentage as a service fee to the guy who moves the money. We could ask for a cut. These are big sums we're talking. Millions of dollars a month. A small cut of that adds up fast. And the beauty of it is, we don't have to get close. We don't touch the powder. We minimize our risks of arrest."

Ramon got up and walked to the balcony of Paco's office. From his perch he could see one of Medellín's landmarks, a statue of La Belle Otero referred to as *the Fat Lady* perched, appropriately enough in the circumstances, on the approach to the Banco de la Republica. He had understood one thing very clearly when he'd cut his deal with the DEA. Ultimately, he would be expected to get a load into the United States. The load would be seized and that would be it. His value as an informant would be at an end. He would go to jail and serve off whatever balance the government and a judge decided should be left on his sentence. At the very least he would have to do ten years.

But maybe this money thing offered some other possibilities. It might go on for some time, and that would be time he'd still be free and out of jail. More important, it would let him get close to the heart of the cartel. That would make him more valuable to the DEA. Then they might want to keep his operation up and running longer than they usually did.

He turned back to Paco. "Listen," he said, "back in '68 when I was in college I had a real good friend. He was an Italian like me. Did you ever hear the word 'wasp'—white, Anglo-Saxon Protestant?"

"Sure."

"Well, at Lafayette, you had wasps buzzing around you every time you stepped out the door. So a couple of *paisanos* like us, we ran together. A natural thing. Then when we got out, he went to Boston University and got a master's degree in finance. I've seen him maybe half a dozen times since we graduated. His father was very heavy, very big in one of those Mafia families up in New York. One night about five years ago we were drinking together; he sort of told me that that was why he went to business school, to help the family manage its money. He suspected I was in drugs. He said, 'Hey, if one day you need some help with moving money, stuff like that, maybe I can put you in touch with the right people.'"

Paco sat slowly back into his leather armchair, giving as he did a little pinch to the tip of his mustache as though somehow that might slow the spread of the contented smile working its way across his countenance.

"Socio," he said, "you might just have something there. I want to bring you up to the compound so you can meet my friend Don Eduardo." The compound was the former city residence of Jorge Luis Ochoa, the place which the principal figures of the cartel used as their in-town office.

"Hey, my friend," Ramon protested, "you know me. I don't like to meet new people. The fewer people you know in this business, the better off you are."

His words were, of course, a smokescreen. Ramon understood the Medellín mentality. Tell a trafficker, "Hey, I'd like to meet some of your friends," and he would start getting suspicious. On the other hand, make a big thing out of not meeting someone and they could hardly wait to introduce you to the guy.

"No, no," Paco assured him, "you're going to like Eduardo. He's a real gentleman, not a slob like Pablo and the Mexican and some of the others. He's a university man." Paco offered that as though somehow higher education was the surest guarantee of a man's social acceptability. "He's got a master's degree in business."

"Let me think about it." Ramon made certain the weakening in his attitude was apparent.

Paco was already squirming like a puppy who's just sniffed frying meat. He always reacted that way to the prospect of making money.

"Sure, sure, think about it. But don't take too long," he laughed. "Time is money."

It was spread all over Kevin Grady's face once again, that taut, chilly smile he reserved for moments of intense satisfaction.

"Guess what?" he asked, entering unbidden into the New York office of his boss, Richie Cagnia. "Our girl's been invited to the senior prom."

"Kev, what the hell is that supposed to mean?"

"Our new CI, that guy Ramon we recruited down in Aruba. He's been invited to the compound in Medellín to have a chat with the guy that moves the cartel's money."

Cagnia pursed his lips and let out an admiring whistle. "A DEA informant inside the compound! Heavy, man, real heavy." He thought for a moment. "We better get that guy

Gomez who briefed us on the money thing on the squawker. This may be something he can run with."

He picked up his FTS line and turned on his conference speaker. Once he had Gomez on the line he let Grady brief him on what Ramon had reported to him from a pay phone in Bogotá.

"Yeah," Gomez glowed, "with a little luck we could make this thing work and work big-time. Although the truth of the matter is we don't have a 'how to do it' kit worked up on these money cases yet. We're going to have to feel our way along here. We don't want anybody making any mistakes and leaving us with a dead CI on our hands."

Lind's Tape

Tony Noriega ascended to the throne of Panama on August 12, 1983. That was the day PK\BARRIER\7-7 took command of Panama's National Guard, which meant, in effect, that he was taking over Panama. For me, as the man who had recruited him for the CIA and run him all these years, that was a moment of considerable satisfaction, a CIA asset taking control of a strategically situated Latin nation. And just at the moment when that nation had become central to our policy concerns.

With characteristic ingenuity, Noriega had arranged his triumph in the name of democracy. He had persuaded his boss, the commander of the National Guard, a general named Ruben Paredes, to call for a presidential election, then resign his commission and run for president himself. Noriega would take over the Guard and deliver its support, he'd promised, to Paredes, thus assuring his election.

Clearly, that watershed in our asset's career called for a visit to Panama, so I flew into Howard Air Force Base the day before the handover ceremony. I tried to call Juanita to announce my arrival. Her phone, alas, was on her answering machine; she was out of the country. Finally, as I was leaving for my flight, I left my agency dead-end number, the one to which an operator replies by reciting the number the caller has just dialed and taking a message, on her machine.

"Your boy's building himself a new office to go with his

new job," Glenn Archer, our station chief, informed me when he met me at Howard.

"So where's his new home?" I asked.

"Out at Fort Amador. In Building 8."

Fort Amador had long been a key U.S. military installation in the old Canal Zone, one of those we'd recently turned over to the Panamanians under the new Canal treaty. It was in Building 8 that Noriega had followed, at our behest, his first U.S.–sponsored course in military intelligence.

"Believe me," Glenn said, "no Southcom GI will recognize the place when he gets finished with it. He's putting in black marble bathrooms, gold faucets—the works."

For our meeting that night Noriega had proposed one of his secret retreats, a former Canal company bungalow known as Building 152 on the causeway stretching out from Fort Amador along the Pacific entrance to the Canal. He used it for drinking sessions with his buddies, for discreet meetings such as ours, or for his regular rendezvous with whatever young lady happened to be his flavor of the month.

If he had been ebullient at our last meeting, there was a new sense of calm, of self-confidence, in the man that night. There was almost a suggestion that our roles had been reversed. He was no longer a supplicant for CIA aid, an asset in need of a helping hand. He was receiving me that evening as the *de facto* head of a sovereign state.

For a while we chatted over our Old Parr, a note of rather fond nostalgia animating our conversation. We reminisced about the first meeting we'd had so many years ago in our David safehouse and the long road we'd traveled together since. I congratulated him on having fulfilled all of the high expectations we'd had for him that night.

When we got down to current affairs, I asked him whether we could count on Paredes' understanding of our contra policy in the event of his election as President.

Noriega scoffed. "Don't worry about Ruben. He's not going to be running *for* anything. *Away* from a few things, maybe.

"Listen," he continued, "I have an idea for a project we could cooperate on. It would benefit us both."

"What's that?"

"I want to set up a modern communications interception system next door to my new headquarters."

His telecommunications specialists, he explained, had

studied the matter closely. All Panama's telephone communications passed through one central switching center at the Post and Telecommunications headquarters in Panama City. What he wanted to do was install a sophisticated computer-run system that would automatically intercept all calls to and from the numbers it had been programmed to monitor. It would then reroute those calls to his interception center, where they would be recorded on voice-activated tape reels.

"Where do we come in?" I asked him.

"We'll need some technical help setting it up. Plus the computers we need are subject to your export restrictions. And, of course, some financial aid."

I smiled and sipped my whiskey. "And what do we get out of it?"

"Access. Your station gives us the numbers you're interested in listening to here. We program them into the computer. Your people can come by each week and pick up the tape reels."

Now that was an offer of considerable magnitude. Sure, the NSA intercepted all the calls coming into or out of Panama on micro-wave links. But the calls on the country's landbased lines, which included Costa Rica, escaped our surveillance. And there was a lot to listen to on them. There were banks, left-wing Latin American revolutionary groups, Puerto Rican nationalists, firms in the Free Trade Zone we suspected of violating our embargo on trade with Cuba, or conspiring to get around our hi-tech trading restrictions with the Soviet Bloc.

Admittedly, Noriega was going to use the system we'd be financing in part at least to suppress his political opposition in Panama. That was contrary to every principle for which the U.S. was supposed to stand. However, this wasn't the U.S. We were playing by a different set of rules here. National security had to be our primary concern, not the niceties of Panama's political situation. And keeping PK\BARRIER\7-7 in power at this critical juncture in our evolving contra war was certainly the key concern here.

"Tony," I told him, "I'll have to get this approved up the line, but my gut feeling is we won't have a problem. Providing we keep it very, very discreet."

He nodded in understanding.

I then ran my idea of placing a CIA officer on the Panamanian diplomatic list in Libya past him.

He liked it. Not only did he agree that they could do it,
but he volunteered the thought that their diplomatic posts in
Eastern Europe might be able to help us out from time to
time with cover and the use of their pouches.

It was, all in all, the most satisfying meeting I ever had
with Noriega. Not only was he taking over, but our relations
with him were moving up to a level of cooperation well beyond anything we had been able to achieve up until now.
°K\BARRIER\7-7 was finally realizing that night his full
potential as a CIA asset..

The handover ceremony the next day was, by Panamanian
standards, grandiose. There were paratroopers, sky divers,
armored vehicles and booming howitzers. Indeed, I doubt
that there was anyone in the country entitled to wear a uniform who wasn't lined up on parade. Needless to say, I
watched it from the discreet distance of the television set in
my hotel room.

Tony concluded the ceremony by embracing Paredes in
the traditional back-thumping Latin bear hug. "Ruben," he
proudly proclaimed, "we give you over to your friends, the
people." He ended shouting out the paratrooper's salute,
"Good Jump!"

Poor Paredes had a good jump, all right—except his parachute didn't open. Two weeks later, he couldn't set foot on
a Panamanian military base without an official pass. His political career as Noriega had predicted was going absolutely
nowhere.

My cup, however, was running over. Late that afternoon,
I received a message informing me a Miss Boyd had returned and was awaiting my call.

Juanita was magnificent, moving through the dials of her
VHF radio with the poise of an American Airlines captain
preparing to take off from O'Hare or JFK.

"Hotel Papa Three Four Zero to Paitilla Ground Control,"
she announced into her radio. "Request runway clearance
for departure Contadora."

"Paitilla Ground Control to Hotel Papa Three Four Zero.
Clearance is granted. Change to tower frequency 118.3"
came the reply. Hotel Papa—HP, Juanita had explained,
were the letters that preceded all Panamanian-registered aircraft. She began to move the knob of her VHF radio with a
series of quick flicks. "I'm going to the tower frequency,

118.3," she explained. "I should get a newer radio in here that would do this for me automatically."

"Hotel Papa Three Four Zero," the tower informed her when she made contact, "you are cleared for immediate takeoff. Zero cross-winds, altimeter setting 29.98. Climb straight out to five thousand feet and contact Approach Control on 119.7. Have a nice day."

"Roger. I ETA Contadora at three-forty Zulu."

Juanita turned from the radio, built up the power on her engines, released her brakes, and sent us skimming down the runway. As the Piper lifted off, I could see to my left the military hangar from which Felipe Nadal was handling the transshipment of our arms from the Colon Free Trade Zone up to the contras.

"I have something a little different in mind for you to-day," Juanita announced playfully as we climbed to five thousand feet and turned into the approach radio frequency. Behind us, the towers of Panama City were receding on the horizon.

"Not *too* different, I hope."

"Have you ever been deep sea fishing?"

"You mean for marlin and things like that?"

"Exactly."

"Never."

"My brother Pedro has a new fishing boat out at Contadora. He's going to give it to us for the day. We'll see how you like it."

"Juanita, with you beside me I'd find fishing for catfish with a bamboo pole exciting."

"Believe me, Jack"—Juanita was laughing with malicious delight—"marlin are not the same breed of fish as catfish are, as you'll discover if you're lucky enough to get one on your line."

Contadora Island, our destination, was a twenty-minute flight from Panama City at the head of the Las Perlas, the Pearl Islands chain. It had enjoyed a brief bout of fame in the late seventies as the island refuge of the dying Shah of Iran. Once the island had sheltered the counting-house in which the minions of the kings of Spain had counted up the treasures of Las Perlas, pearls the size of nuts, according to legend, as they headed off to the court of Castille.

"Do you still find pearls out here?" I asked her.

"All the time. Around the necks of our wealthier visitors."

A jeep met us at the Contadora landing strip and drove us down to the docks where Juanita's brother's boat, the *Quasimodo*, was waiting for us. It was not your smelly Chesapeake Bay fishing trawler or Maine lobsterman. There was a spacious lounge, a galley with microwave ovens and a deepfreeze and, forward, a beautifully appointed master bedroom suite.

The captain was a study in contrast to the elegance of the boat. He was in shorts and a T-shirt, barefoot, with a pair of big toes whose bones bulged out like massive marbles. They, I imagined, were the legacy of all those years clinging to a flying bridge with bare feet in a heavy sea. His face had the texture of old leather; his eyes were tightened into a perpetual squint. We headed off in search of a run of refuse, a trail of flotsam dragged along by an ocean current. Marlin and sailfish tended to prowl the edges of those streams, Juanita explained, pouncing on the smaller fish which fed there.

After half an hour's search, we found the stream we were looking for. The crew buckled Juanita and me into the boat's game-fishing chairs set side by side on the stern. Then they baited our lines and clamped our fishing poles into sockets on the plates attached to each chair. From the bridge, the captain began to maneuver the boat along the fringe of the stream.

I glanced at Juanita. She was taking this, as she seemed to take everything from lovemaking to Panamanian politics, very seriously. She was wearing old blue jeans, loose-fitting these, a man's white cotton shirt, its tails knotted at her waist. On her head she had a tattered straw hat, the loose ends of the palm thatchings which had originally composed it hanging from its brims like spokes. She was tugging her pole backward and forward with a steady, almost mechanical movement.

"How will I know if we get a bite?" I asked. Fishing was not an activity at which I'd spent much time.

Juanita laughed. "If it's a marlin, you'll know, all right. That's why we buckle you into the chair. So he doesn't take you out for a swim in the Pacific."

It must have been fifteen minutes later, I suppose, when my rod suddenly bent into a tight arc and I felt a terrific pull on my line.

"I got one!" I shouted.

Juanita gestured at the locking device on my reel. "Quick," she ordered, "let him have the line."

I flicked the switch on the lock and the line went sizzling out with a high whine.

"When he's pulling on you, let him run," Juanita instructed. "Then as soon as you feel the line go slack, start to reel the line back in," she told me. "You want to avoid slack in the line. That's when they're dangerous. Leave them too much running room and they'll surface, leap out of the water, and snap your line on you."

She had set aside her own line now to coach me with my fish. "Don't fight him," she warned. "When he wants line, give him line. Then you take it back and tug him in a bit each time he eases off. There's a rhythm you're looking for."

As I followed her instructions, she was studying the flat gray Pacific behind us.

"I don't think it's a marlin," she announced. "There's not enough pull on there for that."

The words were barely out of her mouth when a hundred yards or so astern a silver flash shot from the water. For a second my fish was suspended in the air, quivering, seeming to shake the water from his fins as a dog shakes water from his coat when he emerges from the sea.

"The slack!" Juanita cried, seeing me gape in awe at the sight. "Reel in your slack."

Then the fish dropped with a splash back into the depths from which he'd sprung.

"It's a yellow fin tuna," Juanita announced. "Maybe you didn't get a marlin, but at least you got us lunch."

For the next fifteen minutes, I slowly drew the fish to the boat, where a crewman waited to spear him with a gaff. Watching him thrashing out the last gasps of his life on the planking of the *Quasimodo,* I experienced a strange mixture of sadness and exhilaration.

Juanita glanced at him with appraising eyes. "Forty, maybe fifty pounds," she said. "Now you have some idea of what it can be like to have a hundred pounds of marlin on the line."

My yellow-fin, as it turned out, was to be our only strike of the day. Juanita finally decided to order the crew to strike the rods, announcing, "We'll find our sport somewhere else."

We were off Saboga Island, a sparsely inhabited sister isle

of Contadora. She told the captain to put in at one of her favorite coves. It was a place out of a travel brochure: a silver
crescent of beach in front of a dark emerald band of jungle;
aquamarine water so clear you could count the pebbles of
the seafloor fifteen feet below the surface.

Juanita and I decided to have a swim while the crew made
us lunch. I rolled like a lazy porpoise through the warm wa-
er, so different from the icy Atlantic off Long Island in my
youthful summers, while she plunged and twisted beside me.
By the time I finally got out, she'd already gone in, showered, and put on a dry white bikini which set off that tanned,
well-honed body of hers to perfection.

The crew, meanwhile, had laid out our lunch: prawns,
steaks sliced from my tuna, and ice-cold beer. Opening
one, I glanced out at the turquoise sea, then at this stunning
creature beside me. "Boy," I laughed, "a man could get used
o this awfully easily."

I sat down and started to crack open a prawn. "Where
were you the last few days?" I asked.

"In Costa Rica. Visiting friends. I couldn't stand being
here and having to watch that grotesque, ghastly charade
yesterday."

"Noriega's takeover of the army, you mean?"

"The army?" Her words came in a scornful sneer. "The
country, you mean. Can you imagine anything worse? Having your country placed in the hands of a gangster?"

I thought of the man with whom I'd envisaged such a
fruitful future barely seventy-two hours earlier. "A few
things, yeah. There's got to be something good about
Noriega, Juanita."

"Well, you're wrong. There isn't. At least some of the
things Torrijos did really helped the people. Not with
Noriega, though. To him, Panama isn't a country. It's an
economic opportunity."

She snapped the shell off one of her prawns with an angry
gesture, then popped the tail into her mouth. "I get so sick
and tired of listening to Ronald Reagan talking about teaching democracy to the Sandinistas. You're such damn hypocrites, you Americans. If you're so damn interested in
democracy, why don't you start by doing something about
this damn police state you've saddled us with?"

She hurled the remains of the prawn's shell overboard
with an energy that indicated she was probably dreaming of

throwing it at Panama's little-loved leader. Given the baggage I was carrying, this was obviously not a conversation I was anxious to pursue. Trampling on Panamanians' civil liberties, which Noriega was doing on every possible occasion, wasn't an action of which we were supposed to approve, but we needed our Tony for the moment, and the Panamanians were just going to have to wait to get their civil liberties back.

Juanita had apparently mistaken my silence for either indecision or approbation.

"Noriega and those thugs he works with in the military run Panama the way your Mafia runs New York. Launder your restaurant's tablecloths in our laundry or you'll have a fire in here some night. Can you imagine? We now have the *capo de famiglia* of our Mafia installed in our White House thanks to you gringos."

She sighed in anger and frustration. "I'm sorry, Jack. I swore to myself I wasn't going to go on like this with you. You're my good gringo. I know it's not your fault what that damned government of yours does here. It's our problem. And there are some of us who are ready to do something about it."

I felt a chill descend my spine at those words. "What the hell do you mean by that?"

"Jack, if a bunch of gangsters took over your country, would you just stand by and let them do it? Does your freedom mean so little to you, you wouldn't fight for it? That's how some of us here feel."

"Jesus, Juanita!" I remember those words coming out as a gasp as much as anything else. "Be careful about what you're getting yourself into here. People like Noriega don't take prisoners." As I said those words, I looked at this lovely, aristocratic woman. Surely she couldn't be thinking of becoming some kind of urban Central American guerrilla? And warring against the man who was the CIA's most important asset in the area into the bargain?

She stood, up smiling that half-mocking smile of hers once again. "As you've discovered, Jack, I'm a big girl. I know what I'm doing. And right now I'm inviting you down to inspect the forward cabin."

The ocean's gentle swell rocked the cabin with the tenderness of a mother stirring the cradle of her newborn. Its calence provided a haunting counterpoint to the frenzy of our lovemaking during that long afternoon. The curtains across the cabin's two portholes were drawn; an enormous double bed filled virtually the entire cabin. With the door shut and the air conditioning on, it was almost as though we were locked into some mysterious space capsule from which we would not be allowed to emerge until we'd made love to the point of utter exhaustion.

At some moment, I no longer remember when, Juanita reached up into the ledge above the bed and took down something that looked for all the world like a solid silver suppository.

"Coke," she explained. "Do you want a snort?"

I shook my head.

She pointed playfully toward my groin. "They say a little sprinkled there can be very exciting."

"Believe me, that part of my being is getting all the excitement it can handle at the moment."

She placed the silver bullet in one of her nostrils, closed the other with a finger and sniffed. Then she repeated the process with the other nostril.

What effect it had on her, I couldn't tell. We plunged back into another burst of lovemaking. When we'd finished, she took my hand and pressed it onto her breast.

"Feel," she commanded.

The racing beat of her heart pulsated under my fingertips.

"Me?" I laughed.

"No, darling," Juanita giggled. "The coke."

Finally, we both drifted off to sleep. When I awoke, the brightness of the light playing at the edges of the porthole curtain was muted. Outside, the sun must have been sinking to the horizon. For a few minutes I lay there without moving, listening to the measured beat of Juanita's breathing on the bed beside me.

Try not to think, an inner voice was urging me. Wasted advice. Thinking was all I seemed to be able to do. What in hell was I going to do about this obsessive love, passion, lust—call it whatever you like—which had overwhelmed me? Was it something for which I should blow my life apart? Already, it had cast a shadow over my marriage. Sarah Jane had begun to sense the strain. Could I gratuitously hurt her and my sons in the selfish pursuit of whatever it was that was consuming me?

And leaving Sarah Jane would certainly pull the plug on
my agency career. Not only was marriage to a foreign national regarded with something less than enthusiasm a
Langley, but in this case I was getting involved with a
woman who just might be trying to overthrow a man who
was not only a vital CIA asset but my own agent as well.

I rolled up onto my elbow and gazed down at Juanita'
sleeping face. It was as breathtaking in repose as it wa
when she was awake. How could I give her up?

She blinked her eyes open, those soft blue eyes which a
first glance seemed to promise the softness of the angels.
had fallen into the abyss they concealed, and what was wait
ing there was something quite remote from the angel's ca
ress.

She sensed my concern. "What's the matter?"

"Nothing. Everything."

"Jack," she whispered, reading my thoughts perfectly
"don't try to imagine me as something I'm not. Don't try to
picture me as a suburban housewife in Virginia o
Westchester, driving the children to dancing school, worry
ing about the Lobster Newburg I'm going to make for you
boss at our Friday night buffet. That's not me. That's not the
woman you're captivated by."

She flicked my lips with her fingernail, a gesture she liked
to use to get my attention at moments like this. "And don'
start daydreaming about throwing everything over and running off to Panama like a truant. What fulfillment woulc
there be for you here besides our relationship? You'd be a
rich woman's trinket. You'd hate it. Or if you didn't hate it
I'd begin to hate you for not hating it."

"We can't go on like this forever."

"Nothing is forever, Jack. Everything ends."

Why did she have to say that? Why did she have to dis-
concert me with truth when what I really wanted was illusions? Sensing my sadness, she rolled into my arms.

"Don't be unhappy, Jack," she whispered. "After all, is
what we have right now so bad?"

Paco Garrone drove a Jaguar. He felt the car went well
with the elegant yet sporty image he was trying to cultivate
despite the notably unathletic lines that encompassed his
pudgy body. With Ramon sitting tensely beside him, he
whipped the car through the curving traces of the road run-

ning above Medellín's El Poblado neighborhood toward the Tabla, the high plateau. It was shortly past noon. The working days of Medellín's drug barons did not begin at sun-up.

Half a mile farther on, the road dipped and turned right. As it did, they started to run alongside a dark gray cement wall fifteen feet high. It was topped by a crust of bright red tiles strung with barbed wire, and punctuated at intervals with little skull and crossbones designs indicating that the wire was electrified. Paco jerked his head toward the wall. "That's it!" he announced. "The compound."

Ramon stared at the gray wall running as far down the road as he could see. More than anything else, it looked like the perimeter wall of a penitentiary. Under the circumstances, it was not the most comforting image his mind could have conjured up. Another half a mile down the road was the compound's steel gate. A guard tower dominated the entrance. Inside, a pair of guards, making no effort to conceal their automatic weapons, scrutinized Paco's Jaguar. One picked up a clipboard, checked Paco's license plate against a list on the board, and waved them inside.

As the car entered, the gates slid shut behind it. Ramon could sense the worried beating of his heart under his suit jacket and a nervous tightening in his bowels. At the same time, a triumphant thought crossed his mind: he was, without any doubt, the first informant of the United States Drug Enforcement Administration to go through that gate. I just hope, he prayed, I'll be the first one to get back out as well.

Paco drove toward an open area in which a dozen cars and jeeps were parked. To the left of the lot was a large artificial lake, its surface flecked with ducks, geese and a dozen swans. Beyond the lake lay a well-groomed forest. Ramon spotted half a dozen deer darting through its shadows. For some strange reason, a consuming passion for animals united Colombia's drug dealers.

At the entrance to the compound itself was a desk manned by three overweight pistolero/receptionists, their shirt tails hanging out of their pants to cover their sidearms. Paco gave their names. One of the three verified Paco and Ramon against the day's visitor's list, then pointed to a huge sitting room just off the entrance hall.

At least a dozen other supplicants for the cartel's favors were already waiting there. Paco and Ramon settled onto a big leather sofa. A pair of maids in impeccably starched white uniforms moved through the room offering the assembly cups of cafe tinto. Across the room from Ramon and Paco, a trio of teenagers were playing with a MAC-10 submachine gun, taking turns unloading its fully charged clip, then slamming it back into the weapon's magazine.

They were here to offer the cartel their services as hired killers. In Medellín, if you wanted someone killed, all you had to do was pick up the phone. Kids like that took your call.

At the center of the room, a pair of loudspeakers attached to an overhead lighting fixture periodically squawked out a name summoning someone from the waiting room to the cartel offices upstairs.

Finally, the speakers cackled out Paco and Ramon's names. Their summons did not grant them, however, immediate passage into the inner sanctum. They were taken instead to a kind of halfway house, a landing between the two floors where another desk and another armed receptionist stood guard. Once again their identities were checked, they were patted down for arms, then invited to sit down and wait some more.

After another fifteen minutes, a young blond pistolero arrived, announced their names, and led them up half a flight of stairs and down a corridor lined with closed doors. He knocked on one, then opened it in response to a command from the man inside.

"Don Eduardo!" Paco gushed in a tone so deferential Ramon wondered if his associate was going to bow down and kiss the man's ring. Instead, he turned and introduced Ramon to the treasurer of the Medellín cartel.

Eduardo Hernandez graciously waved them to the two armchairs placed in front of his desk. He was slender, medium height, a notably handsome man with glistening black hair cut almost unfashionably short. He was wearing a beige silk suit, beautifully pressed and cut, and an open pale blue silk shirt. Circling his well-tanned neck was what passed for the drug trafficker's Old Etonian school tie, a gold chain. He had on alligator leather shoes, gleaming with the kind of shine Marine Corps drill instructors enjoin their recruits to put on their combat boots under pain of death.

Hernandez took his seat and laid his hands on his desktop, affording Ramon as he did a glimpse of his Cartier Tank watch. A maid, this one notably prettier than her sisters downstairs, appeared with more ritual cups of cafe tinto. Paco and Hernandez gossiped a moment about a mutual friend's purchase of a new estate. As they did, Ramon glanced out Don Eduardo's office window. It gave on to the glade filled with deer they'd seen on their way in.

Looking at it, Ramon felt his hands shaking. Stop it, he shrieked at his inner self. If he let his nerves show, he was dead. Literally. If anyone knew why he was here, if they even suspected he might be an informant, he would be tortured, shot, and probably stuck in a hole in the ground out there in the forest where the deer were nibbling the grass. Staying alive for the next half an hour depended on one thing—keeping his nerves under control.

It was at that instant Don Eduardo turned to him with a warm and encouraging smile. "Our friend Paco has suggested you might be some help to us in our financial dealings," he observed.

"Perhaps," Ramon replied. "It doesn't depend entirely on me." He then went on to outline for Don Eduardo what he had told Paco ten days earlier.

"The thing I can do," he concluded, "if you all agree, is contact my friend and see if either he or his associates would like to become involved in this. I'll have to go up to the States myself to talk to him. You can't do this kind of thing by phone." He turned to Paco. "My socio here can come with me. That way he can meet the guy and vouch for what went on."

Don Eduardo acknowledged the wisdom of Ramon's words with an almost imperceptible wave of his hand. Colombians never used the telephone to discuss business, and Paco's presence in the opening stages of this contact would help assure Hernandez that it was a genuine operation and not some sort of police sting.

"I can't promise you what their reaction is going to be," Ramon went on. "I mean, you hear things about how the Mafia and the Colombians don't get along so well in the States these days."

Don Eduardo laughed and offered Paco and Ramon that engaging smile of his. "I wouldn't worry too much about that if I were you," he assured them. "Believe me, the Mafia would sell used condoms if they thought there was enough money in it. That's something they have in common with us, an affection for money."

He flipped open a folder on his desk. "I see the two of you have done a number of loads together."

"About a dozen," Paco boasted.

"A considerable recommendation." Hernandez now turned the warmth of his smile on Paco. "And you're prepared to be your friend Ramon's Colombian partner, are you?"

In Medellín terms, accepting such a relationship meant Paco was putting both his own life and that of his wife at risk if the operation turned out to be a trap or either of them attempted to double-cross Don Eduardo.

"Sure," Paco agreed.

They then bargained over what percentage Paco and Ramon would receive if their money conduit turned out to be a success. They settled on three percent of the total moved.

"Let me explain to you how this works," Don Eduardo told them. "I am in a sense a financial subcontractor for my associates here in the compound. Let us say Don Pablo Escobar comes to me and says he has 'x' dollars he's accumulated in Los Angeles. I then inform my people. They arrange to take delivery of the cash from Pablo's people and put it into whatever system I am employing to bring it out of the United States. Once Pablo's people have handed the money to my people, it becomes my responsibility. I immediately credit Pablo's account with the sum, minus, of course, the commission involved. In other words, from that moment on, I am exposed for that amount. I am the one who must bear the loss if anything goes wrong."

Again he stopped. The warm smile remained fixed on his face as he studied first Paco, then Ramon, letting the full import of his words register. The man, Ramon realized, was a killer with a Cartier Tank watch. For all his elegance, cross him and he'd be as quick to pick up his phone and call in a couple of assassins—like those baby-faced kids downstairs—as Pablo Escobar would.

"I think you've understood my point," he noted, closing their folder on his desk with just the suggestion of a sigh. "Go ahead and make your contact. If your people are agreeable, I will send one of my senior associates to the States to meet them. Tell them ideally we'd like to be able to make cash deliveries in New York, Los Angeles, Houston and Chicago. And you may assure them that if this works well, there will be a great deal of money involved. A very great deal."

Hernandez stood, indicating that their meeting was over.

This time it was he, not the blond pistolero, who escorted them back down the corridor. Near the head of the stairs was a glass-topped table. Hernandez stopped.

"Hola, Don Pablo," he declared to a dumpy little man sitting in the group at the table. Then he turned and introduced Paco and Ramon. Pablo Escobar made just the barest of efforts at rising from his seat as he offered Ramon a limp, wet handshake. He did not deign to look into the American's eyes.

A few minutes later, the gates of the compound closed behind Paco's Jaguar, and they started their drive back to town. Ramon wanted to shriek out with relief and exultation. He'd been inside the headquarters of the Medellín cartel. He had shaken hands with Pablo Escobar. And he'd gotten back out alive. When was the last time the DEA had had an informant who'd been able to pull that off? He chuckled to himself.

Ray Albright was not a man given to deep political thought. Furthermore, where the flier came from out in West Texas, the term *commie bastard* was employed to describe a wide range of social misfits, few of whom had even a speaking acquaintance with the political thought of Karl Marx.

As a result, this interminable lecture Felipe Nadal was giving him about the *causa,* the courage of the contras for whom he was flying arms and the iniquities of their foes, was producing in Ray a reaction identical to that produced by half a dozen cans of Coors. He was falling asleep.

It was only when he heard the words "you can make some real money here and at the same time help these guys out" that Ray's attention level began to rise.

"Oh, yeah?" he asked. "How's that, Phil?" Wrapping his tongue around *Felipe* required a little more linguistic energy than Ray was prepared to exercise.

Nadal leaned forward. His sidekick, Rene Ponti, who'd come down from the ranch up in Muelle with them, did the same thing.

"Look, Ray," Nadal whispered, "you know everything's taken care of here, right? I mean, you don't have to worry about interception, Customs, the police, no shit like that."

This little guy is a lot closer to the truth than he probably knows, Ray thought. He said nothing, however. He figured he'd let the fucker ramble on until he could see just where he was heading.

"There's a real opportunity here for a little freelancing on your way back home."

So this was why Nadal and Rene had invited him to have a night on the town in Costa Rica's capital, San Jose. They had brought him down to make this pitch to him. Ray smiled. "You mean flying home some cargo that's going to pay a little more per kilo than old Uncle Pedro did?"

"You got it, man," Rene hissed. "We put a couple of duffel bags in your plane, maybe a hundred, two hundred kilos is all. You fly 'em back. You get seventy-five thousand dollars cash for your trouble."

Ray took a pull on his beer. "Now I don't reckon you're going to be filling up them there bags with Aunt Jemima's Pancake Mix, right?"

Nadal leaned closer. "Look, Ray. These poor farm boys fighting the commies in the jungles up there, they don't have enough shoes, they don't have enough food, they don't have enough medicine, they don't have enough arms, they don't have enough ammunition, they don't have enough anything. That Congress we got in Washington doesn't want to vote any money for them. What are they supposed to do, man?"

The Cuban mercenary glanced around the room. The locale he'd selected for their night out was the Key Largo, a well-known San Jose night spot. It was set in what had been the townhouse of one of the nation's oligarchs, built at the turn of the century. Each of its four principal downstairs rooms had been turned into a bar, each equipped with its own staff of resident hookers.

"Sure," he whispered. "We all know what's going to be in those bags. There's a lot of people up there in the States these days that like that stuff. Well, fuck it, man, if they want to stuff that shit up their nose, it's their business, right? This way at least, the money they're spending on it is going to a good cause, you know?"

While Albright might not have wasted much of his life on political thought, he had, over the years, acquired a fairly acute feeling for people. Studying his two hosts so intent on doing good for their Nicaraguan brothers, one thing seemed clear to him. It was most unlikely those barefoot farm boys would ever see any of the proceeds of the operation they were proposing.

Nadal, in the meantime, had carried his pursuit of confidentiality so far he had practically inserted his nose into Ray's ear. "Remember what Reagan said," he warned. "If we don't stop these communists here, before we know it, they'll be swimming the Rio Grande to El Paso."

"Yeah, well, they'll have themselves a lot of company doing that," Ray growled. "Where do you figure on landing this shit?"

"We got a strip in the Everglades," Rene said. "It's where we do some of our paramilitary training. Right on your way into Opa Locka. You just do a touch and go, dump the bags, and you're out of there."

"How do you know the state cops aren't going to come sniffing around?"

"Not to worry, man," Rene assured him. "We're covered. We got a direct line to the Lord on this one."

Albright took another pull on his beer bottle and winked at the pretty dark-haired hooker eyeing him from the bar, running the permutations of this exercise through his mind. A line to the Lord, was it? Well, that guy Lind or Tuttle or whatever the fuck his name was who'd recruited him in Victoria was CIA. That was for sure. The Kentucky farmer up in Muelle had come right out and said he was CIA. These two Cuban clowns, Rene and Phil, you had to figure were on the agency's payroll the same way he was, as hired hands. So the agency was in this up to its armpits.

Out there in Laos, the agency guys hadn't come around screaming at them for flying Vang Pao's dope. If anything, they were probably happy to have them doing their boy Vang Pao a favor. Probably you had the same kind of deal here. As long as you delivered the arms, the CIA wasn't going to give much of a shit about what you brought back. They weren't idiots. They knew the kind of pilots who flew these runs were basically smugglers. Smugglers hated an empty plane the way a good bartender hates an empty glass.

"Listen," he said, "I'll go check out that strip of yours when I get back. If it looks okay, then maybe we can do some business." He stood up.

"For the moment," he announced, "I'm going to check out that little lady in the blue shirt sitting all by herself up there at the bar."

Juan Ospina waited patiently by the Eastern Airlines baggage carousel at La Guardia Airport for his luggage to show up. Ospina had arrived in Miami earlier in the day flying in from Panama City on Pan Am's morning flight. The choice of Panama as his point of departure had been dictated by the fact that he was entering the United States on a Panamanian passport rather than a passport from his native Colombia.

The sale of such passports for thirty thousand dollars apiece was one of the flourishing side enterprises conducted by the Panamanian Defense Forces under the overall supervision of Manuel Noriega. The leadership of the Colombian cartels and the CIA were his two principal customers. Ospina had gotten his because he was the right-hand executive of Don Eduardo Hernandez, the Medellín cartel's money man.

The identities on passports such as Ospina's were taken from the applications of peasants applying for land under Panama's land reform act. Each peasant listed his name, address, date of birth and his *cedula* number, the number he carried on his National Identity Card, on his application. Since those peasants were never going to travel farther than the next village, the officer running the scam had only to make a reasonable match of ages and issue a passport. The result was a perfectly valid document, one which would survive any efforts by Interpol or any other law enforcement agency to authenticate it.

Juan picked up his slightly battered Samsonite suitcase and joined the line of arriving passengers waiting for yellow cabs. There was no Cadillac limo meeting him. The image of Colombian drug dealers working in American cities with huge gold Rolexes hanging from their wrists, screeching through the streets in turbo-charged Porsches, was a fiction manufactured by the producers of *Miami Vice*.

The reality was quite different. The Colombians sent workers to the United States under contract. Their families remained in Colombia, and their basic salaries were banked in Medellín against their return. The marching orders they gave to their people were: Fit in, keep a low profile, don't stand out in the crowd. At one point, they had even employed a former Venezuelan intelligence officer to prepare a security manual for their people. It contained such homey bits of advice as "wash the car on Saturday mornings and be sure your neighbors see you doing it" and "keep the lawn mowed."

Ospina ordered the cab to take him to the Roosevelt Avenue elevated station in Jackson Heights in the borough of Queens. From there he walked to his destination so the taxi driver wouldn't have an address for him, and he could check to be sure he wasn't being followed. Although there was little likelihood of that.

His destination was a simple one-story, bungalow-style home at 8076 Farmwell Road. Before the war, that address had been in the heart of a middle-class Jewish neighborhood. The Jews had long since left, leaving behind them a multi-ethnic quilt: Thais, Pakistanis, Indians, Koreans, Central and Latin Americans. This particular house had been rented in the name of a Colombian couple studying for graduate degrees at Long Island University. Neither the husband nor the wife had set foot in it since the day they'd signed the lease.

Ospina let himself in with the key he'd been given when he left Medellín. The house was sparsely furnished. It had, however, a bed, a television set and a *clavo*—a *nail*—a secret cache for anything Ospina would one day want to hide, like a million dollars in cash.

After breakfast the next morning, Ospina headed for his first stop, a brick six-story Depression-era apartment house at 8050 Baxter Street, opposite the emergency room of the Elmhurst Hospital. The address was well known to a select number of Colombian drug traffickers. Its basement housed two enterprises, the Seoul Driver's school and a firm which advertised "worldwide money transfers."

That was the company which interested Ospina, but not for its financial services. The enterprise offered an additional service, the creation of a false but perfectly legitimate address. Ospina presented his fake Panamanian passport to the Colombian running the establishment and told him he would like to rent a private mailbox. Such boxes were the commodity in which the Colombians dealt. Presumably some people used his service to receive pornographic material or conduct the correspondence of an extramarital affair. Most, however, employed it as Ospina would, as a vehicle for establishing a legal address in the U.S.

After paying the proprietor one hundred dollars for a year rental of his box, Ospina asked for a piece of paper establishing his residence at 8050 Baxter Street. The proprietor obligingly dipped into his desk and drew out a blank Long Island Light and Power Company bill. For another one hundred dollars, he filled it out on his computer for Ospina, listing him, in his Panamanian name, as residing in Basement Apartment A, 8050 Baxter Street.

Ospina's next stop was the New York State Driver's License Bureau Queens office. There he explained to the examiner who greeted him that he spent considerable time in the United States on business, often needed to rent cars, and the car rental companies always made a fuss about the fact that he had an international driver's license, not a U.S. license. He was a New York resident with an apartment he rented to live in on his visits. To substantiate that, he showed the examiner his latest electricity bill.

The examiner gave him a perfunctory driving test. He was then photographed, paid his license fee, and walked out of the building with a brand-new driver's license issued in his Panamanian name listing his home address as 8050 Baxter Street.

He went next to the Chase Manhattan's Jackson Heights branch to open up a checking account. As ID, he gave the platform officer who interviewed him his driver's license. With six thousand dollars in cash, a sum well below the government's ten-thousand dollar reporting requirements, he opened his account. The friendly Chase banker issued him a set of temporary checks. His permanent ones bearing his name and address, printed up in the pretty pale blue he'd selected from the range of samples offered to him, would be mailed to Baxter Street in a week's time.

His final stop of the day was a second-floor shop on Roosevelt Avenue near the elevated station where the taxi had dropped him the evening before. This enterprise, too, was known to his friends in Medellín. Its owners made no effort to conceal what they were selling. "Untraceable cellular phones" they advertised on their front door.

Juan picked out a beeper, one of the new models which could be programmed not to emit a noise but rather to vibrate against the owner's skin to alert him to a message. Then he chose a state-of-the-art mobile phone and arranged for it to be tied in to a cellular phone company. The phone he listed, of course, in his Panamanian name and at his Baxter Street address.

Initially, Gonzalo had suggested they meet downstairs in the lobby of Miami Beach's Hotel Fontainebleau. Ray Al-

bright had seen too many late-night movies in too many hotel rooms a lot scruffier than this one to fall for that trick.
The guy flashed you a peek into his attaché case or gym bag
or whatever it was he was carrying, just enough to let you
glimpse the stack of green bills in there. Then he set the case
at your feet for the swap and wandered off.

When you finally opened up the case, those one hundred
dollar bills you'd spotted turned out to be wrapped around
newsprint cut into strips the size of a dollar bill.

"Well, now, if it's all the same with you, my friend, I'd
just as soon we met in this nice room I got up here," Albright told Felipe Nadal's money courier. He could sense a
flicker of hesitation in Gonzalo's voice. "You sure, I mean,
is okay?"

"I'm okay, you're okay, my friend."

With that, Albright twisted the silencer onto his .38,
flicked off the safety, and tucked it into his waistband beneath his flopping shirt.

Gonzalo arrived carrying a bulging green plastic shopping
bag. Albright looked at it. It came from Harrods in London,
of all goddamned places. He motioned Gonzalo into the
room, put the safety latch on his door, and gestured to his
unmade bed.

"Let's have a look at what you got in there."

Gonzalo shook out the bag, sending a green waterfall onto
the bed. The money was in stacks of tens and twenties, a
hundred bills to a stack, fifty-three stacks in all.

"Holy shit!" Albright groaned. "You must have gone to
every doper in Dade to get this stuff together."

Gonzalo shrugged. They didn't hire him to give explanations.

Albright picked through the stacks, flicking through them
at random. At least no one had tried to stiff him with yesterday's *Miami Herald*.

Once Gonzalo had left, he turned back to the pile of
money on his bed, seventy-five thousand dollars in cash, and
began to laugh. A couple more trips like this, and he'd never
again have to diddle another middle-aged housewife to keep
up her interest in flying lessons.

As it inevitably was on Friday nights, Sparks Steak House
on Manhattan's Forty-sixth Street just past Third Avenue
was packed. The "Thank God it's Friday" singles crowd was

three and four deep at the bar, its dining rooms swarming
with couples in from the Island or Jersey for a night out in
the city.

Juan Ospina, Eduardo Hernandez's newly arrived emissary, was staggered by the dimension of the crowd, his ears
jarred by that peculiar high-pitched din of excited New York
conversation. Almost timidly—and timidity was not a characteristic many of his friends associated with Juan—he approached the headwaiter. That harried and overworked
gentleman looked at him with an expression so sour it might
have curdled milk at five paces.

"Excuse me," Ospina said, "I'm supposed to be having
dinner with a Mr. Jimmy Bruno."

The headwaiter's expression metamorphosed into an instant smile at the mention of the name. "Of course, sir, he's
waiting for you."

With the slightest of gestures to Ospina's elbow, he guided
the Colombian past a dozen diners clamoring for the tables
they'd been promised to a quiet booth along the wall. It was
designed to seat four people. Mr. Bruno was presiding over
it alone.

"Mr. Ospina," he said, rising, "Jimmy Bruno. Call me
Jimmy." There was a dark rumble to Bruno's voice, a
hoarseness that conveyed both a sense of strength and a
promise of intimacy. He grabbed Juan's proffered hand in
two massive hands of his own and drew him toward his seat.
The headwaiter, in the meantime, was snapping his fingers
to a waiter.

"Mr. Bruno," he asked, "would you and your guest like
something from the bar?"

Bruno smiled at Juan. He was a big-shouldered man with
jet black hair and the sort of tan complexion Juan associated
with Sicilians or Mexicans. On his little finger, Juan noticed,
he was wearing a diamond pinkie ring. That was hardly surprising in view of what he'd been told about his associa-
tions.

"Maybe I'll have a vodka on the rocks," Juan replied.

"Make it two," Jimmy Bruno ordered, "and double 'em
up. Stolis."

The headwaiter passed the order to the waiter in a tone
that made it clear Mr. Bruno's drinks order took precedence
over anything else he had to do.

"This is a popular place," Juan declared, acknowledging the obvious.

"Best steaks in the world, right here," Jimmy Bruno assured him. "Brings the people out."

Within seconds, it seemed, their waiter had come scurrying back from the bar with their drinks. "Your very good health," Jimmy said, clinking the rim of his glass to Juan's.

For a few moments they glided through the safe conversational shallows: the weather, Ronald Reagan, the fortunes of the New York Giants, a subject with which Ospina was not particularly conversant.

There were certain rules of engagement that governed conversations such as these, and both men knew them. You didn't pry. You didn't ask personal questions. This was not a forum in which to exchange home telephone numbers, the name of your wife's hairdresser, or the occupation of your mistress.

Finally, when the banalities had been exhausted, Jimmy Bruno, the tone of his voice dropping a register, leaned toward Juan. "My people tell me you'd like some help in certain money matters."

"Right," Juan agreed with the faintest of smiles. "You could put it that way. A question of cash flow."

Bruno's face reflected the legitimate gravity such concerns were meant to evoke. "Basically, what I am is a kind of full-service financial adviser. I can do whatever it is you require: help you in setting up offshore companies, advise you on investments, buy property for you, manage the flow of your money in and out of the country, okay?

"Now," Bruno continued, "we can do all of that in one of two ways. We can do it open and aboveboard in a way I can guarantee you there will be no violation of any U.S. laws, all the forms properly filled out using both our names and so forth. For those services I charge a commission of one-and-one-half percent."

Bruno paused to take a drink of his vodka, noting as he did that his dinner partner seemed less than entranced by the song he'd just heard. "Now, on the other hand, if for some reason you don't want the government to know this money belongs to you ... if you have, you know, problems with that, I can provide you exactly the same services I just outlined for you, but it's going to cost you more."

A flicker of enlightenment had appeared on Juan's face. "How much more?" he asked.

"Ten percent."

"I'd been told it was seven."

"I have to spend more to keep things airtight this way. Attorneys. Setting up dummy corporations in safe tax havens where I know they'll be beyond the reach of investigators here in this country. Being sure we got the right corporate resolutions, the right paper a bank can have on file to satisfy their requirements. Your name isn't going to be on that paper. Nor is mine. But the banker who's holding it, he's got to swallow it. That means he expects a certain reward for his services."

Juan Ospina understood. Clearly, the key was having someone on the inside, a banker you were paying off who made the thing work.

"Tell me, Jimmy," he asked, "how does the bank explain all this cash flow when the bank examiners come around?"

"You've heard of something called the exclusionary list?"

Juan had not.

"Companies that have a big cash flow, like supermarkets, for example, or some oil company that's got twenty gas stations in the area. They get exempted from the cash-reporting requirements. They're put on that list." Bruno circled the tabletop with the palm of his massive hand as though he were a blackjack dealer. "A smart banker knows how to blend an input of cash into that flow."

"I'd like to meet the guy."

"You won't. He doesn't much like meeting people. Besides"—there was nothing particularly friendly about the smile on Jimmy Bruno's face now—"if you knew him, you wouldn't need me anymore, right?

"We work through shell companies, of course," Bruno went on. "That way I can also do some other things for you if you want. You want to buy some property in the States for your business, maybe a couple of apartments here in the city which nobody knows you got or who's living there? Or some trucks to move your product. Or lease a warehouse to keep it in. We can do that."

Bruno allowed Juan to reflect a second or two on that chain of corporate possibilities. "Suppose you want to buy a Mercedes. You walk into a car dealer up in Queens, lay fifty thousand in cash on his desk, which is cash I don't doubt you got, and you've got your Merc. But you've also got some problems. That cash is going to generate some government paper."

Bruno contemplated his heavy hands. "Now, suppose instead we got a corporation here. We put the fifty K into the corporate account, draw out a certified check, I buy the Merc for you in the company name. Now you got no problems. The dealer in Queens hasn't even seen your face."

The waiter appeared to give them their menus. "Give us a couple more of these," Bruno commanded, gesturing to their empty vodka glasses. "You like steak, don't you?" Bruno put the question to Ospina in a tone of voice that indicated he would regard anything other than an affirmative reply as the equivalent of a Carmelite nun's renouncing the Divine.

The two ordered rare New York sirloins, and Bruno again eyed the waiter. "Bring us a bottle of that Stag's Leap 1975," he ordered.

"They got great California reds here," he announced to Ospina, who would have preferred a beer but decided to remain silent in the face of Bruno's enthusiasm.

"Remove is what it's all about," Jimmy continued as soon as the waiter had left, "getting a little space between you and the operation. Take that Mercedes, for example. Suppose some guy, maybe one of your employees, gets stopped by the cops and he's got some product in the car, okay?"

Juan nodded.

"The car may be in your name, but the cops are going to keep the car unless you want to go in personally and have a long and embarrassing conversation with them. They keep the product. The guy goes to jail and you decide to leave town. Now suppose the car's registered to a company. I have my attorney at the police station the next morning telling the cops 'John Smith's a bad guy, okay, but he was driving that car with dope in it on his own. He didn't have any authority from his corporate employers to do that. They're an innocent third party here.' You get your car back. And your name hasn't come up anywhere. You're protected."

The waiter reappeared with their wine. While Bruno and

Ospina looked on, he uncorked it, then decanted it over the open flame of a candle into a crystal decanter.

"Now suppose you want to get that guy out on bail so he can head south," Bruno continued after the waiter had concluded his wine ceremony. "Well, the judge, for, let's say ten kilos of powder, he's going to set a heavy bail. Maybe half a million, two fifty in cash and the rest in a surety bond. Coming up with that kind of money may not be a problem for you. I'm sure you got that money at home. The problem is, how do you bring it into the courtroom and justify that it isn't drug money that's now going to be subject to seizure?"

"Yeah, yeah," Ospina muttered, "I know about that kind of problem, all right. A cousin of mine who runs a restaurant we use for a front in Queens got caught a while ago. We had the cash to make his bail. That was no problem. But, like you say, how do we walk into the court with that in a suitcase? From a restaurant that's showing three thousand a week gross on its income tax returns?"

"You got it," Bruno agreed. "My way the corporation puts up a banker's check for the bail. Because the company feels an obligation for its employees. Your guy gets his bail, what the cops up here call a Colombian acquittal. The next day he's gone. Nobody ever sees him again."

"Yeah, that makes sense," Ospina declared, thinking as he did of an additional advantage Bruno's system offered. If their people felt sure they'd be sprung if they got caught, they'd have less reason to get talkative while they were inside.

"So," Bruno concluded, "those are the kind of services we can provide. Besides moving the money, I mean."

"I'm sure my principals will be interested, Jimmy," Ospina said. "Tell me, how much cash can you handle on each pickup?"

"A hundred thousand minimum. A million max."

"And how many pickups each week?"

"One in each city. Any more than that and you're going to overload my system."

"Can you pick up in the four cities we mentioned?"

"New York and L.A., no problem. We can start there tomorrow. Houston, I got to work on, but it should be okay. Chicago I got to worry about for a while."

"And how long will it take to move the money?"

"Where do you want it? The Caymans? Panama?"

"Panama."

"It depends to an extent on where we pick it up. We have to move it through a couple of institutions here before we can wire-transfer it out. You know how banks are. They like to sit on your money for a while as it goes by. A week, ten days maybe."

"Can't you speed that up?" Ospina asked. "I know my people are going to ask me that."

Bruno shook his head. "Hey, we may not be providing instant orgasm here, but it's safe sex, you know what I mean?"

Before they could go further, the waiter had wheeled his trolley to their table with two enormous sirloins, still sizzling on their hot plates. For a few moments, the dimensions of the task before them stilled their conversation.

When the first phase of their assault on the meat had been completed, Bruno resumed talking. "You know, Juan," he told his guest, "I've been doing this for years. My clients listen to me. They do what I tell them to do because I've learned from experience. But I gotta tell you, if you or anybody else does something I tell them not to do, I stop doing business with them right there on the spot."

"What kind of things are we talking about here, Jimmy?"

"First, your guys who are delivering the cash. I don't want them coming around with open shirts, half a dozen gold chains around their necks, the hair down to their shoulders, with 'dope dealer' stamped on their foreheads. My guys will be in coats and ties. That's how I want your people."

"That makes sense," Juan agreed.

"Do your people use money-counting machines?" Bruno asked him.

"Oh, yeah." Juan was proud of their technical prowess. "Brandts. The new ones that count three hundred bills at a clip."

"That's good. That helps us all get accurate counts."

Soon Ospina reluctantly pushed away the remains of his sirloin. The waiter gathered up their plates and offered them the dessert menu.

"I can't, Jimmy," Juan said, almost gasping. "I haven't got any appetite left at all."

Bruno laughed appreciatively. "A guy's got about as much

chance of walking out of Sparks hungry as he does of walking out of a whorehouse with a hard-on."

The headwaiter appeared bearing a pair of brandy snifters and a dust-encrusted bottle on a silver tray. "Pat would like to offer you and your guest a glass of his favorite cognac, Mr. Bruno," he said. He displayed the bottle to Jimmy. "Rémy Martin Fifty-Year Reserve."

The two new business associates savored the cognac's potent aroma, then took a sip. "You and I, Juan, have got to be very open with one another from now on," Jimmy told the Colombian. "We have to be able to trust one another, because if we don't, both of us are going to lose. What I'll do is assign one of my people to liaise with you. Me, I don't touch the money. Ever. The guy I'm thinking about is a Cuban street kid. Obviously speaks Spanish, which is going to help here. I mean, I don't think we want Colombians working with Italian third parties where we can avoid it. Better for everybody's health that way. This guy delivers the message. He delivers the mail. Don't ask him about banking. He doesn't know. I don't want him to know. Banking questions you bring to me, okay?"

"Got you." Juan smiled as the waiter laid the check at Jimmy's side. He dropped his American Express Gold Card on the bill, and minutes later they were moving past the bar still packed with customers clamoring for a table. Bruno's limo was waiting at the door.

"Nice dinner, Mr. Bruno?" the driver asked.

"The best." Jimmy turned to Juan. "Can we drop you someplace?"

"Thanks, Jimmy," Juan told him. "I'm parked around the corner."

"Okay," Bruno said, extending his big hand. "You know how to get ahold of me if you want me."

"We'll be in touch," Juan assured him, "very soon."

Jimmy Bruno's limousine went up First Avenue to Fifty-seventh Street, turned west, and crossed Manhattan to Ninth Avenue. There it entered the underground parking garage of the modern office building on the corner. Bruno took the elevator to the seventh floor. There he resumed his real identity as Special Agent Eddie Gomez of the Drug Enforcement Administration.

Kevin Grady was waiting for him. Gomez stripped off his suit coat and shirt. "Help me get out of this thing," he said, pointing at the girdle circling his waist like a pouch. It contained a Nagra reel-to-reel tape recorder on which the full details of his dinner conversation were now recorded.

"How did it go?" Grady asked.

"Like a dream. He can hardly wait to get into bed and spread his legs."

BOOK SEVEN

Operation Medclean

Bruno's Financial Management Services, located in Suite 421 at 684 Madison Avenue, basked in the faintly unkempt air of an organization that has been in existence too long to be overly concerned by appearances. In reality, the company's lifespan was reckoned in hours, not years. Kevin Grady and Eddie Gomez had set out to organize it within moments of Juan Ospina's rising to the bait they'd offered.

A few basic operating principles had guided them. The building they picked out was old and relatively small. There was no doorman or receptionist on the premises who could be quizzed about the activities of any of the building's tenants. It had only one entrance, which would make surveillance of Bruno's visitors relatively easy. Furthermore, Madison Avenue ran one way, uptown; any visitor being picked up by a passing car would have to set out in that direction. Cops on surveillance love one-way streets.

The office suite itself had been designed to be just flashy enough to let the Colombians know Jimmy Bruno didn't operate out of a car trunk, but not so flashy that it violated the principles of discreet behavior which they also knew governed Mafia operations. There was a reception room with a receptionist's desk, a coffee table covered with copies of the *Wall Street Journal,* the *Financial Times, Barron's, Forbes* and *Fortune,* and a sofa bracketed by a couple of armchairs.

Jimmy Bruno's office was decorated with watercolors of Amalfi and Capri, framed diplomas, and service citations from the Knights of Columbus and the Sons of Italy. On his desk was a formal wedding portrait flanked by the photos of two adolescent children, the kind the photographer enhances with a touch of hand coloring.

That was the surface display. The decoration also included a lamp in which a wide-angle TV camera was concealed. An omnidirectional microphone was wired into the lighting fixture that hung from the ceiling.

Grady and Gomez had the place ready for business at nine o'clock Monday morning, following Gomez's Friday night dinner at Sparks with Ospina. Ella Jean Ransom was engaged to play the role of Bruno's receptionist-secretary. Like

Grady, she was a frustrated thespian. She could be as raunchy as a bubblegum-chewing Eighth Avenue hooker or as she was here, haughtier than a Bryn Mawr English major imitating Katharine Hepburn.

The occasional agent was ordered to wander in during the first working day to provide a client flow in case the Colombians were watching the place. To no one's surprise, Juan Ospina showed up unannounced shortly before noon on Tuesday. Clearly, he had made his unannounced arrival so he could check out the authenticity of Bruno's Financial Management Services for himself before getting involved any further with Jimmy Bruno. The moment he opened the door, Ella Jean recognized him from a photo taken surreptitiously as he was leaving Sparks. So, she thought, our little pigeon is checking out his cage.

She contemptuously informed him that Mr. Bruno was busy with a client, and that in any event he rarely received callers without an appointment. Finally, in response to his repeated pleas, she consented to call Ospina's identity to her boss in his inner office.

They then let him marinate with his *Wall Street Journal* for half an hour while Gomez finished up with an imaginary client. When he'd walked that gentleman to the elevator, he summoned Ospina into his office. The opening moments of their meeting were interrupted by two phone calls. The first was in Italian, a language Ospina did not speak. The second was from a currency dealer in Zurich with whom Bruno tried to estimate how many pfennigs the Deutschmark would gain on the dollar if the Federal Reserve lowered interest rates by half a point later in the week.

By the time Bruno hung up on the second call, Ospina had bought the operation whole.

"Jimmy," he proudly announced, "my principals are ready to go ahead. We'd like to arrange for our first cash pickup in forty-eight hours or so."

"Where?"

"Right here in New York."

"No problem." Gomez leaned against the support of his high-back desk chair. This first exchange, he was sure, would be a test run involving a minimal amount of cash so the Colombians could check out the system and, above all, try to pick up any sign that somebody was watching. Well, hey wouldn't pick anything up on this one because Gomez was going to stand down the surveillance.

"There are a couple of things we got to set up here for our modus operandi. First, I got to get you together with the liaison guy I told you about, Cesar Rodriguez. He's the guy who makes the pickups for me. Ella Jean," Bruno called out, "see if you can beep Cesar to come in here and meet a new client.

"The next thing we got to decide is where and how we hand over the money. I find the best thing is to have Cesar rent a motel room someplace. Your guys bring him the dough and they can count it together." For the benefit of one of our cameras, Gomez was thinking, which makes lovely viewing for a jury further on down the line.

"Why not just hand over the suitcase?" Ospina asked.

"No problem. We can do that. But then how do we know how much money you got in there?"

"We tell you."

"Yeah, sure, Juan, and we'll believe that just like you and believe all that stuff they taught us about the virgin birth, right?"

"Well, I don't guess you want to count it right out there on the street, do you?"

"Not really. If we're going to do a suitcase swap, we got to agree on one thing right here and now. We both got to accept that the count for the money in that suitcase is the one the bank gives us when they get the money, okay?"

"I guess we could do that."

"And don't forget, a million bucks in twenties weighs one hundred twenty-five pounds all by itself. You know that?"

Ospina started in surprise.

"From what I hear, there's a lot of people out there pay for your powder in twenties."

"Oh, yeah, you're right, we got twenties like you wouldn't believe."

Bruno smiled warmly. That was an admission he'd wanted recorded on his tape machine. "Maybe you'd better find yourself an Arnold Schwarzenegger to lug that shit around."

"Or how about we make the exchange at one of our places?"

Jimmy Bruno made a grand gesture with his hands. That was exactly what, eventually, he hoped these guys would suggest. "Maybe later when we get to know each other better we could do that, you know what I mean? For now, better we use the motel room or the suitcase. You tell me what you want and where you want to do it."

"Well, for the first time I guess a suitcase will be the best. How about over in Jackson Heights Friday morning?"

The fact Ospina wanted to pass just one suitcase confirmed Gomez's earlier suspicion about a test run. He leaned forward and let his voice wind down into the hoarser regions of confidence. "No offense, Juan, but what they got over there in Jackson Heights is Little Colombia. The cops know that. You've got patrol cars, plainclothes and uniform, coming by all the time." He nodded out the window toward the busy traffic of Madison Avenue. "Right here in midtown Manhattan is the best place. All we got here is the traffic patrol, the brownies handing out parking tickets." It was also inevitably very busy and therefore ideal for a surreptitious filming of the exchange.

Jimmy's understated office, his prudence, his effort to insulate his operation from any contact with law enforcement, all impressed Ospina. This guy, he told himself, is really tight. "Look, Jimmy, I'd like to use my own liaison man to work with your friend Cesar. Ramon, the guy who knows one of your friends."

For just a second Jimmy Bruno appeared baffled. "Oh!" he said, "you mean Ray Marcello, the *gumba* that went to school with my associate's friend. I got no problem with that." None at all, he glowed. "Now, where do you want this money to go?"

Ospina pushed a piece of paper with a series of numbers written on it to him. "To this account at the Banco de Occidente in Panama City."

The transfer finally took place at 10:30 Friday morning in front of 333 East Fifty-sixth Street. The Colombian courier recognized Cesar Rodriguez from his description and the number plates on his car. He opened his trunk, took out a suitcase, and passed it to the DEA agent. Across the street in a Ryder van, another DEA agent filmed the transaction.

Cesar, who was also a DEA agent assigned to the New York DO's Group Six, put the suitcase in his car and drove off, hoping the Colombians were following him. If they were, they'd see he went straight to the bank with no stopovers anywhere.

As Gomez had predicted, the sum in the suitcase, 101

thousand dollars, was small by Colombian standards. It went into the account of a Panamanian corporation established by the DEA some weeks earlier, than began to work its way through the banking system, moving through two U.S. banks with their knowledge and cooperation before being wire-transferred to Panama. Every step along the way was legal. Seven working days after Cesar had deposited the money, Clara Mendez, the manager of the Banco de Oecidente's Panama City branch, called her friend and client Don Eduardo Hernandez in Medellín.

"The transfer you've been waiting for has arrived," she said, giving him the sum deposited in his account.

Hernandez was more than pleased. The transfer had taken time, but the amount was accurate and the procedure had worked exactly as it was supposed to. They were onto an important new vehicle for moving money out of the States.

"Where did the wire transfer come from?" he asked.

"The Morgan Guaranty Trust in New York."

Hernandez couldn't help smiling. Mr. Jimmy Bruno bent first-class bankers. That was smart. The one place the U.S. government was never going to look for a bent banker was in an institution like Morgan Guaranty.

Lind's Tape

Everyone has known moments like it, moments that imprint themselves with such clarity on our memories that we can summon them up in abundant detail whenever we wish. Some are associated with public events. Ask any American over the age of ten on November 22, 1963, what he was doing when he heard the news that President Kennedy was assassinated.

Other moments, like that terrible instant for me when Juanita's brother Pedro's telephone call arrived, define the watersheds of our private existences. I'd just come down from lunch that day and started to read my NSA Restricted Circulation Bulletin, the twenty-four-hour take of top secret intercepts out of my Latin American parish. Since most major figures in the world have known for years that all micro-wave link communications are intercepted by three or more intelligence agencies, they say little of consequence in such calls. The result is intercepts that tend to contain titillating revelations about the lives and peccadilloes of second-echelon figures. Great intelligence they are not, but they can easily become addictive reading. When George Bush was running the agency, you couldn't get him away from the transcripts of Leonid Brezhnev making baby talk to his mistress.

I had just started my reading that day when my assistant walked in. "A Mr. Pedro Boyd just called on the cut-out line," she informed me. "He says he has to speak to you urgently. I must say, he did sound rather agitated." She laid a piece of paper on my desk. "He'd like you to call him back on this number."

There was only one way Pedro Boyd could have gotten my cut-out number—from his sister Juanita. If he wanted to get hold of me urgently, it had to be because she had asked him to. But why? Why not call me herself?

I returned the call immediately.

"Mr. Lind!" The name seemed to come out in a gasp. "Thank God you've called. Something terrible has happened to my sister Juanita!" His concern gushed in full flood over the telephone line.

She's crashed that damned airplane of hers, I thought. Or gone missing at sea on the *Quasimodo*. "What is it?"

"She disappeared without a trace three days ago!"

"Jesus, no!"

"Si, si. I just found out what happened to her. She's been arrested. With two of her friends."

"Why?"

"For conspiring to overthrow the government."

"I don't believe it!" The shock my voice conveyed was real; the sentiment of disbelief, alas, was not. I recalled with nausea gripping my stomach her words to me on the *Quasimodo* about fighting for freedom. Evidently, she had meant them. She and her friends really had been trying to get rid of Noriega.

"They've thrown them into prison without a trial! For five years!"

"How the hell could they do that?"

"The son of a bitch of a dictator who runs this country just passed a new law," her brother declared. "Anyone, *any-one,* accused of calumny against the state is automatically sentenced to five years in jail. No trial. No conviction. Nothing. All they need is the accusation and you're condemned. That's what he's done to them," he continued, his voice beginning to break. "Mr. Lind, my sister will never survive five years in a Panamanian prison!"

He didn't have to tell me that. I knew enough about the kind of penal system PK\BARRIER\7-7 was running to realize he was not exaggerating. The canons of justice in Noriega's Panama were the kind that gave the accused the right to remain silent as long as he could stand the pain.

"I've called the American ambassador for his help," Boyd continued, "but Noriega never listens to him. The only people he listens to are the generals at the Pentagon and his friends at the CIA. Don't you know some general in the air force from your work who could help her, Mr. Lind? Please, for God's sake, can you do something to help her?"

"Mr. Boyd," I replied, still trying to assimilate the enormity of what he'd told me, "I certainly will help all I can, believe me."

I hung up and sank, stunned and shaking, into my chair. Outside, the late January cold had leached the sun's rays of most of their force, converting the afternoon sunlight into a pale shroud.

Panamanian prisons under the regime of my asset Tony Noriega were citadels of bestiality and brutality. They would have tossed Juanita into a common cell reeking of urine, feces and sweat the way meat is tossed to a gaggle of baying hounds. A wink from some sadistic matron would have let Juanita's cell mates know that this rabiblanco princess had been shorn of her protective cloak because she was a political prisoner. And the guards? They'd get the word she was for the taking in the dark hours of the night.

How could I possibly let that happen to a woman I loved so passionately? How could I allow that body which had given me so much to be so brutalized and degraded? For a moment I sat there, alone with that most uncomfortable of companions, my conscience, debating what to do.

There was one thing I knew I could do. I could tell Hinckley I had urgent business in Panama, go out to Andrews Air Force Base, and get a flight down to Howard. Once I was in Panama, I could contact Noriega and tell him I needed to see him urgently.

If I asked him to free her, he would do it in a flash. Not out of compassion for her. Not out of friendship for me. He would do it because that would give him something far more precious than whatever he might have gained by keeping Juanita and her friends in jail.

Noriega collected other men's weaknesses as a lepidopterist collects rare butterflies. He treasured those flaws, saved them, hoarded them as tools that he would one day employ to compel other men to do his bidding. Ask him in strictest confidence to render me that personal favor and I would be adding my flaw, my point of vulnerability, to his collection. I would have put myself in debt to him, and Noriega never forgot or canceled a debt. The day would come when he would call it in.

Professionally, going to see Noriega would be in flagrant violation of every canon the agency had, of every principle that was supposed to govern my behavior as a clandestine operator. The instant I asked Noriega for that favor, our roles would be forever altered. I would become the controlled rather than the controller.

Indeed, it would be so outrageous a breach of agency regulations, a transgression so severe that, if it were ever known, it would lead to my instant dismissal from the CIA.

What the agency expected of me in this situation was stoic silence, no matter how painful or how trying such a course of action might be. We ran in a cruel world. We were supposed to have developed a set of calluses on our souls that we could call on for protection in moments like this.

Suppose I resigned and then went to see Noriega? He'd laugh at me, first for being so stupid and second, because I would then be useless to him. A Samson shorn of his hair. Yet if I sat here and did nothing, how could I ever look this woman I loved in the face again if she survived her jail term? For that matter, how could I ever look at myself in the mirror again?

The telephone interrupted my anguished meditation. This time it was a regular switchboard call from Sarah Jane. She was in a bubbling good mood, which was rare enough these days. My preoccupation with Juanita, my remoteness, my indifference to our relations, had begun to cast a long shadow over us.

"I've decided to try the recipe I got for that new salmon mousse for dinner tonight," she informed me.

I had completely forgotten we had invited her friend and fellow gourmet, Toni Esterling and her husband, for dinner.

I stood up and carried the phone over to the window. For a moment I looked out at the gloom of the countryside shrouded in the kind of cheerless light Utrillo put into his paintings of winter scenes.

"Jack?" she called suddenly. "Are you there? Did you hear me?"

"Yes, darling, I'm sorry. I was listening. It's just that something very major has just come up. I've got to leave town."

"When?"

"Right now."

"You sound upset."

"I am. Very."

Sarah Jane sighed. Like most agency wives, she had long ago learned to live in the certain knowledge that the unexpected would be the norm of her existence. "Will you come home before you leave?"

I kept an emergency flight kit in the office for moments like this. "I don't know."

"Well, I guess we'll just have to try that recipe out some other time."

Beepers, Ramon thought. How the hell did people traffic dope before they invented the beeper? He was standing beside Juan Ospina in the second-floor Radio-Telecommunications store on Roosevelt Avenue in Queens that specialized in the sale of those indispensable adjuncts to the drug trade, untraceable cellular telephones.

"Now, this is the newest beeper we got,". the salesman was explaining to Ospina. "It bounces its signal off a satellite, which means it can be tied into all the cellular nets in the country. There's practically no place you're going to go wearing this thing where you'll be out of touch."

He laid the device into Ospina's hands with the reverential gesture a Forty-seventh Street diamond merchant might reserve for a prize stone. It was, Ramon noted, not much bigger than a remote control for your TV.

"The beauty of this thing is that it's got a twelve-digit display panel," the salesman purred. "What's the significance of that, you ask? I'll tell you. You and I can work out a code between us which nobody knows. I got a beeper, you got a beeper. We want to have a private conversation, maybe pay phone to pay phone, right? You beep me, punch in a code that tells me where to call, when to call. You go to your corner pay phone, dial the number I gave you which is another pay phone and, bingo, there I am. We can have our little chat and nobody's listening, know what I mean?"

You'd have to be an asshole not to, Ramon thought. Everyone in the drug trade, from Pablo Escobar down to the kid with the Reebok hi-tops in Bed Stuy, loved these things.

"So how much does that thing cost?" Ospina asked.

"$129.99."

"I'll take a dozen."

You would think, Ramon told himself, that the salesman would at least have smiled at an order that size. He didn't. He acted as though he sold a dozen beepers at a crack half a dozen times a day which, the CI told himself, just might be the case.

Ospina paid cash, which didn't seem to surprise the salesman either, and they walked back onto Roosevelt. "Come on," he said, pointing across the boulevard, "let's have a beer at the Chibcha."

"For Christ's sake, it's four o'clock in the afternoon!" Ramon said. "They're closed."

"Not for me. The owner's a paisa. They'll let us in."

The nightclub was deserted. Hanging from a far wall, Ramon noted, was a pennant of the Nacional Football Club of Medellín. The club's owner was Pablo Escobar. Ospina picked out a booth at the back and ordered two beers.

"Listen, Ramon," Ospina said once they had their beers, "I've been talking to our friend Don Eduardo. He sends you his warmest regards. He thinks this Jimmy Bruno thing you put us onto is going to be very profitable for us all. He wants you to know he's very pleased with the way things are starting to work out."

Ramon took a drink from his bottle of beer and nodded. He knew, of course, about the first trial pickup. If Ospina was giving him a stroke like this, it was because he was about to lay something heavy on him and, sure enough, he did.

"We need someone up here to coordinate the operation for us. To work with Jimmy Bruno's people to make sure everything goes smoothly." Ospina was leaning across the table the way its usual nighttime occupants did to communicate over the din of the music. "Don Eduardo and your friends down in Medellín would like to ask you to do that for them."

"I thought that's why they sent you up here."

His Colombian interlocutor shook his head. "I've got other stuff to do."

It was the way they worked, the Colombians, keep themselves out of the front lines. Ospina, Ramon knew, was not making a request. He was issuing an order, one it wouldn't be wise to refuse. Not with a wife and two children sitting back there in Bogotá. He'd wanted to find a way to string this informant business out, to make himself more valuable to the DEA. Well, he'd found it. It was located between a rock and a hard place. On the other hand, suppose he tried going to Kevin Grady and saying, "Look, I can't handle this."

Grady would say, "Okay, can you handle twenty-five in Marion?"

"Of course, Medellín will see that all your expenses are covered, very generously," Ospina assured him. "And remember you and Paco are getting your cut on everything that goes through the channel."

Ramon gave Ospina the sort of silly grin that had always been for him the hallmark of defeat. "So when do we start?"

Lind's Tape

In view of the fact my arrival in Panama was both sudden and unannounced, I decided to avoid the downtown embassy and work out of our station at Corozal. There was no reason I could think of to let the ambassador know I was in town and planning to meet with Noriega. Setting up my session with him, however, proved to be a little more difficult than I'd anticipated. Tony was in Chiriqui Province with one of his American friends, a former Chicago mobster named Hank Lerner, to whom Noriega had given the slot-machine concession in Panama. They were building a luxury hotel together.

We finally met late one evening at his secret hideaway, Building 152, the old Canal Company bungalow on the causeway running along the entrance to the Canal. The place had the kind of vaulted wooden ceilings you find in seashore cottages in Maine. Curiously, in view of its primary function, it was equipped with twin beds. One of them was undone, and that special odor that blends cheap perfume and recent sex permeated the atmosphere when I arrived. Clearly, our meeting had yielded pride of place to a rendezvous of a different sort. Well, no one had ever accused PK\BARRIER\7-7 of not having his priorities straight.

Since I didn't want to make the real reason for my visit any more evident than necessary, I started out by reviewing our work in progress to make it appear our meeting, however impromptu, was just another of our periodic get-togethers. Our station, I told him, would be coming to him for three more Panamanian diplomatic passports within the next fortnight. We were using those passports very effectively as cover for some of our agents circulating in Eastern Europe and the Third World. Noriega assured me they'd be ready.

Then I reviewed the progress on the installation of the electronic eavesdropping operation we'd discussed on our last visit. We'd gotten the necessary approval and funding, I informed him. The agency was ready to coordinate the building of the installation with his technical people.

The third and final item was more delicate but would feed quite naturally into my request for Juanita's freedom. Noriega's rule was becoming an embarrassment in certain circles in Washington. After all, we couldn't very well go on screaming to the high heavens about the Sandinistas' failure to restore democracy in Nicaragua, while ignoring the fact that our satrap was running a military dictatorship in Panama. Panama was as much an American satellite as Nicaragua was a Soviet one. Indeed, we'd probably gone the Soviets one better here. Danny Ortega was a Marxist crackpot, but I doubt he had ever been on the KGB payroll.

As a result, voices were now being raised in Washington suggesting it was time for democratic elections in Panama and a return of the nation to civilian rule. That did not surprise Tony. The problem both we and he faced, he pointed out, was twofold. On one hand we had to find a candidate who could win an election; yet on the other he had to be docile enough or dumb enough to leave the real power in Panama where it now was, in Noriega's office. We simply could not afford to find ourselves with some left wing wacko as President of Panama, screaming out about the misuse of our Canal Zone bases to support the contra war. Tha would blow what was already an increasingly controversial program right out of the water.

"I've been thinking about it," he assured me. He'd already considered and rejected two possible candidates, he told me. Did we have any suggestions?

There was, in fact, one name circulating in Washington, that of Ardito "Nicky" Barletta, a distinguished economist and officer of the World Bank who'd been a graduate student at the University of Chicago when Secretary of State George Shultz was teaching there. He wasn't docile but he was politically naive, and after sixteen years of indulgent military rule, Panama could certainly use the discipline of a good economist.

"I've heard of him," he said. "I'll have a look at him."

The time had now come to press Tony's button. I took a long swallow of my Old Parr and then a deep breath, knowing I was about to commit the gravest professional sin of my career.

"Tony," I said, "I have a favor to ask you. It's strictly personal. It's got nothing to do with the agency."

"No problem."

I explained the situation of Juanita and her two friends and asked if it would be possible to get them quietly released from his prisons.

A scowl darkened his features. To this day I don't know if it was caused by anger at my request, at the displeasure hearing their names had provoked, or whether he was just trying to figure out who they were and why he'd clapped them into jail.

"Oh, sure," he said finally, "I know who you're talking about now. You know her?"

"Yes," I acknowledged. "She's a friend of mine."

Those black reptilian eyes of his flickered. The notion of a platonic relationship between a man and a woman was foreign to his thinking, so there was no doubt in his mind as to the nature of our friendship. I think he was only surprised and angry that his spies hadn't already made him aware of our affair.

"It will be a bit awkward to explain, but for you, Jack, I'll do it," he told me.

With that he got up and walked to his phone. He got through to someone at PDF headquarters and instructed him to release all three prisoners immediately. Furthermore, he ordered him to have Juanita driven home to her apartment in a police vehicle.

"Don't ask me why," he snapped into the telephone. "Just do it."

He sighed, poured us each another scotch, clinked his glass to mine, then winked. "They were a bunch of amateur troublemakers. But do me a favor, will you? Keep her out of my hair from now on?"

We chatted a few more moments, then Noriega glanced at his watch. "She'll be home in a quarter of an hour. You better get over there to enjoy her gratitude," he leered.

At the doorway, he looped a fraternal arm around my shoulder, a gesture he would never have allowed himself before that moment. More than anything else, it spoke to the changed nature of our relationship.

"Women," he laughed, a malicious smile creasing his saturnine features. "They can really mess a man up, can't they?"

I swept Juanita into my arms the second I opened the door to her apartment. She was strangely indifferent to my embrace. Had some horror overtaken her in prison and broken that independent spirit I so admired? For a second I dismissed the thought, and savored instead the immensity of my relief at having her, alive and well, back in my embrace, feeling the outlines of her body pressed once again to mine.

We kissed, then slowly drew apart. She looked at me, hurt and sorrow, other mementos, no doubt, of prison, filling her eyes. Curious, I thought, she should be surprised to see me but she didn't seem to be. If anything, it was as if she'd been expecting me.

"Your brother Pedro called and told me what happened. I grabbed the first flight I could to Howard and talked to an air force general I know over there. I hope it did some good."

Wordlessly, she slipped from my arms and walked toward her living room sofa. She was wearing the clothes she'd been arrested in, a pair of blue jeans encrusted with dirt and grime, a cotton shirt, the top two buttons missing, ripped off, I assumed. It, too, was filthy. She had no makeup, of course, her hair was unkempt, and I knew from one deep breath that she hadn't been able to wash for days. That was hardly surprising. Her face was pale and drawn, but studying her body and clothes I saw no indication of bruises, no telltale patches of dried blood. Her scars, apparently, were on her soul.

She sat down, leaned her head against the couch, and looked at me with a regard so distant the most charitable adjective I can think of to describe it is dreamy.

"Jack," she said, breaking the uncomfortable silence that had grown between us. "It's time to stop the charade. I know who you are. I know who you work for. I know why Noriega let me go."

"How do you know all that?"

"Because Noriega called me ten minutes ago to tell me."

The son of a bitch, I thought. Part of his motivation was, I had no doubt, sheer viciousness. He would have assumed Juanita didn't know I was CIA. Why leave her in ignorance of a reality that was sure to upset her? It would also have been his way of telling her what powerful friends he had. You and your pals are tilting at windmills trying to overthrow me, he was saying. The gringos will never let me fall.

For a while I didn't answer her. What was I supposed to say? Denying her words would be a waste of breath. Should I tell her, 'I'm sorry if I'm an officer of the CIA'? I wasn't. Employment with the agency had its disadvantages, but as far as I was concerned, being ashamed of what we did wasn't one of them.

Finally, I acknowledged the obvious. "It's true, Juanita. I'm an officer of the CIA. But I wasn't hiding that information from you to take advantage of you, or because I thought if I told you it would mean the end of our relationship. It was because we don't go around shouting, 'Hey, I'm an officer of the CIA' from the rooftops. Silence is the rule of our game. You know that."

"What I know, Jack, and what pains me deeply, is that the man I thought I loved turns out to be an agent of the nation and the organization that has handed my country over to tyrants."

"Juanita, if Noriega is such a tyrant, why did he let you and your friends go free tonight?"

"I'm not sure I ever want to know the answer to that question, Jack, but he's a tyrant, all right. Do you know about the law he used to throw us into jail for five years? Without a trial? Without a conviction? With only an accusation? And from an unidentified accuser, at that. If a man who will do things like that isn't a tyrant, then please give me a better definition of one."

I walked over to the balcony on which we'd stood that first night when we'd come back from our tour of Panama, and looked out, as I had then, at the moon-flecked sea, at the ships waiting to enter the Canal. Had we reached the end of our affair? Was the end of our love the price I was going to have to pay for saving her from Noriega's jail? There was a terrible yet not inappropriate irony in that, wasn't there?

"Juanita, there are other considerations here besides Noriega and his rule." I was, I guess, pleading now for her understanding or at least her acceptance of our actions.

"Of course, there are other considerations at stake here, Jack. What is at stake are America's goals, America's interests, not ours. Because you're bigger and stronger, because you're convinced you know better, because you think that you have some God-given global vision, our concerns have to be subordinated to yours."

"Size and strength isn't what it's about, Juanita. It's principles."

"Principles, is it, Jack? Which principle of American democracy are we talking about here?" At least, her old fire was back now, I thought. That was a meager enough consolation, but it was something, after all.

"Is it freedom of the press? Of expression? Of the right to free elections? To express political opposition freely and openly? Because you won't find any of those principles working in Panama, Jack. And who's deprived us of them? A military dictatorship your government and the CIA has supported, backed and anointed with a shower of gold for fifteen years."

She had gotten up from the sofa and marched out to the balcony to join me, her arms folded defiantly across her chest, her chin thrust angrily upward as it must have been when she faced Noriega's interrogators.

"Fundamentally, Jack, you're a good man, and that's what troubles and puzzles me so. How is it good men like you can delude themselves into accepting and tolerating acts of evil, crimes even, in the name of some higher, redeeming validity?"

"Juanita, let's try to at least keep a sense of proportion about this, can we? This is Panama, not Nazi Germany, for God's sake."

"Oh, I agree, Jack. Ours is a small, insignificant evil, only a minor sore on the earth's misery-filled surface. But why should it hurt us any the less for that?"

"There are other evils out there, evils that make this one pale."

"Please don't invoke those buffoons the Sandinistas you're fighting to justify that declaration, Jack, dear."

"How about those lovely people the Sendero Luminoso? The ones who rip peasants' arms and legs off in public when they disagree with their wonderful Marxist theories? Are they evil enough for you?"

"Tell me something, Jack. Do you know how the Sendero finance their activities?"

"I have an idea," I replied, but she wasn't listening or if she was she didn't want my answer interrupting the flow of her own logic.

"They put a tax on every coca leaf that leaves Peru on its way up north. Which makes them silent business partners in the cocaine traffic with guess who? That nice man you went to see tonight to get my freedom, Manuel Antonio Noriega."

Again I tried to intervene, but I could have saved my breath.

"You hear things in prison, Jack, you learn things. Noriega is in the cocaine traffic right up to his neck. Probably with some of your brave contra freedom fighters."

"I don't believe it."

"You don't believe it because you don't want to believe it. Because it's inconvenient for you to believe it."

"I don't believe it because nobody has ever given me a single shred of evidence to support that charge." In the heat of our discussion I had, perhaps conveniently, forgotten the accusations against Noriega we had quashed back in the early seventies.

"Jack, I haven't thanked you yet for freeing me. I'm sure it was a difficult and even dangerous thing for you to do. I'm grateful. I really am. And do you know how I'm going to show you my gratitude?"

"Gratitude isn't necessary, Juanita. I'd rather have understanding than gratitude."

"I'm going to get you the proof of Noriega's involvement with the drug traffic, Jack. Then, because I know you are a good man, I know you'll give that proof to your government. Maybe, at last after that, you Americans will stop supporting that son of a bitch."

"For Christ's sake, Juanita! Be careful about what you're doing from now on. I was able to help you once. I'm not sure I'll be able to do it twice."

Her face was drawn, her eyes encircled with the pallor of fatigue. Suddenly, she let her head slump on my shoulder. "I need someone to hold me in his arms tonight, Jack," she whispered. "Will you give me your arms?"

I wrapped them around that lovely body of hers. "Of course, Juanita."

She spent twenty minutes showering, scraping off the dirt and memories of prison. When finally she emerged from the bathroom, snapped off the lights and slid beneath the covers, she was trembling. She folded her body into mine more in resignation than in passion.

"Once I thought I loved you, Jack," she murmured. "If there's anything left of that, it's here in this bed that we're going to find it."

"What Ospina did," Ramon explained to the little gathering, "was send ten of those beepers we bought back to Don Eduardo Hernandez in Medellín. Hernandez passed them on to Escobar, the Ochoas, Kiko Moncada, I don't know who else. They sent them back up here to their money couriers in New York and L.A., okay?"

Kevin Grady studied Ramon with a conflicting blend of emotions. In part, his feelings were those of a hardened cop watching a CI for any sign of evasiveness or hesitation; in another part, they were similar, perhaps, to the thoughts of a father watching his prodigal son take the first steps on his journey of return. He'd begun to like this guy. Ramon, as far as Grady could tell, was playing the game. He was doing the right thing without being prodded or pushed. It wasn't as though you had to yank out his back teeth to get something out of him the way you did with most CIs.

He looked around at the team he had assembled in the office of Bruno's Financial Management Services: Ella Jean Ransom, coolly appraising Ramon; Eddie Gomez, more Jimmy Bruno than DEA agent inside these premises; Cesar Rodriguez, the youngest agent in their group.

"Ospina assigned each beeper a number," Ramon was saying. "That number corresponds to a telephone number on this list he gave me." Ramon laid a sheet of paper on Bruno's desk. "I don't know who's going to be at the end of any of those phone numbers, who the guy works for. I don't even have a name for the guy—or guys—who got the beeper."

He paused to be sure the DEA agents were following him through this cartel-constructed thicket. "The way it works is this. I get a call on my beeper, right? The guy leaves his beeper number, say three, along with a time and a day of the week. According to my list, beeper three, which in fact happens to be the first guy who called, is identified as area code 718, telephone number 9352768, I called that number from a pay phone on the day and at the time number three left on my beeper."

"I presume," observed Eddie Gomez, "all the numbers on that list he gave you are for pay phones."

"Right," Kevin Grady said, taking over, "we've got the locations of all ten of them pinned down, five here, five in L.A. Like Ramon said, the first guy to call was number three, which is for a booth at the corner of Northern Boulevard and Prince Street in Flushing." Grady had pulled out a notepad. "We put the booth under surveillance at the time the guy had requested for his call and followed him when he finished talking." He glanced down at his notepad. "He was driving a gold Thunderbird, New York number plates 9408Y6. It's registered to a Miss Cindy Velasquez, a part-time psychology student at Queens College. Apparently, she's the guy's girlfriend."

He flipped a page of his notebook. "We followed him to what appears to be his residence, 7101 Sutton Street. The apartment's leased in the girl's name. She's Colombian-born, naturalized U.S. She came up NADDIS negative on the computer. As far as we can tell, she has no priors. She may or may not be involved here."

"How about the guy?" Gomez asked. "What do we know about him?"

"Right now, not a lot. According to the super, his name is Ricky. Been living there with her for about three months. The mailman hasn't had any mail for him, so we haven't got a last name on him yet."

"You think that place might be a cash stash-house?"

"No. We put a stake on it. There's not much traffic going in. My guess is he's the delivery boy. Hopefully, he'll pick

up the money at the stash-house and take it to whatever delivery site we give him."

"Are we going to put a wire on the phone?" Cesar asked.

"Fuck no!" Kevin gave the young agent a contemptuous
glance. Well, he was a new kid on the block; what could you
expect? "Why would we waste time doing that? You better
understand one thing right now, kid. Colombians never use
their home phones. It's all cellular phones and beepers. Get
a court order to tap that phone and all you're going to hear
is the Velasquez girl complaining about her menstrual pains.

"Now," he announced, snapping a cassette into the tape
recorder before him, "here's the recording of our friend Ramon talking to this guy Ricky. As you'll see, Ricky's not
much into small talk."

"Hola."

"Hola."

"Ramon?"

"Si."

"I've got 925 shirts ready for you."

"Okay."

"For Z3 370.142."

"Right, Z3 370.142."

"I'd like an appointment around noon Thursday."

"Okay. I'll talk to Jimmy's friend. I think he's staying in
a motel up there somewhere, okay?"

"Okay."

"I'll call you back on this number at six tonight."

"No, you won't. I'll beep you at six and give you the
number I want you to call me on. In exactly fifteen minutes
after my call. Got it?"

"The Z3 number is for a numbered bank account at the
Banco de Occidente in Panama City," Grady explained,
shutting off the recorder. "Each beeper has at least one.
Some have two or three. The number 925 means they want
to pass us 925 thousand dollars."

Ella Jean whistled appreciatively.

"Yeah. A million bucks means they're going to play now.
The good news here is they've agreed to exchange inside a
motel room where we can film the operation. There's a Best
Western on Interstate 278 above the Hunt's Point market.
Cesar, you're going to get your ass out there and book a
room. Ramon will give this guy your room number and the

location when he calls him back at six. The technical people will come in tonight to wire the place up."

He turned to Gomez. "We have the NYPD running the stake on Ricky. We explained there'll be a residual in this thing for them—shared arrests, arrests they can generate themselves. They'll get their share of all the assets we seize to pay for all the overtime they're going to be clocking on surveillance. Now, hopefully, our guy will stop by the cash stash-house to pick up the dough on his way to the motel tomorrow, so we'll have that for openers."

Kevin stood up and stretched, popping up on the balls of his feet. He loved the excitement, the sense of engagement and challenge that always came when you started on a promising operation. This was anything but a game, yet Kevin knew a part of his leader's role was to keep the enthusiasm level of everybody up. "Hey," he concluded, "I think we're on to something major here. Maybe very major. Let's not any of us fuck it up."

As the meeting broke up, Grady sensed Ramon was hanging back, as though he had something on his mind. He walked over to his CI and casually looped his arm over one of Ramon's shoulders. "That wasn't the place to say it in there, Ramon, but let me tell you I think you're doing a terrific job for us. We're not going to forget it."

His words produced a flicker of gratitude in the CI's eyes. Those dark eyes were set into deep sockets in his angular face; now their depth was underlined by the dark pouches of troubled sleep. The guy is worried, Grady thought, the strain is beginning to show. Ramon's next words confirmed his observation. "Can we talk? In private?"

"Sure. I was just going across the street for a cup of coffee with Ella Jean. Is it okay if she comes along? She's one of us." Kevin, in fact, had not been planning to have a cup of coffee with Ella Jean or anyone else. It was standard DEA practice, however, to have two agents talk to a CI wherever possible. It cut down on the chances of any misunderstandings coming up later.

Ramon hesitated just a second, then agreed. They took a back booth in the Madison Avenue Coffee Shop. Ramon laid his concerns on the table as soon as the coffee had arrived. "I'm worried about my wife and kids in Bogotá. I wonder if I shouldn't get them out of there." Then he reviewed his conversation with Ospina and the potentially lethal implications of the liaison role into which he'd been drafted.

"Did your wife know you were into the drug traffic?" Grady asked him.

Ramon shook his head.

"So she doesn't know you're working with us now?"

Again, Ramon shook his head.

"How do you explain all your long absences to her?" Ella Jean wondered.

"I tell her I'm away on business. Real estate."

"And she doesn't want to know everything about where you are, what you're doing?"

Ramon gave the black female agent a deferential smile. "Latin wives. They don't ask a lot of questions like that."

"Ramon," Grady said, "I told you down in Aruba that if things got hot we'd bring your wife and kids up here and put them in the witness protection program. I meant it. We're ready to do that. But before we can, you're going to have to come clean with her about what's going on here."

Ramon was silent. This was a reality he had not yet contemplated. Like a lot of the realities that seemed to be closing in on him these days from every side of the box called life.

Kevin sensed very clearly what was going through his CI's mind. "There's another thing here, Ramon, and I'm not trying to lay something on you when I tell you this. An undercover operation always works best when everything stays one hundred percent normal, nothing changes in anybody's routine. Those guys in the cartel have no reason to suspect you've changed sides. You've never been arrested. As far as they know, you've never even been indicted. I want to keep it that way."

"Yeah, but what happens when you start arresting people?"

"That's not going to be tomorrow. The idea here is to hold off, build up as long a list of felons as we can, get a strong case then, bang, come down in one swoop. Sure, the local police in New York and L.A. are going to bring people in. But they'll be fringe people, nobody who's seen or who worked with you.

"Now, suppose we get your wife and kids up here next week. Your pal Paco's wife calls your wife to find out how she's doing and, oops, nobody's home. The folks have disappeared. You don't think that's not going to set bells ringing in Medellín? They haven't got the wife and kiddies anymore, but they sure as hell have got you. And about two thousand hired guns any one of whom they can stuff onto a plane to come up here and do their dirty work for them."

Ramon massaged his throbbing temples with his fingertips. "Yeah, well, I don't know. I just don't know. Maybe you're right."

"This is your first undercover penetration, Ramon. I've run fifty of them. Believe me, they work best when no one breaks the mold, when things bounce along just like they always have."

Ramon squirmed. Worry seemed to have taken up permanent residence in his brain these days. He glanced at Ella Jean for some kind of feminine comfort or guidance.

"Will your wife be able to deal with all this if you tell her what's going on?" she asked him. "She's not going to flip out and spoil the party, is she?"

Her question shook Ramon. It was another point he hadn't faced. "I think she'll be okay."

"Does she love you enough to throw everything over, her friends, her family, her country, to come up here and live with you for the rest of her life?"

Ramon groaned softly. Where was the exit? Where was the way out? "I just don't know," he mumbled.

Ella Jean laid a compassionate hand on his shaking wrist. "Let me suggest something." She glanced at Grady before going ahead. "When you think you're ready to tell her, you come to us and let us know. We'll give you the name and twenty-four-hour number of our DEA country attaché at the embassy in Bogotá for her. You tell her that if something comes up and she has to run, all she has to do is call him. He'll take over and she's out of there."

She studied the effect of her words on the worried CI. "You've also got to tell her that if she ever, and I mean *ever* gets a call from him, she grabs the kids and leaves everything, the soup on the stove, the laundry in the washing machine and heads straight to the embassy. That will take care of an emergency which hopefully never is going to happen here. Then just before things start going down on this operation, we can quietly move her and your children out of Bogotá."

"Yeah," Ramon said. "You're right. That's the only way,

isn't it? I'll have to tell her what's going on the next time I go back."

Ella Jean gave his wrist a reassuring squeeze, then withdrew her hand. "I like you," she told him. "I like your concern for your wife and children. That's not something we see in many of the people we run into in this business."

Ramon left a few minutes later.

"What do you think of him?" Grady asked Ella Jean when he'd gone.

"First, I really do like him. Second, you can trust him. He's playing the game."

"What makes you say that?"

"Because he's already anticipating the downside of his involvement with us. Looking ahead to how he's going to protect his family when the shit hits the fan. Now that has to tell you he's going to do what he has to do."

"Yeah," Kevin acknowledged, "you got a point there." Ella Jean was wearing an emerald green dress topped by a high Chinese style collar she'd set off with a single gold chain stretched around her neck in a choker. The dress's cut was not so tight as to be provocative, but not so loose that the outlines of the trim figure it concealed were lost, either. Kevin glanced at her, trying not to let his eyes linger too long on the lithe outlines of her body. Yet what was so attractive to him in Ella Jean was not the sensual promise of her figure, but the tenderness, the sense of compassion that lay just below that tough street kid's outer shell of hers.

He reluctantly averted his gaze and drained the last of the coffee from his cup. Since that painful morning when he'd thrown a final, symbolic fistful of dirt on his wife's casket, work had been about the only emotion driving him forward. His friends had made the usual gestures friends make with a bereaved widower: come to dinner to meet this charming divorcee Suzy; we're dying to have you meet Peggy who's just arrived from Chicago. You're going to love her.

Except none of it had taken. The scars left by his wife's death were too fresh. Now, sitting here sipping coffee beside this attractive black colleague of his, he felt for the first time in months the stirrings of desire. Ella Jean Ransom might be about as far away from his boyhood in Irish Catholic Queens as you could get, but the attraction was there.

He let his hand give a tentative brush to Ella Jean's.

"Hey," he said, "you did a terrific job with that guy. Thanks."

Then he offered her what was meant to be a playful wink. "You know, not only are you a good-looking lady, but you're a smart one, too."

Ella Jean arched a feline eyebrow. "Poor Kevin," she laughed, "what's the world coming to for nice honky guys like you? Not only are there smart women out there now, but some of them are even black."

The trick to flying at night in weather over water, as Juanita Boyd well knew, was not to let your eyes wander too far from the instrument panel. With her Piper Seneca being tossed around by the gusting winds, the horizon shifting and frequently obscured by drifting clouds, it would be all too easy to slip the plane into a down angle without even realizing it had happened. She had double-checked her QNH, the barometer-based settings which ensured the accuracy of her altimeter, with the Paitilla control tower before taking off from Contadora Island fifteen minutes earlier.

Ahead of her now she could see the lights of Panama City reflecting against the opaque underbelly of the cloud mass hovering over the capital. She would be approaching Ten Miles Out, the contact point at which she would come under the Paitilla tower's approach frequency. One eye on her altimeter, the other on the instrument that displayed the plane's alignment to the horizon, she began to flick through her radio's frequencies toward the one which she wanted, 118.3. Suddenly a voice came squawking through the darkness of her cockpit.

"Okay, my friend, everything is ready for you here. The truck will pick you up at the end of the runway as usual. Go over to Tower and get your landing instructions."

"Roger, will do. See you in a few minutes," a second voice answered.

Juanita glanced at the frequency setting on her radio. It was 123.0. She'd stopped short of her goal and had picked up some private exchange by mistake. With a twist of her finger, she sent the radio up to the proper setting, 118.3. As she did she heard the voice that had just said "Roger, will do" talking to the Paitilla tower.

"This is Hotel Kilo Three Four Seven Niner ten miles out,

level at five thousand feet, inbound from San Blas. Request landing instructions."

HK, *Hotel Kilo,* was the call sign for aircraft registered in Colombia. What, Juanita wondered, was a Colombian plane doing coming into Paitilla at this time of the night? From San Blas off Panama's seacoast?

For the moment she had other things on her mind, however. Once the other aircraft had gotten its landing instructions and moved into its approach, she moved up onto Ten Miles Out and radioed the tower in turn for her landing instructions.

"Altimeter setting 29.88," the tower informed her. "We have winds out of the southwest at twenty knots gusting up to thirty. You are cleared to land straight in. Call back when you are in visual."

Three minutes later, Juanita set her Seneca smoothly onto the rain-slicked Paitilla runway. As she rolled to a stop, she noticed another aircraft, its wingtip lights blinking, being led up the row of hangars to her left by a vehicle of the Panamanian Defense Forces. Toward the end of that line of buildings there was, she knew, a hangar reserved for the exclusive use of the PDF. It also housed Noriega's personal jet.

As she started her own turn off the runway, the second plane passed under the glow of a lamp. She caught a glimpse of its registration—HK 3479. It was an Aerocommander 1000. Why was that Colombian aircraft slipping into Paitilla in the middle of the night, then rolling up to the PDF hangar under a PDF escort?

Of course. It confirmed the whispers she'd heard in jail about Noriega and the PDF's involvement with the Colombian drug traffic.

She taxied to her own hangar, closed down her aircraft, and got into the car she had left there in the morning when she had taken off for Contadora. As she was heading for the airport exit, a crazy idea grabbed her. Why not just drive past the PDF building and have a look at what was going on?

She turned away from the gate and drove up the arm of the airport running toward the building, set a bit apart from its neighbors. As she approached it, a sentry emerged from the shadows into the path of her advancing headlights. He held up one hand summoning her to stop. In the other, to give bite to his order, he waved an Uzi.

He walked over to her window. "Where do you think you're going?" he asked.

She offered him her most fetching smile to bolster the credibility of the lie she was about to utter. He did not appear impressed. "I'm looking for the exit."

"Let me see your papers," he demanded.

She was about to protest but thought better of it and handed him her cedula, her national identity card and her driver's license.

"Don't move," he ordered, and disappeared into the hangar with it. He came back a few minutes later and handed her back her papers. With a disdainful wave he pointed back in the direction from which she'd just come. "Turn around," he told her, "the exit's back there."

The gold Thunderbird rolled out of the parking lot at 71-01 Sutton and poised an instant at the curb like a hunting dog sniffing the morning air for a promising scent. Ricky Mendez was studying the street for any unusual activity that might indicate police surveillance. Satisfied there was none, he turned right toward Kissena Boulevard.

Half a block away, two detectives of the New York Police Department's Narcotics Squad crouched in the rear of the panel truck emblazoned with the logo of Goldstein's TV Sales and Repairs, and watched the flashy sports car rumble by. Ricky was driving that vehicle in violation of the canons of the Medellín cartel, and the fact did not escape their notice.

"That's the first Colombian I ever saw trying to make life easy for us," one muttered, picking up his radio. "Contact. Kissena. Ten twelve," he announced. That told the other surveillance vehicles in the operation that the Thunderbird was out of the garage and headed for Kissena Boulevard. A car was already stationed in the parking lot of an Exxon station on Kissena from which its occupants could monitor the flow of traffic coming out of Sutton. Minutes after the first signal, its driver saw the Thunderbird turning north on Kissena toward Flushing.

"Contact Kissena toward Flushing," he noted into his radio as he slid his car into traffic. One of the surveillance cars, a Honda carrying a pair of female detectives, was already leap-frogging ahead of the Thunderbird. The other, a Pontiac, brought up the rear.

Kevin Grady and Eddie Gomez followed the progress of the tail from the office of Bruno's Financial Management Services, grabbing at each of the few scraps the police offered up on their police net.

Ricky drove up Kissena past the Queens campus of the City University of New York toward Flushing.

"With any luck," Gomez grumbled, "the bastard's headed toward a cash stash-house to pick up the money for our meet."

During the next fifteen frustrating minutes, the radio was silent. The two agents had to assume their New York colleagues were holding eyeball contact on the T-bird. Finally, their phone rang.

"Our guy just called in from a pay phone to stay off the net," the police communications desk informed Grady. "Your friend stopped at a two-story residential dwelling at 92-12 Sanford Avenue in Flushing. Beeped his way into the garage and closed the door behind him."

"That's it!" Gomez chortled. "We got the cash stash-house!"

When Ricky came out an hour and a half later, Grady alerted Cesar and Ramon to the fact he was on his way, then requested the NYPD to drop their surveillance since this time they knew where Ricky was going.

In Room 207 of their Best Western motel, Cesar and Ramon gave a last check to their surroundings. The motel's primary function was to provide short-term accommodations to the hookers working the truck drivers delivering fresh produce to the Hunt's Point market. When Cesar had taken the place, he'd found it littered with the mementos of its regular clientele: splotches of mascara in the wash basin, Kleenex tissues blotted with lipstick in the ashtrays, artificial eyelashes scattered over the rumpled bedcovers, an empty bottle of Johnson's Baby Oil in the waste basket. He'd left them all in place. Keep the decor authentic, he'd decided.

The two men gave a final check to their hidden video cameras and recorders. They worked without a sound. Satisfied, Cesar sent Ramon out to the parking lot to wait for the Thunderbird.

As the car rolled to a stop, the CI strolled over to it.

"Hola. You got some shirts for me?"

Ramon sensed the driver hesitating, probably running the sound of his voice through some audio filtering system in his brain to compare it with the voice he'd heard over the phone.

"Ramon?"

"Yeah, man." Ramon underlined his words with a playful wink. He saw the reassurance lightening Ricky's darkly handsome Latin features. Funny, Ramon thought. If things go the way they're supposed to here, I'll be eyeballing this guy across a courtroom one day, setting him up to do fifteen to twenty. How reassured is he going to look then?

Ricky unsnapped the latch of his car's luggage compartment. It contained four white Samsonite suitcases. "Give me a hand here," he asked Ramon.

The CI picked up two suitcases and led the way up the outside staircase to Room 207. Carefully, he set the Samsonites at the end of the bed, where they would be in the center of the hidden camera's angle of vision.

"So what have we got?" Cesar asked.

"A little more than I said. We had a delivery last night. We make it $1,006,500."

"Okay, let's have a look."

They snapped open the suitcases. They were crammed with greenbacks, stack after stack of them, wrapped with rubber bands and filling every corner of each Samsonite.

Cesar picked up a couple of the bundles and flipped through them.

"I brought a couple of money counters," Ricky volunteered.

The DEA agent tossed a stack of hundred dollar bills onto the bed like it was a pack of Oreo cookies. "So let's start counting."

Ricky's Brandt money counters took three hundred bills at a time. The bills were stacked sideways on a metal slide which flicked them through a slot one by one, registering the count on a display counter as each bill passed through the machine. The key to the operation, of course, was making sure that all the bills in each stack were the same denomination.

The job was slow, tedious and boring. Many of the bills were filthy and rumpled. Some couldn't get through the machine and had to be hand-counted.

At one point, Cesar picked up a particularly filthy fifty dollar bill and sniffed it.

"Shit," he said, "you could get high smelling this damn

thing. Can't your people at least try to clean the goddamned powder off before you bring us this stuff?"

Ricky winced. "Listen, some of the stuff these guys bring us you wouldn't believe. We have to use surgical masks when we work with it. I kid you not."

They were counting the contents of the third suitcase, working on a stack of particularly filthy twenties, when Cesar exploded. Five of the bills in the stack had already been of the wrong denomination, three fives and two tens. Every tenth bill, it seemed, stuck in the machine. Cesar grabbed the remaining stack out of the Brandt and hurled the bills at the walls of the motel room.

"Jesus Christ!" he shouted at Ricky. "This is the last fucking time I do this for you. I gotta take this money to a bank, a good, legitimate bank. I gotta put it into a legitimate bank account. What the hell do you think those bankers are going to think when they see this filthy stuff with your goddamn coke powder all over it? What the hell are they going to think about our operation?"

Ricky rocked back on his heels under the buffeting of the Cuban American's angry salvo. "Hey, man, why you rattling my cage here? I'm just the delivery boy."

"Yeah?" Cesar snarled. "Well, you go back and tell those guys you work for the next time they send us money, they send it the right way. The fives together, the tens together, the twenties together, exactly five thousand bucks in each bundle, all clean, all counted, none of it mixed up. I'm telling you right now that if it doesn't come in that way, fuck you, you're out the door. I don't touch your goddamn money. You hear me, hombre?"

"Yeah, yeah. Get off my case, will you? I'll tell them. Listen, it's tough. They got guys bringing this stuff in from all over the place. Maine, Albany, Boston. What do those guys care they got a little coke on their dough?"

Son of a bitch, Ricky was thinking as he said that, this guy's a piece of work. At least you know one thing. He's no cop. A cop, he'd take the money any fucking way. What does he care how it's packaged?

The rest of the count continued in angry semi-silence. It came out to $1,004,900, which was 1600 dollars short of the total Ricky had announced on arrival, a shortcoming Cesar noted with a caustic comment. The three signed a joint receipt, and Ricky, delighted to have this operation behind him, was out the door like a shot.

Ramon and Cesar left separately. They met later at Bruno's Financial Management Services. Once again the money came out of the Samsonites and was assembled stack by stack on Eddie Gomez/Jimmy Bruno's desk. Gomez produced a Polaroid camera. Kevin, Cesar, Ella Jean and Ramon proudly circled the mound of money for a group photo, their eyes illumined by wonder. There is, after all, something about the sight of a million-plus dollars in cash sitting on a tabletop that can inspire a sense of awe in almost anyone.

Ella Jean sighed and squeezed Kevin's hand. "You realize," she whispered, "you're going to give the twenty best years of your life to the G, and in all those twenty years working for them, they aren't going to pay you as much money as we got sitting right there in front of us on that table?"

Pedro del Rica stalked along in the footsteps of Manuel Antonio Noriega as the general strolled proudly through the ante-room of his newly remodeled headquarters in Fort Amador's Building #8. One whole wall of the room was lined with a glass case housing Noriega's private gun collection, presentation pistols from his military admirers around the world and enough submachine guns, it occurred to del Rica, to equip a battalion of paratroopers. His employer was not a man likely to be caught under-gunned in a coup d'etat.

On a table in one corner of the room, displayed in a glass case as a traveler might display a shrunken human head he'd brought back from the Amazonian rain forests, was the kepi Noriega had worn as a cadet at the Peruvian military academy.

The general threw open the door to his inner sanctum and waved the man with the permanent scowl into the armchair beside his desk. He circled around behind it, pausing as he did to play for a second with one of the pieces on the chessboard he had set up beside his computer, then sat down.

"So," he asked, "how did it go last night?"

"We had a little weather, but they got in all right."

"How much did they bring?"

"Five hundred. All of it was for our hangar. None of it was for their Inair operation this time." Del Rica reached down, lifted up the black leather suitcase he'd been carrying and laid it on the general's desk.

Noriega spun through its combination lock and flicked its latches open. It was filled with bundles of hundred-dollar bills.

"It's all there," del Rica assured him. "I counted it."

The general snapped the lock shut again and set the suitcase on the floor beside him.

"No problems?" he asked del Rica.

"No, everything's smooth here on our end. The Colombians are happy. It's going out of Costa Rica slowly. It all depends on which of those gringo pilots are flying down the arms. Oh, there was some woman who came poking around the hangar area last night after the plane came in, but . . ."

"What is a woman doing around our hangar at Paitilla at two in the morning?"

"She said she was lost which maybe she was. Looking for the exit gate. Maybe she was nosy, I don't know. Anyway, the sentry got her cedula number and the registration of her car."

"Let me have a look."

Del Rica took a notepad from his inside pocket, flipped through it, then laid it, open to the page he'd been looking for, on Noriega's desk.

Boyd, Juanita Boyd. Where the hell have I heard that name, Noriega thought. Then he remembered. It was the woman who was Lind's mistress, the one he'd released from prison to keep him happy. If she was driving past their hangar at two in the morning, it was not because she was lost.

"Thanks," he told del Rica, tearing the page from his notebook. "I'll hold on to this."

Half an hour after del Rica had left, Noriega walked next door to Building #9 where, with the aid of the CIA, he was installing his electronic eavesdropping station. When the young West Point–trained officer he'd put in charge of the project had finished briefing him on its status, Noriega gave him a piece of paper.

"I want this number added to your Listen List when you start operations," he ordered. "But the tapes you run on it are to go to only one person—me."

The Taco Bell was just off Sepulveda, a twenty-minute drive from Los Angeles International Airport. It was set in one of those suburban L.A. sprawls that reminded Ramon of the song he'd sung as a kid about all those *ticky tacky houses* standing in a row, street after street of anonymous one-story bungalows, each with its identical attached garage. For all its banality, however, that kind of neighborhood was the perfect environment in which to conceal a stash-house.

He contemplated the nachos on his plate with a minimum of enthusiasm. Ramon disliked Mexican food. He could sense the acid indigestion this snack was going to produce just from looking at it. Again, he scanned the restaurant for any hint that the courier he was supposed to meet here had arrived. Detecting none, he took a bite of his food.

Both Kevin and Cesar had assured him that the money exchanges in L.A. would be even easier to manage than they had been in New York. Ramon had rented a Buick at Hertz when he'd arrived at the airport. It was out in the parking lot of the Taco Bell. The courier would "borrow" it for half an hour or so, take it to wherever the money was hidden, stuff the money in the trunk, then return the car and the keys to Ramon.

The DEA's L.A. district office had fixed one of their tiny radio transmitters to the inside of the car's fender with a magnet to make surveillance relatively easy.

Ramon was well into his nachos when the courier, carrying a cup of coffee, sat down at his table.

"Ramon?" he asked.

The CI nodded.

"The car in the lot?"

"The blue Buick four-door parked in the slot in front of the trash cans." Ramon slipped him the keys as they talked.

"Okay, read your paper. Relax. I'll be back in half an hour or so."

Ramon watched him go, then tried to concentrate on the *L.A. Times* crossword puzzle. He couldn't. His mind was on the courier who'd just left. His was another face he would one day have to confront across a courtroom. You would have thought some sense of pain, of regret for that might have animated his being. It didn't.

The fact was that Ramon had begun to enjoy this undercover role of his—the danger, the duplicity, the sense of participation in something important which Grady and Cesar were trying to convey to him. But most of all, he just liked the excitement. In its strange way, the kick he was getting here wasn't all that different from the kick he'd once gotten out of brokering loads. I'm a damned excitement junkie, he thought.

The courier was back in forty-five minutes. "It's locked in the trunk. We double counted it and it's $925,000 on the button. If there's any discrepancy in the bank's count, call me." He paused to slip Ramon a piece of paper along with the car keys. "It goes to three different accounts. They're listed on here with the amount each one gets."

That's all there was to it. Two hours later, Ramon and Cesar were posing for yet another Polaroid shot in front of another mound of money on an agent's desk in the L.A. district office. Looking at it, Ramon realized the DEA wasn't going to lose this operation just to seize one load of coke coming out of Medellín. He had found his long-term employment with the U.S. government.

The South Bronx hallway was long and poorly lit, the shadows along its route dark pools of undefined menace. Even the friendly weight of his Glock automatic in his shoulder holster did little to reassure Kevin Grady. As they got to the end of the corridor and started up the long flight of stairs toward their destination, Kevin saw a hostile black face eyeballing him from the darkness of the stairwell. Clearly, it belonged to a sentry standing guard on the operation they'd come to visit.

Jack Tompkins led the way. He moved with the assurance of a man who'd been in and out of these premises many times, as indeed he had. He was black, a former New York beat cop whose friendship with Kevin dated back to their days together in the Police Academy. Now he worked for the New York State Bureau of Narcotics running an organization he had developed and pioneered himself. It was called the Street Research Office, and its task was simple: to find out everything there was to know about the drug scene; what was in and what was out; what was happening to prices; what was in favor; what were the latest techniques for consuming drugs; where the action was at now and where it was likely to shift to. Tompkins was a walking encyclopedia of the drug underworld, and there was no one in the city for whose knowledge Kevin had more regard.

Therefore, when Tompkins had called and suggested this visit, Kevin had agreed immediately. "Something new has just hit town," he had warned Kevin. "You better get a look at it, because I think we got a disaster coming our way."

Jack did not make arrests, which gave him the access that allowed the three of them onto these premises unmolested. Both Kevin and Ella Jean marching up the staircase at his side were here *ex-officio* to learn, not to function as DEA agents. The intelligence they could get here would far outstrip the value a single bust would offer.

Ella Jean, dressed down for the occasion in a Long Island University sweatshirt and blue Adidas warmup pants, pointed at the dark stain on the step above them, spilling over onto its riser. It was blood, barely coagulated. Whoever had left it there had left it in the last hour or so.

"Would you guess their debt collectors don't believe in extending credit?" she whispered to Jack.

When they reached the landing, Kevin sniffed a sour odor. It reminded him of the bitter smell in his high school chemistry lab on Thursday afternoons before they began their weekly experiments. Ahead of them, a steel-plated door creaked open a few inches. Kevin saw a dark face topped by a seventies style high-pile Afro stare first at Jack, then shift his glare to him.

"Who be the fuckin' honk?" he hissed.

"He's okay. He's with me," Jack growled.

The man unlatched his protective chain and opened the door a few reluctant degrees. Their genial host was wearing a floral shirt flopping over what appeared to be, in the dim light, his boxer shorts and a pair of sandals.

"Five bucks," he muttered to Ella Jean and Grady. "Five bucks you want to come in."

The first thing that overpowered both Kevin and Ella Jean when they entered the room was the smell. It was a sickening blend of smoke, sweat, urine, semen, every form of human excrement and filth imaginable. The big sitting room was half-light and shadows, its occupants moving at half-speed—if they moved at all—as though they might be extras depicting one of hell's stages in a theatrical representation of Dante's Inferno.

As Kevin blinked to adjust his eyes to the smoke and light, he noticed a girl lying on the floor to his right lift her head from the crotch of a man on whom she'd obviously just been performing fellatio. She was a teenager and a young one at that.

"Come on, man," she whined to her partner. "Gimme my rock. They no juice left in that dick."

The contentment writ large on the man's features attested to the accuracy of that observation. He reached into his shirt pocket and pulled out a little plastic vial. He shook it for a moment, then passed it to the girl. She half scampered, half crawled crab-legged across the room to another girl who sat slumped against the wall.

Her arrival galvanized her friend into action. Kevin watched as she took what looked like a square cut out of a window screen, set it on a little stand, broke open the vial and shook the crystal it contained onto the screen. She capped it with a kind of glass beaker, then lit the crystal on the screen with a cigarette lighter.

As the crystal began to glow, the first girl knelt over the opening in the beaker and drew a deep breath. She held it in her lungs as long as she could, then leaned back against the wall while her friend leaned over the beaker and repeated the process. A third, gaunt older woman crawled out of the shadows to stare at the crystal's dying glow.

"Sisters," she begged, "let me sniff that, please."

Kevin studied the first girl leaning against the wall. She was a little wide-eyed, perhaps, but otherwise he could detect no sign of the effect the drug was having on her. Whatever was happening, was happening somewhere in the recesses of her brain.

"Keep your eye on her," Jack whispered. "In ten minutes she'll be sucking someone else's dick to get another rock."

He led them through the room. From somewhere in the distance came the whang of metallic rock. Voices, male and female, in Spanish and ghetto jive, drifted through the gloom. One man was on the floor groaning softly. Well, Kevin told himself, thinking back to his first visit to a heroin-shooting gallery, at least you know he's not dead. On the sofa, a couple copulated, remarkably indifferent to their act. His, Kevin realized, was the only white face in the room, a fact to which its occupants appeared largely indifferent.

"Let's go out into the kitchen where they make the stuff and we can talk," Jack suggested, turning toward a door leading off to another corridor.

The kitchen was well lit and, compared to the living room, relatively clean. A young black man was industriously mea-

suring baking soda onto a balance. He resembled a carica-
ture, with his black leather baseball cap, its peak turned
backward on his head, and a glistening gold tooth illuminat-
ing his friendly grin.

A second, somewhat less engaging black male sat at the
kitchen table, a .38 in his lap, a blue bandanna wrapped
around his head. He nodded to Jack.

"This here's Kevin and Ella Jean," Jack informed him.
The young man shrugged at that apparently useless information.

"So what the hell is that stuff they're doing in there?"
Kevin asked.

"Out in L.A. where it comes from they call it rock.
Around here they call it crack because it makes a popping
sound when it burns. It's Medellín's newest gift to us good
folk here in the Big Apple. It's cocaine in a form you can
smoke."

Kevin whistled softly. "We got trouble."

Jack chewed his lip as though the gesture might help him
marshal his thoughts. "I've never seen anything move like
this, Kev. I saw it for the first time over on Fulton Avenue
in the Bronx seven weeks ago. Now it's all over the city."

"Just in the ghettos?"

"Kevin, whoever made this stuff made it for the ghettos.
You talk about your designer drugs. This stuff was designed
by some son of a bitch somewhere just to reach the kind of
people we got out there in the next room."

"How the hell do they make those little rocks? Everybody's been saying for years you could never smoke coke."

"That's the killer, Kev. It's easy." Jack waved toward the
kid measuring the baking soda onto his scale, like a turn-of-
the-century grocer making up a blend of tea or coffee for a
customer. "This stuff's so cheap because it's so strong. One
of those little rocks, they tell me, gives you a hit at least as
strong as freebase, maybe stronger. They use that baking
soda to step on it before they dissolve it in ammonia and
heat it up. Instead of boiling away all their coke, what
they're doing is essentially converting it into another form,
those little crystals. No waste production. So instead of having to sell powder for a hundred bucks a gram, they can sell
off those little crystals for ten, fifteen bucks apiece. They
give the customer a much bigger bang than that whole little
sack of powder ever did. And the dealers can make four

times as much dough with it as they would from the same amount of powder."

Kevin eyed the ceiling in despair. The genius of man for securing new and better ways to hasten his own destruction never ceased to amaze him. "Who was the bright guy who figured all this out?"

"I don't know but our friend Arnaud here, he's a member of a Los Angeles South Crips gang which accounts for that blue bandanna he's wearing. He's got a few interesting ideas on the subject, don't you, Arnaud?"

Arnaud turned to them with a gesture of infinite weariness. It would not be healthy, Kevin told himself, to underestimate the young man's apparent fatigue any more than you'd want to misjudge his indifference to their conversation.

"All I know is what I see."

"Which was?"

Arnaud waved his .38 by its barrel like it was a ping-pong paddle. "We had this key man"—a key man was a dealer who sold cocaine in kilo lots—"this honky spic, Carlos his name. One day he comes by our house, he says, 'Hey, I gonna show you some new shit.' So he shows us how to cook up this rock stuff, right? 'You get your customers started on this shit' he say. 'Give it away. Free samples. Man, they'll be coming back for more before you can walk away. This stuff gonna make you millionaires. You gonna be the Michael Jacksons of the drug business.' "

Arnaud lowered his voice and tilted his head toward Jack as if his next words were a secret meant only for him. "He be right, brother."

"This stuff's going to make heroin look like Gerber's baby food, Kev. It's an epidemic already. I've contacted Houston, Chicago, Kansas City, Detroit, Pittsburgh. You name the city, it's there. Six more months and we're going to have a firestorm on our hands."

"Who's bringing it?"

"Brothers like our friend Arnaud here. The Crips and the Bloods passed the word from city to city, from ghetto to ghetto. A regular little missionary society they were."

"Which explains why this stuff is only showing up in the inner cities so far," Ella Jean noted.

"Sure. Our friend Arnaud isn't going to exactly blend in up there in Scarsdale, is he? Besides, this is the ideal environment for this stuff. The price is right. All we've got in these ghettos is unemployed teenage males. Crack is an equal opportunity employer. They got jobs for everybody—guards, couriers, steerers, cookers, errand boys, name it, man."

Jack rubbed his eyes with his thumb and forefinger and shook his head as though he was chasing some vision off his mental screen. "You've never seen anything like this stuff, believe me. It's so addictive, I've seen people get hooked on just one hit. One fucking hit!"

"You know something I noticed?" Ella Jean asked. "I saw a lot of women out in that room."

Jack sighed in sad acknowledgment of the wisdom of her observation. "Almost fifty percent. For some reason it seems to turn them on."

"If the women go, who the hell is going to hold our people together, Jack?"

The older man shook his head. "Nobody, girl."

Kevin got up. "What a fucking depressing business this can be. Let's buy half a dozen of those vials," he said to Ella Jean. He'd checked out office funds to make a DEA "monitor buy" on whatever drugs they found on the premises.

As they were walking back out through the crack house parlor, Kevin noticed the teenage girl he'd seen on the way in. Jack had been right. Her head was buried in the lap of another client, furiously working her way toward another rock.

"Hey, it's going to be like shooting fish in a barrel the day we start taking these guys down," Eddie Gomez chortled. Together with Kevin Grady, Ella Jean Ransom and Cesar Rodriguez, he was reviewing for the benefit of Richie Cagnia, the Group Supervisor of the New York DO's Group Six, two months' activity in Operation MEDCLEAN, the code name assigned to the DEA's money-laundering scheme.

Cagnia's job was to play the devil's advocate, trying to pick out the errors Kevin Grady and his team had made in their work. Ultimately, he would have to decide whether to authorize them to continue with the operation or order them to close it down.

"In two months, we've laundered twenty million dollars for them," Gomez proudly noted.

"Twenty million bucks!" Cagnia barked. "Holy shit! Can

you imagine what the media's going to do to us when they get their hands on that figure?" Few things rankled DEA sensitivities quite so much as harsh criticism from an uncomprehending media.

"Listen, Richie," Gomez pleaded, "we got 1.2 million in commissions for our services. That's all in a government-controlled bank account that's financing the whole rig. This operation hasn't cost the G a quarter, not a quarter."

"We are running into some problems here, though," Kevin Grady admitted. "Medellín is beginning to complain that we don't service them fast enough. The money always gets through. They like that. But their man Ospina's on Jimmy Bruno's case twice a week about trying to speed up the flow. The other thing is that they want us to do more pickups."

"Wait a minute!" Cagnia waved an angry arm toward his office ceiling. "We're not going to launder a hundred million bucks for these guys, for Christ's sakes! We've got a very delicate problem here. The U.S. government is using its facilities to launder drug profits for drug traffickers knowing full well that money is going to wind up in the pockets of Pablo Escobar. We're providing these guys with a criminal service. Laundering twenty million bucks is bad enough. A hundred million—forget it! How the hell do you think that's going to play in Peoria when we come to trial? We got to decide when enough's enough and start taking these guys down. Maybe this thing hasn't cost the G a nickel, but what the hell are we getting out of it?"

"The penetration we've gotten out of this so far has been terrific," Kevin assured him. "Eight out of those ten beepers Ospina sent south are back up here and in play to our sting. That means we got eight stash-houses for openers. We've put them all under twenty-four hour surveillance. Everybody that comes to call leaves with a tail. We do number-plate checks on the cars. We've got film units on site at most of those houses. So as a result, we found out who's bringing the money into those collection depots. That brought us down to the second-echelon people. From there, we spread down to the third level, the people who work with the street scum. Since they never keep the powder and the money in the same stashes, we then switched across and started working our way up the powder side of the pyramid."

Kevin paused, pretending to study his notes, actually trying for a little dramatic effect. "The result of all that is we now have 162 targets, suspected felons, on which we got or are getting enough evidence to convict on a conspiracy charge. Here's an example of what this operation is turning up. You remember the first stash-house we got on Sanford Avenue in Queens?"

Cagnia made a scratching noise with his throat which was meant to indicate that he did.

"Well, it turned out to be some kind of a regional stash-house. We spotted cash deliveries coming in there from twenty-three different places, all over New England. Upstate, Jersey, even northern Pennsylvania. With the local police in those places we've already identified sixty-seven targets out of the deliveries to that one stash-house alone."

"So how are you going to take them down without blowing your whole operation?"

"The local police don't arrest these guys when we turn the information over to them. They put them under observation on their own, set up wiretaps, follow them until they've built up their own, independent probable cause which allows them to get a warrant from a judge or an indictment from their grand jury based on the results of their follow-up work, not on what we gave them. Then they put them in the sack. That way it doesn't come back to us. The New York and LAPD's are working that way, too."

"So how many of those guys are inside? Right now?"

"Nineteen, but, Richie, you don't want to judge this rig in the conventional 'how many people did we put away' mode."

"You know any other way Washington is going to look at it?"

"What we really have here, Richie," Kevin pleaded, "is a unique opportunity. If we use this vehicle right, it can get us inside the cartel's money operations. Get in there and maybe we can find out how they move their money around the world. And much more important, where they're keeping it. And who the hell knows? Maybe we can pick up something on the movement of our kingpin targets down there if they ever decide to leave Colombia to visit their friendly bankers."

"Why do you figure you'll be able to do that?"

"Because we know those cowboys down in Medellín have got a lot of respect for our Jimmy Bruno. He delivers. They want to get in closer to him, which is just what we want

them to do. We figure that's our next step here. This Banco
de Occidente they use down in Panama is Colombian-
owned. It's rotten. But if we can worm our way into these
guys, then maybe we find out where their money goes when
it leaves Panama. Switzerland? Liechtenstein? Luxembourg?
The Caymans?"

"Who tells you they love you down in Medellín, the CI?"

"Yeah."

"How do you know he's not double banging you?"

Kevin gave his boss his icy little smile. "The same way I
knew he was going to be a winning ticket when I wanted to
put the arm on him, Rich. The street cop's flair."

Cagnia groaned. "The new administrator is FBI, remember? You know what those bureau guys think about street
cops' flair. The only flair they know about comes out of a
computer."

"This CI isn't like the scum we usually deal with," Grady
assured his boss. "He really is into this thing. He wants his
time down, sure, but it's more than that for him now. He's
playing the game. He's switched sides and he means it."

Cagnia offered his subordinate a doubter's dour glare.

"Rich," Kevin pleaded, "this is a rare opportunity for us.
One like this hasn't come along before and another one may
not come along again for a long time. Sure, there's a risk
leaving the operation running. We'll have to move another
ten, twenty million of their dollars."

"And get raped in every paper and on every TV station in
the country for doing it."

Grady shrugged. "The price you pay. But if we can get in
there, find out how their money flow works, think of the list
of assets and bank accounts we'll have for seizure and forfeiture. Maybe we will have laundered thirty million of their
bucks, but we'll wind up seizing three hundred million. You
don't think that's worth it? Besides, if we don't launder
those bucks, you can bet your ass someone else will and
then we won't have any idea where they went."

At about the time the meeting in Richie Cagnia's office
was breaking up, on the other side of the continent, in West
Hollywood, California, an officer of the Los Angeles County
Sheriff's Office was watching a Buick LeSabre slide out of
its garage and start off toward Sunset Boulevard on its journey across the sprawling city.

The officer, driving an unmarked car, slipped into the traffic stream behind the Buick. Its driver was almost halfway across the city before he made the error for which the policeman had been patiently waiting. At the intersection of Airdrome and Crescent Heights, he slowed down as he approached a stop sign and then, seeing no one was coming, reaccelerated to his normal speed. The officer put on his hat, slapped his red roof light onto the top of his car and went after him.

"Excuse me, sir," he said to the Buick's driver, a swarthy Latin male at least fifteen years his junior, "you just failed to come to a complete stop at that stop sign back there."

"B-b-but there was no one coming, officer," the young man babbled.

"That's the law, son, traffic or no traffic. May I see the car registration papers and your motor vehicle operator's license, please?"

"It's a rental car, sir. Hertz." The driver gestured to the Hertz sticker on his windshield as verification of his words.

"All right. Then let me have a look at the rental agreement."

The driver swiftly and obsequiously complied with his request.

"Right. And your driver's license, please?"

That request, unlike its predecessor, produced a long and awkward silence. "I don't have one, sir. I'm a foreign visitor."

The reply came in a whisper so low it came and went with the swiftness of a puff of air.

"How were you able to rent a car without a valid driver's license?"

"A friend of mine rented it, sir. He loaned it to me, sir." The *sirs* were coming in a quickened cadence now as the awkwardness of his situation became increasingly apparent to the young man.

"Did he just?" smiled the officer, who now had what he'd been looking for, reasonable grounds to pursue a search of the vehicle. "Would you mind getting out of the car?"

The young man complied, his movements hesitant with pain and perplexity. He was wearing a black suede jacket and pale jeans. His dark Latin features, the cop noted, enjoyed the regularity of those who've been untouched by life's sufferings. That, he mused, just might be about to change. He looked inside the car, then pointed to the trunk.

"Would you open that for me?"

The request seemed to puzzle the young man. "Uh, sir, I don't know. *No tengo las llaves.* I don't have the keys," he muttered.

The cop pointed to the keys dangling in the ignition. "There."

The driver stretched a reluctant hand to them and, shaking slightly, opened the trunk. It contained two gray suitcases.

"Those yours?"

"No, sir."

"Who do they belong to?"

The young man shrugged. *"No lo se. Mi amigo.* I don't know. My friend." It had just occurred to him that, in the circumstances, he might be better off taking refuge in Spanish.

"Mind if I have a look in them?"

The only reply the driver could make was a despairing shrug. The cop snapped open one of the cases. It was stuffed with neatly wrapped bundles of hundred-dollar bills. The cop whistled softly, then turned back to the driver. To his immense satisfaction he saw that he'd gone so pale he might as well have dropped a Ku Klux Klan hood over his dark Latin features.

"Sure this isn't yours?"

The driver barely had the force to shake his head.

"Then it belongs to the Los Angeles County Sheriff's Office for now. If your friend wants it back, he'll have to come in and claim it." The cop couldn't resist punctuating this remark with a smile. "And explain to us when he does just where and how he got it."

Lind's Tape

As much to please the U.S. as for any other reason, Tony Noriega finally succumbed to our pressures to go through the motions, at least, of conducting a democratic election in Panama. As you can well imagine, we at the agency had very little to do with those pressures, as did our friends at the Pentagon. They came principally from State, whose officers were constantly finding themselves embarrassed by the difference between the lofty democratic principles we were urging on the Sandinistas and the authoritarian rule we were so cheerfully supporting in Panama.

The man finally anointed to be Noriega's candidate was Ardito "Nicky" Barletta, the economist who'd been at the University of Chicago while Secretary of State George Shultz had been teaching there.

Once the decision had been taken to go ahead with the election it became vital for PK\BARRIER\7-7, as well as for us, that Barletta win the damn thing. The reason for that was that Barletta's opponent was to be Arnulfo Arias, known to everyone in Panama by his first name, Arnulfo. He was the man the military had thrown out of office with their coup d'etat in 1968. He was a nasty bit of work, a demagogue, a populist of the most craven kind, an admirer of the Fascists with whom he'd worked as a diplomat in Europe in the 1930s. But worst of all, he loathed us gringos and the Panamanian military with equal passion. Elect him president of Panama and Noriega would be gone in a flash, and along with him all of our hopes for continuing Panamanian support for our contra war against the Sandinistas.

The forthcoming election was the occasion for my next trip to Panama and my next meeting with Juanita. To run Barletta's campaign and make sure his man won, Noriega had brought in a bunch of American political whiz-kids, recommended to him by Hamilton Jordan, who'd become a great admirer of Torrijos during Jimmy Carter's administration. Arnulfo's Achilles' heel, the whiz-kids assured Noriega, was his age, eighty-two. They shot a whole bunch of TV spots subtly designed to show Barletta's relative youth and vigor: Nicky playing basketball with his kids, Nicky plunging into the surf, Nicky striding purposefully through a morning constitutional.

His opponent watched it all for a while, biding his time. Then Arnulfo delivered his reply. He began showing up at all his political rallies with his busty, 33-year-old mistress hanging adoringly on his arm. So much for the wisdom of our hot-shot American political geniuses.

Fortunately, Noriega's confidence in our whiz-kids was not unlimited. He also engaged an ABC-trained polling expert to teach his staff how to run an exit poll. There was no use, he reasoned, learning you'd lost an election hours after the count was in. Then it was too late to do anything about it. You needed to know you might lose it in time to set the necessary corrective measures in motion.

On election day I was at headquarters in Langley, ready to coordinate any actions that might be required in the wake of the elections, although Noriega's prevote polls gave us a small but comfortable margin of victory. I was stunned, therefore, when Noriega rang me in my office shortly after noon Panamanian time, something he almost never did. He was furious.

"Listen," he shouted, "this idiot you had us run for president has gone and lost the goddamned election!"

"Tony," I said, "how can you know that? The voting's still going on."

"Because I know as much about elections as you gringos do. Those guys we trained to do exit polls show we're going to lose by at least 40,000 votes, probably more."

In an election in which a total of 640,000 votes were cast, that was not an insubstantial margin.

"Arnulfo's going to take over this country. He's going to throw me out on my ass and half the PDF along with me. He's going to throw you out, too. Forget about training your contras here! Forget about running in arms through the Free Trade Zone! Forget about that guy in my embassy in Libya! Forget about every goddamn thing I've done for you in the last five years! You and your contras have had it. You'll never get anything out of Panama as long as that bastard Arnulfo is president."

I let him rant for a few more minutes to vent his rage, then said, "So what do we do, Tony?"

"Look," he said. "I'm going to do what has to be done down here, and you guys are going to have to go along with it. You, my friend, are going to have to make sure that government of yours keeps its goddamn mouth shut about what we did. Just tell them to smile and say everything is fine down in Panama."

Tony was furious about what was happening, but angry as he was he would never have employed that tone with me before the day I'd come to him asking for Juanita's freedom.

"When you have a heavyweight title fight and it's a draw, who wins?" he stormed on. "The champ, right? Well, tell your people 40,000 votes down here, that's a draw so we win."

Clearly, the matter had gone well beyond my authority.

"Tony," I said, "I'll talk to some people up here and get back to you."

Five minutes later, Hinckley and I were in Casey's office. After I'd given them a summary of what Noriega had told me, Hinckley turned to the Director.

"Bill," he said, "as you well know, without the unrestricted use of our Southern Command military bases in the old Canal Zone, without unlimited use of our intelligence and electronic facilities down there, what Noriega says is right. Our contra effort is doomed. So are our efforts to support the government in Salvador. If we know one thing about this guy Arias, it is that he will do absolutely nothing to advance U.S. interests in Central America. For once, we have a clear choice here: we advance the democratic process in Panama or we advance American policy in Central America. It's got to be one or the other."

Casey sat there glowering for a couple of minutes. "Let me handle it," he said finally.

In Panama, Tony started to cook the electoral books without waiting for a reply from us. The counting of the votes was supposed to be held in a public hall. His first move was to order a bunch of his goons to start a riot around the hall. In their zeal they killed three people and injured close to a hundred, but the trouble they stirred up was enough to allow Noriega to declare that, for reasons of public safety, the count would go forward in a private residence under the eyes of a group called the Tallying Board, which he controlled.

They managed to dither for a couple of days while the count from the remote Guayami Indian District in Chiriqui was "rectified." Then, the Tribunal announced that Barletta had won by 1,713 votes, a figure a lady member of the Tribunal had pulled out of the air.

It was a well-run exercise except for one problem: The United States Embassy knew exactly what was happening. They had a hot-shot political officer there, a guy named Ashley Hewitt, who knew Arias had won by 60,000 votes. He drafted a dispatch announcing the result to Washington. Ted Briggs, the ambassador, signed off on it. Next morning everyone in authority in the State Department from George Shultz on down knew who had won the election. Ambassador Briggs congratulated one of Arnulfo's allies on the victory personally. He announced to the papal nuncio that the

U.S. knew Arias had won and was going to live with the result.

No, we weren't. Casey had done his job. The State Department did an adroit about-face. Their spokesman announced Barletta's victory to the world press at his daily briefing and said that the stolen election represented the return of the democratic process to Panama. Briggs sorrowfully informed the papal nuncio he'd been ordered by Washington to recognize Barletta's victory despite the fact he knew it was fraudulent. Ronald Reagan invited Barletta to the White House. Finally, Secretary of State George Shultz was ordered to put the U.S. government's Good Housekeeping seal of approval on Noriega's thievery by going to Panama for Barletta's inauguration.

It was a pretty sordid exercise in hypocrisy, about as sordid as any I was called on to witness in thirty years of government service. Still, it had produced the results we were after. PK\BARRIER\7-7 remained firmly in command of Panama. Nothing was going to disrupt our war against the Sandinistas.

Casey ordered me to Panama to make sure no post-election traumas disrupted the smooth flow of events and, more important, to prepare the way for a secret visit he intended to make to Panama at the end of July. He was, after all, anxious to meet the man for whose theft of a democratic election he had just secured our national blessing.

Noriega, I found, was still fuming over how close we'd come to disaster with that election. The whole thing, he now maintained, had been a futile and unnecessary exercise.

He wasn't the only one fuming. Juanita, like most Panamanians with a modicum of intelligence, had no doubts about who had really won the election. My arrival so soon after the results had been officially announced only served to confirm her conviction that Noriega had stolen the election with the agreement and connivance of the U.S. government and the CIA. Like many people south of the border, she tended not to make much of a distinction between the two. What could I say to that? Congratulate her on being right?

Sensing the coolness in her welcome, I decided to take her to dinner at Las Bovedas, the restaurant in which we'd eaten the night we met. Perhaps, I told myself, those surroundings would awaken in her a nostalgia for the passion we had once shared.

As she always did, she surprised me that night. Rather than launch into a furious tirade against the electoral theft, she seemed to accept the result with a cynicism I hadn't seen in her before.

"Of course," she observed, "why argue? You'll just say stealing elections is as traditional a part of life in Latin America as the Sunday *paseo*." The paseo was the Spanish family stroll through a city's main street on pleasant evenings or after Sunday Mass. I started to make a *pro forma* reply, but she interrupted.

"This will come back to haunt you," she promised. "I know Nicky Barletta and he's not going to be as accommodating as you and your friend Noriega seem to think. But what really interests me is what I talked to you about the last time we met. You and your genius friends at the CIA have gone and stolen an election for a drug dealer."

"Why do you say that?"

"Because now I know Noriega's involved in the cocaine traffic."

All sorts of warning lights blinked on in my mind at her words. "Juanita, please don't tell me you're getting involved in that."

"Just as an observer." She then described to me her late-night arrival at Paitilla ten days earlier. "What was a Colombian aircraft doing landing at Paitilla in the middle of the night and going to Noriega's hangar under a PDF escort?"

"Good question, Juanita, and I don't know the answer." Damn right it was a good question. That PDF hangar, although she didn't know it, of course, was the building we were using to transship our contra arms up north. Her discovery might mean nothing. People obsessed by their convictions, as Juanita was with her hatred for Noriega, are apt to rush to judgment on the flimsiest scrap of evidence.

Still, her observation opened up a very disturbing possibility. Was someone mixing up our arms flow to the contras with the coke traffic? Is that what was going on in that hangar? If it was, it could lead to an unmitigated disaster. Let the news that CIA contractual employees and some of our contras were running cocaine into the United States reach the media, and our efforts to save Salvador and Nicaragua would be destroyed overnight.

I had better find out what the hell was going on here before anybody else did. A little heroin flowing out of the Golden Triangle was the price we'd been ready to pay for good intelligence on communist China. A little heroin out of Long Tien was the price we'd been ready to pay for Vang Pao's cooperation in Laos. Maybe a little coke flowing into Florida was the price we were going to have to pay for ridding the hemisphere of the Sandinistas.

For the moment, however, my concern was Juanita. "For the love of God," I pleaded, "don't get yourself mixed up in that drug stuff. Those people are killers. They murder people who look at them cross-eyed. Can you imagine what they'd do to someone like you if they found you getting in their way?"

Juanita laid her hand gently on mine. As it happened, I needed a little detective work done on Noriega, and she was determined to do it whether I liked it or not.

"Jack, I appreciate your concern," she assured me. "Just as I appreciated what you did to get me out of jail. I'll be all right. But start thinking about what you're going to do when I put the evidence of Noriega's drug trafficking in front of you."

"Ramon, I want to come clean with you. I think you've earned that with the job you're doing for us." Kevin Grady measured out his words with the care of a chemist preparing a potentially explosive mixture. "First of all, I've got to tell you this money operation we're running is the most important single case the DEA has going at this moment. We have it because of one person and the opening he brought us. That person is *you*. You're the only guy we have, or indeed have ever had, who's actually in there in Medellín talking to these guys."

Ramon seemed to shrink under the enormity of the responsibility Kevin Grady's words had laid on him. The DEA agent sensed his CI's apprehension. For Grady, indeed for the DEA, this talk was the turning point of Operation MEDCLEAN. A telephone call from Paco Garrone to Ramon had triggered it. Don Eduardo, Paco had informed Ramon, wanted to chat—immediately. If Ramon went, Grady had reasoned, then they might be able to find their way into secret financial worlds into which they'd so long sought entrance. If he didn't agree to go, then they would have no choice except to make whatever arrests they could and close the case down.

So important did Kevin feel the meeting was he had brought Ramon for the first time into the headquarters of the New York DO, using an unmarked car and the underground garage to get him inside unseen. Kevin was enough of an old-fashioned, second-generation immigrant patriot to sense a majesty to these premises: the flags of the United States and the administration in the entry, the portraits of the President and Vice President by the receptionist's desk, the plaques and awards given to New York DO agents for valor or special achievement, the gallery of honor with its portraits of DEA agents killed in the line of duty.

He had set the meeting in the big corner office of the SAC, the Special Agent in Charge, with its breathtaking view of the Hudson River. Kevin wanted the session to blend awe and intimacy, to combine a sense of the authority and power of the United States government with the notion of friends hatching a conspiracy.

"Let me lay it on you as frankly as I can. It is very, very important to us that you go to that meeting in Medellín with Don Eduardo. Because if you don't go, then the operation is over, finished. Closed up tight."

Kevin watched Ramon very closely. He was as tightly wound as a sprinter waiting to hear the starter's gun.

"I also know that in sending you back into that compound we are putting you in harm's way. We are taking a gamble, a big gamble that the reason he wants to see you has nothing to do with your role working for us as an informant."

"You're taking a gamble with my life is what you're doing," Ramon snapped.

"That's right. That's exactly what we're asking you to do. Take a gamble with your life."

Grady took a piece of paper from the coffee table in front of him. "And now I've got to tell you something else you're not going to want to hear."

The bastard, Ramon thought. He's going to tell me how many years I'll have to do if I refuse to go.

That was not the case. Kevin was under no legal obligation whatsoever to reveal to Ramon the contents of the paper in his hand. He was doing it because he felt he had a moral obligation to reveal it to his CI and he was doing it to the fury and consternation of his superiors. But revealing that material was a concession Kevin had demanded for going ahead with this. If he was going to ask Ramon to risk his life by going up to the compound in Medellín, he was not going to ask him to take that risk ignorant of the information the paper he held contained. It was the report of the arrest of the money courier in L.A.

Ramon gasped when Kevin finished reading it. "That's it! That's why they want me back down there!"

"No." Kevin tried to infuse his words with all the measured wisdom of which he was capable. "If I thought that was the case I wouldn't let you go even if you wanted to go. There is no reason whatsoever for them to tie this to you. That courier had been under surveillance for two weeks. The L.A. cops saw him borrow the rented car from a friend to make the pickup because his own car was in the garage. They knew that the name on his license and the name on the rental agreement weren't going to match, which would give them reasonable grounds for searching the car. As it turned out, the asshole didn't even have a driver's license, so they could book him for that."

"Oh, come on, Kevin, those guys in the compound in Medellín weren't born yesterday. Of course they're going to lay that on me."

"The courier was going from a collection point in West Hollywood to the stash-house off Sepulveda where your first L.A. pickup came from. That house hasn't used you in ten days. They haven't even beeped you to ask for a pickup. There's no way they're going to tie you to this. They want you down in Medellín for something else. Because, I'm convinced, they want to expand this operation."

Ramon's head shook almost spastically. "I can't do it, Kevin. I just don't think I can do it."

"Why?"

"I'm tired. And I'm scared. I haven't been able to sleep since Paco called. Every time I close my eyes, I get nightmares. Just look at me. Anybody with any sense can see I'm at the end of the line."

"It's because you're scared, Ramon. What I'm trying to tell you is you don't need to be scared. They're not onto you. When you start believing that you'll get your old confidence back."

"When I start believing that, I'll be the world's biggest

asshole. What good is it going to do me to get half my life back if I'm already dead when you give it back to me?"

"Ramon, I'll promise you one thing. It's the only thing I can promise. If you go down there for us on this one, I'll do everything in my power to see you never spend a day in federal prison. Not a day."

The CI stared at Grady, blinking back tears of fear and strain. This guy is my savior and my executioner, all wrapped up in one person, he thought.

"You know what they do to people who betray them down there? *Before* they decide to be nice and kill them?"

The SAC coughed. He had strongly opposed Kevin's demand to reveal the information about the L.A. arrest to the CI. His own philosophy in these matters was simple: you can never ask a CI to do too much. That information had probably pushed this guy over the edge. Now he had to intervene here for legal reasons.

"Look, Ramon, it's my duty to tell you that if you refuse to go back down there, we'll understand. We'll accept half a loaf here and ask the judge for the best deal we can get for you."

My cyanide pills, Ramon thought, the ones I took to Aruba. I still have them.

"And if I do go down there and get back out, you give me the rest of my life back, right?"

"We go to bat for you one-thousand percent with the U.S. Attorney's office and the judge for just that," the SAC assured him.

"Okay," Ramon whispered. "I'll go."

He stood up, then turned to look back at Kevin. The DEA agent expected to see anger or hatred in his eyes. He didn't. He saw something else, some echo of a fraternal bond.

"Don't forget what I told you about the wedding ring."

Paco Garrone whipped his Jaguar through the curves of the high road skirting the mountain crest above El Poblado, laying down the rubber with the verve of an aspiring racing driver. As he shot past them, he gestured exuberantly at the forest of cranes and derricks, the luxury high-rise apartments under construction along their route.

"Prosperity!" he shouted. "Boom times in Medellín! All thanks to coke!"

Ramon barely grunted.

Paco glared at him. "Christ, you're a moody bastard this morning."

Ramon started as though he'd just woken up from a daydream. Or, more appropriate to his case, a nightmare. He'd been stewing for days in the terror this forthcoming meeting inspired. He still had no idea what lay behind this imperious summons to the compound. All his socio had been able—or willing—to tell him was that Don Eduardo wanted to talk business urgently.

"Ah," he lied, "I was brooding about all this traveling I've been doing. I'm getting fed up with it."

Paco braked to stop at the compound entrance. While the guards checked out their car, Ramon tried to quell his nerves by studying the plaque on the wall beside the gate. "Londono LTDA Constructores" it read. There was a smart guy. Get rich off the drug traffic but never go near the drugs.

The gate opened and they rolled in. This time they did not have to wait in the crowded reception room. The blond pistolero who'd escorted them on their first visit was waiting for them. Wordlessly, he took them upstairs to the cartel's working headquarters, then down the corridor to Don Eduardo's office.

Listening to their escort's knuckles strike the door, a curious thought flashed through Ramon's mind. It was a line from Macbeth: "Hear it not, Duncan, for it is a knell that summons thee to heaven, or to hell."

Don Eduardo yanked opened the door. He stood there an instant staring and blinking. Then he grabbed Ramon in an *embrazo*. His greeting could not have been warmer if he had been Queen Isabella welcoming Columbus back to the court of Castille.

He swept his visitors into his office, called for the ritual cups of cafe tinto, bombarded Ramon with questions about his trip, Juan Ospina, their work in New York and L.A.

"Let me tell you right now how pleased we all are with the Jimmy Bruno operation," he gushed. "Everything has gotten through. It's slow but it's reliable, and that's what counts."

He paused to sip his coffee, then bestowed on Ramon the kind of smile a game-show host reserves for a contestant who's just won a two-week trip to Hawaii. "The reason I asked you down here is this. We've got to find a way to convince Jimmy Bruno to move more money."

This, Ramon imagined, savoring the exultation sweeping through his system, must be how the Hindus feel when they levitate. A second before, he had been desperate to conceal his fear from these two men, to prevent them from sniffing out the emotion's special odor on his person. Now he could barely contain the jubilation engulfing him. I've won, I got my life back, I'll never have to go to jail. "Look," he heard himself mumbling, "Jimmy's a very cautious guy. He doesn't like to take chances."

Don Eduardo wasn't even listening. "We're generating over a hundred million dollars cash a month up there now. This new crack thing is phenomenal. We can't get the money we're taking in out of there fast enough. Would you believe I've got forty million in cash warehoused in L.A. waiting to move?"

From what Kevin Grady had told him, Ramon could. "Christ!" he whistled.

"We can deliver Jimmy Bruno a minimum of eight million dollars a week if we can convince him to take it."

"Like I said, Jimmy plays it tight. He worked with the Mafia for years. Probably still does. They've got companies, corporate accounts they use that handle big cash flows all the time so the IRS doesn't watch them too closely. They don't want to upset that apple cart by overloading the system."

"Indeed," Don Eduardo interrupted. "I'd like to find out more about the system he uses and how he gets those dollars into his accounts and out of the United States. Not the names of the banks or the corporations, of course. Just the system."

"I don't know how forthcoming he's going to be about that," Ramon warned. Not until the day he puts the cuffs on you.

"Well, I have something to offer him in return." Don Eduardo smiled. "Another system that may be even better than his is."

"'I doubt that," Ramon replied, thinking as he did, what system could be better than the U.S. government?

"It's called *La Mina,* the mine."

"The mine?"

"A gold mine. And believe me, a real gold mine."

Fueled by his restored confidence, Ramon's mind was

now in overdrive. "Look, Don Eduardo, there's only one person who can convince Jimmy to do this. *You.*"

"Me? I can't go up to New York."

"No, and I doubt he'll want to come down here either. But you guys could meet someplace in the Caribbean or the Bahamas so it would look like he was going on a vacation."

"Could you set that up?"

"I could try."

"Do it. There's just one last thing. One of our idiot couriers out in L.A. got caught driving without a license with a million dollars in his car. The police have seized the money. Do you suppose Jimmy Bruno could help us get it back?"

In DEA jargon, the operation was called "orchestrating the surrounds." The two DEA technicians had flown from Washington to Amsterdam, where the administration's country attaché had provided them, courtesy of Interpol, with a pair of Danish passports. Thus covered, they flew KLM to their final destination, the island of Aruba off Colombia's Caribbean seacoast.

Now, settled into their sixth floor suite at KLM's Golden Tulip Hotel, they carefully unpacked their hi-tech electronic gear. The hotel had two suites to a floor; the sixth was the top floor. Before deciding which of the two they'd like, they'd asked the reception clerk to show them both suites. They wanted to compare their views, they'd told her, to see which was more romantic.

Convinced she was dealing with a vacationing gay couple, she'd obliged. Their interest in fact was not the view but the furniture. As they had hoped, it was virtually identical in both suites. Mr. Jimmy Bruno, aka Special Agent Eddie Gomez, would be occupying the other suite in twenty-four hours. Their task now was to doctor up two pieces of furniture in their room with audio equipment and a fiberoptic video camera which they would swap with the identical pieces of furniture in Bruno's suite moments after he'd arrived. By nightfall, the equipment was ready.

The island of Aruba had been Don Eduardo Hernandez's choice for his meeting with Jimmy Bruno. Colombians didn't need visas to enter the island, so there would be no record of his passage here. He flew into the island from Cartegena with Ramon, who would serve as his interpreter. The two men went straight to the Golden Tulip Hotel, where

Jimmy Bruno and Cesar Rodriguez, who'd come in from Panama City forty-five minutes earlier, were waiting for them in their $560 a night suite.

Kevin Grady flew in independently from Florida and stayed in another hotel. His job was to provide communications, backup and supervisory oversight if any was needed.

The first minutes of their meeting were crucial. It was essential for Eddie Gomez to get the Colombian to relax, to put him at ease, to reassure him if he had any suspicions that he'd been lured into a sting.

It was a task in which Gomez delighted. He loved his Jimmy Bruno role. He wore the deceit it called for as comfortably as most people wear a pair of old shoes. By the time Don Eduardo reached his suite, Gomez had installed a full bar and ordered up a coffee service. That was meant to get them all into coffee and an early morning beer right there in the suite. The idea was to start the conversation rolling in front of the DEA's microphones and cameras before the Colombian might suggest leaving the DEA's well-wired environment to go down to the bar or restaurant. The worst-case scenario would be to hear Don Eduardo suggest they put on their bathing suits and go for a stroll along the beach.

It was debatable how much conversation actually suitable for courtroom use a recorder concealed in a jock strap would pick up. Furthermore, as one technician had pointed out to Gomez, "Go for a swim wearing one of those things, and if it short-circuits, you probably won't be making love for a month or two."

As it turned out, Don Eduardo harbored no suspicions about their meeting or Jimmy Bruno's character. Why should he suspect a man who'd already moved twenty million dollars out of the United States for the cartel? Besides, Jimmy Bruno exuded a kind of conspiratorial air that invited confidence. Within five minutes, Jimmy had Don Eduardo ensconced in an armchair, his coat off, his tie undone, a bottle of Heineken beer in one hand, a Cuban cigar in the other.

First, they exchanged compliments like the satisfied business partners they were. Then Hernandez moved the conversation to Jimmy's operations. The American was remarkably forthcoming.

"The key thing," he told his Colombian colleague, "is that I got my people inside the fence. Very trusted people in certain banks we're using. Now, these people are high enough up in things so that they can cover our cash deposits and watch over the transfers. But sometimes they have business elsewhere, they have to travel, take a day off. When that happens we have to hold up operations, and that's what accounts for the slowdowns we sometimes run into."

Don Eduardo, working through Ramon because his English was limited, assured Jimmy that he understood the problem. But, he pressed, couldn't Jimmy increase the amount of money he was processing by his system?

"The problem," Bruno told him, "is that under our laws, a banker has the responsibility to know his customers and know what's generating his cash flow. Now, suppose some of my accounts generate four, five million a month, month in, month out, right? All of a sudden, bang, that's up to forty. Bells begin to ring. I'm going to maybe put some of my trusted people into a very embarrassing situation, you know what I mean? You also got to understand I work with some other people. Do something that might jeopardize them and you run into some very unhealthy factors. Like you can get yourself killed, which is about as unhealthy as things can get."

Jimmy belched, an ejaculation that was more a manifestation of his good spirits than the state of his stomach. "We also gotta be very careful here not to get our friends in law enforcement curious about what's going on. Because whether your boy Juan up there is moving ten keys of coke or I'm moving the money from ten keys of coke, the fact of the matter is the law says we're equally guilty. We both go to jail for the same time. So increasing the flow like you suggest isn't easy for me."

The undercover agent waved his half-empty bottle of beer expansively. Gomez knew nothing begets a confidence quite like a confidence shared. "Now if you guys got any bright ideas about a better way to do this, I'm all ears."

His words triggered just the response he was looking for.

Basking in the warmth of Jimmy Bruno's trust, Don Eduardo leaned forward and declared, "There are some other people I'm working with who have a system. A real system. A gold mine."

"A gold mine, for Christ's sakes!"

"Right, a gold mine down in Uruguay, a real one. It exports gold to the U.S. and Europe. It also owns a gold refinery in Hollywood, Florida."

Jimmy Bruno looked appropriately puzzled but didn't interrupt his Colombian associate.

"Let's say gold is selling for $350 an ounce. That's 5600 dollars a pound. Twelve million plus dollars a ton, okay?"

The undercover agent had no trouble following the Colombian's math, although his colleagues liked to joke that he couldn't balance his checkbook.

"Suppose our mine is shipping a ton of gold a week to the States. That's roughly 600 million dollars a year. The gold comes in officially, openly. It's declared. The duty's paid. The tax is paid. It's insured for its full value. It goes to the company's refinery in Florida, where it's melted down and refined. From there it's shipped to jewelers we do business with in New York, L.A., Miami, Houston. They sell it, make it into jewelry, whatever, deposit the money they got for it in their banks and tell their banks to remit the money to the refinery's bank. The refinery orders it wire-transferred back to the mining company down in Montevideo, or maybe to a gold broker we use in London. In other words, all they're doing here is exporting the proceeds from the sale of their gold plus a legitimate profit. If the U.S. government asks where the money comes from, it's legal, aboveboard and there's paperwork to cover every step along the way."

"Great," Jimmy said, "so you're in the gold business, not the money-moving business."

"Wrong, my friend, because what was in those crates marked 'gold' wasn't gold. It was lead."

Now Jimmy sat up. "Lead!"

"Oh, maybe we'll gold-plate the top level or two of ingots in the crates just in case some Customs inspector decides to look inside one day. But the result is we've declared we've imported 600 million dollars worth of gold into the country when in fact we're out of pocket maybe ten million in lead and paper charges. So that leaves us with a shortfall of 570 million dollars we can now cover with the proceeds from our coke sales."

Ramon listened to their exchange with awe and fascination. Here was Don Eduardo, supposedly one of the smartest men in the cartel, coughing up the organization's most precious secrets to a DEA agent. He'd fallen for the DEA's sting hook, line, and sinker. But then, why the hell wouldn't he have fallen for it? After all, Jimmy Bruno and the U.S.

government had laundered twenty million dollars for the cartel, and never lost or misplaced a nickel of their money.

"And that business of melting the stuff down in Florida and shipping it out to your dealers is all just bullshit, a book transaction?" Jimmy continued.

"Oh, they have a few real ingots in there they smelt down so the place looks perfectly legitimate if anyone comes to call. But basically what happens is that our money couriers deliver their cash to the jewelers we work with in New York and L.A. at those big jewelry trade offices they have in those cities. Once they're in there, there's no way to know which of the thirty or forty jewelers they've got in those buildings they're going to see. The jewelers take the money in cash and put it into their regular business bank accounts. Anybody asks about it, it's no big deal. After all, a lot of people pay for jewelry in cash."

"Yeah." Jimmy Bruno growled out his approval of the scam. "Guy goes to the track, makes a killing, wants to buy the girlfriend a diamond, he uses the winnings. Pays in cash. That way, how's the wife to know, right?"

"Of course. And in the States, lots of people, particularly the Orientals, like to buy gold with cash from their businesses. They put the gold under the bed. That way the IRS doesn't see the money go by."

Jimmy Bruno reached over and slapped a warm and congratulatory hand on Don Eduardo's knee. He couldn't believe his good luck. The damn fool Colombian had just laid in his lap a money-laundering operation twenty-five, fifty times more important than their little sting was meant to be. And all for the benefit of the DEA's hidden mikes and cameras.

"Now, that's what I call a system," he enthused. "Hell, I can buy straw hats in Singapore for fifty cents a hat, bring them in here, overvalue them, tell Customs they're worth fifty bucks each, pay the duty—what the fuck does Customs care what they're really worth as long as I pay their duty—and I've got a money-export factor of a hundred percent there."

Don Eduardo beamed. He liked quick learners.

"And you've lined up jewelers to work with you?" Jimmy asked. He knew he was on dangerous ground with that question, but he felt Hernandez was so absorbed in their talk that he was prepared to take the risk the Colombian wouldn't realize he was fishing.

"Armenians," he answered. "They're big in the business all over the United States. We've got them lined up in New York, L.A., Houston and Miami. They're like us paisas. Everyone's a cousin of everybody else."

They continued to talk for another hour. Jimmy promised he would investigate the possibility of using one of his corporations to set up a dummy import-export operation along the lines Don Eduardo's description of La Mina had inspired. By the time they went downstairs for a long poolside lunch, everything of value that was going to happen had happened, right in front of the DEA's recording equipment.

After lunch, the two younger men, Cesar and Ramon decided to check out the girls by the beach while Jimmy and Don Eduardo had coffee.

"We're going to Panama tomorrow," Ramon told Cesar. "He wants to introduce me to the woman who runs their business at the Banco de Occidente. We'll be staying at the Marriott."

"Okay," Cesar said. "Go. I'm sure that's what Kevin would say. He'll figure out a way to get there and be in touch." He paused, chuckling. "You may be going to Panama, but if this goddamn Mina thing really exists, we're going to the Super Bowl in Washington when they see and hear those tapes we made this morning."

Ramon stared up at the three centuries old stones piercing the hazy moonlight above him as though they were a giant's skeleton or the trunk of some prehistoric tree. It was well past midnight. These ruins of Old Panama were deserted, peopled only by the ghosts of the conquistadores who had once lived here and the pirates who came ashore to slaughter them and raze their city.

He leaned up against the stones and lit a cigarette. They were the base of what had once been the bell tower of the cathedral of Old Panama. Somewhere in the darkness around his feet were the remains of the altar at which Pizarro had knelt to receive communion before setting out to conquer the Incas for God, for gold, and for Spain.

So absorbed was he in his thoughts that he didn't hear the footsteps edging toward him through the high grass blanketing the ruins. By the time he turned, Kevin and another man were there beside him in the shadows.

The DEA agent grabbed his hand. "You did it, pal. Congratulations."

"I got my life back, right?"

"You bet. Washington is so excited about the meet in Aruba nobody can talk about anything else." He gestured to the man beside him. "This is Fred Hines, our country attaché here."

"You pick interesting spots for your meetings," Ramon observed.

Hines looked off into the solitude. "Nobody comes near this place at night. Not too many people come in the daytime either, for that matter."

"So how did your meeting go at the bank?" Grady asked.

"Great. First of all, that bank is in their pocket one hundred percent. Hernandez told me, 'Look, we never have any problems with these people. They're here to take care of us. They understand that. They know what their job is.'"

Grady had expected to hear as much.

"This woman Clara Mendez who runs the accounts? She's really in tight with them. She calls Escobar 'Don Pablito.' I mean, how tight can you get?"

Ramon flicked his cigarette onto the stones of what had been the cathedral's floor. "What's really interesting is this. I told her I wanted to open a couple of accounts just like you said to, right? I said to her, 'How can I be sure they'll be safe if the gringos at the DEA come sniffing around?'

" 'Not to worry, man,' she tells me 'We're covered here.'

" 'What do you mean by that?' I asked her.

"She said: 'We pay the man here for protection.'

" 'Noriega?' I said.

" 'Who else?' she told me. 'If the DEA wants to seize any of our bank accounts, his people give us a twenty-four-hour warning. We clean ninety-five percent of the deposits out of them so that all the DEA winds up with is the leftovers. You're a friend of Don Eduardo. Don't worry about your money. We'll protect it the same way as we protect Don Eduardo and his friends.' "

Grady leaned back against the ancient stones of the church tower. He was staggered by what he'd just heard. "Noriega!" he whispered. "What a target he'd make!"

"That's just the beginning, man," Ramon told him. "I was

talking to Hernandez about him back in the hotel room tonight." He pulled a microcassette out of his pocket and
passed it to Grady. "I taped it. It's on here. In Spanish."

"Jesus Christ, Ramon, that's dangerous! You shouldn't be
taking risks like that."

"It's no risk, Kevin. You were right up in New York.
These guys trust me a hundred percent."

"So what did he say about Noriega?" Hines asked.

"Well, it's all on there, but I'll paraphrase it for you. He
said: 'That son of a bitch Noriega! He gets four thousand
dollars for every kilo of coke we pass through Panama.'

"I said, 'Does that come to much?'

" 'Much?' he said. 'It's a third of what we're moving.' "

"And that's there, on that tape?" Grady was still wrestling
with the enormity of what he'd heard.

"Sure."

Noriega, the darling of the Reagan administration? The
guy George Shultz had said was so wonderful because he'd
just run an election everyone said was crooked? The dictator
those bastards at the CIA, at the Pentagon, were so proud of.
That guy was taking a skim on a third of the cocaine going
into the United States? It was mind blowing. And it was the
target of a lifetime.

"Listen, Ramon," he said. "I think the time has come to
get your wife and kids out of Colombia. Bring them up quietly, discreetly, like you're all going to Disney World. We'll
have the U.S. Attorney's Office set it up with the Marshal's
Service. The DEA guy at the embassy will help. I'll meet
you when you arrive, and we'll put them right into the
witness-protection program."

BOOK EIGHT

A Package from Medellín

Lind's Tape

"This is dynamite!" Glenn Archer exclaimed, walking into the office the station had given me for my stay at Corozal. "Thank God you're here. We need a quick decision." He dropped the embassy cable form he was clutching on my desk as though it had just burned his fingers which, figuratively speaking, it had.

"The coding room downtown sent this out to me. It's a DEA cable. They have standing orders to route their traffic through us. I've ordered them to hold up transmitting this damn thing until you've cleared it."

I picked it up. It was typed on standard DEA stationery.

From: SA Fred Hines Country Attache
To: Fred Gustafson
Cocaine Desk
DEA Headquarters Washington

Following information obtained in debriefing SCI-83-0021 in Panama City May 12 1984 by SA Kevin Grady:

1. SCI-83-0021 was informed in private conversation by Eduardo Hernandez, a Colombian national residing in Medellin, Colombia and an indicted target of ongoing DEA investigation MEDCLEAN NYDO SCI-85-0112 that Manuel Antonio Noriega, commander of the Panamanian Defense Forces, receives a payment of U.S. dollars four thousand for every kilo of cocaine transshipped by the Medellin cartel through Panama to the U.S. Noriega in return guarantees cocaine shippers physical security of shipments and freedom from arrest. Hernandez has been identified by the New York DO as the principal financial officer of the Medellin cartel. Tape recording of private conversation between SCI-83-0021 and Hernandez in which allegation is made being forwarded to DEA HQ Washington via diplomatic pouch.

2. SCI-83-0021 was further informed in private conversation May 12 1984 at the Banco de Occidente Panama City with Clara Mendez, a Panamanian national not cur-

rently the subject of a DEA investigation and the aforesaid Eduardo Hernandez, that bank pays protection
money to Manuel Antonio Noriega and the PDF and in
return receives advance notice of DEA plans to seize or
freeze bank accounts in Panama.

On the basis of the foregoing information, we request
permission to initiate an investigation for criminal conspiracy to import cocaine into the United States against
the aforesaid Manuel Antonio Noriega with the objective
of obtaining a criminal indictment against the aforesaid
individual before the Federal Grand Jury of the Southern
District of New York.

"Holy Christ!" I groaned. "This is all we needed! Can you
imagine?" I asked Glenn. "The CIA and its Director personally have just finished stealing an election for a man another
federal agency wants to indict as a common criminal? Our
best asset in Central America is identified as a drug trafficker at a time when we have Ronald Reagan running
around the country rattling on about his war on drugs? When
Nancy is telling the boys and girls 'just say no'?"

"Unfortunately, Jack," Glenn told me, "I can imagine it.
You hear a lot of gossip around town. This could be a disaster in the making."

"You may be right," I agreed. "The first thing we do is sit
on this cable until I've had a chance to discuss it with Langley. Send a copy 'Top Secret Eyes Only' to Hinckley and ask
him to call me on the secure phone as soon as he's read it."

Glenn took the cable and set off to do just that, leaving
me to ponder once again its contents. Grady, I thought,
where the hell have I heard that name? Then, of course, it
came back. He was the narc I had met on my flight up to
Vientiane, the one who'd tried to seize Vang Pao's load of
heroin. How come he was still working for the government?

Hinckley was predictably furious when he called through
half an hour later. "Grady!" he barked. "He was the guy
who got in our way out in Laos. Trying to seize that Air
America DC-3. What I want you to do is call him and that
other DEA agent into the station chief's office right away
and order them to cease and desist their investigation of
Noriega immediately. And I mean immediately. We're not

going to let something like that go forward at this critical juncture in our Central American activities."

"On what authority am I supposed to do that?"

"On your authority. On the agency's. Just tell them there are larger national security concerns at stake here. End of story. You know as well as I do that their activities are subordinated to our concerns outside of the United States."

There was no way, Hinckley declared, we were going to have Bill Casey flying into a secret meeting with a man who was the subject of a criminal investigation.

"All right, I'll set it up right away," I agreed.

"Good. While you're doing that there are one or two things I want to check out up here before we decide how we're going to handle Noriega. But you back those two agents off this as fast and as hard as you can."

Grady recognized me the moment he walked into Glenn Archer's embassy office on the floor immediately above the DEA's three-room office suite. Puzzlement, then anger flashed across his face. Grady hadn't changed a great deal since we'd met on that hair-raising flight from Bangkok to Vientiane. He was graying a bit at the temples, but he still had that lean, hungry look about him, the Bobby Kennedy aura that had struck me the first time I saw him. Like Bobby, he kept his shoulders hunched and his upper body tilting slightly forward. There is an old Irish wish: *May the wind be always at your back.* Kevin Grady looked to me like a man who'd spent his life walking into the wind rather than with it.

I waved the two of them to the chairs we'd placed in front of Archer's desk, displaying what I meant to be an absolute minimum of cordiality. You could handle a situation like this in one of two ways—Mr. Nice Guy or Mr. Hard Ass. Remembering my earlier contact with Grady, the latter had seemed more appropriate here. I slid their unsent cable across the desk.

"How the hell did you get your hands on that?" Grady snarled.

I ignored him. "Your request to open an investigation into the activities of General Noriega is hereby denied. You will immediately cease and desist all your activities in that regard. Should you or anyone else uncover any further information on the subject of General Noriega, you will convey it to Mr. Archer and to no one else. Do I make myself clear?"

Hines, the country attaché, was severely shaken by my little ultimatum. You could tell just by looking at him that no one was going to be able to mention Noriega's name in his presence from now on. Grady was another story. He was boiling.

"Who the hell are you to tell me, a federal law enforcement officer, who I'm going to investigate and not investigate? The trail leads right to this guy. He's in it up to his armpits. I'm going after him."

"No, you're not. Forget it."

"Why the hell should I?"

"Because you don't know the whole story. Because there are larger national security concerns at stake here."

"Just like there were in that DC-3 full of heroin?"

"Exactly. And I don't think I need remind you of the outcome of that confrontation."

For a second I thought Grady was going to soar out of his chair and leap at me across the table. "National security concerns?" he snorted. "Listen to me, you pompous asshole, if you want to see national security concerns, you should have been with me two weeks ago up in New York. In a lovely new institution they got up there. It's called a crack parlor. They're going up all over the country. They smoke cocaine in them. The cocaine your great pal Noriega is helping the Colombians to pour into the country. It's killing people. It's driving them batty. It's destroying their lives."

He barely paused for breath as he roared on at me from across the desk. "You want a national security concern, a real one? That's it. That's what's going to destroy our society, our country. Not whatever half-assed concern it is that's leading you CIA guys to play footsy with a second-rate Latin American dictator."

"Mr. Grady." I had iced my tone of voice down to its most disdainful pitch. "Your government career apparently survived one brush with us. It most assuredly will not survive another. I am not asking you to stop your investigation of General Noriega. I am ordering you to stop it."

Grady sat there an instant, clenching and unclenching his fists, a stream of pure Celtic fury pouring from his eyes. Then he sprang from his chair, spun around and started for the door.

"Mr. Grady," I called out. "Come back here."

"Fuck you!" he shouted and slammed Archer's door behind him so hard he almost jarred it off its hinges.

Poor Grady. I felt genuinely sorry for him after that meeting. You had to admire that capacity of his for righteous indignation. It harked back to another more innocent time, when things were black and white, decisions simple and clear-cut, and moral ambiguity did not have to cloud our decision making. I was meditating on that when the phone rang. It was Hinckley calling back. I reviewed the meeting for him.

"Good," he said. "I found out from our people over at the DEA what I wanted to know. The information in that cable comes from one of their informers, this SCI-83-0021 they refer to. He's a drug smuggler, a guy from Philadelphia who lives down in Bogotá now. His name is Raymond Marcello. Apparently he has good contacts with the Medellín cartel."

"Sure," I replied, "that's how they usually work, through informers."

"Right. Well, what I want you to do is set up a meeting with Noriega right away. The first thing you've got to tell him nice and discreetly is to cool it. We saved his ass in 1972. We saved it again today. We're not going to make a career out of doing that. For the time being we need him more than he needs us, so we'll just pretend this didn't happen. But you've got to make him understand that the one thing we cannot afford is to have a drug scandal break out. The congressional opposition to the whole contra program is so damn vociferous up here, just a whiff of a scandal would destroy us. Got that?"

"Right."

"The second thing you're going to do is quietly pass him this guy Marcello's name and let him handle that problem."

"Ted, you know what Noriega is going to do with that information, don't you?"

"No, I don't know and neither, for that matter, do you. Nor do I want to know. I just want to make sure that the most important asset this agency has in Central America is not taken out of play at a time when his function is vital to the accomplishment of the agency's—and the nation's—mission."

Talking overseas on a secure telephone requires a certain

technique. It's a bit like talking from ship to shore; you can't talk while the other party's speaking. It's fine for transmitting orders, but something less than ideal for a debate, as I was now discovering.

"Ted, I know Noriega. I know exactly what he'll do with that information. He'll have the guy murdered."

"No, Jack, you don't know that and neither do I. Don't pretend to a knowledge you don't have. Don't create a reality where one doesn't yet exist and may never exist. All we're doing here is executing our mission. We're performing for a valuable asset exactly the service we would expect him to perform for us in similar circumstances."

How I would have preferred to have had that argument with Hinckley face to face instead of having to utter my thoughts into the abstraction of a telephone.

"Oh, come on, Ted, that's just discussing how many angels can dance on the head of a pin."

"Look, you remember we had this same discussion back in 1972 when that guy Ingersoll was accusing Noriega of shielding the heroin traffic, didn't we? We warned him then someone was ratting on him. He dealt with the problem and we didn't hear another word about Noriega and drugs until today, did we? And look at what Noriega has been able to do for us since 1972."

I was awfully glad even the NSA couldn't monitor these secure conversations of ours. "There's a big difference between what we were dealing with in 1972 and this situation. In 1972 we only had a generalized suspicion. This time we're dealing with a specific individual. And an American citizen to boot."

"We're dealing with a scumbag, just another guinea dope dealer. An informer trying to weasel out of the jail time he so richly deserves. Screw him. Just weigh him in the balance against the things Noriega's doing for us and is going to do for us and see where you come out."

"There's something else at stake here, Ted. I'm not a lawyer, but I know it's a firm principle of criminal law that any individual who incites another to commit murder, who furnishes him with the lethal weapon to kill someone, is guilty of the crime as much as the killer is. Giving Noriega this man's name puts us in that position. Furthermore, let's face it. We're executives of the U.S. government and we're actively participating in the violation of the nation's laws."

"Who the hell is talking about murder? Who the hell is talking about crime? You sound like some damn Jesuit-trained lawyer. None of that is at issue here."

"It is unless you've stuck your head in a barrel full of sand."

"Jack, what Noriega does with the information we give him is his moral responsibility. Not yours. Not mine. Not the agency's. All we're doing is providing him with information he, as one of our valuable assets, is entitled to have. What he does with it is his business alone."

"Rubbish, Ted. Now you're the one who's talking like the Jesuit-trained lawyer."

"I've been with the CIA longer than you have, Jack. Since its founding, practically. There is implicit in the agency's mandate a dispensation to suspend the concerns that are troubling you when the national security requires it. That's what's happening here. So forget about those worries of yours and get on with the job."

"It's not that easy, Ted."

"Listen to me, Jack. Listen carefully. Look at the big picture here. The President wants his contra policy advanced. Casey wants it advanced. Are we supposed to be martyrs and go against the President and the Director? Hell, no. Our job is to execute their policy and, believe me, keeping your asset Noriega in play is a vital part of that. Act in the best interests of your country, Jack, not in those of some sleaze-bag drug dealer. That's what you're paid to do."

I started to reply, but Hinckley cut me off. The tone had changed dramatically. "If you're not going to protect your asset yourself, Lind, then let me tell you this. I'll fly down there tonight and tell him myself—while you're packing your bags to open up our new station in Ulan Bator."

My meeting with Noriega took place later that same evening at La Playita, his seaside cottage. It was only the second time I'd been there. I went, my heart heavy with doubts and misgivings about what I was going to do when I got there, but I went nonetheless.

Fortunately, the encounter was brief, barely the time we needed to work our way through two glasses of Old Parr. Noriega was preoccupied with the aftermath of the elections, with stifling the outrage of his political foes, who knew full well he had stolen them.

When we got to the reason for our encounter, I could not detect the slightest reaction on those dour features of his. He just sat there a second, absolutely expressionless, digesting my little lecture on the evils of the drug traffic. Then he snorted.

"You don't really suspect I'd be involved in something like that, do you?"

"I certainly hope not, Tony. Because if you are there may come a time when we can no longer help you, however much we might want to."

He scowled but said nothing.

"There's just one other thing," I said, and slipped Mr Marcello's name and function into our conversation. He reached for a notepad from the table beside him.

"How do you spell that guy's name?" he asked.

It was only as we were leaving that he finally lightened up a bit. Half playfully, he punched me on the arm. "I gave you one," he smiled, "now you give me one. That is how it should be."

Driving back to Corozal, I was a deeply troubled man. What I had done in asking Noriega to release Juanita was a thoroughly unprofessional act accomplished for an honorable end. What I had just done was a thoroughly professional act accomplished for a most dishonorable end. I thought about Kevin Grady and that capacity of his for moral outrage. Once, I'd been able to feel outrage too at the tawdry side of our business, at the agent sacrificed to the higher gain. No more. Somewhere along the line, I'd lost that. The calluses had indeed grown thick upon my soul. My concern back at Corozal was not the possible consequences of what I had just done in passing Marcello's name to Noriega, but in getting a report on our conversation into a ciphered cable for Langley as quickly as I could.

The black cleaning lady wearily shoved her trolley down the corridor of the Jewelry Mart at 220 West Fifth Street, two blocks from the steel and glass canyons of Los Angeles's financial district. She was just another sister in that enormous and faceless sorority of women, mostly blacks and Hispanics, who labor nightly to clean those buildings while their white daytime tenants slept.

It was 2:30 a.m. and the building was empty except for the security guards downstairs and the roving patrol who'd just greeted her as he worked his way down to the fifteenth floor. She entered the back office suite of the Larmex gold and jewelry outlet and prepared to go to work. Larmex was owned by a pair of Armenian brothers, refugees from war-torn Beirut, where they'd been active in the gold and jewelry trade.

Normally, her first action would be to empty out the room's wastebaskets. Here, however, she clambered onto a desk just under the closed-circuit TV camera that provided security for the Larmex premises. She unscrewed the rear of the camera's control panel, and extricated a small cassette, which she tucked into her ample bosom. She inserted a new one in its place, screwed the cover back on, and climbed down from the desk to start emptying the wastebaskets.

In fact, the most important aspect of her night's work had just been completed. The cleaning lady was a DEA agent working undercover, one of the dozens of agents now assigned to the enormous operation that had grown out of Eduardo Hernandez's revelations on the island of Aruba about La Mina. Just as Cesar Rodriguez had predicted to Ramon on the beach that day, Hernandez's information was leading the DEA straight to the Super Bowl of money laundering schemes. It was by far the largest ploy of its kind ever uncovered by U.S. law enforcement.

So big had the operation become that it now involved the FBI, Customs, Treasury, the IRS, as well as the DEA and the local police departments in the cities involved. Inevitably, the sprawling size the operation had taken on meant that Kevin Grady's role in it had been substantially downgraded. Essentially, he was now the contact to the CI who had started the whole ball rolling.

Watching the paper flow generated by the operation crossing his New York desk, he couldn't help marveling at what they'd uncovered. The most recent estimates of La Mina suggested that at least half a billion dollars a year in laundered cash was flowing through its jewelry outlets. The joint task force now had jewelry stores in six cities and the gold refinery in Hollywood, Florida, under surveillance. The link appeared to be Armenian refugees from Lebanon like the brothers who owned Larmex. Those who had settled in the States had retained ties to cousins and uncles who'd chosen South America for their place of refuge. The mastermind, DEA intelligence had determined, was an Uruguayan financier named Raul Vivas, who owned a money-changing firm called Cambio Italia. His principal associate was another Uruguayan called Sergio Hochman, whose firm Lectra S.A. appeared to be the holding company controlling the spider's web of dummy corporations involved.

It was about as promising as operations got, Grady thought, and almost enough to make him forget the target he'd wanted to go after, Manuel Antonio Noriega.

As he was thus consoling himself, Ella Jean Ransom walked into his office. "I've got Joe Abrams, the country attaché down in Bogotá on the line," she said. "They're ready to move Ramon's wife and children. They'll be coming in Wednesday on Avianca's Flight 020. They get into La Guardia at 9:30 at night."

"Great," Grady said. "Let me have a word with him.

"Joe," he told his colleague in Colombia, "thanks for handling that. We appreciate. How's the CI?"

"He's fine. He's going up to Panama City tomorrow with Hernandez for a final meeting at the Banco de Occidente, then he'll fly on back up to New York via Houston. He'll be getting in a little bit after his family."

"Okay. Be sure he checks in with Hines in Panama."

"Don't worry. He's well clued in."

It was 7:30 in the morning, but already Panama's humid heat made jogging along the Pacific sea-front below the Marriott Hotel an ordeal. Next time, Ramon thought, I'll have to find a less strenuous way to handle my meets. He carefully checked his six o'clock as he always did as a matter of routine although he knew it was no longer necessary. His Medellín colleagues' confidence in him was now complete.

Up ahead, he could see the figure of Fred Hines, the DEA country agent, plodding slowly forward. He caught up with him and for an instant the two men matched strides.

"How's it going?" Hines asked.

"No problems. I'm meeting Hernandez at the Banco de Occidente at ten o'clock. He's opening some new accounts we're going to be using from now on in the Jimmy Bruno operation."

"How long do you figure it will take?"

"An hour maybe. Then I'll go back to the hotel, have lunch and head out to the airport."

"Okay. Just be sure you check in with me before you leave for the airport. Ciao."

Ramon accelerated his pace and left Hines behind. Their exchange had not lasted more than thirty seconds.

Forty minutes later, he was showered and dressed and marching into the downstairs breakfast buffet at the hotel. To Ramon's delight, Panamanians had apparently never heard of things like cholesterol-free, all bran and fiber breakfasts. Every form of delicious calorie-ridden food imaginable was on display: eggs, bacon, ham, cheeses, a dozen kinds of fruits and fruit juices, Danish, banana bread, nut bread, rolls, croissants. With the appetite fueled by his early morning run, Ramon served himself twice from a wide variety of those treats. Finally, at 9:10, he went up to the entrance and asked the doorman for a cab to the Banco de Occidente.

The bank was located in Little Switzerland, a gleaming gulch of glass-and-steel towers clustered around the Via España, monuments to coke money and Panama's bank secrecy laws. There was virtually no bank in the world worthy of the name that was not among the one hundred twenty-five banks in the area. A cynical U.S. Treasury estimated that sixty percent of the money passing through that banking community was generated by drug sales.

In his crisp dark blue suit, clutching his black attaché case, Ramon was as much the prosperous banker as any of the other visitors entering the Banco de Occidente's air-conditioned lobby that morning. He was heading for the elevator bank when an equally well-dressed young man approached him.

"Señor Ramon?" he asked.

Ramon was surprised to hear someone address him by name. Before he could answer, the young man palmed a gold police badge at him.

"I'm Captain Luis Peel, the liaison officer between the DEA and the police here. Freddy Hines sent me to bring you an urgent message. He doesn't want you to go to this meeting. Washington just cabled him that it looks like it's a trap. He wants me to bring you back to the embassy where we know you'll be safe. He's waiting for you back there."

"Jesus!" Ramon said, feeling his intestines tighten. "Thank God I didn't get here early!"

"Yes," Peel replied, "that's fortunate. My car's waiting just outside."

Lind's Tape

Hopefully, my warning had put a little fear of God into Noriega, but there remained the real possibility that some of our CIA contractual employees, our UCLANs, or some of the contra leadership were moonlighting in the drug trade. We had to stop it if we could and be damn sure we could cover it up if it was going on. Let the word of that kind of activity get into the public domain and, as Hinckley had pointed out, it would blow the President's favorite foreign policy initiative sky-high. Have Talmadge assemble our key UCLANs for a meeting at the secret air base the agency was building at Aguacate in Honduras, Hinckley ordered. Get up there and read those guys the riot act. Have them cool it before any of that stuff can get public.

Gary Ellis, our station chief, met me at the airport when I arrived in Tegucigalpa, and we set off for Aguacate, which was in Olancho province on the border with Nicaragua. As we left the capital and started rocketing through the highlands toward the frontier, I noticed how often we were passing wooden crosses implanted on the shoulders of the roadway.

"They mark the place where someone died in a car crash," Ellis explained. "The Hondurans believe the dead person's soul is trapped there until a priest comes to say a Mass on the spot and plant that cross. Tells you something about how religious these people are."

"Tells me more about the way they drive," I said.

Olancho province was pretty country, gently rolling land with jacaranda and acacia trees blooming everywhere. The poorer campesinos' huts were sided with palm fronds; the wealthier covered theirs in composition brick. All, however, were roofed with red tiles made from a local clay. They looked a bit like the rooftops you'd see in a Van Gogh oil of the Provençal countryside. Our destination was a village called Catana, where the macadam ran out. From there it was a twelve-mile run over a dirt track out to our air base.

Twice our Toyota four-by-four had to ford streams that came up to our hubcaps. The foliage lining the roadside grew more dense as each kilometer passed. There was no sign of human life.

"Nice country," I remarked.

"Gets worse," Ellis informed me. "There's sixty miles of solid jungle between the Nicaraguan border and the camp. The Sandinistas aren't apt to come by for a visit unannounced."

Finally, the dirt track simply ran out in front of a wall of forest.

"This is it," Ellis proclaimed "welcome to your friendly CIA's Aguacate Air Base."

A slope led down from the track to a dried-out riverbed which had been paralleling our course for a mile or so. Off in the distance, I could hear the clank and scrape of bulldozers and see the twisters of dust their blades were raising in the dry soil. At the base of the slope, hidden in a clump of trees, was a guard post. A pair of kids in jungle uniforms, Adidas sneakers and carrying AK-47's almost as big as they were, emerged from the bush offering me my first glimpse of our contra warriors.

One of them volunteered to lead us to Talmadge. The Duke was at the far side of the runway the bulldozers were cutting into the countryside, keeping an eye on a group of contras unloading long wooden crates from a DC-6 with Panamanian markings.

"Spare parts for your John Deere tractors?" I asked.

The Duke wasn't around the day they put the humor gene into the DNA chain. "AK-47's," he growled. "From Poland via Tel Aviv, La Paz and Panama City. Thanks to your boy Noriega."

Talmadge led us back across the runway toward a wooden hut which was his field headquarters. He gestured off toward the horizon and the sound of the bulldozers.

"Right now this strip can't handle anything bigger than a DC-6," he observed, "but when we finish lengthening the runway we'll be able to take in C-130's."

There were no Honduran military at the airfield. The Honduran authorities had no precise idea what we were doing up there, how many planes we were bringing in, what they were carrying, where they'd come from or where they were going to. It was, for our purposes, ideal.

We settled down around the Duke's wobbly wooden desk. On the wall he'd hung a U.S. Army Corps of Engineers map of Nicaragua, little red pins indicating his contra raiders' deepest penetrations inside Sandinista territory. Outside, in the distance, we could hear the crackle of small-arms fire and the *whump* of mortars coming from the ranges on which he was training his fighters.

I explained to him Hinckley's concern about some of our UCLANs or the contra leadership getting into the drug traffic.

"What the hell does Hinckley expect?" the Duke snarled. "It's his damn fault anyway. Contract out our war, that was his idea, wasn't it? Use the private sector. Don't have any American CIA officers around so Congress can't find out what we're doing. Well, without agency officers around, who's exercising control? Nobody is. And when you run an operation without proper control, you'll get into trouble every time."

I told him—without mentioning Juanita—about my fears that there might be cocaine getting mixed up with our arms flights out of Panama.

"I don't doubt that for a moment," the Duke said. "The place I'd keep my eye on is that strip we're using over in Costa Rica near Muelle, with that farmer who's freelancing for us. He has money troubles and there are no agency officers up there. It's all UCLANs. Old Felix Rodriguez down in Ilopango is okay. I don't think he'd mess with dope. When I'm here I think this place is clean. When I'm not?" He shrugged.

We then trotted in half a dozen of our contractuals, Felipe Nadal in the lead. I read them the anti-drug smuggling gospel. You've never seen so many expressions of hurt innocence in one room as we had in that little office.

"Juanito," Felipe declared with the fervor of a nun taking her final vows, "I swear to you on the head of the mother of my children, never, never would I get involved in such things. Never. I would kill with my bare hands any one of my men who touched that stuff." There was a general outpouring of Latin oaths from the rest of the assembly to give strength to his declaration.

We then spent the next two hours reviewing Black Eagle operations and the other aspects of our contra program.

"So," I asked the Duke when they'd all left, "do you think we did any good?"

"Oh, hell yes," he laughed. "From now on they'll be much more careful about covering their traces."

Kevin Grady had spent his lunch hour in Macy's shopping for presents, a Barbie and Ken doll set for the little girl, a remote-control model of a Formula One racing car for the boy. He'd had them gift-wrapped, but now he couldn't resist undoing the packages to show the toys off to Ella Jean.

She gave him a sadly tender look. "What a pity you never had kids, Kev. You'd make a great father."

Grady shrugged. "Bachelors don't make the best of fathers."

"A lot of bachelor mothers doing pretty well out there."

"I guess."

"Trouble is the way you're living since your wife died, Kev, the first woman you're going to meet will be playing the organ at your funeral."

Grady tried his best to smile. "True enough. I think you're the only girl I know, Ella Jean. The only one I care about, anyway."

"And the only one who gives a damn about you."

Kevin had just begun a clumsy effort to wrap his gifts back up when the phone rang. It was Fred Hines calling from Panama.

"Kevin," he gasped, "Ramon, your CI's gone missing!"

"What the hell do you mean?" Grady sank on his trembling knees into his chair.

"He never came back from his meeting with Hernandez at the Banco de Occidente. We checked out his hotel room. His things are still there. His flight to Houston just cleared. He didn't get on it."

"How about Hernandez?"

"Checked out of his hotel room at nine this morning. Nothing since."

"And that woman, what the hell was her name, Clara, at the bank?"

"Says there was never any meeting scheduled as far as she knows."

"He's been set up!"

"I'm afraid so. I've been on to my liaison over at the PDF, Luis Peel. He's promised to do everything he can to help."

"Dear God!" The words came out half as a prayer, half as a cry for help. He turned to Ella Jean. "What ever am I going to tell that poor woman and her children at the airport?"

"I just had a call from our little friend Felipe," Pedro del Rica informed Noriega. "That CIA guy Lind called all their

Cuban Americans to a meeting at that airport they're building up in Honduras this afternoon. Gave them a big talk about not smuggling drugs. Said he thinks somebody may be mixing up coke in the arms flights we're running for them."

Now where the hell would Lind have gotten that idea, Noriega thought. Unless it was from the nosy little girlfriend of his. I should have kept the bitch in jail after all.

"I wouldn't worry about it too much," Noriega assured him. "Just be sure everybody is extra careful."

Ella Jean Ransom cast a worried glance at Kevin Grady in the chair beside her. His tie was askew, his mouth stretched taut, his whole expression that of a man struggling to hold in a violent outburst of anger. His meeting with Ramon's wife and children at La Guardia had been an ordeal, he'd whispered to her, slipping into his seat for this meeting. The decision had been made not to inform them of Ramon's disappearance until the DEA had some firm indication of what had happened to him.

For the moment, both agents were caught up in the tensions generated by this high-level midnight gathering in the office of the New York DO's special agent in charge. Everybody was there: the FBI, Customs, Treasury, Richie Cagnia, Eddie Gomez, and, finally, the deputy administrator of the DEA for Operations, flown up specially from Washington to preside at the meeting. Its purpose was to try to determine what had happened to Ramon and what consequences his disappearance was going to have on their ongoing operations.

"Okay," the deputy administrator for Operations said, declaring the meeting open. "First question. What do we figure happened to this guy?"

"He was set up," Richie Cagnia declared. "The cartel people figured out he was double-banging them, they got him into a corner, put a gun into his ribs, dropped a bag over his head and off he went. It's as simple as that. If you ask me, he's already dead."

"The Panama country attaché found the cab driver who took him to the bank. Everything was normal. He walked straight into the bank. That's our last sighting," Ella Jean reported.

"Why are you so sure he was set up?" the deputy pressed

Cagnia. "Maybe he double-crossed us. Maybe he's on a plane to Rio right now."

"On the day he sent his wife and kids up here to get into the witness-protection program? It doesn't make sense."

"Maybe he wanted a new wife."

"That's most unlikely," Ella Jean emphasized. "We knew him pretty well. The whole reason he was performing as a CI was because of his family."

"He sure as hell isn't going to be heading back to Colombia," Cagnia laughed. "Not when his pals in the cartel find out what his work with us is going to cost them."

"So you've all read the New York office's paper." The deputy administrator was anxious to wrap up this part of the discussion. "Anyone here who doesn't think the guy was set up?"

That was when Kevin exploded.

"For Christ's sake! What are we sitting here picking our noses for? Why are we having this stupid debate? Of course he was set up. That's not what counts. What counts is who set him up. You all think it was the cartel. You're wrong. It was the CIA."

A silence as embarrassed as it was pained greeted his accusation. Ella Jean looked at Grady, his chest heaving under the pressure of his anger. He's really put his foot in it now, she told herself. The FBI representative was, at the same time, nodding to his colleague from Treasury. What can you expect from these people they have at the DEA, his expression seemed to say. The New York SAC looked out at the city lights so he wouldn't have to contemplate the deputy administrator's fury.

Kevin himself seemed oblivious to the consternation his remarks had prompted. He angrily described Ramon's last report and his confrontation with Jack Lind.

"That son of a bitch passed his name on to Noriega and Noriega did him. That's what happened."

"You'll note, Mr. Grady," the FBI man purred, "that the Panamanian police are cooperating fully with your DEA investigation. That hardly indicates Noriega was involved in this."

"That indicates you don't know fuck-all about how those people work."

Oh, oh, Ella Jean thought, poor Kevin's just made himself another enemy.

"There is not a single shred of hard evidence, Grady, to support such an allegation." The New York SAC was anxious to get the discussion off this treacherous ground as fast as he could. "We're fighting the Medellín cartel here, not another agency of the government."

"Don't count on it," Grady retorted.

"Let's forget about the CIA for the moment." The deputy administrator was well aware of the niceties of Washington politics. The last thing his boss wanted or needed was a fight with the agency. Those were fights the DEA inevitably lost. "We all seem to agree our CI was set up. There is only one conclusion we can make from that. All our operations in which he was a player are now compromised, right?"

There was a murmur of concurrence around the room.

"That means we've got to close up shop on all of them tonight. Everything, MEDCLEAN, La Mina, the works. We've got to get search warrants on all those jewelry stores and the refinery, all the identified stash-houses, cash and dope. We've got to unseal all our sealed indictments and make arrangements to pick up everybody we've named in them. We've got to get arrest warrants sworn out on all our unindicted suspects. We've got to get seizure orders on every bank account we're watching and get in and seize those accounts the moment the banks open their doors in the morning. The U.S. Attorney's staff will have to put in triple overtime on this. And the whole thing has to be timed and coordinated like we were Eisenhower landing in Normandy. It's going to be a mammoth job. Nobody sleeps tonight, my friends."

He paused just a moment. "Except maybe you, Kevin. You've been under a big strain here. Losing a good CI always hurts."

The Piper Cheyenne settled easily onto the asphalt runway of Pablo Escobar's favorite homestead, the Hacienda Napoles, and taxied toward the three-plane hangar which served the ranch. The pilot turned to the two men guarding their cargo behind him.

"Everything okay?" he asked.

"No problem, man. You made it seem like a bus ride."

The pilot shrugged. Indeed, for him, this flight between Escobar's Colombian ranch and the landing strip at Panama's Coronado Beach was little more these days than a bus trip. He guided the plane up to the big double doors of the hangar. As he reached them, he saw the stumpy figure of his boss, his little straw hat perched on his head, waiting for them.

"Hey," he hissed to the men behind him, "Don Pablo's here."

He shut down his engine, opened his window, and waved obsequiously to his employer.

"No problems?" Escobar asked.

"Everything went fine, Don Pablo."

As the pilot answered, a mechanic was already opening the plane's door. The first passenger sprang to the ground. He turned and began to tug at their cargo while the other passenger shoved at it from inside the plane. It was a man wrapped tightly into a mental asylum straitjacket, his mouth gagged with adhesive, his head, bruised and bloody, sticking out from above the jacket's collar. His eyes were puffed, their sockets blackened from beating, but they could still flicker with terror at the sight of Pablo Escobar's advancing figure.

"So," Escobar smiled, "our pajarito—*little bird*—has come home for his reward."

Raymond "Ramon" Marcello had returned to Colombia.

Kevin Grady was exactly where Ella Jean had expected him to be, by himself on a bar stool in a corner of Desmond's on 57th between Eighth and Ninth avenues nursing a bourbon and soda. She walked down the bar and slid onto the stool next to his. Maurice, the barman, came up to her. "What's your pleasure, Miss Ella?" he asked.

"A Diet Coke. I'm driving."

"How's it going up there?" Kevin said.

"It's going to be huge. At least two hundred good folk if we manage to pick them all up. Millions in seizures. Plus some big dough in those stash-houses."

"His monument."

"Yours, too."

Grady shook his head. "You know why it hurts so much? I really got to like that guy. What balls he had, going back into the compound for us. I mean, how often do you give a damn about a CI? Who cares if most of them live or die?"

"I know. I liked him, too. He was different."

"And facing that poor woman with her two kids tonight.

Pretending, oh yeah, everything's fine, Daddy'll be along in a day or two, not to worry."

"What's she like?"

"Spooked out at the moment. I mean she's been hit by their trinity of terror in the last few days. Her husband was doing drugs. Her husband got caught. Her husband's doing the one thing you never do, cooperating with the gringos."

"She speak English?"

"Not a word."

"Life's going to be tough on her for a while."

Grady tightened his grip on his whiskey glass a second, then raised it to take a long swallow.

"Why the hell didn't I order him to blow that meeting in Panama and come right back up here?"

"You had no reason to suspect anything was wrong."

"I should have. My Irish street cop's flair deserted me. I should have sniffed out that bastard Lind."

"Tell me something, Kev." Ella Jean leaned into the bar, set her elbow onto its surface, and turned so her dark eyes could focus more closely on Grady. "You don't really believe that bullshit about the CIA shopping him to Noriega, do you?"

"Of course I do. And I'll bet that guy Lind is the one who did it."

"There are just too many other ways it could have happened, Kev. They might have picked up the surveillance on one of the La Mina jewelry stores. That would have given it to them in a flash. Or one of the Jimmy Bruno cash stashhouses. A dozen things."

"I don't believe it. I believe the agency is protecting Noriega and closing their eyes to his drug stuff because he's doing something big for them. Just the way Vang Pao was out in Laos."

Ella Jean rested her dark hand on Grady's, the long red fingernail of her index finger flicking quizzically at his watchband. For an instant she contemplated their two hands, black and white, resting on each other on the bar. "Kev, dear," she muttered softly, "let me tell you something. You're not going to advance that promising career of yours by going around this building making war on the CIA. The gray flannel suits have a lot of powerful friends in high places."

"He was my CI. And he was my friend. One day I'll get the bastard who did him."

Ella Jean sighed and withdrew her hand. "Boy, they sure put thick heads on you Irishmen, don't they?"

Desmond's only other customer was at the opposite end of the bar, slouched over his drink like a slag heap collapsing in a downpour. The barman had stationed himself halfway between his clients, one eye on his TV tuned to a John Wayne World War Two epic with the sound off, the other on the clock, waiting for three and the moment he could close up. The melancholia of late-night New York drifted like fog through the bar. It was an hour for exchanging confidences with a stranger, confessions with a friend.

Kevin slipped an arm around Ella Jean's slim waist. "Taking advice isn't what I do best in life, El. But I appreciate it, your giving it to me. I appreciate an awful lot about you. Since she died, you're about the only person I really feel close to. You know that?"

"I feel it sometimes."

He pressed gently at her waist. "Maybe we should just get the hell out of here."

Ella Jean's dark eyes glowed with compassion and wisdom. She looked at him for an instant, then leaned her face close to his. "Maybe we shouldn't, too." She kissed him tenderly on the cheek. "Some things are better left undone, Kev."

The package arrived at the New York DO by Air Mail Special Delivery twenty-four hours later, as Kevin was preparing to leave for Panama on a temporary assignment to investigate the circumstances surrounding Ramon's disappearance. It was addressed to him. There was no return address. Its postmark indicated it had been mailed from the Central Post Office in Medellín.

He was about to open it when Richie Cagnia intervened. "Don't touch that damn thing," he warned. "Who knows what they might have put in there? What we want to do is get that downtown to the NYPD's bomb disposal people. Let them open it for us."

Grady stared at the package with new and sudden horror. "You really think it might be booby-trapped? A letter bomb?"

"How many friends you got in Medellín who'd be into

sending you CARE packages? Let's send it down to Police Plaza."

The Bomb Disposal people, in the form of a plainclothes police sergeant, brought the package back three hours later. Kevin called Cagnia and Ella Jean in to witness along with him what it contained. Laying the opened, then resealed package onto Kevin's desk, the plainclothes sergeant seemed almost embarrassed. "Boy," he noted, "they got some real weirdos down there in Medellín, don't they?"

He broke open the new seal and reached into the envelope. "We dusted for prints before we opened it just in case," he informed them as he was pulling out a sixty-minute audiocassette which he set on Grady's desk. Then his hand went back into the envelope.

It came out clutching a wooden box about six inches long and two inches wide. It was handcarved into the shape of a coffin, a replica accurate down to the little handles screwed into its side panels. Fixed onto its surface was a small brass plaque. The initials *R.M.* were etched onto the plaque.

"Christ!" Kevin gasped.

Ella Jean stifled a sharp cry.

"You going to open it?" asked the sergeant.

"I don't know if I want to."

"I think you got to."

Grady reached over and gingerly pushed open the lid of the coffin with his thumb and forefinger. Inside, preserved in formaldehyde inside a glass tube, was what appeared to be at first glance a long, reddish-brown worm. It was a human tongue.

He groaned and let the cover drop back onto the miniature coffin.

"Those bastards!" he whispered.

For almost a minute the three agents stared silently like the mourners they were at the miniature coffin. Finally, Kevin reached out for the audiocassette.

"You guys listen to this thing?"

The police sergeant shook his head. "We figured if it's evidentiary material, which it probably is, you ought to get the first crack."

"I'll get my Walkman," Ella Jean muttered.

Kevin, his fingers shaking, snapped the cassette into the player. He pushed the volume button up full, stretched the earphones out in front of them so they could all hear, and turned the machine on.

It was a recording of Ramon's final agony, his voice clearly identifiable as they followed his calvary through every shriek and scream and cry and whimper down to his dying groan and Pablo Escobar's guttural laugh of triumph.

"I think I'm going to be sick," Ella Jean said.

Grady sat in shock at his desk, his head in his hands, weeping silently.

Ella Jean had come back when, at last, he drew open the center drawer of his desk. He took out a box which had once contained one of his dead wife's rings, snapped it open, and removed a simple gold wedding band.

R.M. to C.A. 10-8-76 was inscribed on its inner surface.

He looked at it for a long moment, then slipped it into his pocket and stood up.

"Excuse me," he said, "I have a promise to keep."

BOOK NINE

The Woman in Suite #51

Lind's Tape

B ill Casey coveted secrets the way a courtesan covets jew-
els. He simply reveled in the hush-hush aspects of our intelligence world. I think it brought back to him something of
the excitement, of the heady sense of engagement, he had
known in his World War Two days in London with the OSS.
He routinely cloaked his overseas trips—of which he made
many—with an air of such secrecy you would have thought
we were protecting the mysteries of D-Day.

Our trip to Panama from July 31 to August 2, 1984, so he
could meet Noriega personally, was typical. Takeoff from
Andrews Air Force Base was set for after sunset. By leaving
at that hour, we would both depart Washington and arrive in
Panama under the cover of darkness. No one outside half a
dozen people at the agency and the White House even knew
we were going. Everybody in the traveling party left his office normally after work and went home. Each of us was
given an elaborate disguise to cover our trip to Andrews: I
was off to a tennis game, someone else to a neighbor's out-
door barbecue.

Once we were airborne, however, Casey relaxed, undid
his necktie, put his feet up on the table, and called for his favorite predinner drink, a scotch and water. For some time he
had been impressed by what PK\BARRIER\7-7 was doing
for us, not only in Panama but in the rest of the world as
well. Casey had decided it was time to meet him. After all,
Casey had just exerted in Washington the pressures that had
allowed Noriega to get away with stealing a national election. Why wouldn't he be anxious to meet the man?

Our party that night, besides Hinckley and myself, included a new boy in school, a Marine Corps light colonel
assigned to the National Security Council named Oliver
North. North's office in Room 302 of the old Executive Office Building across from the White House was only a few
steps from Casey's in-town office. That was how he had
caught the Director's eye.

North had been made in heaven, I think, for Casey. He
was all stand-up-straight, salute and charge-up-the-hill Marine. You never got any sophisticated requests or embarrass-

ing questions out of Ollie. It was just snap to it and get the job done. Casey loved him for that.

He was going to take the Duke's place as the Director of the Central American Task Force. The Duke's blunt, take-no-prisoners manner had offended one congressman too many. The change, as Casey explained, taking up his drink, was part of a new and important turn in our contra policy.

"Those bastards over on the Hill think they're going to shut down our contra program," he growled. "Well, I've got news for the fuckers. In this country it's the President, not the Congress, that makes foreign policy. Ronald Reagan wants this program and, by God, he's going to get it."

Casey's manner was gruff—rude, his detractors claimed. I never agreed. It just reflected a kind of blunt heartiness that was a part of the man's character.

As he rambled on, it began to become clear to me that he had bought Hinckley's concept of an off-the-shelf covert operations capability—lock, stock and barrel. Essentially, Casey was going to run his war without congressional oversight or approval by setting up a kind of parallel CIA, a free-standing secret apparatus at the private disposition of the President and the Executive Branch.

"You ask where do we get the money if we don't get it from Congress?" Nobody had, but he obviously thought someone should have. "Congress thinks they're the only source of money around. Well, they're not. We'll go to the Saudis. We'll go to the Sultan of Brunei and ask them to cough up. There are things they need from us. This will be their way of helping us out in return. We keep the money we get in Switzerland, in Panama. It never sees the inside of a U.S. bank. So what oversight rights does Congress have on it? None at all."

Hinckley was listening to him with the pride of a school-teacher listening to his prize pupil recite the poem he's memorized for Class Day. North was wide-eyed with admiration.

"Second thing we do is increase the Israelis' management role here. They're our best source of arms anyway. And the third thing, and this is the reason for our trip, I want to get Noriega involved more deeply in this effort. He can provide us more training facilities for the contras. We ought to be moving more of our arms to the contras through Panama. He's good on this end user certificate business."

He looked at me. "Did you know he just gave our contras n Costa Rica $100,000 cash?"

I glanced at Hinckley. He was old stone face. Yet in view of what we'd learned in the last three weeks, I took it as an absolute given that that $100,000 cash Noriega had passed o the contras had been drug money from Medellín. Clearly, hat was not a subject for discussion around this table.

"No sir," I said to Casey, "I didn't know that."

"Yeah. A damn fine gesture."

Casey remained buoyant and cheerful all the way to Howard Air Force Base. On a recent trip to Germany, he'd insisted on dragging his escorts on a tour of the local girlie oints and gin mills. I was afraid, in view of his radiant energy, we'd have the same request here. Panama is, after all, well equipped in that regard. Fortunately, however, he headed off for a good night's sleep at the station residence where he was going to hole up during his stay.

His meeting with PK\BARRIER\7-7 took place on the following night. Hinckley and I briefed him for it. We told him about the 1972 drug allegations and the more recent ones. Needless to say, we did not go into any detail about our clash with the DEA.

"Yeah," Casey growled, "I'll talk to him about that."

Many people at the agency who dealt with Noriega tended to do so with an imaginary clothespin over their nose to ward off the man's offensive moral odors. Not Casey. From that first encounter, he developed a genuine regard for the man.

Noriega certainly made it easy for Casey to like him. I know, because I translated for them on that occasion; Noriega was reluctant to use Panamanian translators so as to limit the number of Panamanians who were aware of just how close he was to the CIA.

I don't think there was anything Casey wanted from Noriega that night that he didn't get. Certainly, part of the reason for PK\BARRIER\7-7's willingness to be so forthcoming was his realization that the closer he got to our contra activities, the more completely he became involved in the program, the less likely it was that we would—or could—go after him if the news of his other activities got out.

He agreed to expand training facilities for the contras, to increase his and Panama's role as a way station moving arms

to them. He volunteered Casey the services of his lawye
and business adviser in Geneva, Juan Bautista Castillero, t
help move his offshore money and set up dummy corpora
tions for us. He promised to intervene to smooth the ruffle
feathers of one of our prize contras, Eden Pastora. Whe
Ollie North suggested we might build a CIA air base i
Costa Rica similar to the one we had at Aguacate, he offere
help in that.

The meeting lasted three hours and was cordial from sta
to finish. It ended with the usual display of back thumpin
affection and *hasta la vistas*. It was only after Noriega ha
left that I realized that Casey, whether through intent or in
advertence, had never once mentioned drugs.

Later, I called Juanita from my hotel. She did not seen
surprised to hear my voice. Rather, I detected in her tone
note of sadness, nostalgia perhaps. She was leaving fo
Costa Rica early in the morning, she told me, to see a clos
friend in San Jose, the capital. I suggested I might come b
for a nightcap. I was aching to see her, to make love to hei
to do anything I could to re-ignite that passion we had onc
shared. Our last lovemaking on the night she'd been release
from prison had been a tenuous groping after what we had
known. We had not found it. I was desperate to find it again

I sensed her hesitating, debating with herself. I imagine
her on the terrace of her flat wrapped into that red mini
kimono she so liked to wear before going to bed.

"It's late, Jack," she sighed finally.

"I know it's late, my darling. That's what bothers me.
don't want it to get any later."

Again, there was a long pause as though she was wonder
ing what to reply. Was she staring out at the ships waiting
their passage through the Canal? Leaning against her bal
cony rail, her black hair knotted behind her neck, hei
makeup off, her blue eyes alight with that luminosity tha
glowed all the more intensely when it was not set off by
mascara?

"Perhaps another time, Jack. When I come back maybe
You're part of the reason for my trip to Costa Rica."

"Me? There's only one trip I want you to take, Juanita
It's right here in Panama, and I want to take it with you."

Once again she sighed. "We'll see. It's my turn to offe

uotes, Jack. You know what the Bible says. 'To every thing
ere is a season.' Maybe our season has come and gone."

Her words chilled me. How could they not? Were they her
ay of saying goodbye to what had existed between us?

"*Hasta la próxima,*" she said softly. Then, with a gentle
ut deliberate movement, I heard her set her receiver back
to its cradle.

"Trying to fly an airplane without a proper altimeter is
bout as much fun as trying to fuck with a limp dick, my
iend."

Ray Albright tended to be long on homey advice and, the
ld Air America flier thought, the young flier beside him
ıre seemed to need a little sound advice. Albright gestured
t the purpling mountain crests circling the horizon beyond
ım Tulley's ranch in northern Costa Rica. "You seen them
ills coming in, didn't you? That's about all they got be-
ween here and the coast."

Sunset and the hour the two men were scheduled to fly
ıeir aircraft back to Florida was fast approaching.

"Maybe I could go out visual. Ride on your navigation
ghts."

"Sure you could. Right up until the moment we hit one of
ıose nice Caribbean thunderstorms. It ain't worth the
hance, my boy. Nothing is."

The two men had flown their Black Eagle flights into
Muelle twenty-four hours apart from Opa Locka in Florida.
Their planes were now both poised on the edge of Jim
ulley's dirt strip ready, except for the younger pilot's faulty
ltimeter, for their return journey.

"I can't figure out what happened to it. It was fine on the
vay down."

"I'll tell you. One of these clowns they got here whacked
 with the edge of a crate or some damn thing while they
vere unloading your cargo. Broke the damn seal. I got a re-
air kit in my plane." Albright, veteran flier that he was, was
eady for most emergencies. "Who the hell knows? Maybe
 got me a spare altimeter in there somewheres."

The two men clambered into his Aerocommander. His
raft, like the younger man's, had a stripped-down interior to
naximize its capacity to load cargo. Unlike the younger pi-
ot's aircraft, which was empty for the homeward-bound

journey, however, Albright's was stuffed with olive-drab
U.S. Army duffel bags, each of them firmly padlocked.

Albright crawled to the front of his aircraft, unclamped
his emergency repair kit, and began to paw through it under
the glare of a flashlight's beam.

"Shit," he lamented, closing the box, "I got everything i
there except an altimeter."

He turned back to his younger colleague. "Listen, kid, I'
tell you what we're going to do. You go down to San Jose
the capital of this here country. They got a bar there the
call the Key Largo. Filled up with a lot of pretty young la
dies just waiting to make a handsome fella like you happy
Settle in with one of them for forty-eight hours while I fl
back to Opa, order you up a new altimeter, and air-freight i
on down to San Jose, okay?" Ray beamed at the eminer
wisdom of his suggestion. "God ain't yet invented the air
plane ride that's worth getting killed for."

"Yeah," his fellow aviator agreed. "I guess that's what
got to do. I hate to lose the dough that downtime means
though."

The two started back out of Albright's plane. The younge
man gestured to the duffel bags. "What they got you runnin;
back?"

Albright kicked the sack. "Oh, this here's free enterprise.'

The younger pilot's eyebrows arched and his glance re
turned to the duffel bags. He'd heard the gossip. There wer
ways to make a few extra bucks on the trip back home if yo
knew the right people.

"Happy powder?" he asked.

Albright snorted. "It ain't soap powder."

"Risky, no?"

"Not the way this thing's set up, it isn't. It's covered. Yo
remember what they used to say about that good-old-boy ra
dio station—'covers Dixie like the dew'? That's the wa
they got this covered." Albright laid his heavy hand on hi
fellow pilot's shoulder. "You're interested, talk to little Phi
over there," he said, indicating Felipe Nadal talking at th
edge of the runway to Jim Tulley. "Maybe he can fix yo
up."

As investigations went, Kevin Grady's efforts in Panam
to determine just what had happened to Ramon were abou
as close to a total failure as it was possible to be. A week o

unrelenting digging in Panama City had added virtually nothing to the DEA's already limited knowledge of the circumstances surrounding the disappearance of his CI.

Grady had stationed himself between 9:00 and 9:30 in the lobby of the Banco de Occidente every morning for five days showing everyone who entered a photo of Ramon. No one recognized him. The only private aircraft that had left Panama for Colombia that day belonged to the cartel's financier, Eduardo Hernandez. His plane had taken off from Paitilla before Ramon had even been deposited at the bank by his taxi driver. It was as clear as it could be: his friend and CI had dropped through a black hole on that fateful morning because he'd been set up. Someone had passed the word on his role to the cartel's leadership.

The DEA's Panamanian Police liaison, Captain Luis Peel, was obsequiously helpful, although it seemed to a wary Kevin that he was almost as interested in what progress Grady was making in his case as he was in advancing his work.

Finally, after a week in Panama, Grady invited Freddy Hines, the country attaché to lunch at the Marbella, a seafood restaurant on the Avenida Balboa not far from their embassy office.

"I just can't believe that the cartel is going to pull a stunt like this in Panama without Noriega's blessing and help, Freddy." Frustration tugged at the edges of Kevin's voice. "Certainly not a snatch as clean as this one was."

His fellow agent ate silently for a mouthful or two, as though Kevin had just gotten into some areas he was not anxious to enter. "Do you know what the official line at DEA Headquarters in Washington is on Noriega, Kevin? The one that gets relayed to me down here?"

"How the hell would I know that?"

"Well, it's that Noriega may be a crook, but he's not a drug crook, so he's not our concern. You're not going to get a very sympathetic audience up there, Kev, if you go around shouting, 'Noriega did it.'"

"Listen, Freddy, how can you say that after what the CI told us out there in that churchyard or whatever the hell it was?"

"Hernandez may have just been blowing smoke to magnify his own role."

"Hernandez wasn't lying. I know enough about him to

figure that out. He's probably the guy who counts out Noriega's money."

Hines split open the shell of a fried shrimp, employing an almost delicate gesture of his fingers to do it. "Kev, Noriega is very helpful to us. Whatever I ask him for, I get. I want his navy to seize and search a ship we think has drugs on it, he orders it up for us. I see some American around here I wanted extradited to the States, I ask Noriega and, bang, he's on a plane out of here. I want a bank account seized, whammo, it's seized."

"With how much money in it?"

Hines shrugged.

"He gives you the guys you want, does he? I hear Ochoa and Escobar are spending a lot of their time up here now that things are hot down in Colombia because they shot up that minister. Noriega offer to hand them over to you yet?"

"Washington's never asked for them."

"And suppose they did?"

Again the country attaché gave an indifferent twist to his shoulders. "Listen, pal, do me a favor, will you? Don't upset the apple cart. You heard what that agency guy Lind said. Higher national security concerns, right?"

"Boy, this guy Noriega has a lot of friends, doesn't he? The CIA. You."

Hines slowly masticated a shrimp as though its flesh was going to be a source of special wisdom in these trying circumstances. He swallowed and drew closer to his fellow agent.

"Listen," he mumbled, "I never told you this, okay?"

"Sure."

"If you're really interested in Noriega, there's a guy up in Costa Rica you ought to go see, a Panamanian. His name is Hugo Spadafora. He's a wacko, okay? An Indiana Jones type, a kind of freelance ideological warrior. He's a doctor, went to medical school in Italy and got himself all mixed up with the leftists. I mean, this is not a guy Ronald Reagan is going to be in love with."

"What does all that have to do with Noriega and drugs?"

"Wait. The Sandinistas start their war against Somoza, Spadafora forms a battalion of Panamanian volunteers and jumps in beside them. Now he's decided he doesn't like the Sandinistas, so he's fighting against them with the Mesquite Indians. But the thing is this. He's going around up there saying he has the proof Noriega's involved in drugs. Hard proof. Why don't you go up and see him?"

"Maybe I will. But why don't you want me to tell anybody where I got the bright idea?"

"Look, Spadafora tried once to reach out to us. The station chief here squashed it. Like they did with us and your guy Ramon. It was 'don't put your cotton-pickin' fingers on Noriega.' I have to live with these CIA guys down here. I don't want to make waves. I want a long, quiet career and retirement after my twenty. So keep my name out of this, okay?"

Of all the many charms of San Jose the most original, Kevin was discovering, was that streets didn't have names and the houses on them didn't have numbers. Directions were: Go to the water tower, turn left, go three blocks. On your right will be a house with a high red wall around it. Go left, take your second right, and it's the house with the blue shutters at the end of the street.

To his surprise, that original way of navigating through the city was working remarkably well. Grady would have preferred to have met Spadafora in a hotel downtown. Meetings in hotels with their in-and-out traffic were more discreet than going to someone's residence in a clearly identifiable building and neighborhood. Spadafora, however, had insisted, even after Grady had suggested it might be risky. "I'm comfortable with it," he'd assured the DEA agent.

The Panamanian was a handsome and charismatic man, tall, lean, with wavy hair and the warm eyes of a man who was as at ease seducing a beautiful woman as he was at converting someone to whatever was his political passion of the moment. His wife, Ari, a lanky woman in minishorts and a T-shirt several sizes too small, served drinks, then disappeared. For a long while the two men simply talked, getting to know each other, Spadafora recounting his adventures to his American guest.

Boy, Kevin wondered, can this guy be for real? Could anybody have led a life like his? Finally, Spadafora turned to the business that had brought Grady to Costa Rica.

"Now I tell you about Noriega," he began. "He's in thick with the Medellín cartel. Have you ever heard of someone named Felipe Nadal?"

Well, Grady thought, at least he doesn't beat around the

bush. Nadal's name, he admitted, was one he hadn't heard before.

"He's a Cuban-American who works for the CIA. That's why nobody will touch him."

"How do you know he works for the CIA?"

"I work for the CIA. They give me arms for my Indian fighters. The CIA man who works with me introduced me to Nadal. If he wasn't around, he said, then Nadal would help me with arms."

"Okay, that's fair enough. So how are Noriega and the cartel involved here?"

"The cartel flies their cocaine into Paitilla airport from Colombia. They store their drug in Noriega's private hangar there. The CIA also uses that hangar to warehouse arms for the contras which they are bringing in through the Canal Free Trade Zone. Do you follow?"

"So far you make it very easy."

"From Paitilla, they fly the arms up north, to Honduras and to a couple of airfields here in Costa Rica. On some of the flights they bring in both cocaine and arms."

"How do you know that?"

"I saw the cocaine once at a ranch we use north of here in a place called Muelle."

"Why are you sure it was coke?"

"One of our people on the ranch told me it was."

For the moment, that was an explanation Grady could accept. He nodded to Spadafora to go on. "So how does it get to the States?"

"They have planes flying into the same ranch from the States with other supplies. It goes back in those planes. Nadal is in charge with about half a dozen other CIA employees. Which means that, either wittingly or unwittingly, your CIA is involved in the operation along with Noriega and the cartel. That is why everyone here is afraid to talk about it."

"Do you have any proof of all this?"

"Listen, Kevin, that isn't all." Spadafora was the kind of man who glided rapidly into first-name friendships. "They have a second operation that's even prettier. You know we Panamanians have a shrimp and lobster freezing and processing plant in Vacamonte, south of Panama City?"

"I'm not aware of that, no."

"One of our biggest customers is the Cubans. They're not

allowed to export their shrimp and lobster to your country because of your embargo. But we are. So we buy their shrimp from them, process it, then ship it up the States as though it was ours."

"Fine, Hugo, but my business is drugs, not fish."

"Some of those shrimp get sent up here to our Pacific port Puntarenas to a company called Gelaticos. Nadal is a partner in it, together with a bunch of your contra leaders. They repack the frozen shrimp in Costa Rican packaging, add in cocaine and ship it to their distributors in Miami and New Orleans. The word is they use the profits to help arm the contras."

The frozen-food ploy, Kevin knew, was a classic. In order to open a case for inspection, Customs inevitably had to spoil the merchandise. If they got the wrong case, the G wound up with a big bill and Customs with embarrassingly empty hands. As a result, you weren't going to find Customs inspecting frozen food crates without a very good reason for doing so.

"You can be sure of this. This is fact." Spadafora articulated his words with the conviction of the political ideologue he was. He now pushed a piece of paper at Kevin. "These are some of the banks they use. The ones I know of."

Grady looked at the list. It included the Israeli Discount Bank, the Korean Exchange Bank, the Banco de Central America, the BCCI.

"Mostly, they use the BCCI," Spadafora declared.

Kevin twisted in his chair, worrying about how to evaluate Spadafora and what his next move should be. First, he reasoned, a little stroke for his host would be in order. Spadafora was obviously the kind of man who would respond well to a little flattery.

"Hugo, I believe you. Even if some other people may not."

"Yes," Spadafora lamented, "they are all afraid to do anything because of the CIA."

"I'm not afraid of the CIA, Hugo. That's not my problem."

"What's your problem?"

"I'm a cop, not a politician. What may be proof to you is just talk to me. My job is to indict someone for a crime. When I do that, I damn well better have rock-hard evidence, because the next step is going to be the courtroom. You give me the bullet I need, and I'll fire it at Noriega. And the CIA. I promise you that. But you've got to give me the bullet first."

"What do you need?"

"Proof. Evidence. I need photographs, tape recordings. I need people who saw things who are willing to swear to a deposition, to stand up in an open courtroom and testify."

"I can get you some of that."

"How?"

This time it was Spadafora's turn to squirm in his chair, debating whether or not he could trust Grady.

"I have some of that material you're looking for. Hidden away in a safe place in Panama. One of my old girlfriends was here twenty-four hours ago. She knows where that material is hidden. I could ask her to get it out of its hiding place and bring it to you."

"That would do it, my friend. If that stuff is what you say it is, that could be our bullet."

"Okay," Spadafora extended his hand to Grady's to set the seal on their deal. "Her name is Boyd. Juanita Boyd. She'll call you when she's got it."

Half an hour after Grady's departure Spadafora consulted his private telephone book, then drove to a pay phone in downtown San Jose. He was a cautious man, and there was always the chance his home line was tapped. From there, he dialed 610237 in Panama City.

As he did, 320 miles away in Building #9 at Fort Amador where Noriega's CIA-financed electronic eavesdropping center was headquartered, a reel-to-reel tape recorder began to turn.

Receptionists and telephone operators at all U.S. embassies have standard instructions on how to deal with anyone calling with drug-related information. Be welcoming, be polite, never ask for any potentially embarrassing information like the caller's name, and put him into contact with a DEA agent as expeditiously as possible.

That was how Kevin Grady happened to field a call from an anonymous informant at the San Jose embassy on the morning following his meeting with Hugo Spadafora. Normally, the country attaché would have taken the call, but he was away for the day so Grady acted in his place.

"You the drug guy?" a clearly nervous voice demanded when Grady picked up the call.

"Sure am, sir," he said. The voice rang with youth, so Grady felt that *sir* might bolster his ego a bit. "How can I help you?"

There was a long pause, one of those awkward moments every DEA agent experiences when a potential informant hovers on the brink, wondering whether he has the courage to continue or whether to hang up the phone and retreat back into the warm and comforting womb of anonymity.

"There's something I saw," the voice ventured finally, "I think I should tell you about."

"That's very good of you, sir. We're grateful for all the help we can get from honest and concerned citizens like yourself. Would you like to come in and have a cup of coffee at the embassy? Or if that's a problem for you, we can meet in town somewhere."

Again, the caller paused. "I think I better not go near the embassy. When you hear what I have to tell you, you'll know why."

"Can you give me just a rough idea what it's about?"

"An airstrip near a place called Muelle and some things that are going on up there. That's all I want to say now."

Muelle. That was the place Spadafora had mentioned, where the CIA had an airstrip they used for arms deliveries to the contras and from which, Spadafora had claimed, cocaine was being shipped back to the States.

"Sure. You here in San Jose?"

"Yeah."

"Well, there's a hotel downtown where we could meet called the Amstel. Suppose I check into a room down there. You could come in and join me."

The Amstel was almost next door to the Key Largo, and its bar came equipped with a full-service array of hostesses. It was the kind of environment in which someone on the fringes of the drug world was likely to feel at ease.

"Okay, I'll be there. But come alone."

"My name's O'Brien. Suppose I check in about one. Could you come by at 1:30 or 2:00?"

"Yeah, that ought to be okay."

It was after 2:30 when the man showed, but Kevin had counted on that. He'd probably been walking around the block trying to screw up the courage to come up to the room. As his voice had indicated, he was young, perhaps thirty, with Ray-Ban sunglasses, a suede jacket and a nervous tic agitating his left thumb.

"Hi," Grady said. "I'm Kevin O'Brien."

The man took his hand. "How you doing?" he asked. He didn't offer his name. Kevin didn't press for it. It was too early for that. He gestured to the room-service tray of beer and coffee he'd ordered up to lubricate the flow of their conversation.

"How about a beer? Coffee may be a bit cold by now."

The man grabbed a beer bottle, popped off the top, and drank a swig directly from the bottle. Kevin did the same.

"So what can I do for you?" Kevin asked. His smile was as inviting as he could make it.

"I'm a flier. I don't want to get into details about what I fly or who I'm flying it for, okay? Except I can tell you one thing. There's never any drugs on my plane. Never."

Kevin nodded with all the solemnity of a priest offering absolution.

"Maybe sometimes some of the things I do aren't strictly kosher," the flier continued, "but drugs, no. I had a cousin back in Baton Rouge, like my big brother. He OD'd on heroin. So you better believe, I hate fucking drugs. And I hate the people who sell them even more. Last night some guy offered me a shot at flying a load of coke into the States."

Kevin stirred and hunched forward in his chair. "What happened?" he asked in a tone a mother might use to ask a son how he'd stubbed his toe.

The pilot explained the incident which had occurred the evening before at Muelle when he'd boarded Ray Albright's plane in search of a spare altimeter to replace his own broken instrument.

"Well, that's very interesting. I'm grateful to you for that. Did the pilot give you the name of the guy who was supposed to fix you up with a load if you wanted one?"

"Nadal, Felipe Nadal, but he called him Phil."

Bingo, Kevin thought, Spadafora wasn't bullshitting me. "Costa Rican, was he?"

"I think the pilot said he was Cuban. Anyway, he was a Latin type. They all look the same to me."

"What does he do up there in Muelle?"

"He's sort of the flight-line boss. Tells you where to park your plane, runs the crews that unload your cargo."

"Did you talk to him?"

"Hell, no. Like I said, maybe I like money, but I got my own reasons to hate dope."

"And the pilot? Do you remember his name?"

The man hesitated. Now he was going to be giving up a fellow American and, worse, a fellow flying adventurer. That was not the same thing as giving over some Latino's name. Kevin sensed his hesitation and didn't press, letting the man come to it himself.

"Ray Albright."

"Do you know how you could get hold of him in the States? Have you got an address or phone number on him?"

"He's out of Texas, but we're doing contract flying for the same outfit out of Opa Locka in Miami. They'd know how to reach him."

Grady stood and walked to the window with his beer bottle clutched by the neck in his hands. He was in shirt-sleeves with his tie undone. He looked at the pilot, doing his best to radiate fraternal warmth and sincerity.

"Look, I want to really thank you for coming in and telling me this. It takes some balls, which obviously you got. Believe me, I appreciate it. I sure wish we had more people around like you."

He paused to let the young man wallow in the warmth of his praise.

"Now, we can do a couple of things here. We could let it go at this, but I'd really hate to do that. Let me ask you something. Would you be willing to take a lie-detector test on what you just told me?"

"Why the hell not? It's the truth."

"I'm a hundred percent sure it is. This is just one of those bureaucratic things government agencies like mine get into. When are you going back to Miami?"

"Oh, three, four days."

"We could meet again back there if that's convenient for you. You go about your business here, repair your plane's altimeter, there's no risk of anyone ever seeing us together. In Miami I can guarantee you nobody will ever see us."

The pilot reflected a second. "Yeah, I guess we could do that."

Kevin smiled and offered the pilot another beer. The lie detector test was just the first and the most innocent of the favors he intended to ask this young man. The rule, however, was to bring them along slowly, step by step until you had them up and running. Besides, who wasn't going to take a lie detector test to prove to you he's telling the truth, which Kevin figured this guy was.

What he was really doing, however, was shifting this case north to the States. If he registered the pilot as a potential informant here in Costa Rica, there was a vetting process with which Kevin would have to comply. He would have to expose both the man's name and his information to the CIA station chief before he could start an investigation. That did not apply in Miami. There, the CIA could not get its hands on the pilot's name as long as Kevin was careful to keep it out of his official documents as he once had done with Ramon's name. There wasn't going to be a line in the DEA files in Costa Rica on this meeting. He simply wouldn't make a record of it. That way he would be under no obligation to inform the ambassador or the CIA of what he was doing.

The *pushbutton motel* is a uniquely Panamanian institution. Fundamentally, its function is to provide the community's adulterers with rigorously anonymous yet comfortable, even luxurious accommodations for an hour or two. The genesis of the pushbuttons is a source of constant amusement to Panamanians. They can be traced back to a Spanish priest, a Padre Condomines.

The good father was one of the first people in Panama to employ garage doors that could be opened from a car by an electronic command. A friend visiting the padre one day—to have his confession heard, the story suggests—marveled at the system, and in a flash of creative brilliance, the pushbutton motel was born.

There are now ten pushbuttons in Panama City with names like Lindo Sueño—*Pretty Dreams,* or Campo Amor—*Field of Love.* Whatever the name, however, the principles on which they operate are the same. They are constructed roughly in a U shape with a series of fifty to seventy-five garages set side by side. Each garage adjoins its own air-conditioned private bedroom suite complete with a large double bed, a closed-circuit TV and a bathroom with a bath, shower and bidet. Some of the more luxurious suites come equipped with an array of strategically placed mirrors. At the center of the U is a kind of central working area to service the suites.

A pair of prospective clients circle the U until they find an open garage door. They drive into the garage and the driver presses a button on the garage wall, which automatically closes the doors of the garage behind them. Now no one can see the car of the couple who are employing the motel.

At the same time, the button has set a red light flashing in the central service corridor which tells the attendants on duty that a client is waiting in the garage behind that particular bedroom suite. An attendant enters the suite and opens a small panel on the wall between the bedroom and the garage. The client lays a ten dollar bill—U.S. dollars are the currency of Panama—into the panel, which will be his or her rent for ninety minutes. The attendant takes it and leaves the suite, locking the door behind him as he goes. The gesture also unlocks the door joining the garage to the suite. The happy couple can now come in. They can watch the latest porn movies on their TV, or order in drinks from the bar, which are passed to them through another two-faced sliding panel no larger than a champagne bottle. They can even order up a telephone, which can be plugged into a jack for local calls so they can call home to report they'll be late because they're caught in a traffic jam.

When they're finished, the couple leaves, gets back into their car, and opens the garage door behind them with the button on the wall of the garage. They drive off.

The button has also set a green light flashing in the service corridor to inform the staff the room's guests have left and it's time to prepare the suite for their next clients.

From the time they've arrived until they're back on the highway heading into town, no one has seen the happy twosome. So private are the pushbuttons that their driveways are lined with thick shrubs high enough to prevent a car entering the premises from seeing a car on its way back out.

Not surprisingly, boom times for the pushbuttons are 5:00 to 7:00 weekdays and Friday night, which by tradition in Panama is a husband's night off from his marital duty.

On a stifling hot Friday night in early August 1984, the Paradiso, one of the capital's newest and most luxurious pushbuttons, was doing a land-office business. The cleanup crews were running late; fifteen to twenty minutes usually elapsed between the time the client pulled away and the mo-

ment the cleaners arrived to make up the suite for the next
clients. It was always like that on Friday nights.

The two elderly cleaning women who opened the door to
Suite #51 at 12:15 that night found the lights out and a curious, ammonia-like smell permeating the room. The first of
the pair turned on the lights, then screamed in horror.

Lying on the bed, nude except for a black silk brassiere,
was one of the room's two previous occupants. Her facial
features were twisted, her mouth contorted as though she
had been gasping for air, her eyes had rolled back up into
her head, her black hair was splayed on the pillow with a violence like that of her death. She was motionless.

The cleaning lady's scream brought half a dozen of her
fellow attendants rushing into the room to gawk at the body
sprawled on the bed. Finally, the night supervisor arrived
and thrust his way through their ranks. He went to the bed,
picked up the woman's wrist, feeling for a pulse. There was
none. On the bedside table he noticed a pair of broken glass
vials and a plastic envelope with traces of white powder still
clinging to its interior.

"She's dead," he told his stunned cleaning crew. "Have
the office call the police—and an ambulance." The latter, he
knew, was a formality. "Lock the room and don't let anybody in until the police get here."

They were there in fifteen minutes—a medical examiner, a
police sergeant and a corporal. The medical examiner's first
action, pronouncing the victim dead on arrival, was routine.
While he was offering a cursory exam to the dead woman,
the sergeant had started to study the broken vials and the envelopes on the bedside table. He bent over and sniffed the
vials.

"Amino-nitrate," he informed the medical examiner. He
pointed to the plastic envelope with its traces of white powder. "They were doing cocaine and poppers."

The medical examiner studied the bedside table in turn. "I
suppose we'll have to do an autopsy, but I'll tell you right
now what happened," he said. "Cocaine and those poppers
can make a bad mix. She went into a cardiac seizure. The
bastard got scared, pulled on his pants, and got the hell out
of here leaving her to die."

"Sure," the sergeant agreed. "Probably some married man
who was scared to death his wife would find out he was

screwing around." He turned to his aide. "You find any ID around? Anything that will tell us who the hell she is?"

"Nothing," the corporal replied. "It looks like the guy who was with her picked the place clean."

"We could at least arrest him for leaving the scene of a crime," the sergeant said.

"You could if you ever find him," retorted the medical examiner. "To do that we've got to figure out who she is."

The younger policeman leaned over and looked into the dead woman's face. "Maybe she was a *puta* from downtown."

"Look again," the medical examiner told him. "When was the last time you saw a puta like that around the Ancon Inn?"

"Maybe we can take her fingerprints and see if they match anything in our files."

"You can," the doctor sighed, "but I don't think it will do much good. Put her in a bag and take her down to the morgue. And inform Captain Peel we've probably got a drug-related death on our hands. He'll have to oversee the investigation."

It was not until late the following morning that the police resumed their investigation into the woman's death. Her body, in the meantime, was stored in the cold lockers of the morgue, waiting for the autopsy scheduled for noon. Three men were assigned to the case—the sergeant who'd been dispatched to the scene at the Paradiso, a Panamanian Defense Forces lieutenant assigned to the police as an investigator and, because drugs were found at the death scene, Captain Luis Peel, the officer of the PDF who investigated most drug matters.

The sergeant was missing when the two others convened for coffee and cigarettes in the lieutenant's office. "Well," he said, "let's take a look at what we've got without him."

At that moment the sergeant burst through the door. "Sorry I'm late."

"Anything new?"

"Yes, sir. We have an ID for her. I just got it. We had her fingerprints on file after all. In fact, we had her in prison a few weeks ago on political charges."

"A political!" the lieutenant said warily.

"Yeah. Her name is Boyd. Juanita Boyd."

The name Boyd commands respect in Panama the way Rockefeller does in mid-Manhattan or Astor in Mayfair. Its aura converted the lieutenant from a bored investigator into a worried bureaucrat.

"You know," Peel warned him, "this could be embarrassing for her family. To have their daughter found in a place like the Paradiso. With drugs around. Why don't we just forget about the autopsy so we can give them back her body unmutilated? We all know how she died. We'll keep her ID a secret in here until they've been able to give her a quiet, private burial."

His proposal put the lieutenant in a quandary. "The regulations say we should have an autopsy."

"Let me handle that. You guys try to find out—*quietly*— who she might have been with last night." Peel snickered. "That may be a big investigation. From what I hear, she was a very active lady."

Sitting around a first-class hotel room in Panama City on a government expense account, lounging all day by a swimming pool watching a bunch of air hostesses get a suntan, are not activities that would throw most DEA agents into a stuttering rage. Five days of that, however, five days of waiting for Juanita Boyd to call with the word that she was ready to deliver the material Hugo Spadafora had promised him, was driving Kevin Grady crazy.

He was anxious to see the material. He was equally anxious to get back to the United States so he could contact his flier in Miami before the young man could develop confessional chilblains. Finally, on Wednesday afternoon, his hotel room phone ended its long silence.

"This is the brother of the man you met in Costa Rica," a voice announced.

"Great. I've been waiting for his lady friend to call."

"I'm afraid she won't be calling."

"Why?"

"She's dead. She was buried yesterday."

Grady was sitting at the writing desk in his room on which his phone rested. He slumped forward almost as though someone had slapped him on the back of his head.

"I don't believe it. What happened to her?"

"I don't know. Her family isn't saying anything about how she died. The funeral and burial were private, which is rare here in Panama. My brother is convinced she was murdered by people who wanted to stop her from giving you that material of his."

"Where is it, do you know?"

"No. I was in charge of it, Mr. Grady. I was the only person who knew where it was hidden. Not even my brother Hugo knew. Juanita called me with a password Hugo and I had set up. I knew her. Not well, but I knew her. I got the material out of its hiding place Friday afternoon. She came by to pick it up from me at 9:00 on Friday night. She told me she was going to give it to you Saturday. The announcement of her death said that was the day she died, Saturday."

"Did it say anything else? A time? Where?"

"No, but that's not unusual. Anyway, Hugo's material seems to have disappeared. It might be in her apartment, but how do we get in there to find out? Unless we can convince her brother to let us go in and search the place for it."

"Do you know what it was?"

"No, it was in a sealed package."

"Look, could you call her brother and see if you can convince him to let us into the apartment to look for it? Tell him you gave her some important papers for a friend and the friend needs them urgently."

Five minutes later, Spadafora's brother called back.

"We can't get in. Her apartment's been sealed by the police. Apparently they're investigating the circumstances surrounding her death. I tried to ask her brother why, but he doesn't want to talk about it. Something happened to her they're very embarrassed about, but he's not saying what."

"Sure, well, murder can be embarrassing, all right, particularly if it happens to you. Let me make a couple of inquiries on my side and I'll get back to you."

Grady was ready to dial another number, then thought better of it. The DEA office would still be open. He went downstairs and took a cab to the embassy.

The office was on the second floor, protected by a door that opened only in response to an electronic code tapped into a control panel on the wall. Hines was more than a little surprised to see him. Grady had not bothered to inform his colleague of his return from Costa Rica.

"So how was San Jose?"

"Okay. Can you do me a favor?"

"Sure."

"Reach out to your contacts in the police and find out what they know about the death Saturday of a woman called Juanita Boyd."

"I'll call our friend Peel." Hines switched on the speaker button of his phone so Grady could listen to their conversation.

"Officially," Peel replied to his query, "I can't tell you anything. It's a criminal matter under active investigation by the police."

"What's the charge?"

"Probably negligent homicide is going to be our best bet."

"And unofficially what can you say?"

"It's a real dirty business. She was apparently screwing her brains out in a pushbutton with some guy, doing coke and poppers. She got a heart attack, he got scared, ran out and left her to die."

"Did you do an autopsy?"

"No. We didn't want to chop her to bits and hurt the family any more than they'd already been hurt. They're big people here."

"Do you know who the guy was?"

"He didn't leave any clues, which means it could have been half of male Panama. She was a real player."

Hines glanced down at the note Grady had just passed to him.

"You remember my friend Grady who was working on the disappearance of that CI? He thinks this woman might have had something for him. Do you suppose you could let him have a look at her apartment?"

"Grady? No problem at all."

Lind's Tape

I received the news in the mail. It came in an envelope addressed to "Mr. Jack Lind, c/o The United States Embassy, Panama." Some meticulous clerk had, I suppose, ran it past the embassy's various offices until it fetched up on the desk of our station chief, Glenn Archer. I flicked it with my fingernail. It was like those cards people employ to invite you to a dinner or a cocktail party.

Tearing the envelope open, I saw immediately the black

border rimming it, and, further down, the black cross embossed at its head.

"Señor Hector Vasquez Castillo y Boyd y Señor Pedro Jaime Suarez y Boyd," it began, "are deeply pained to have to inform you of the untimely death of their daughter and sister, Juanita Maria Angelica Suarez y Boyd."

I wanted to weep, but I was too shocked. I snatched at the card's few remaining lines through the filmy haze of the tears swelling in my eyes: the date of her death and the date of her funeral mass and burial later the same day in the Cemetery of Saint John the Baptist in Panama City.

What could possibly have happened to her?

Clearly, the card must have been sent by her brother Pedro. I grabbed my phone logs and found his number from the call he'd made to me announcing that she had been jailed.

He was in mourning for his sister's death, a servant informed me, and was not in Panama. Did I wish to leave a message? Numbly, I expressed my condolences. Then I drafted a cable for Glenn Archer in Panama.

PERSONAL FOR ARCHER STOP WOULD APPRECIATE ANYTHING YOU CAN LEARN CONCERNING DEATH SATURDAY TWELVE AUGUST JUANITA BOYD PANAMANIAN CITIZEN RESIDENT MONTE CARLO APARTMENTS PAITILLA PENTHOUSE LEFT STOP MATTER IS PERSONAL REPEAT PERSONAL NOT AGENCY CONCERN STOP DISCRETION APPRECIATED REGARDS JACK

Langley is not an appropriate environment for grief or mourning. We have one of those ghastly nondenominational meditation centers down in the basement, but I have never seen anyone using it. That may reflect on the spiritual life of most CIA officers or, more likely, the uninvitingly sterile nature of such places.

In any event, we tend to share our joys but mourn privately. And there was certainly no one at Langley with whom I was going to share my grief at Juanita's death. I went out to the parking lot, got into my car, and drove down to the George Washington Memorial Parkway to a lay-by looking down on the Potomac River. There I wept alone.

BOOK TEN

The Samurai's Choice

For Kevin Grady, the feel of his Eastern Airlines Boeing's wheels bouncing down the tarmac of New York's La Guardia Airport was as soothing as his dead wife's fingertips had once been massaging the knotted muscles of his neck after a particularly nerve-racking day. He was home, delighted to leave the humidity and poverty of Central America behind him. He could find all of those qualities he needed right here in the city he loved.

Officially, his trip had been a bust. His investigation into Ramon's disappearance had produced nothing but a handful of smoke. Unofficially, however, things looked more promising.

Captain Luis Peel, full of his usual obsequious gestures and flattering words, had personally escorted him to the Boyd woman's apartment to look for Spadafora's missing material. He didn't find it, of course. That was not the surprise of the week. That surprise he'd found in the dead woman's bathroom, glancing through her medicine cabinet. There he had noticed two things. There were no birth-control pills among her medicines. In all probability, therefore, she didn't use them. He had noticed, however, a diaphragm case on one of the shelves. Was that, he wondered, the device she employed? He had opened it. The diaphragm was inside.

Does a woman going out for a night of frantic screwing leave her diaphragm behind, he'd asked himself. And if she'd wanted to spend a wild night balling some guy, why not do it here in her lovely apartment instead of in some tawdry motel room?

Peel had been waiting on the balcony looking out to sea, ignoring him while he'd gone through the apartment. It seemed clear he didn't expect him to find anything in there. Spadafora's papers were supposed to contain the rock-hard evidence of Noriega's drug trafficking. Who ran the police in Panama? Noriega. The police had the damn papers, Kevin had told himself. That was why Peel had been so accommodating in letting him search the apartment. That was why he was standing out there on the balcony without a care in the world. That was why there had been no autopsy. She hadn't died of a heart attack. They'd killed her, grabbed the papers, and stuffed her into the motel room, knowing Peel would be called in to run the investigation and would run it the way the boss wanted it run.

Ramon. Now this Boyd woman, Kevin mused. It seemed that every time you pushed out toward the edge of the envelope, getting close to Noriega, a curtain dropped. Then it parted just enough to let someone shove a body through the opening. This last murder told him one thing, at least. Spadafora had been telling the truth. If they had killed the Boyd woman to get their hands on his papers, then the evidence they'd contained must have been overwhelming. Fortunately, he still had one last card left in his deck he could play.

"Welcome to New York," the Eastern Airlines stewardess chirped merrily. "The time is 7:20 and the outside temperature is seventy-eight degrees."

Kevin was still meditating on the ramifications of Juanita Boyd's murder when he plunged out of the plane's passageway and into the crowded lobby. There, next to the Eastern Airlines ground hostess, was Ella Jean.

"Hey!" he said, happiness bursting like a bolt of lightning across his face. "This is the best surprise I've had since I left. I hope you haven't come out here to tell me I'm being transferred to Philadelphia."

"No such luck. I just wanted to see if that ugly face of yours got any better-looking down there. Which it hasn't."

They settled into her car parked in front of the terminal thanks to the DEA card on the dashboard. "So how did it go?"

"As far as Ramon is concerned, I didn't learn zilch. I learned some other things, though. How'd you like to pull a few days' temporary duty with me down in Miami?"

"So I can get a nice suntan?"

"Yeah. And help me convince a young man to do something he'd be a perfect fool to agree to do." Kevin sketched out a few basic details of his meeting with the flier in San Jose.

"The first thing I want to do is put him on the box and verify his story."

"Why didn't you do that down in San Jose?"

Kevin leaned back against the headrest of his seat and glanced at Ella Jean maneuvering her car through traffic with a skill that was almost athletic. "The guy is obviously flying arms to the contras. He's probably working under a CIA contract whether he knows it or not. I asked the country attaché about the strip they're using. It's a contra operation, all right. The attaché wanted to tiptoe in and install one of those twenty-four-hour cameras we have that can film everything that goes on for a full day. The CIA guy whistled him dead."

"He admitted it was a CIA operation?"

"Oh, hell, no. You know how those guys pussyfoot around the truth. He said, 'Ahem, well, er, it's authorized. For the *causa.*'"

"So what's your plan?"

"Convince the pilot to go back and talk to the guy Albright who told him all this. With a wire on this time. If he confirms it, then we try to run a penetration on that guy Nadal. He's got to be an American citizen, so we can demand his extradition."

"Boy, you never learn, do you, Kevin? You remember how the bosses reacted when you dropped those three lovely initials CIA on the table that night? Now you want to go out and indict some agency guy? Who's sitting right in the middle of one of their big operations?"

"Why the hell not? Where does it say the law doesn't apply to them?"

"Oh, no place where you're going to read it. Just where it counts." She honked furiously at a taxi driven by some wild-haired Middle Easterner who'd just cut in front of her with the disdain of a veteran New York hack. "I certainly am going down to Miami with you. Somebody's got to protect you from yourself."

"Thanks, pal. Remember, we don't breathe the initials CIA to anyone in the office until we absolutely have to."

"Unfortunately, my friend, we live and die by the damn lie detector at the DEA. It's a professional deformation. We don't leave home without it." Shep Baker, the young pilot—he'd finally given Grady his name—stared moodily at Kevin. "We have to find a way to separate fact from fiction real fast. You wouldn't believe some of the wild stories people come in and tell us. For every stand-up, serious guy we see like you we get ten weirdos."

"Thanks a lot," Baker replied. The flattery wasn't taking.

His sour expression revealed just how much he regretted his presence here in the DEA's Miami office and his agreement to take the lie detector test. "So how does it work?"

"Ever had an electro-cardiogram?"

"A couple of times."

"Well, they wire you up a bit like that. Then they ask you some control questions. Ideally, they'd like to get you to lie. 'Do you ever cheat on your wife?' "

"I'm not married."

"Or your girlfriend. Or the IRS. Everybody does that. The idea is to get a reaction pattern they can use when it comes to the real stuff."

Baker looked increasingly despondent. Kevin, who'd bought his story without reservation was, for the first time, entertaining a doubt or two.

At that moment Ella Jean entered the conference room. "This is my associate, Ella Jean Ransom."

Ella Jean gave the young man the full court press. "Kevin's told me all about you, Shep." She glowed, grabbing his hand in her two hands, gushing as though she'd just been introduced to Magic Johnson or Kevin Costner. "It's just great what you're doing for us, real great."

Gently, she took him by the hand into the next room as an operating theater nurse might bring a patient in to prepare him for surgery.

In twenty minutes it was over. The examiner came out first. "Clean as a whistle," he told Kevin. "Not a single blip in his story."

Ella Jean followed, her arm through Baker's. "He was wonderful. Just wonderful."

Mr. Baker himself had a relieved smile spread across his face. You'll lose that fast enough, my young friend, Grady thought, when you hear the exciting plans we have in mind for you.

Shep Baker's prize for being a good boy and passing his lie detector test with high marks was lunch, courtesy of the U.S. government, at Joe's Stone Crab, a Miami Beach landmark. Grady ordered a couple of bottles of first-class California chardonnay to give the occasion the celebratory note he wanted it to have. Ella Jean alternated between bathing Baker in admiring glances and regaling him with inside stories of life on New York's mean streets.

Kevin concentrated his attention on his potential CI, trying to figure out if maybe he should take Baker's story about his cousin who'd overdosed at face value. A DEA agent is disinclined by years of experience to take the first story he's told as the gospel truth. After all, the kind of people he deals with have usually thrown off a dozen lies before they've had their breakfast coffee.

Still, that could be what was driving Baker. Not once had Baker asked, "What's in it for me?" He didn't seem to think the preacher was at the door and that he needed a little forgiveness. Never had he suggested a deal to expunge some crime from his past record. Did he have a political ax to grind? If he did, it hadn't surfaced yet.

Grady eased their conversation toward his own memories of the black girl who'd killed herself because she could see no other escape from her heroin habit. Telling the story, he caught a telltale flicker in Baker's eyes.

Ella Jean, sensing where Kevin was at, moved the conversation into the new crack rage ravaging the nation and the ghastly human toll it was beginning to exact. By the time their double espressos arrived, Kevin was ready for his move.

"We could always leave this thing where it is," he assured Baker, "but it would be a real shame not to make just one more step forward."

"What do you mean?"

"Albright, the pilot."

"What about him?"

"Suppose you give him a call. Thank him for getting that altimeter down to you so fast. Tell him you owe him a drink."

Baker shrugged. "Why not?"

"You guys meet someplace, have a couple of drinks, and then you slide the conversation around to the operation in Muelle. You tell him, 'Hey, I'd like to get in on that, but I got to know a couple of things. I don't want to talk to Nadal. I don't trust Hispanics. I need to talk to someone like you.' "

"What's the idea of all that?"

"We have you wired up when you go for that drink. So we have whatever Albright tells you on tape. Corroboration, real tight corroboration. That will give us a case no defense attorney is going to bust open on us."

Baker paled. Now he knew why everything had been so warm and friendly at lunch. "That could get me killed."

Grady chuckled. "Don't worry. Ella Jean here will be sitting in the bar when you meet him, looking out for you. She can put a .38 round through a gnat's asshole at twenty yards."

"I'm not talking about in the bar, for God's sakes! When he gets the good news I've set him up ... What happens then?"

"Nothing, because by the time Mr. Albright finds out you were wearing a wire, he'll be wearing a pair of lovely gray prison denims."

Ella Jean laid her hand on Baker's. "Remember that cousin of yours in Baton Rouge, Shep? Think of how many people's lives are going to be destroyed by the crack that will come out of the cocaine Albright's flying into the United States. Think about those people, then tell me what you want to do."

Ella Jean and a Cuban-born agent of the Miami office had been detailed to stake out Smilin' Jack's, the bar near the Opa Locka airport, where Ray Albright had agreed to have a drink with Shep Baker. A third agent would watch the parking lot in the unlikely event of trouble.

Kevin had briefed Baker on the points he wanted him to cover, then stripped him down and fitted him out with a four-thousand-dollar Nagra tape recorder. The recorder was as flat as its manufacturers could make it. Its edges were curved. The machine fit snugly into an elasticized girdle which Grady taped to Baker's groin underneath his boxer shorts. The microphone was not much bigger than a pen-filler. Baker would not be able to pass a serious pat-down wearing the device, but no one expected he would have to.

Once Baker had left for the bar, Kevin had only to sit in the office the Miami DO had assigned him, ready by the phone for an emergency, hoping everything would go right. The phone, like several in the office, was equipped with a tape recorder which was automatically activated when the receiver was lifted. That was so that in an emergency, when a caller had only seconds to get his message across, none of it would be lost through carelessness or inadvertence.

Kevin used the time to ponder his next move. If Albright came through on tape, then he would try to convince Baker to go back to Costa Rica wearing a Nagra girdle and set up a dope deal with Nadal. The ideal would be to fly back a load on that first trip. Then they could jump all over the load on whatever field it was they were using to bring the stuff in.

The phone rang. He grabbed it. It wasn't his agents at Opa Locka, as it turned out, but the New York DO call-forwarding service passing him a call.

"Mr. Grady?" a female voice said. "Just a moment please."

"Good evening," his caller announced, coming onto the phone, "this is Jack Lind calling, Mr. Grady."

"Lind!" The words exploded out of Grady's mouth. "What the hell do you want?"

"I know this call must be an unpleasant surprise for you, Mr. Grady, just as the reason for it will be. I'd like to ask you a personal favor."

"You want to ask me a favor? After what you've done to me—twice? I got to tell you, Lind, if you went blind and were banging your white cane on the curb, I wouldn't help you across the fucking street."

"There are no national security concerns involved here."

"Yeah? It must be the first time in your life you don't have them to hide behind. How does it feel?"

"Painful, because, as I said, my concerns are purely personal. They involve a young woman whose death I understand you were looking into in Panama, Juanita Boyd."

"Juanita Boyd? Why are you interested in her?"

There was an awkward silence on the phone. Grady could sense how difficult it was for his caller to articulate his answer to that question.

"Because I was in love with her." The words came in a tone of voice Grady recognized. It was like the sudden rush of a felon coughing up the admission his interrogators had been after for hours. "What do you think happened to her, Mr. Grady?"

Why should I go gently with this guy, Grady thought. "She was murdered."

"Why do you believe that?"

"Because I'm a cop, not a spy like you. I live in the real world, not in some make-believe fairy tale. She was bringing me the evidence that would have let me nail that son of a bitch who's such a friend of yours, General Noriega, to a criminal indictment for drug trafficking. She picked up that material for me at nine o'clock Friday night. At twelve-thirty she was dead and the stuff was missing. Now, how would you read that? Do you think she gave it to the guy she was supposed to have been screwing that night?"

Lind was silent.

"Let me ask you this." Grady tried, not altogether successfully, to muffle some of the hostility in his voice. "If you were in love with her, I presume you made love to her. Did you?"

"Yes." The reply was almost a whisper.

"Did she use a diaphragm for birth control?"

"Yes."

"Always?"

"As far as I know. She had had problems with the pill, she told me, and her doctors advised against a coil. So."

"Do you know where she kept it?"

"On the shelf of her medicine closet in the bathroom."

"Then tell me this, Mr. Lind. If she was planning to go out that night and spend the evening shacked up with some guy, why didn't she take her diaphragm with her?"

Grady could sense the question had shaken Lind. "How do you know she didn't have it with her?"

"Because I saw it right where she left it when she went out to get those papers for me. On the shelf of her medicine closet. Your girlfriend was murdered for those papers, Lind. She was done by goons working for your great pal Noriega. Then they dumped her in that motel to make it look like she'd blown herself away on too much coke. And Noriega buried the whole thing in the police investigation."

"Thank you," Lind gasped. "I think I'd better go now."

It was only when he hung up that Grady realized the tape recorder had been running on their conversation. He snapped out the cassette, put it in his pocket, and replaced it with an unused tape.

It was mid-morning the next day before the Miami DO's typists prepared a transcript of Baker's tape-recorded conversation with Ray Albright. Ella Jean read it first.

"These are pure gold," she declared, laying the pages in front of Grady. "I've indicated the good stuff in a pink marker pencil." Grady swept up the papers and let his eyes go quickly to the passages she'd underscored.

BAKER: Hey, I've been thinking about what you told me in Muelle. The powder, you know?

ALBRIGHT: You didn't talk to Nadal?

BAKER: No. Hispanic guys, I don't know, I just don't trust them 100 percent, you know what I mean? I mean, I'd like to get in on that but I got to be 100 percent sure first. I got to be sure it's safe. You know, I got a wife and kids to worry about.

ALBRIGHT: My friend, like I told you. You don't have to worry. Everything's taken care of here.

BAKER: Well, you know, Customs ...

ALBRIGHT: Let me clue you in, pal. Who do you think this outfit we're flying for, First Aviation, is? It's fronting for the CIA. I flew for guys like that out in Southeast Asia. Air America. I know how these things work. They want to keep this whole arms for the contras business a big secret, right? So they drop a blanket over the whole goddamned thing. Forget about Customs. They've been taken care of.

BAKER: Can you really trust these guys? Nadal and all. I mean do they really pay you like they say they're going to? They don't try to screw you?

ALBRIGHT: Always paid me. Bring me a nice bag full of money right to my hotel room.

BAKER: How much do they pay?

ALBRIGHT: Seventy-five grand a trip. Flat rate.

BAKER: No matter how much you take?

ALBRIGHT: Two hundred keys max.

BAKER: You know, guys around here, they say the rate's five hundred bucks a key. That's a hundred grand for two hundred keys.

ALBRIGHT: Well now, that shows you got some smart friends in the business. The thing of it is though, they're not wired into a real safe deal like this one. They gotta worry about Customs and the DEA.

BAKER: Yeah, that's true, I guess. So I talk to Nadal. Not that guy Tulley, the one who keeps telling you what a big CIA honcho he is?

ALBRIGHT: Forget Tulley. He's all hat and no cattle. That guy's so dumb you spit in his face, he'd think it was raining.

BAKER: Doesn't say much for his vision, either. I'll talk to Nadal next trip. I guess he's got to be agency, too.

ALBRIGHT: Oh, shit yes. There's a whole bunch of them down there that are in on it. On a contract like everybody else. Cubans mostly. Part-time employees doing a little moonlighting on the side just like the rest of us. (Laughs)

BAKER: They got to be making a pile of dough.

ALBRIGHT: Hell, yeah. I mean they'll feed you a line of horseshit if you're dumb enough to swallow it about how the money goes to the *causa*. Buy M-16's to kill communists. Believe that and you believe in Santa Claus. What it buys is condos on the beach but what the fuck, that's their look out.

BAKER: Hey, listen, the guys on the strip you go in on. They know what they're doing, right?

ALBRIGHT: Oh yeah, they been doing it for years. You touch down, open the doors, kick out your duffel bags and you're outta there.

BAKER: What happens you got weather when you get in?

ALBRIGHT: You figure out your overhead, open the door, and kick the stuff out. It misses, fuck it, little Phil done lost a load of dope.

BAKER: Great. Watts tells me he's got a trip for me the end of next week.

ALBRIGHT: I'm going down on Thursday.

BAKER: Well, listen, tell Nadal if you see him. I'll play. I'll talk to him when I get down there.

Grady emitted a triumphant *yip* when he'd finished reading. "Great!" he exulted. "Now we have a case! Everything Baker told us we've got corroborated on that tape. Already, with that, we could put Baker up in front of the grand jury. But I've got a better idea."

"What's that, Mr. Genius?"

"Baker gave it to us on that tape. We run a penetration on Nadal. We convince Baker to fly back down there to Muelle with a wire. Nail Nadal and the whole damn operation!"

Ella Jean stood up, her coffee mug in her hand, and walked to the window looking off toward the gleaming glass and steel towers of Miami's banking district running south out Brickell Avenue. The avenue coke built, she thought bitterly. She turned back to Kevin.

"I'm awfully glad I'm here, Kevin. Someone has to rein in that mad Irish enthusiasm of yours. There is no way, re-

eat, no way, you're going to go charging after those people
n Costa Rica until we've laid this all out in front of Richie
Cagnia and the SAC in New York."

"Why the hell not?"

"Because you're not the Lone Ranger. You're not a one-
man DEA. We know what those trips to Costa Rica are all
.bout. We know who's in charge down there. There's no
vay I'm going to let you light out after them until you've
covered your ass up the line. You may not like it, Kev, but
hat's what the book says you got to do."

"What the book says we've got to do and what we should
lo aren't always the same thing, Ella."

"Maybe not, but this time we do what the book says. You
emember what you told me when we came down here? 'We
lon't breathe the initials CIA until we have to?' Well, this is
vhen we have to, baby, this is when we absolutely have to."

At a certain point in their rise up the civil service ladder,
he United States government tends to compensate its senior
employees for the meagerness of their paychecks with the
grandeur of their surroundings. The New York SAC's office
vith its wide windows looking out at the Hudson was a to-
:en of that. He welcomed Kevin and Ella Jean into it with
he fulsomeness of a senator welcoming a major contributor
o his re-election campaign.

"A great job," the SAC said, lifting Grady's report in his
ands. "A great job."

That, Kevin knew, was the obligatory stroke before he got
lown to the serious business. "Clearly, it is now our
obligation—or my obligation—to bring this whole matter to
he attention of the Administrator before we proceed any
'urther." The Administrator was the head of the DEA. "I am
ure he's going to feel he has to take this over to the Attor-
ey General and expose it to him. After all, this is not a rou-
ine investigation we have here. By any means. This goes
vell beyond routine. This involves major misbehavior by an
employee, maybe even an officer, of another federal agency.
And not just any federal agency, either."

"Boss," Kevin said, "they'll throttle us. The CIA will step
on us if we do that." His protest, he knew, wasn't going far,
ut he felt he had to make it anyway.

"The CIA isn't going to tell us to stop, Kev. They'd never
lo a thing like that."

"Of course they wouldn't. What they'll do is, they'll send the information back down the other side and squeeze off our investigation that way."

The SAC exhaled a deep breath. He had not reached this level of the DEA's hierarchy without having a finely developed sense of the political niceties of his business. "Whatever the outcome, Kev, it's my responsibility to put this in front of the Administrator before it goes any further."

The Attorney General of the United States followed the report of the Administrator of the DEA with all the happiness of a man hearing his doctor inform him he has a malignant tumor of the prostate.

"Thank you very much for your information," he told the Administrator when he'd completed his account of the possibility that there was a drug-smuggling operation in Central America involving contractual employees of the CIA. "What is your next step?"

"We'll try to use an informant to penetrate their operation on the ground in Costa Rica through that man Nadal."

"Good," the Attorney General sighed. "Please keep me informed of your progress."

Lind's Tape

Hinckley made it a point of pride never to let his emotions show in public. Or in private, either, as far as I could see. There were some cynics at Langley who suggested that was because he'd never known any emotion in his life other than a sense of expediency. In reality, it was, I am sure, all part of that desire of his for control: control of himself, of the people around him, of his operations.

I say this because inside he must have been boiling that day not so long ago when he called me up to his seventh-floor office. On the outside, however, he was icy calm. My recollections of the meeting are detailed because it came almost immediately in the wake of my traumatic telephone call to the DEA agent Kevin Grady about Juanita's death.

"We have a disaster on our hands," Hinckley announced as I sat down. "Our friend over at the National Security Council just called. The Attorney General warned him that the DEA is on to a cocaine-trafficking ring inside our contra supply operation. And most particularly, in Costa Rica. They've asked for the go-ahead to penetrate it with an informant."

"Did he give it to them?"

"Of course he did. What was he supposed to do? Say 'Let them go ahead and break the law'? We've got to shovel this under the carpet, Jack. Cover it up. If this should ever get out, if even a whiff of it ever gets out, the scandal will destroy the whole contra program. We'll never see any more funding out of Congress."

"We're not getting much from them now," I noted. "According to Casey, it's the Saudis and the Sultan of Brunei who are paying for our war."

Hinckley gave me that sour look he reserved for those who interrupted the flow of his logic with inconvenient points of order. "You know perfectly well what I'm getting at, Jack. This war of ours is unpopular enough as it is. Let this out and the whole thing will blow up in our faces. There'll be such a public outcry the White House will be forced to close it down. Not even Ronald Reagan will be able to stop it. We'll wind up hanging our contras out to dry just like we hung out all those poor Vietnamese. I did that once in my lifetime. I'm not going to do it twice."

"Well, what do you suggest we do about it?"

"The only name the DEA has right now is Felipe Nadal's." At that, I saw Nadal in front of me in Honduras, swearing his innocence on the high altar of his wife's head. Well, I thought, maybe he's divorcing.

"We've got to make sure," Hinckley continued, "that the DEA never gets the material to build its case."

"Then we'll have to pull Nadal and some of the others out of there. Fast." My conscience still pained me at what I had done at Hinckley's insistence in giving that informer's name to Noriega. I didn't know what had happened to him, nor did I wish to know. But I wanted to push Hinckley toward the least violent resolution possible of this crisis.

"That's exactly right," Hinckley agreed. "You go down to Howard right away and get them out of there. Nadal. The Dwarf. The lot. Assign them on temporary duty to the station in Puerto Rico. Let them sit on the beach down there in the sunshine where the DEA can't find them for the next six months."

"On full pay?"

"Of course on full pay. How else are we going to keep their mouths shut? Once this has all blown over, we'll close them out and take them off the payroll. But for now just be sure the DEA doesn't get its hands on them."

"They must have some evidence if they've gotten their investigation this far along."

"They've got a pilot. They can have him. One individual doesn't matter. When he claims we were involved, we'll simply stonewall. Suggest he's trying to involve us as a way of bargaining his time down. And we'll let him know that won't work."

The assignment was just what I'd been looking for for the past twenty-four hours. I'd pack up Nadal and company, then go to Panama and confront Noriega with Kevin Grady's accusation that his people had murdered Juanita.

She had probably been the most beautiful woman in Panama, Noriega thought. How ironic it was, then, that the last sight her eyes had looked upon on this earth was the face of perhaps the ugliest man in the country. Pedro del Rica was sitting beside him in the big leather armchair from Harrods that Noriega had positioned by his desk at his seaside hideaway, la Playita. Del Rica was like a good servant or the obedient child of an earlier age; he never spoke unless he was spoken to. He was hunched there now, a whiskey glass in his massive killer's hands, his scar contorting his features into their permanent sneer, a morose and menacing man awaiting his master's summons to perform some violent action.

Noriega despised him. But he was efficient and silent, two attributes the Panamanian much prized in those around him.

"How did they kill her?" he asked. "Without leaving a trace?"

"It was simple. Something the Mafia uses in the United States. You take a long, sharp steel pin . . ." Del Rica looked around the room for an object that might help Noriega envision the tool he had in mind. He found none. "In New York, they use an ice-pick. My people used a long needle, like a knitting needle. You put it in her ear, than give it a hard whack that drives it three, four inches into her brain. That's all."

"No marks?"

"Only a touch of blood in her ear. Nothing you could find without doing an autopsy and looking at her brain." Del Rica shrugged. There had never been, of course, any question of anybody performing an autopsy in this case.

The image disgusted Noriega. Why had he even asked the question of this hired Doberman of his? He should be above all that.

"You said you had a problem to discuss?"

"Lind, the CIA man."

Lind? Noriega was fully focused at the sound of that name. It was vital that he, of all people, swallow the story about Juanita being in that motel room using coke and poppers. She had used those drugs. That information had been gathered by his secret police and lodged in her file. If she'd done it with her other lovers, she'd probably tried it out on Lind, too. At least, that had been the assumption on which they had worked when they'd decided to park her body in the pushbutton and leave evidence of drug use around the room. "What's your problem with Lind?"

"He's raising hell up in Costa Rica. The word I have is that the DEA has smelled out our operation. Lind is in Muelle pulling everybody the agency thinks might be involved out of there so it doesn't get exposed. Nadal. Rene. Most of the people we were working with are gone or are going."

Now, why hadn't Lind mentioned that to him? Or why hadn't someone from the local station informed him? Was it because they suspected he might be involved? Was it possible the CIA was in some way connected with the effort to get hold of Spadafora's material? That seemed extremely unlikely. Otherwise, why would they have warned him about the DEA informer? He thought back to the details of the tape-recorded conversation they'd brought him from Building #9, the one in which Spadafora had told Juanita to get his papers and hand them over to a DEA agent named Kevin Grady. There was no mention of Lind or the CIA in there. No, he concluded, this didn't concern him, and he was going to make sure it stayed that way.

"We're going to close that operation down. Right now. Completely. Before the gringos get on to us, too."

"Are you afraid of the gringos?"

"Of course I'm not afraid of them. I'm too important to them. I know too many things now." He cupped his fingertips in a little knot as though he might be grasping a rubber ball between them. "I have them by the *cojones.*"

He sat back, satisfied with his decision. It was, he was sure, the right one. Why risk everything he had on a secondary operation? Things were going so well now. He'd calmed the storm of angry protest that had followed his stolen election. His power in Panama was unchallenged. Barletta, his new president, was so worried about the economy, he never looked up from his papers to see what was really going on in the country.

Most satisfying of all, he was becoming a respected international figure. His newfound friend Bill Casey had just invited him to pay an official visit to Washington. He had had a secret meeting at Howard Air Force Base to discuss the contra program with Vice President George Bush.

The French government of President François Mitterand was beginning to woo him. He'd made an important financial contribution to his electoral campaign. They were talking about his supplying them with end user certificates to cover the secret shipment of some of their arms to Iraq. He liked France. He'd already bought an apartment in Paris. He was looking for a chateau in the south. One day, he'd find a way to get them to award him their Legion of Honor. That would give him, a poor orphan from the slums of Terraplen, social access in Paris, wouldn't it?

Financially, his situation was secure. He had substantial accounts at the BCCI in Miami, London, Paris, Luxembourg, the Cayman Islands. This was not a moment to take risks. He'd reached the station he'd sought in life and nothing was going to separate him from it now. Nothing.

"Close it down tight," he warned del Rica. "I don't want anything leaking out."

He walked his Doberman to the door, del Rica trailing a rigorous two paces behind him as any faithful mascot might. "Spadafora," Noriega mused, "one day we'll have to do something about him, too."

He watched del Rica's hunched figure stalk out to his car, then went back to his office. He poured himself a glass of Old Parr, and sat in front of his television set debating whether or not to turn on the world news broadcast by the Armed Forces Network, which serviced the American troops in the old Canal Zone bases.

He began to think about Lind. If the American ever discovered what had really happened to his girlfriend, he was going to become a problem, a real problem. The way you took care of problems was to deal with them before they came up. How could he take care of Lind? The ideal would be to find a way to get the gringos to do the job for him. Let his superiors know about his plea for Juanita's freedom? Tell his new friend Casey he wanted another controller?

Then, it came to him, as all his good ideas did, in an almost mystic flash. It was perfect. He went to his desk diary and found the date he was looking for. With it, he leaped up and rushed to the basement control room in which all the audiotapes from the tape recorders monitoring the house were stored, all the film footage of his weekend romps, were kept. He had film in there to blackmail a whole battalion of U.S. military officers.

He worked through the audiotapes until he found the date he was looking for. Fingers shaking with excitement, he threaded the tape into his playback machine and turned it on. It was there all right. It was perfect.

He cut out the vital segment, reeled it up on a smaller tape and rushed back upstairs. At his desk, he slipped the tape into an envelope, wrote out a brief note of instructions to go along with it and called for his driver.

"Take this to the Foreign Ministry," he ordered. "I want it to go in the diplomatic pouch to the consulate in New York in the morning."

The waiting is the worst part of a DEA agent's life; the waiting for a CI or undercover agent to make contact; the hours on stakeout watching for one figure to arrive, for the one gesture, the one sign that might mean something was going down. Putting on the blue raid jacket, hammering down the doors, shouting "Freeze!" the way they do in the movies, was almost the easy part. It certainly was the most fun.

Kevin Grady was playing the waiting game now, sitting at his office desk since 4:00 a.m., looking out at the Hudson, at the stirring city, waiting for the damn phone to ring. Ella Jean had come in, too, to share the vigil with him, ruining her intestines along with his consuming endless cups of black coffee.

They knew one thing. Their CI Shep Baker wasn't bringing back a load. He hadn't flashed out their coded radio sig-

nal which would have told them as soon as he was airborne
that he had coke on board.

It was after nine o'clock when the phone finally rang.
Grady made such an impulsive grab for it, he almost
knocked the instrument onto the floor.

"Shep! You okay? How did it go?"

A weak and exhausted voice replied. "Lousy."

"What do you mean, lousy?"

"Nadal's disappeared. They've got a whole new crew. You
mention the word powder to any of them and they take sick.
Apparently some CIA guys came in there and scrubbed the
place out. The one guy who would talk would only say, 'The
party's over. The word is out.' "

Kevin slumped in his chair, his face gray, an air of such
overwhelming disappointment scarring his face that Ella
Jean came over, took the phone from his hands, squeezed his
neck, and said, "Shep, this is Ella Jean. You still did a great
job. Thanks. We'll be in touch."

She hung up the phone and continued to stroke Kevin's
neck. "It was bound to wind up this way, Kev. You were
right the other day. This is the way they do things. Look at
it this way. Maybe we didn't put anybody away. But at least
we shut them down."

Grady could only sit there slouched in his chair, shaking
his head in sadness and dismay. It was at that moment that
the receptionist entered the office. "Mr. Grady, this is for
you." She handed him a manila envelope.

"What the fuck is that?" Grady snarled.

Rudeness was so uncharacteristic of Grady that the
woman almost leaped back in fright. "I don't know," she
babbled. "A bicycle messenger just delivered it."

Grady looked at the envelope. There was no return address, just his name and *New York Office, DEA*.

He opened it and spilled the contents onto his desk. It
contained a three-inch reel of audiotape. "What the hell do
you suppose this could be?" he asked Ella Jean. "Let's go
down to Technical Services and see if they have a machine
we can run it on."

The tape turned out to be a conversation between two
men—in Spanish, a language neither Ella Jean nor Grady
spoke.

"We better listen all the way through anyway," Grady
said, "maybe they'll switch into English." They sat there lis-

tening. It occurred to Grady that one of the two voices sounded vaguely familiar. Although, how could that be, since he didn't speak Spanish?

Suddenly, both he and Ella Jean sat up and looked at each other. "Rewind it a couple of feet and play it back," Grady ordered the technician. "Let's see if we heard what I think we heard."

This time the sound was unmistakable. "Raymond Marcello" one of the two men said, then seconds later "Ramon." It was at that instant that Kevin thought he recognized the voice of the second speaker.

"That's Jack Lind, the CIA guy!" he roared. "We've got to get this translated right away."

The two rushed down to the office of the Hispanic translation service with their tape and reel. "Look," Kevin pleaded with the heavyset woman guarding access to the place like some forbidding head nurse on a busy hospital ward, "I need an urgent translation of a tape. The full typed text can wait. I just need to have a rough idea of what we've got on here fast."

The matron lifted her 195 pounds reluctantly from her chair and surveyed her busy brood of translators. "Gloria," she said, "you help these people, please."

She pointed Kevin and Ella Jean toward the young lady. "Rush," she lamented, "always they are in a rush here."

"They're talking about an election," Gloria said as the tape began to roll. "Maybe in Panama. Yeah, in Panama. This tape, he made in Panama maybe a month ago."

"Are there names being used?" Kevin asked.

Gloria listened a while more, then stopped the machine. "One man, he call the other General."

She started the tape again and listened in silence. "Hey," she announced suddenly, "this for you. They talking drugs." She rewound the tape and started it forward again. "I do a rough translation, okay?

"First man say 'The DEA suspects you may be involve in drug trafficking. They have informer, very close to cartel of Medellín who say you receiving protection money for allowing their product to pass through Panama on its way to the United States.'

"Now the general speaks. Hey, he call first man Jack. He say 'You don't really suspect I be involve in something like that do you, Jack.'

"Now Jack talk. He say 'I certainly hope not, Tony'—he call him Tony—'because if you are there could come a time when we can no longer help you however much we might want to.'

"Jack again. 'The informer's name, by the way, was Marcello. Raymond Marcello. They call him Ramon.' "

Kevin leaped from his chair. "Thanks, Gloria, that's great. That's all we need." He turned and gave Ella Jean a frantic hug. "We got him, babe!" Then he glanced up toward the ceiling. "This one isn't going to get away, Ramon, I swear to you."

"What are we going to do, Kev?"

"You're going to fly this down to the Office of Special Services in Maryland right away to have one of their voiceprint analysts establish that the second voice on that tape is Lind. And then we're off to the races."

"But, Kev, to do that, we've got to have a second, independent tape of his voice."

"We've got one."

"We do?"

"Up in my desk. The son of a bitch called me last week down in Miami on one of those phones that automatically tapes incoming calls."

Identifying and analyzing a voiceprint in a criminal procedure is similar in many ways to identifying and analyzing a set of fingerprints. The two tapes of Lind's voice Ella Jean brought to the DEA's Office of Special Services just off the Beltway in Maryland were passed individually through a computerized electronic filtering system, which broke the sounds produced by the speaker's voice on each tape down into their component parts such as timbre, resonance, and the unique guttural tone of each speaker's voicebox in his larynx.

Then, while Ella Jean watched, the white-coated DEA voiceprint expert projected the computer-enhanced breakdown of those basic sound characteristics onto a split computer screen which allowed him to compare them side by side in his search for identical matchups.

Where fingerprints are concerned, most states and federal criminal proceedings require a matchup of at least thirteen swirls, those curlicue tracings characteristic of a fingerprint, in order to establish legally that a set of prints found on a gun, for example, match those of a suspected killer.

With voiceprint analysis, there is no legally defined number of matchups required for a legal identification of the speaker. The expert running the analysis must be sure enough of his identification, certain enough of his evidence, that he is prepared to go into a courtroom and testify to the validity of his identification of the speaker.

Voiceprint experts, therefore, whether they are employed by the DEA, the FBI or a police department, tend to be very independent-minded people. Their reputations and their credibility are at stake in each of their identifications. They do not react favorably to overzealous prosecutors or agents.

Recognizing that, Ella Jean sat silently on her stool while the DEA expert worked, watching him pass projection after projection through his computer, studying them as intently as a microbiologist might study the slides of microbes under his microscope.

Finally, after an hour and a half of intensive effort, he sat back, rubbed his exhausted eyes and dropped his pencil onto his clipboard.

"No question," he said, "you have a matchup. About as good as they get."

"Even though he's speaking Spanish on one tape, English on the other?"

"It's the sounds that matter, miss, not what the sounds mean."

An hour later, Ella Jean had an official affidavit from the Office of Special Services, signed, witnessed and sealed, attesting to the fact that the voice identified as that of Mr. Lind on tape one and that identified as belonging to a man called *Jack* on tape two, were in fact the voice of one and the same person.

She rushed to National Airport and caught the one o'clock shuttle back to La Guardia. By three o'clock, she was standing in front of Kevin.

"They match!" she declared, handing Grady the affidavit.

Grady studied it. What overwhelmed him reading it was not a sense of triumph or exultation. It was rather a sensation of profound relief, rather like an enormous burden sliding from his shoulders. He saw Ramon on the seawall in Aruba pondering suicide, marching off alone to risk his life

in the cartel's compound in Medellín. He saw the shattered
woman to whom he had had to return Ramon's wedding
band. We got him for you, Kevin thought. It was all we
could do. But we did it.

He looked up at Ella Jean. "I'm going to make an ap
pointment for us tomorrow morning at the U.S. Attorney's
Office for the Southern District. I guess we'll also have to
tell Richie and the SAC what we're about to do."

The SAC received them thirty minutes later. Nodding sol
emnly, he read through the file Kevin and Ella Jean set be
fore him. Finally he put it aside.

"There's no question this time, Kev. Lind's gesture was an
overt act in the furtherance of a criminal conspiracy. On the
strength of what you have here, a federal judge is certainly
going to be prepared to issue an arrest warrant for him.
When are you going down to the U.S. Attorney's Office to
start the process?"

"Tomorrow morning."

"Good. Go ahead. I've got to inform the Department of
Justice of what we're doing as a matter of courtesy, but the
case goes down."

At 9:30 the following morning, in the office of Assistant
U.S. Attorney Eddie Rhodes in the U.S. Attorney's office
opposite the Federal Court House in Foley Square, Kevin
Grady and Ella Jean Ransom began to fill out their request
for a warrant for the arrest of John Featherly Lind IV, em
ployed as an officer of the Central Intelligence Agency,
Langley, Virginia, and residing at 3051 Baxter Lane, Fairfax,
Virginia, and The High Cliff, Half Pone Point, Maryland, on
the charge of conspiracy to obstruct the furtherance of a
Federal investigation.

Lind's Tape

I was ready to board a flight out of San Juan, Puerto Rico,
for Miami, and then down to Panama to confront Noriega on
Juanita's murder, when Dick Mills, our local station chief,
caught up with me in the terminal building. He handed me
a new ticket.

"You've been rebooked from Miami to Washington instead of Panama. We just got an urgent-action cable in from Langley. They want you back there right away. You'd think they couldn't live without you. Ain't it great to be loved?"

I remember those words all too well. How ironic they proved to be in the light of the events of the next twenty-four hours. As usual, I got into the office early the following morning. I had my feet and my coffee mug on my desk, the *New York Times* and *Washington Post* in my lap, when Hinckley called.

"Jack," he said, his voice unusually solemn, "would you come up immediately, please? Bring your coffee. You may need it."

As I walked into his office, it struck me that he looked about as cheerful as a priest administering extreme unction. He guided me to a chair with such thoughtfulness, I wondered for a moment if he might even offer me a cigarette. He didn't.

"Jack," he announced, "I have terrible news. Simply terrible news."

"What is it?"

"A federal judge in the Southern District of New York is about to issue a warrant for your arrest."

"My arrest?" I gasped. "Why, for God's sakes?"

"On two criminal charges, the unauthorized revelation of secret material relevant to a federal investigation and conspiracy to interfere in the pursuance of a federal investigation. Each charge can carry a jail term of twenty years on conviction, Jack."

Stunned disbelief. Incredulousness. Think of any expression you want. They all would have fit my reaction at that moment. I simply could not comprehend what Hinckley was talking about. "You must be joking!"

"I wish I were."

"On what possible grounds, Ted?"

"That you revealed to Noriega the fact that he was being investigated by the DEA for drug smuggling and gave him the name of the informant they were using. The man was subsequently murdered, by the way."

I felt, quite literally, dizzy, as though I'd just stepped out of a cable car at 13,000 feet. "How in God's name does anybody know that?"

"They have a tape recording of your conversation wit
Noriega."

I felt a tide of nausea rising up in my intestines, a flarin
concern that I might be about to vomit. How could the DE
have gotten hold of that tape? From Noriega, of course. Wh
else could it have been?

"Ted, you gave me a formal order to pass that informatio
to Noriega."

"Maybe I did, Jack, but nobody has a tape recording c
me giving you that order. The NSA can't record secur
channel communications."

That bland, expressionless look of Hinckley's, the one tha
had earned him his nickname, the Pale Rider, had once agai
congealed his face into an icy mask. I understood. He wa
hanging me out to dry. I could hear his testimony in a court
room or before a board of inquiry: "I certainly never gav
Lind any such order. He took that information to Noriega o
his own accord. As a consequence, probably, of the relation
ship that had grown up between them. There is always
very special bond that exists between an agent and th
agency officer controlling him." You bastard, I thought, i
you have a conscience it should be troubling you right now

It wasn't, however. I don't think Hinckley came equippe
with that particular piece of the human machine. He wa
into damage control.

"I've taken this up with the Director," he explained. "I
view of your long and valued service to this agency, h
wants to do all he can to help you. Go downstairs, and writ
out your letter of resignation right now. He'll accept it an
guarantee you that you and your family will receive you
full retirement pay and benefits. We'll also do what we ca
to help out with your legal expenses."

"In other words, I'm supposed to lie down, roll over, an
take the risk of spending the rest of my life in a federa
prison, a prison of the country whose best interests you tol
me I'd be serving when I passed that information t
Noriega."

"Jack, you know as well as I do that the Director can ter
minate an officer's service like that." Hinckley snapped hi
fingers to make his point. "He doesn't owe an explanation t
anyone. Not to you. Not to the Civil Service. Not to Con
gress. Not to the President. Is that what you want? Have hir
give you the sack, rip the medals off your chest and orde

you marched out to the gate under armed guard? We're trying to offer you an honorable way out here, Jack."

"Honor? If you knew what the word meant, Hinckley, you'd stand up like an honorable officer and admit that you gave me that order. That you and Casey and I and a whole bunch of us in this building have been knowingly, deliberately and systematically breaking the laws of this country, defying the express will of Congress for the last two and a half years. That's what honor calls for here. If you had a shred of decency in you, that's what you'd do."

"Look, Lind, we are not going to have those bastards from the DEA standing out at the front gate with a battery of television cameras going, waiting for you to come out so they can have the pleasure of slapping an arrest warrant on a serving officer of the CIA. You're not going to bring disgrace on this agency. You know what a samurai does when he's been compromised? He falls on his sword. Be a good samurai, Jack."

"Be a fall guy for you is what you mean. Take the rap for you and Casey and everybody else in this house who's been breaking the law because of this God-given mission of ours to stomp on the Sandinistas, no matter what the cost."

"Jack," he replied. "Look at the big picture here. We have a job to accomplish. And we are going to accomplish it. No one individual, not even an officer as valued as you are, can be allowed to stand in the way of that."

I wanted to shout. Dear Jesus, no one will ever know how many crimes we in the agency had justified in the past forty years by the absolution implicit in those five words, "Look at the big picture."

Hinckley got up and looked at his watch. "You have five minutes to decide what it will be, Jack. Either you go downstairs and write up that letter of resignation to the Director, or the Director fires you and you're escorted from the building under armed guard."

It wasn't much of a choice. I resigned because I felt I owed my wife and sons the right to my retirement benefits. At a few minutes before noon, I drove away in disgrace from the agency I had served so long and, I thought, so well. The George Washington Memorial Parkway was a blaze of gold and crimson fire. I was in despair and the capital I loved was alight in the glories of its finest season.

I started home, then changed my mind and drove down

here to Half Pone Point instead. I could not bear to face my wife and sons in my hour of dishonor. Thinking back, I am sure that as I walked through that officer's parking lot for the last time, Hinckley would have been peering down at me from the window of his seventh-floor office, wondering how I could have been so dumb as to commit the unpardonable sin of getting caught, how I could possibly be so naive as to feel guilt or anger for what we had done.

When the rest of us are scorned as pariahs or in federal prison or an early grave, old Ted, our Pale Rider, will still be up there, serene and composed, in his seventh-floor office. That's only natural. The Hinckleys of this world never do get caught, never do pay the price, do they? From the Bay of Pigs to involving the Mafia in our attempts to kill Castro, from Vang Pao and his heroin to Noriega and his cocaine, Hinckley glided through it all and never left a set of fingerprints anywhere.

I suppose, Kevin, that this tape will eventually fall into your hands. There is a certain poetic justice in that. It will complete that circle we started flying on our DC-6 to Vientiane so long ago. By the time you listen to it, it will no longer have legal validity in a courtroom for you because of the circumstances in which you will have found it. Justice, however, is not dispensed in courtrooms alone, and unless I have very seriously misread your character, you will know how to employ the material on this tape in the pursuit of justice.

Please do not look upon it as some kind of an Augustinian justification *pro sua vita*. The balance on the scales does not weigh in my favor. I have upon my conscience the blood of that murdered DEA informer of yours; so, too, do I have upon it the blood of a woman I passionately loved. He, I killed with my words; she, I helped to kill by my silence, by my refusal or inability to hear her exposition of what was right because I was deafened by the thunder of my professional logic.

How did it happen? How did I delude myself into the acceptance of acts I knew to be profoundly wrong?

Part of that answer must lie in the very nature of an organization such as the one I served. Hinckley was right when he said that implicit in the charter of the CIA was a kind of special dispensation to suspend the law, the nation's law or God's law—if there is such a thing—when we felt we needed to do so to protect the national security. Expediency became our religion in the pursuit of that goal. Yet was this nation ever so insecure that its survival had to depend on doing what was expedient rather than what was right?

We who reached a certain level in the agency tended to regard ourselves as America's mandarins. We were convinced we knew both the interests of the rulers we served and the people whose destinies we guided better than they did.

Did we?

(Sound of bell ringing)
(Sound of receding footsteps)
(Sound of approaching footsteps)
(Sound of drawer opening)
(Sound of gunshot)

END OF TAPE

Since Then...

General Manuel Antonio Noriega continued to enjoy close relations with the Reagan Administration and the CIA for some years after the death of Jack Lind. In November 1985 he was personally invited to Washington by CIA Director William Casey. His visit included sessions at the Pentagon, the National Security Council and an entire afternoon at CIA headquarters, including a two-hour meeting with Casey. His Pentagon escort was excluded from all his meetings at the agency.

In February 1986, as the crack epidemic was beginning to ravage America's inner cities, Casey briefed Arthur Davis, the newly appointed U.S. Ambassador to Panama. When queried by Davis on Noriega's possible involvement in drug trafficking, Casey assured the ambassador that "if anyone should know about this guy's involvement with drugs it's us and we have no proof at all that he's involved." Casey, Davis concluded leaving his briefing, was "in love with the guy."

Late in the summer of 1986, however, a meeting took place at a social evening at the Broward Country Club north of Miami, which would radically alter the course of Noriega's relations with the United States. It was between Dan Moritz, an officer of the DEA and Richard C. Gregorie, an Assistant U.S. Attorney assigned to the U.S. Attorney's Office for the Southern District of Florida.

"I've got a guy who can give you Manuel Noriega," Moritz told Gregorie. "Will you take the case?"

Gregorie would. He was the kind of Federal Prosecutor Kevin Grady dreamed about. He began intensive work on the case in February 1987. The guy referred to by Dan Moritz was Floyd Carlton, Noriega's personal pilot. Carlton had been involved in ferrying cocaine from Panama to Costa Rica, arrested and was prepared to reveal what he knew about drug trafficking in Central America in return for a reduced sentence. Despite Carlton's cooperation, Gregorie's job was not easy. A box of critical evidence shipped by the DEA's Panama office to Gregorie via diplomatic pouch disappeared en route. Its disappearance has never been explained.

While Gregorie labored, Senator John Kerry of Massachusetts opened public hearings into Noriega's ties to both drug trafficking and the CIA before his Senate Foreign Affairs sub-committee on Narcotics, Terrorism and International Communications. The hearings focused public scrutiny for the first time on the Panamanian dictator's activities. Noriega's period of usefulness to the U.S. government was drawing to a close.

On February 2, 1988, Gregorie and his boss U.S. Attorney Leon Kellner laid out their case before the National Security Council. The CIA's representative at the meeting made a *pro forma* effort to protect the agency's asset but the case compiled by Gregorie was so overwhelming it could not be dismissed. Kellner and Gregorie received the go-ahead to lay their charges before a federal Grand Jury in Miami. On February 4, 1988, the Grand Jury handed down its indictment. It was unsealed at noon the next day.

Noriega managed to convince himself, however, that with the nomination and election of George Bush, a former director of the CIA with whom he had met on at least three occasions, he would escape prosecution. "Now I'm safe," he told a friend on the evening of Bush's inauguration.

He was not. In May 1989 Noriega and the PDF once again stole a Panamanian presidential election. This time, however, the theft was carried out in front of the world's television cameras and without the blessing of the U.S. government. Despite the controversy surrounding Noriega, however, the CIA maintained its close working relationship with the Panamanian dictator. The agency offered him a New Year's present on January 1, 1989, a handsome hand-carved Peruvian board game. CIA officers continued twice a week to collect the tapes of the wiretaps being made on the agency's behalf at Noriega's electronic eavesdropping center in Building #9 at Fort Amador.

On the weekend of December 16–17, 1989, a young marine lieutenant was shot and killed after he and three fellow officers ran a PDF roadblock in downtown Panama. The same evening, PDF officers brutally beat a U.S. Naval officer in front of his wife. President George Bush gave the order to mount Operation Just Cause, the invasion of Panama and the arrest of Noriega as quickly as possible.

On Tuesday, December 19, 1989, despite the fact his nation was being swept by rumors that an invasion was imminent, Noriega left Panama City for Colon to inaugurate a new crane at the port's container facility. Shortly after three o'clock that afternoon, he received a call from Colonel Rafael Cedeno, his liaison officer with the CIA and U.S. military intelligence. Cedeno informed Noriega that he had just received a telephone message from their top source in Washington. There was not going to be any invasion of Panama, the source had assured him. The troops flying into Howard Air Force Base were part of a pre-Christmas rotation. The CIA had just administered the Kiss of Judas to the man who had once been the agency's most prized Central American asset.

To celebrate those glad if false tidings, Noriega returned to Panama, ordered up a bottle of Old Parr and a blond young lady at the Ceremi, a military recreational center near the airport. He was there when the invasion began. He took refuge first in the home of Jorge Krupnik with whom he had once negotiated the purchase of arms for the contras, then in the apartment of his secretary's sister. Finally, on the day before Christmas, wearing blue Bermuda shorts and a baseball cap, hidden under a blanket in the back of a Toyota van, he was driven to asylum at the Papal Nunciature of Monsignor Sebastian Laboa.

On the evening of January 3, 1990, he surrendered to the U.S. forces surrounding the Nunciature and was flown to the United States to stand trial. The trial opened before Judge William C. Hoeveler in the United States District Court for the Southern District of Florida in September 1991, and lasted nine months.

In keeping with U.S. legal practice and precedent, Judge Hoeveler rigorously excluded testimony concerning Noriega's work for the CIA on the grounds that it was not relevant to his guilt or innocence of the crimes of which he stood accused. Only one of the many CIA officers with whom Noriega had dealings during his long career as an agency asset was allowed on the witness stand.

Nor did any of the material uncovered by the U.S. invasion force in his or the PDF's files appear during the trial. A team composed of representatives of the State Department, the CIA and the Pentagon's Defense Intelligence Agency (DIA) had been assigned to review and catalogue those documents after the invasion. They quickly discovered documents relating to General Noriega's ties to the CIA, documents which, in the words of one of the men who saw them, "were most embarrassing to the agency."

The State Department's representatives were thereupon excluded from further study of the documents. The task of reviewing them was left solely in the hands of the two agencies which might have an interest in repressing the information they contained.

Noriega was convicted on eight of the ten counts against him and sentenced to forty years in federal prison by Judge Hoeveler on July 10, 1992. He is currently serving that sentence pending the appeal of his conviction.

Kevin Grady was promoted to the post of Assistant Special Agent in Charge of the New York District Office of the DEA for his work in the Medclean Operation. After a number of highly successful prosecutions in New York, he was reassigned to the DEA's Washington Headquarters Cocaine Desk, then transferred to a senior position in the administration's Operations Office. He is currently on undercover assignment somewhere in Asia.

William J. Casey suffered a massive stroke in his office at CIA Headquarters shortly after 10:00 a.m. on Tuesday, December 15, 1987. Ironically, his personal CIA physician, Dr. Arvel Tharp, had just finished checking the Director's chronically high blood pressure when he was stricken. He was taken to Georgetown University Hospital where neurological tests revealed that he had developed a tumor on the left side of his brain. The tumor proved to be cancerous and a five-hour operation to remove it left Casey in a substantially diminished state, largely unable to communicate with those around him. He died without ever having recovered his faculties, on May 6, 1988, just as the publicly televised Congressional hearings into the Iran-Contra affair were beginning. Death had silenced the voice of the man who knew more than any other person alive about the events which had preceded and produced the so-called Irangate scandal.

Ted Hinckley retired with honor from the CIA in 1989. At his retirement ceremony he was commended for his service in Laos with General Vang Pao, his work with the police in breaking the Tupamaros guerrillas in Uruguay and with the military in Argentina during the military junta's so-called Dirty War against the nation's Marxist urban guerrillas. He now lives in the Greater Washington area where he runs a private security consulting firm styled very much on the lines of the off-the-shelf covert operations capacity he urged on Bill Casey at the outset of the contra program.

Duke Talmadge was reassigned by the CIA to Western Europe after he was withdrawn from the contra operation. His departure jarred his Central American associates who had come to admire greatly his professional capabilities, capabilities they found notably lacking in his successor, Lt. Col. Oliver North. After completing postings in the Hague and Berlin, Talmadge retired from the CIA. He now lives in northern California where he continues to enjoy good Cuban cigars, California cabernets and the attention of a number of female admirers to whom he is still a U.S. version of James Bond. Charged by Lawrence Walsh in the Iran-Contra affair, he was one of those who benefited from President Bush's Christmas Eve pardon in 1990.

Ella Jean Ransom has continued to pursue her career in the Drug Enforcement Administration. She is currently the Assistant Agent in Charge of a major district office of the DEA on the eastern seaboard, one of the highest posts held by a woman in the DEA.

Hugo Spadafora left San Jose, Costa Rica, in late September 1985, to return to Panama and get for the DEA himself the material proof of Noriega's involvement in the drug traffic. He was taken from the bus on which he was traveling to Panama City by a PDF sergeant in the Panamanian border town of Concepcion, brutally tortured and murdered. His body was stuffed into a gray U.S. Postal Service mail sack and dumped on the Costa Rican side of the frontier separating the two Central American nations. The news of his murder stirred a furor in Panama, a furor which started the process that ultimately led to Noriega's downfall. Noriega later admitted to his political counselor Jose Blandon that it was he who had given the PDF commander in Chiriqui Province the orders to seize and murder Spadafora.

* * *

Gerardo "Kiko" Moncada, the man whose genius helped deliver the blight of crack cocaine to America's cities and streets, was invited by Pablo Escobar to a conference in Escobar's luxurious jail in the hills above Envigado, adjacent to Medellín, in early July 1992. The drug lord accused Moncada of taking advantage of his incarceration to move in on some of his U.S. territories and demanded several million dollars in compensation from Moncada for his lost revenues. Moncada refused to pay him. Forty-eight hours later, Moncada's mutilated body was found stuffed into the trunk of a car on the outskirts of Medellín.

Jorge Luis, Juan David and Fabio Ochoa Jr. handed themselves over to the Colombian authorities in June 1991 after lengthy negotiations. They are currently serving five-to ten-year sentences for drug trafficking. Each has given the Colombian government a formal undertaking not to resume their trafficking activities once released from jail. In return the Colombian government has agreed to make no move to confiscate their property and other financial assets earned as a consequence of the drug traffic.

Pablo Escobar followed the example of the Ochoa brothers and turned himself in to the Colombian authorities in the late spring of 1992. He was jailed outside his fiefdom of Envigado, in an installation so comfortable it was baptized the Medellín Hilton. Ironically, the building had been designed as a rehabilitation center for addicts of basuco, the crude form of smokable cocaine used in Latin America. Following Moncada's murder, Colombia's Attorney General decided to transfer Escobar to a more secure prison. Tipped off of the coming move, the drug lord escaped and became Colombia's—and perhaps the world's—most famous fugitive. In late autumn of 1993, he tried to secure visas for his wife and children to the United States but was refused. He sent them to Germany but there, too, they were refused entry and returned to Bogotá. Escobar contacted them from an Envigado pay phone at their Bogotá hotel on their return. His call was traced and undercover agents of Colombia's National Police sent to the area to try to locate him. They did and on December 2, 1993, police raided his hideout. Escobar was shot and killed as he attempted to flee over the rooftops adjacent to the building in which he was hiding.

His death effectively brought to an end the activities of the so-called Medellín cartel which had dominated the cocaine traffic in the 1980's. Medellín's place has been taken by the Cali cartel which, according to DEA estimates, now controls approximately eighty percent of the world's cocaine trade.

The CIA/DEA Rivalry continued unabated until the end of the Cold War. Interestingly enough, it was President George Bush, a former director of the CIA, who took the first moves to improve relations between the two U.S. government agencies by ending the DEA's systematic subservience to the CIA in its overseas operations. Beginning in 1990, DEA Country Attachés were no longer required to submit the names of the targets of their investigations or of their potential informants to the CIA Station Chief for clearance before initiating any action. Bush was also the first president to invite the administrator of the DEA—at the time John Lawn—to participate in meetings of the National Security Council on a regular basis. With the fall of the Berlin Wall, the CIA set up its own division to participate in the war on drugs. Its early efforts were less than successful. DEA agents resented the CIA's intrusion on their territory, and a tendency of many of the CIA agents working in the area to treat them in a disdainful and condescending manner. One of the agency's first recruits was General Raoul Cedras of Haiti who was supposed to keep the agency posted on drug trafficking in his nation. Instead, Cedras did exactly what Noriega had done before him—pocketed the agency's money while taking a fee from drug traffickers for each kilo of drugs he allowed to transit Haiti en route to the United States under his protective wing. Under the leadership of R. James Woolsey as Director of the CIA, the relations between the two agencies improved considerably. The CIA now works closely with the DEA and the FBI in penetrating drug trafficking and organized crime around the world.

The Crack-Cocaine Epidemic continues to ravage the inner cities of the United States. The origins of most of the criminal justice problems plaguing the nation—the proliferation of automatic weapons in the nation's cities, the rash of teenage violence, the random killings haunting our streets—can be traced to the crack-cocaine epidemic. Three quarters of the violent crimes committed in the nation last year were drug related. In the vast majority of cases, the drug in question was crack-cocaine. By late 1994, thanks to the combined efforts of law enforcement, more dynamic educational programs in inner city schools, the political and religious leadership of the black community, and Partnership for a Drug Free America, there were signs that crack consumption in the nation's ghettos was at last beginning to decline. Its devastating effects, however, will haunt the nation for years to come. One figure alone is graphic evidence: roughly 350,000 babies are born each year in the United States to mothers addicted to drugs. The vast majority of those mothers are addicted to crack-cocaine and an alarming percentage of their offspring are born with brain lesions which give them learning disabilities, a tendency to antisocial behavior, and irrational outbursts of anger and violence. Unfortunately, there is no indication that intensive counseling and specialized education can undo the damage done to their brains by crack while they were in their mothers' wombs. As they mature, they risk becoming permanent wards of society in either a jail cell or an institutional bed. Nothing might more completely vindicate Kevin Grady's angry declaration to Jack Lind that the real menace to U.S. society in the mid-1980s lay in the proliferation of drugs, not in the political ambitions of a group of barely competent Marxists in Nicaragua.

Acknowledgments

The preparation and research for *Black Eagles* would not have been possible without the help and guidance of many friends in various walks of life. It is, unfortunately, impossible to list them all here, but I would like to acknowledge particularly my debt of gratitude to a number among them.

First, of course, my thanks go to my friends old and new, active in or retired from, the DEA: Paul Knight who first introduced me into the arcane world of narcotics law enforcement in Beirut in 1958; Kevin Gallagher who had what was certainly the most dangerous job in the organization when I met him, representing the DEA in Marseilles during the breakup of the French Connection; Bill Ruzzamenti who guided me on this project; Peter Bensinger, Bud Mullen and John Lawn, all former administrators of the DEA; and, most particularly, a number of active DEA agents in New York, Hartford, Atlanta, the Middle East, Central America and Colombia. Anonymity is an important part of their job, however, and I would do them no favor by citing them here. Finally a word of thanks to the man who inspired the character "Ramon" and to Assistant U.S. Attorney Buddy Parker in Atlanta for opening to me the files of the Eduardo Martinez case.

In Panama, I was much helped by Michele Labrut, Jose Blandon, ex-president Barletta, Pat Janson, Mario Rognoni, Vicky Amado and many others.

Jonathan Winer and Jack Blum of the Kerry Committee, Ambassador Arthur Davis and his daughter, Susan, our most engagingly original ex-Commissioner of Customs William von Raab, were among the many who offered their good counsel in Washington.

So, too, did a number of my friends of many years standing, retired officers of the Central Intelligence Agency. I hope they will not take offense at these pages; my criticisms

are not of the institution they all served so honorably but o
the small number in its ranks who went astray.

Dr. Gabriel Nahas helped me to understand the devastat
ing effects of crack cocaine on the brain; Ansley Hamid, it
implantation on the streets of our cities; Dr. Pierre vor
Bockdtaele, its effects as seen on Saturday night in the emer
gency room of the Harlem Hospital; the Good Samaritans o
Phoenix House, what can be done to save the lives shattere
by the drug.

Gregg Lockwood in California and John Sutin gave me
figuratively speaking, flying lessons. Gerald Meyers, the
Court Recorder of the U.S. District Court in Miami, and hi
wife Pilar did wonders getting me the transcripts of Genera
Noriega's trial. My thanks also go to my old *Newsweek* col
league Kevin Buckley, himself the author of an excellen
non-fiction account of Noriega's downfall, for sharing sc
many of his sources with me.

Finally, and most important of all, my thanks to my wife
Nadia for her support, understanding and patience in the
long months I labored on this book.

Thoughtfulness and help was the gift of all of the above
and many others. Any errors, misinterpretations or misjudg
ments in these pages are mine alone.

TERROR ... TO THE LAST DROP

OFFICIAL RULES

NO PURCHASE NECESSARY TO ENTER OR WIN A PRIZE. To enter the SEE HOW AR A GOOD BOOK CAN TAKE YOU SWEEPSTAKES, complete this official entry rm (original or photocopy), or, on a 3" x 5" piece of paper, print your name and omplete address. Mail your entry to: SEE HOW FAR A GOOD BOOK CAN TAKE YOU WEEPSTAKES, P.O. Box 8012, Grand Rapids, MN, 55745-8012. Enter as often as ou wish, but mail each entry in a separate envelope. All entries must be received by ovember 29, 1996, to be eligible. Not responsible for illegible entries, lost or isdirected mail.

Winners will be selected from all valid entries in a random drawing on or about ecember 31, 1996, by Marden-Kane, Inc., an independent judging organization hose decisions are final and binding. Odds of winning are dependent upon the umber of entries received. Winners will be notified by mail and may be required to ecute an affidavit of eligibility and release which must be returned within 14 days notification or an alternate winner will be selected.

One (1) Grand Prize winner will receive 25,000 American Airlines AAdvantage iles. Approximate retail value: $500.00. Five (5) First Place winners will receive ,000 American Airlines AAdvantage miles. Approximate retail value: $200.00. Ten 0) Second Place winners will receive 3,000 American Airlines AAdvantage miles. pproximate retail value: $60.00. Thirty (30) Third place winners will receive 1,000 merican Airlines AAdvantage miles. Approximate retail value: $20.00. Approximate tail value of all prizes: $2,700.00.

Sweepstakes open to residents of the U.S. and Canada except employees and the mmediate families of Penguin USA, American Airlines, its affiliated companies, vertising and promotion agencies. Void in the Province of Quebec and wherever se prohibited by law. All Federal, State, Local, and Provincial laws apply. Taxes, if y, are the sole responsibility of the prize winners. Canadian winners will be quired to answer an arithmetical skill testing question administered by mail. inners consent to the use of their name and/or photos or likenesses for vertising purposes without additional compensation (except where prohibited). No bstitution of prizes is permitted. All prizes are nontransferable.

American Airlines may find it necessary to change AAdvantage program rules, gulations, travel awards, and special offers at any time, impacting, for example, rticipant affiliations, rules for earning mileage and blackout dates and limited ating for travel awards. American Airlines reserves the right to end the dvantage program with six months notice. AAdvantage travel awards, mileage crual, and special offers subject to government regulations.

Winners agree that the sponsor, its affiliates, and their agencies and employees e not liable for injuries, loss, or damage of any kind resulting from participation or m the acceptance or use of the prize awarded.

For the names of the major prize winners, send a self-addressed, stamped velope after December 31, 1996, to: SEE HOW FAR A GOOD BOOK CAN TAKE U SWEEPSTAKES WINNERS, P.O. Box 714, Sayreville, NJ 08871-0714.

Penguin USA • Mass Market
375 Hudson Street, New York, N.Y. 10014

Printed in the USA

American Airlines and AAdvantage are registered trademarks of American Airlin

WIN A TRIP

With American Airlines® AAdvantage® Miles!

**Enter the
See How Far a Good
Book Can Take You....
Sweepstakes!**

Name_____

Address_____

City_____State_____Zip_____

Mail to:
SEE HOW FAR A GOOD BOOK CAN TAKE YOU SWEEPSTAKES
P.O. Box 8012
Grand Rapids, MN 55745-8012

No purchase necessary. Details on back.

⊘ Signet ® Onyx ◈ Topaz

AAdvantage